Legananny Legacy:

The Selfsame Moon and Stars

By Dorothy MacNeill Dupont

For Dad, without whose storytelling skills,
Lizzie and the Twomblys of Newton Lower Falls
would have been lost to us.

For Ma, who quietly urged us,
"Listen to your father."

You are the bow from which your children
As living arrows are sent forth.

The archer sees the mark upon the path of the infinite,
And He bends you with His might,
That His arrows may go swift and far.

Let your bending in the archer's hand be for gladness,
For even as he loves the arrow that flies,
So He loves also the bow that is stable.

– Kahlil Gibran, *The Prophet*

The Women of the Legananny Legacy:

Elizabeth (Beth) Frazer Cockburn
(The Winds of County Down)

|

Margaret (Maggie) Jane Coburn Heenan
(The Winds of County Down)
(The Selfsame Moon and Stars)
(The Scent of Smoldering Bridges — fall, 2015)

|

Elizabeth (Lizzie) Jane Heenan MacNeill
(The Winds of County Down)
(The Selfsame Moon and Stars)
(The Scent of Smoldering Bridges — fall, 2015)

|

Clara (Claire) MacNeill Thayer
(The Scent of Smoldering Bridges — fall, 2015)

PREFACE

The Legananny Legacy is written as a fictionalized chronology of real people and their experiences. The stories were brought to our generation by my father, Raymond H. MacNeill, whose talents for story-telling made this collection of family lore stick in our minds, bonding the struggles of our daily lives with that of the four generations before ours. Through his repetitive, dramatic weaving of stories, we *saw* our grandmother venturing to America, becoming an indentured servant, then master of her fate, living and loving full out, with the bruises and scars, triumphs and defeats, anger, shame and compassion by which all human life is characterized.

As the stories were written, it became most logical to present the work in several volumes, highlighting three generations: Maggie, Lizzie, and Claire. The genealogy and timelines in the story, set in the social, economical and political climate in which our ancestors lived and by which they were influenced are true, and I stand by them. There are relationships among this cast of characters which have no

i

basis in fact, and they are enumerated at the back of each book, in the annotation, *The Truth and The Fantasy.*

This second book of the *Legananny Legacy* series, *The Selfsame Moon and Stars,* begins in 1892, continuing the stories of Maggie, Lizzie, and Eliza. It is a study of personalities, tough decisions, strength, and vulnerability. The portraits are painted on a canvas of social and historical events, influenced by the acceptance or rejection of the common beliefs and attitudes of the times.

The women in this volume each have a particular strength of their own; strength as different from the others, as if they had invented the word to have separate meanings when applied to them: Maggie strength, Eliza strength, and Lizzie strength.

There is a vulnerability laid bare in each woman, against which she wages her personal war. The spoils of that war are: strength, dignity, and self-reliance. The consequences of fighting that war too long and too hard are cynicism, hyper-vigilance, and loss of compassion and joyful spirit. Each woman finds her own balance, in the attributes to which she aspires, and the blessings of which she may be unaware.

The writing and research of this novel has been long, sometimes arduous, at most times daunting, but never without a satisfying hope, never without boundless reward. I am eternally grateful for the challenge to record these stories, connecting the events within the framework of time and *mores* of the day.

My Aunt Edith's mother, Louisa Paun, once said to my father, "If you don't bring your children to see us, how will they know who they are?"

To that end, it is my pleasure to introduce you to our family.

— *Dorothy MacNeill Dupont*

Elizabeth (Heenan) MacNeill
The Crossing – 1892

Chapter One

On the rough road to Belfast, neither the cold mist of the early April dawn, nor the uncertainty her future, could dampen Lizzie's spirits.

Ever'one seems sae serious, she thought; *as if they are girdin' themselves up ta face certain doom.* Her half-brother, Johnny and the Reverend Mister Denison were sitting in the front of the spine-jarring wagon, while Cousin James, Eliza, and Lizzie were huddled in the back, among the well-worn bags containing their most valued earthly possessions, meager as they were.

Ever since her church announced the American clergy and government were looking for people willing to immigrate to their country, her mind was made up. This was her chance to take charge of her own life in a new country.

Lizzie tried to cajole her half-sister out of her foreboding. "Come, Eliza, we're no' droppin' off the edge o' the earth! Try being a *wee bit* cheerful. It's a grand adventure we're takin'.

1

"We'll see wondrous things an' have great experiences other folk jes' dream o'. We'll feel the warm spring sun on our faces in jes' a few weeks, an' it'll be the selfsame sun as here, though we're half a world away! Imagine it, Eliza. We'll see the other side of the world!"

"Lizzie, ye make ever'thin' sound lak' yer was goin' ta a tea party. I'm near scairt ta death, an' yer jumpin' in with both feet. Are ye no' afraid o' nothin'?"

"'Course, she's no', Eliza. *That* would take a brain ta think wit'!" shouted Johnny, gleefully from the front of the wagon. "She's 'way too excited ta have any *sense* about it."

Eliza put her arm around her protectively, while Lizzie fumed at the perceived injustice.

"You *will* have to exercise some caution, Miss Heenan," counseled the Reverend Mister Denison. "The Devil is about, and will trip you up if you do not keep a watchful eye. When we go on the ferry, please stay close together. There are ruffians who prey on children like yourselves."

"Aye, Mister Denison," the travelers answered obediently. *Children*, scoffed James to himself, *the man is no older an' has seen less o' the world than I have. He's likely been cloistered away in some secluded seminary an' knows little o' real men, let alone the evil they do. He's ne'er got his hands dirty doin' an honest day's work, I'll wager. They oughta make a man work fer a livin' afore they sic him on God-fearin' folk, tellin' 'em how ta live.* He clenched his jaw showing his irritation with the young minister. *Are there a special set o' classes in arrogance ye take at thet seminary, or is it born ta all clergy?* He sighed, quoting his father's oft-spouted opinion to himself, knowing it was unjust, but enjoying it all the same. His father and he did not see eye to eye on much, but although his old man did not agree with his *'runnin' away ta 'Merica'*, neither did he stand in his way.

Belfast was in full bustle when they drew down on the

coastal city. The three travelers in the back sat up peering over the front seat at the throng of people already rushing to destinations unknown. The mist had dissipated, and the sea wind was whipping up the debris in the street.

They watched amused, as a tall, elegantly dressed gentleman chased his hat, caught by a sudden gust. The streets were crowded with carriages, wagons and horses all vying for space. The drivers shouted greetings and curses at other drivers and pedestrians. Lizzie was absorbing it all. Well-attired ladies with colorful hats carefully stepped from carriages, assisted by footmen. There were somberly-dressed maidservants scurrying along with baskets of bread and small packages wrapped in butcher's parchment.

A knife-sharpener and his assistant had set up shop on the corner, announcing their expert services to passersby. Lizzie was charmed by their formal, if tattered and dusty clothing. The sharpener sported a tall, slightly crumpled hat jammed down to his shaded eyes, giving him an air of mystery.

After the sleepy countryside of Legananny, the noise of the city was deafening. A local constable grabbed a little boy who looked up at him with angelic eyes, while hiding a wallet behind his back. The angry, shouting victim demanded hanging for his offense.

Lizzie stole a glance at her half-sister to see her reaction. Eliza's eyes were wide with wonder and fear. She was clutching Lizzie arm as if the wind and the noise might carry her away. Just then, a young man waved and shouted at his companion, "Look, the one with the fire-red hair! I'll take me some o' *thet* ta keep me warm at night!"

This action prompted the young minister to sternly admonish Lizzie, saying, "Miss Heenan! You must cover your hair more modestly while you're traveling. It is an occasion of scandal to let it fly about like that. That kind of attention can only end in calamity."

Lizzie flushed and quickly shoved her hair into her somber black bonnet and tied it tight under her chin. Although she did as she

3

was told, she glared angrily at the back of the clergyman's head. *Jes' because thet brash young man was rude beyond understanding, should I be held accountable fer his actions?*

Soon, the wagon turned down a sloping cobblestone street toward the dock and the waiting ferry. Once the wagon and horses were safely at the livery, the five sojourners approached the ferry.

"Step lively, now. There is no time to waste." Mister Denison went to the gangplank and handed the tickets to the sailor standing there. "Come up the walk quickly. We are about to sail."

Eliza whispered to Lizzie, shyly. "Is this the ship, then?"

"No Eliza, it's only the ferry. Be careful how ye walk. Ye don't wanna fall. Looks like they's more cattle than people here. *Whew.*" Lizzie wrinkled her nose at the smell.

"As a matter of fact, Miss Heenan," began Mister Denison as he drew himself up to impart his knowledge on the subject, "There are many more cattle than people on this ferry. It is a matter of commerce. It is monetarily more advantageous to transport animals to market than to ferry passengers. So, most experienced passengers would not object to share the ferry with them for so short a journey."

"Mister Denison, ye are right, o' course," Lizzie replied devilishly. "Perhaps ye will admit 'tis less than desirable fer the human passengers ta share the deck wit' the creatures however, when ye examine the heel o' yer boot. You seemed ta have stepped in some residue o' thet *commerce.*" James ducked behind the minister to hide the grin and the barely-contained laugh she inspired at the humbled minister's expense.

When the young man, now embarrassed, went to the rail to scrape his boot clean, Eliza said in a low voice, "Lizzie, please don't tease him anymore. I knae he seems insufferable, but he's takin' us all the way ta Liverpool." Then she added, "He *is* a man o' God, after all."

"Don't worry, Eliza. I'll apologize an' attempt ta be *thoroughly* contrite." Lizzie walked straight to where Mister Denison was still trying to get the offending mass off his boot.

"Mister Denison," Lizzie said with all the humility she could muster, "I apologize sincerely fer causing ye any discomfort. Please accept my apology an' share the poor victuals I have."

"Apology accepted, Miss Heenan. I would be delighted." Then, with a surprising twinkle in his eye, he added, "*up*wind of the beasts, of course."

"Of course, Mister Dennison, let's stay upwind." Lizzie smiled broadly, acknowledging his attempt at humor. They moved with their bags to the other side of the ship as it was beginning to move. They were awkward in their movements, owing to the sudden motion of the ship and to their careful avoidance of clumps of 'commerce' strewn in their paths.

Once there, they spied a small built-in chest where they could sit and have a bite. Eliza declined, but Lizzie insisted she have a small biscuit and watch the horizon. She sat there for a long time, silently watching the median where the dark Irish Sea met the dull, gray sky. James, noting her pallor, sat beside her and talked quietly, almost mesmerizingly to her.

Mister Denison and Lizzie moved toward the rail and engaged in their first meaningful conversation. "Ye were educated at Eton, Mister Denison?"

"Oh my, no, I went to a small seminary in Bath. They were poor, but thorough, and I was fortunate to have been taken in. I was orphaned by a fire at twelve and lived there until I was ordained. The instructors were very good to me, although they had no real hope of my becoming a clergyman. I'm afraid I was not very tractable. How they put up with my mischief, I'll never know. I suspect I gave them some relief from their solemn and pious lives though," he admitted, ruefully.

5

"I'm sure ye were a handful. I knae I was, an' *am,* I'm afraid. You've already been served a dish o' my rude behavior, for which I am truly sorry," said Lizzie. She marveled at the ease in which he revealed his tragic childhood. "It musta been lonely fer ye ta lose yer parents sae young."

"It was at first, but the Anglican priests each brought me into their homes, and for a semester at a time, I had a family. Some were difficult to appease, others were truly generous with their time and their patience. It taught me to adapt to most situations." His round face turned sad as he answered, a melancholy shrouding his stocky frame. He shook his head as if to rid himself of remembered ghosts, then smiled brilliantly.

"So nae ye will take Mister Coburn's place as assistant, while he succeeds the Reverend Mister McKay. How's he farin' these days? He seems verra tired," Lizzie said.

"He is. He's ill and has been for a while. How he drives himself, I don't know. He won't rest. He says he has much to do before his time is up. We've urged him to let us take over now, but he wants to work until his last day, if he can. He's a wonderful man of God. I only hope I can be half the shepherd he's been."

"I'm sure ye will be. No one is born knaein' the right thin' ta do all the time. Mister McKay has had a lang time ta be the great man he's become," Lizzie said solemnly, then smiling, she chided, "But don' ferget ye sense o' humor."

"You're wiser than your years would indicate, Miss Heenan. When Mister Coburn sent me to bring you three to Liverpool, I was overwhelmed by his trust in me, I'm afraid I forgot it wasn't me that was important, but the task itself. I'll do my best to remember that."

"My mother al'ays said, 'There are new lessons ta be learned ever'day an' ev'ry person ye meet is your teacher.' Sometimes ye learn from yer ain mistakes, sometimes from another's folly, an' sometimes yer learn from a thin' done right."

"She raised a clever child. What have you learned today?" he challenged.

"Mm-m, today I learned yer kin neither knae a man by yer first look, nor a book by its first page. Ye have ta give them both time ta prove themselves." Lizzie tipped her head coyly, and looked at him through her lashes. *He canna be any older than James. He's got a kind face when he's not o'er serious an' if I weren' goin' ta America...*, she mused. *Ach, who would I be foolin'? I could ne'er be a minister's wife! His church would turn on him like an English regiment on a Dublin man. I've ne'er been able ta keep my mouth out o' trouble fer two minutes, nor I fear, would I be willin'.*

"Then, praise God, Miss Heenan. It's surely been a good day for both of us," replied Mister Denison.

The three and a half hour journey from Belfast to the Isle of Man passed pleasantly for Lizzie and Mister Denison. Not so for Eliza, who seemed to have trouble focusing on the horizon as bidden. She was never really sick, but never well. James spent the time talking to his ashen-faced cousin, trying to keep her mind off the undulating vessel. By the time they docked, the skies were bright with the afternoon sun.

"We'll only be here for a short while, then we will continue to Stranraer. You may want to walk around a little, but I don't recommend leaving the ship," said Mister Denison. "Your sister may feel better if she can get up and move around. Perhaps you can persuade her to eat another biscuit?"

Lizzie went to where Eliza was sitting, stoically hanging onto Johnny's arm. Encouraging him to take Eliza for a walk, Lizzie sat with their bags. "Would you like a biscuit, Mister Denison? I couldn't get Eliza ta take one yet. Perhaps when she an' Johnny come back, she will." The young clergyman took one and the gulls diving near the ship took interest. As he was talking, waving the biscuit in his hand, a diving gull seized the opportunity and snatched it away.

7

"Huh? Well, that was unkind," laughed the young man.

"It was, indeed. If I give you another, will you promise me ye will take better care o' it?" laughed Lizzie.

Then smiling, she said, "I should spell Johnny a bit wit' Eliza. 'Tis hard ta imagine we've spent all this time talkin'."

"It has been very pleasant, Miss Heenan. It makes the time go quickly, doesn't it?"

"Ye kin call me Lizzie, if that's agreeable to ye. We're no' likely ta be meetin' a parishioner ta take offense."

"You're very kind, Lizzie. Call me Alfred, if James doesn't think it too familiar." James was staring out to sea.

Lizzie said in a low voice, "James is unlikely ta object. Besides, I've won a battle or two from the likes o' him. So he'd best behave himself.

"Look, they're comin' back." She called, "Johnny, I'll sit wit' Eliza a while, so ye kin look around more, if ye like."

"Thank you, Lizzie. Ye don't mind, Eliza? I'd like ta see a bit o' the ship. Would ye join me, Reverend Denison? Ye will have ta watch ye step, though," he teased.

Lizzie patted the seat next to her and Eliza sat down. As the two men were walking away, Eliza asked, softly, "What on earth did ye find ta talk about wit' Mister Denison, all thet time?" James snorted hearing her question.

"He's a verra interestin' man, Eliza," she said, smiling wickedly. "An' if I were no' goin' ta America, I'd pay him more attention. Once ye git ta knae him, he kin be quite charmin'." James rolled his eyes and muttered to himself.

'Lizzie, he's a man o' the cloth! What're ye sayin'?" Eliza said shocked.

"I'm sayin' he's a *man* first. He's quite nice. I'm no' gonna marry him, but he's verra nice."

"Lizzie Heenan, if Johnny heard wha' yer sayin', he'd be as shocked as I am. What mus' Cousin James think o' ye talkin' thet way about a clergyman?"

"Cousin James thinks very little of it, I assure you," the handsome young man asserted, wryly.

"Let him be shocked. It's all verra innocent," said Lizzie hiding her smile behind her gloved hand. "He's had a hard life. He's very serious about his callin', but he's no' wit'out a sense o' humor."

"I wish I could talk ta people as easy as yer, Lizzie. Ye don' let anyone hush ye up."

"It comes wit' a price, Eliza. Sometimes, I say things bes' left *unsaid*. Promise me, you'll never let me say anythin' ta hurt yer. Ye must tell me straight away, if I do. Ye are my sister, an' my dearest friend, Eliza. I'd no' wanna hurt yer fer the world."

"I promise. But ye ne'er would. I think I feel better nae. Talkin' ta yer is better than listenin' ta Johnny talkin' about farmin' an' the fallin' price o' crops." Seeing Lizzie grin, she added, "An' about *Janie* this, an' *Janie* that, an' *Janie* is m' darling'."

"Poor Johnny, he longs ta be in America. Joseph didn't have two words ta put t'gether 'bout it after he got hame. He musta been worried about the farm. I think if Johnny could gae, Joey would.

"Ye think ye kin eat a biscuit fer me nae, Eliza?"

Her color was back to nearly normal now and so was her hunger. Lizzie hoped the sea would stay calm for the next part of the ferry ride. It was just a short train ride after landing and then they'd be in Liverpool. She'd be glad to be on dry land for a while.

Eliza, James, and she talked about what the big ship would be like. This one was bigger than they had ever seen, but Mister Denison, *Alfred*, she corrected herself, claimed it was like a whole city on the water, with a library, a fancy dining room, and a theater on the upper decks. They would not be allowed up there, but they

9

would be able to go out on the lower decks for fresh salty air and a look at the horizon.

She was going to mention that the Earl of Annesley told her about his experiences on the ocean, but she wanted to keep that to herself for a while. It was her secret, only the Earl, her mother and she knew..., and *Mórai*. She felt selfish, withholding it from Eliza, but it felt warm and special to have a secret. Lizzie sighed. *Eliza wouldna believed me anyways. She'd think I made it up in my head, like the made-up stories we told each other when we were wee girls.*

The next few hours seemed to drag. When Johnny and Alfred came back from their tour of the ferry, they were excited to tell the girls all the mechanical wonders they found. The giant steam engine that propelled the ship, the smoke stacks, the captain's cabin, and the front deck were all described in great detail. Lizzie asked just enough questions to keep the stories flowing.

"I suppose ye goin' ta be a steamship captain nae, Johnny?" teased Lizzie.

"Nay, but I think I'd like ta knae one," he said with a smile. "I've questions upon questions I'd like the answers ta."

"Miss Heenan, ye look a bit more chipper, than earlier," noted Mister Denison. "I hope that's true."

"Aye, Mister Denison. I am feelin' better, thank you," Eliza said shyly. "Lizzie al'ays perks me up. Thank yer, fer sittin' sae lang wit' me, James. I think it helped, jes' ta have ye both there wit' me."

"My cousin is more gracious than most. It was *she*, puttin' up wit' me, I'm afraid," said James.

"Nonetheless, it's pleasant to see a family who gets along so well. If I ever have children, I can only hope they will do as well," said the Reverend Denison.

"Oh ho, 'twas not al'ays thet way, sir," said her brother, laughing heartily. "These two conspired evilly against me at ev'ry turn. How I survived, I'll ne'er knae." As Johnny rolled his eyes heavenward in exaggerated suffering, Lizzie cuffed him playfully.

10

Alfred Denison looked from one to the other, smiling at the amusement in their eyes. *They're remembering some childhood prank I cannot share. How I envy their familiarity with each other! Will I ever share a secret remembered life with another? Lizzie, I wish you were not leaving now, when I've only just met you.*

Nearing the end of the ride, the sun burst through the gray clouds, painting a warm picture of blue skies, sandy beaches and sea foamed waves at the landing.

The ferry ride over, they boarded a train at Stranraer, and by the time they arrived at Liverpool, the little group was sad to leave Mister Denison and Johnny behind. Eliza and Lizzie stood by the sea wall, marveling at the docks and warehouses lining both sides of the Mersey yards. It seemed every dock was teeming with people coming and going in a great rush.

"We'll only have a few hours ta gae afore we sail away on the *City of New York*. Ye kin see it down thet way, the huge one near the end." James pointed through the myriad of black cranes and freight barges loading and unloading.

The workmen were shouting orders to lesser laborers who scurried about like ants around a crust of bread. Lizzie was fascinated with the apparent chaos resolving itself to neat stacks of goods both on land and ship. The noise was even greater than in Belfast. Cranes screeched in protest, as their loads were set down on the pier.

The shift whistle screaming into the late afternoon skies, assaulted her ears. Clumps of workmen intent on their task suddenly broke apart, grabbed their gear and ran toward the warehouse buildings. The entering workmen strode calmly with their pails toward the ships while foremen yelled directions. The night shift had begun. Gas lights were lit and the ship lights took on an eerie glow. Low in the sky, the sun threw red and purple streaks on passing clouds, as a last reminder of its brilliant performance.

11

The docks were still crowded as the five travelers walked down the giant wharf. "Stay very close together now. These are honest, hard-working, but rough men and they will have their sport with you if you attract their attention. The dock at the great ship is filling up. Hold your papers as if your future depends on it, for it does," said Mister Denison.

Lizzie's excitement grew as the crowd gathered pushing and shouting toward the enormous floating edifice. There were people of every size and class, sitting on their bags, mother's hands hanging onto their children's coats, and young men milling about, waiting for instruction. Mister Denison urged them toward the front of the human mass. "Be careful! They will push you right into the water if you get too close to the edge. The gangway will be dropped over here. Soon, the ship's master and his aide will stand up there, ready to take your information and examine your papers. Don't take them out until you reach the top. It will be very windy up there, so hold them fast."

Lizzie now admired his commanding air. She had been told about the crowded dock and the procedure to get on the ship, but to have someone like Alfred here was a Godsend. She had no concept of the magnitude of the event. The ship was taller than any building she had ever seen and there were more people than she'd seen on Market Day in Castlewellan. The colorful swarm represented every walk of life, attired in tatters to grand finery.

A fight broke out behind them. Lizzie clutched her papers in panic. She was shoved from behind. Mister Denison caught her. "Easy, Lizzie," he said, "Hang on to me for support. This crowd would carry you away." She remembered the Earl had predicted they would set up a fight to distract the waiting passengers while pickpockets pushed through the crowd.

The nearness of him made her wonder if he knew what she was thinking. She was glad the lights were dim enough to mask her reddening face.

12

The fight over, Lizzie straightened up and said, "Thank you, Mister Denison. I'll be fine now." She tipped her head so the bonnet would hide her face and not betray the heighten confusion she felt.

"Of course, Miss Heenan, I hope I haven't overstepped my bounds. I merely wished you to be safe."

Lizzie peeked from under her bonnet at the soft brown eyes that revealed concern and dismay. "On the contrary, Mister Denison, ye may have prevented a disastrous outcome ta this part o' our journey. Look, we should be able ta gae aboard, nae."

"If I may be so bold, Miss Heenan, would you do me the honor of writing to me? I would like to know how you fare in America and what your reaction to the process is."

"I should be delighted, Mister Denison. I don't know how long the post might take, but it would be my honor to write to you." Lizzie matched the formality of his speech and felt shy with the impending departure.

As she came closer to the walkway, she could see Eliza far ahead in line. Her half-sister was looking around frantically, panic written on her lovely face. Lizzie jumped up and waved. When Eliza spotted her, Lizzie waved her forward.

"I have ta get up ta her," she said, looking directly into the clergyman's eyes. Impulsively, she kissed his cheek and ran up the walk away from him. When she looked back at him he was smiling, looking rather bewildered, and touching his cheek with his gloved hand. Lizzie smiled and turned up the walkway to the captain's clerk.

She saw James shake hands with Mister Denison and follow her, several passengers back.

On deck, Lizzie and her fellow passengers filed past two men she determined were the medical officer and his assistant. He looked at each passenger from head to toe without stopping the line, except when he spied a symptom of concern. He would then make a more thorough examination and pass or reject that person as he warranted necessary.

At yet another station, an officer and a clerk addressed each passenger and asked for their papers.

The weary clerk was brusque. "Papers, Miss." Lizzie ceased her daydreaming, handing her sheaf of papers to him. He searched through them for some bit of information. When satisfied, he stamped them with a number and returned them.

"Move on, lower deck, steerage, quickly. *Next*," he shouted.

A sailor stood at the juncture of two lines. He pointed to her, then to the right. In the jostling crowd, Lizzie saw Eliza turning a corner, being swallowed up into the ship. She rushed to reach her. She hardly had room to pick up one foot and find a place to put it down again. Her bag was caught on another's straps and she dropped it. The crowd pressing forward nearly knocked her down.

"Tarnation, woman! What 'ave you got in there, bricks?" the injured man yelped. "I'm not trying to steal your bag, but please try to keep it off my poor toes!" He thrust the offending bag in her direction. A boy squeezed under her arm looking for protection. His mother, in a panicky voice, screamed his name, and yanking his arm, pulled him back.

"I'm sae sorry, sir. I beg ye pardon. Please forgive me." Lizzie grabbed her bag and headed through the doorway that had swallowed up Eliza.

As she entered the dimly lit corridor and down the steep stairs, she heard, "Dim-witted Irisher."

Keep yer temper, Lizzie, yer no' at hame, nae. Jes' try ta find Eliza. She must be scairt witless.

At the bottom of the stairs was another even steeper flight, more of a ladder than stairs. The crowd of passengers were elbowing, shoving, and reaching over each other to keep their families together. They were shouting in various accents and

14

languages trying to signal their children, mothers, fathers, aunts, uncles, brothers, or sisters.

Lizzie couldn't stop nor change direction. *We're movin' like cattle, no' knaein' where, jes' goin'.* As if he could hear her thoughts, a man beside her sputtered, "If we was cows, we'd be protected fum harm. The steamship comp'ny's gotta pay a fine fer injurin' *cattle.*"

At the bottom of the second stairs, the passengers were divided again. Single women were relegated to the farthest room. The room was the full width of the ship, divided into smaller cabins, holding four to sixteen bunks. The narrow bunks were attached with iron posts to the floor and ceiling, one over the other. The outside perimeter of the room was lined with benches and the front of the room had several doors indicating wash rooms and storage.

The only light was from small gas lamps on either side of the portholes and the lights outside.

There was room for about ten women in that room. They would have to share if there were not enough beds, since there were more passengers to come at Queensland. Most of the women were English, cleanly, if poorly, attired. *At least the room looks clean,* thought Lizzie. *It smells a wee sour, but it's been scrubbed clean.*

"Lizzie!" As she turned her head, she saw Eliza flattened against the wall, clutching her bag to her chest. Eliza's face was joyous in her relief at seeing Lizzie. "I thought I los' yer fore'er! Ye kept gettin' further an' further away."

"We'll stick together like melted candle wax from nae on, I promise," said Lizzie, knowing how terrified she must have been.

Eliza and Lizzie found a bunk near a porthole, as the Earl said. Lizzie looked out to blackness, then turning her head to the farthest viewpoint; she could see a narrow crescent moon. As her eyes became accustomed to the dim light, she saw the edge where the water touched the sky.

As a cloud moved, it revealed a scattering of distant stars in the dome of the sky. *Ma's seeing these same stars. She's thinkin' about us an' our grand adventure. Imagine how many times Da saw this very sight, sailin' away ta America!* "*Watch fer the light o' the moon an' stars,*" he used to tell her. "*They's the selfsame moon an' stars I'll be lookin' at, thinkin o' yer, m' darlin'.*"

One by one, each woman came in, plunked down her bag and herself on a bunk, tired, but satisfied she had made it through the process of boarding. Having paraded through the first room, which was designated for the men, then a middle corridor of cabins assigned to married couples and families, Lizzie had noticed a doorway to the outside between the cabins. *At least we don't hafta go through the men's bunks ta git outside.*

"Are we really expected ta sleep in here wit' all these other women?" asked Eliza, tremulously.

"I was tol' we'll sleep here an' ta get a bed near a porthole. They wash down the floorin' daily, sae don' leave yer bag on the floor. Keep yer bag under yer head or in yer sight al'ays. Keep yer papers on yer person," said Lizzie.

On each bunk, there was a straw mattress, a coarse blanket, a set of two tin plates, a *pannikin* they called it, a knife, a fork, and a spoon. "Make sure ye keep ye food kit together fer all ye meals. Wash 'em yerself an' keep 'em sep'rate from all the others," she said, remembering the words of the conversation she had with her mother's friend.

Lizzie noticed several of the other passengers were eavesdropping as she went through the list of precautions. She figured if they knew how well-prepared Lizzie and her half-sister were to protect their belongings, perhaps their listening neighbors would not cause too much trouble.

Returning to the porthole to see the sea and small passing boats, she said, "Eliza, anytime ye need ta settle yer stomach, look fer the horizon out this round winder here. We'll figure out other things as we need 'em. Ye an' I will take this bottom bunk. I have more biscuits if ye've a mind ta eat."

When she turned to look at her, she saw Eliza huddled at the edge of the bed, sound asleep. Lizzie smiled, contentedly. *We're off ta the greatest adventure o' our lives, an' Eliza chooses ta sleep through it. Good fer her. Maybe her stomach will stay calm if she's sleeping.*

Lizzie sat on the edge of the rough bunk, watching Eliza sleep for a while. She felt the ship move off the bar where it had been anchored, slipping out of the channel of the Mersey. She hoped the sudden movements and rocking of the ship wouldn't wake Eliza. The rest of the women tended their nightly routines as best they could in their new surroundings. They found a water closet at the end of the room with bars of yellow soap and running water for washing.

The ship moved forward with a shutter, its balance restored once on the open sea. Now, all she could hear was the noise of the engines, thrumming in rhythm with the sea. The passengers were silent, and in the dim light, the journey took on an ominous portent. *They's no turnin' back, nae.*

Lizzie pondered the life she left behind in Legananny, the village where she was born in Northern Ireland. Her invalid mother, her grandmother, and her uncle stayed on the farm leased to them by a grateful soldier-baron, for the saving of his life.

Her half-brothers ran another farm their grandmother left them, scratching each year for the rent and taxes. *Nae, I've abandoned them, an' taken their sister Eliza from them,* she thought ruefully.

Remembering her promise not to leave Eliza alone, Lizzie resisted her overwhelming curiosity to explore the deck. *T'marra's another day. We'll see James after breakfast.*

17

The striking of bells indicated the passage of time she knew, but the time they marked was beyond her understanding. *T'marra, I'll find out. Right nae, I am more tired than curious.*

Chapter Two

It was the ship's bells that woke Lizzie the next morning. It was almost dawn and as she opened her eyes, Eliza's big brown ones stared back at her. "Well hello, fellow traveler," she said, amused at Lizzie's surprise.

"Well, you seem much better this mornin', Eliza. Ye musta slept well. I think t'night, we should wear our nightdresses, an' no' sleep in our bes' clothes," she said ruefully. "They will no' last the eight days journey if we rumple them up ev'ry night."

"Laurie Mahon, o'er there, say we'll gae ta breakfast at eight o' clock in the women's dining room, out this door an' through ta the next," said Eliza, excitedly. "Then we'll be able ta gae out on deck an' see James. We're gonna stop at Queensland fer more passengers, too."

Lizzie was glad Eliza found someone to talk to on her own. Eliza had always hung back and let her do the talking, following whatever Lizzie thought they should do. A part of Lizzie selfishly wanted to keep her sister-friend to herself, but she was happy with the more adventurous Eliza she was seeing. Although older and often wiser, Eliza stood behind Lizzie's bold demeanor and waited for her to make friendships, take action or seize the adventure.

19

Maybe this leap o' faith' is jes' what Eliza needed ta stand on her ain.

"I told her all the thin's ye were tellin' us, 'bout the ship an' the horizon. Where did ye learn all thet, Lizzie? I ne'er knew anyone who sailt anywheres, nor did James. Well, 'cept fer the fishermen comin' in ta Castlewellan ta sell their catch. "An' they's no' much fer talkin'. I wouldn't dare ta ask, anyways," she admitted.

"I learned about ocean travel from a world traveler and a gentleman," Lizzie replied smugly. She knew she need no longer exclude her sister from her mother's secret friendship. The knowledge could no longer harm her mother, nor the Earl for that matter, if the two girls were in America. To take the edge off her hoity tone, she said, "I'll tell ye ever'thin' when we meet James on deck, later."

Eliza stared at her in wonder, knowing if she pressed her, Lizzie would shut her off and she would never get the answer. *It's bes' ta let her tell her story in her ain way, I s'pose.* Lizzie always seemed to have the upper hand when it came to Eliza. *She's bustin' at the seams ta tell somebody, but she'll draw it out jes' ta tease me.*

Breakfast was signified by eight bells. It was simple fare, but plentiful. Lizzie was shocked at how very hungry she was. She slipped an extra few biscuits in her pocket for later. She smiled when she noticed most of the other women were doing the same. *If this continues, I will no' fit inta my clothes by landin'. Mother's friend said the salt air would increase my appetite and ta eat well while I am able. Well, I've al'ays been able ta eat, haven't I?*

As they all filed out of the women's dining area, they discovered each of them had the same destination in mind. The sisters, finding the rail filled, decided a walk around the ship would afford them some private conversation and much needed exercise as well. They finally spotted James further along the rail. As they strolled together, intending to walk around the ship, they discovered half way around the ship, the walk was roped off from the deck to

20

the ceiling, to prevent the third class passengers from peering in at the saloon patrons. Disappointed that their plan had been thwarted, the three found an unoccupied bench on which to sit and talk about what they had seen. Soon, the conversation came back to Lizzie's secret advisor.

"Sae, Lizzie, who's this world traveler in yer acquaintance? An' why haven't I met him?" asked Eliza, skeptically. "He's a member o' the House of Lairds, perhaps?"

"It's the Earl of Annesley an' aye, he *is* a member of the House of Lairds," Lizzie replied with her satisfaction spreading proudly over her features. "He's an auld friend o' *Mórai* an' Ma's."

"Horse feathers, jes' because ye heerd o' him, an' maybe even seed him, doesn't make him a *friend* o' yer fam'ly, Elizabeth Jane Heenan." Lizzie watched with glee at the surprise and confusion stamped on James' darkening face.

"It's the truth o' it, James," Lizzie hastened to tell them about her grandmother's brothers, William and Peter, who saved Laird Hugh's life in the Crimean War. She told them about the pact for the land her grandmother and mother leased, and the friendship he had with Maggie. "He's al'ays been right there on the edge of ever'thin', but I ne'er knew why." When she finished, the two listeners stood in stunned silence.

"Sae he's the one that told ye all about sailin' an' America?" Eliza finally said. "I saw him at Da's funeral. I didn' know why he was there. Da didn't like him much, I'll tell ye thet."

James scowled as he turned away from her, leaning on the rail. Lizzie put her hand on his shoulder and asked him what was troubling him.

"My father wanted me ta be a farmer like him, but I had no taste fer it. Against Da's will, I apprenticed myself ta a carpenter at sixteen an' when I was released, I had *sech* plans! The Earl was plannin' a new Church o' Ireland in Castlewellan an' sought my master's counsel in the constructin' o' it. When the designs were

21

ready, he asked thet I be put on the job, but the Earl hired men from London instead. None o' the local men were e'er engaged in the project."

"Oh, James, I'm sorry thet happened. Thet was Laird William, his brother, no' Laird Hugh. Well, ever'thin' happens fer a reason, they say. If ye got the job, ye'd no' be goin' ta America wit' us nae, would yer? We need ye wit' us, James Heenan, so perhaps it's God's will."

James turned toward the sea for a long moment. Then he sighed. Smiling sadly at her, he said, "Aye. Yer as wise as a red-haired child kin be. *If* there be any such thin' in this world."

Impulsively, Lizzie hugged her cousin's neck. She was glad to have him on this journey. "I promise, 'twill be better in America, James."

The three faced the impossible blue hues of sky and sea, dreaming of bold new lives in a land they had never seen. Lizzie prayed her promise to James would be true. She knew her cousin's way through life was hard fought and he wanted a fresh start.

As she pictured herself in America, it occurred to her, *When no one knaes who ye are, ye kin be anybody ye wan' ta be.* She chuckled to herself. *Sae, I'll be the one who gits wha' she wants. I'll have a new land, a new life an' nothin will git 'n my way, thet I canna handle.*

Giving voice to her thoughts, she said to them, "I knae what James wants. He wants a new life, some land o' his ain, a wife, an' babies. Eliza jes' wants a family, but she doesn't care if he's a farmer, or a teacher, or a shopkeeper. Me? I want a good husband, a whole bunch o' babies, a farm, a good business, and enough money ta no' worry 'bout *havin'* enough money."

"Wouldn't *thet* be the life? Find yerself an earl o' yer ain, Lizzie. He prob'ly won't care about a farm, but wit' all yer money, yer could buy one an' hire a farmer, how's thet?" teased James. "It might be hard ta find an earl in America, but maybe ye kin find a

22

gov'nor or some other 'high 'n mighty ta marry ye. 'Course, 'tis said, when ye marry fer money, ye earn ev'ry penny o' it."

Lizzie, laughed, "While *I'm* doin' the wishin', I might as well wish ta make my *ain* money an' no' be dependin' on how rich *he* is."

"Keep wishin', Lizzie. But what will ye be *doin'* fer this grand money ye earn? I dinna think it's by doin' *laundry*, ye will be gittin' rich, girl." James ducked as his fiery cousin swung at his head.

"If I had my bag with me nae, ye'd be laid out cold on this deck, James Heenan, cousin or no'!"

"Look, we're comin' inta Queensland," Eliza interrupted her squabbling companions, nervously.

"You ladies better git ta ye bunks ta protect ye belongings. The folks boarding here are a seedy lot, by the looks o' it. There seems ta be some *bumboat* women among them (women who sell wares and sometimes conduct questionable business aboard any ship in port), sellin' cakes, an' biscuits, an' *more*, if ye have a penny," said James, winking as he leaned over the rail.

There were about seventy more passengers for steerage, plus some brash, elbowing women with trays, hawking their wares. At the far end of the ship, about a dozen first class passengers picked their way carefully up the gang-plank trying to keep their pristine gloves unsoiled.

Later, when the ship pulled out from Queensland, James and the girls went up on deck again. While still in the calm of the sea on the leeside of the Irish coast, the sun was warm and the colors bright. The new steerage passengers, primarily young girls, entertained themselves with Irish dances and old tunes. Upon hearing the songs accompanied by a young man with a melodeon (accordion), some of the Liverpool passengers, also from Ireland, brought out their fiddles, tin whistles, and a *bodhrán* (Irish drum) to join in. The feeling was festive and nostalgic, bringing tears to the eyes of many of the on-deck passengers.

"Git ye fiddle, James!" commanded Lizzie, excited by the impromptu dancing.

"Nay, Lizzie. I'm no' lookin' fer a fight. These are Cat'lic children. They won' be hearin' the likes o' the Orange in their tunes. 'Sides, 'tis pleasant jes' ta be listenin' fer a change," replied James. "It's no' like they have no music o' their ain ta keep time wit' their steppin'. Jes' enjoy it an' sing along."

One old man had a shaft of white clover in peat that he cradled in his arms. He was bringing shamrocks to his son in California, he said. He was surrounded by young Irish girls who, though having just waved goodbye moments before, were already lonesome for home and family.

In this atmosphere of good will and celebration, some played cards, others just sat on benches chatting and the children chased each other up and down the deck. There was an occasional squabble among the card players and the children, but for the most part, the voyagers were agreeable.

Clouds rolled in after a while and the wind became bitter. The joyful passengers gathered their cloaks around them and headed down to their quarters. James and Eliza moved inside with the rest of the passengers, leaving Lizzie to stand vigil for the last sight of the Irish coast. Lizzie held out as long as she dared, knowing confinement would magnify the growing choppiness of the deepening gray ocean waves. When icy rain began to pelt her face, she relinquished her watch and headed down the steep ladder.

The darkness inside the hatchway always surprised her. The floor below was now slippery and she banged into walls and doors, feeling her way to the women's quarters. The door ahead was swinging freely, affording a low intermittent light as she moved toward it.

As she reached for the door, her feet lost their purchase and Lizzie found herself held face to face with a young steward. "Pardon me, ma'am. Ye shouldn't be walkin' 'round about 'ere by yerself. Not dangerous by 'alf, it is. Please stay in ye quarters 'til dinner's called." The young man half-dragged her to the entry, deposited her unceremoniously inside the women's quarters and slammed the door behind her. Lizzie could hear several thumps behind the door, a string of English curses and more bumps fading away down the corridor.

"Lizzie, are you all right?" asked Eliza. She did not wait for the answer, however. She turned her head toward a large open barrel and promptly emptied her stomach.

The stench of the quarters was overwhelming. The seasick women were lined up to get to the water closet, most of them stopping at the barrel.

"Eliza, git ta the winder an' look fer the horizon, nae." Lizzie grabbed a girl who was about ten and dragged her to the barrel just in time. "You there, comin' out o' the water closet, git a wet towel an' wash this child's face. The rest o' ye, when ye gae in there do the same. First wash yer ain face then, see ta som'one else."

Lizzie put the little girl back in her bunk. When she looked up, she saw one other woman that seemed not to be sick. "Why aren't ye sick? What helped yer no' be sick?" she demanded.

"I-I don' know. I watched out ta winder, like ye said. I dint eat nothin' this mornin'."

"Good. Remember thet t'marra, then. It don' mean ye will ne'er be sick, but it does seem ta help. Do what ye kin fer these others." Lizzie ran to the front of the room and threw her head over the barrel. She wasn't immune, she just wasn't as sick as the others. *The motion doesn't git ta me, it's the smell! First chance, I've gotta git ta the deck agin.*

The women seemed to respond to the cold cloths and several were resting in their bunks, if not comfortably, at least without

25

violent upheaval. Eliza was still watching out the porthole, afraid to leave the sight of the blackening sea meeting the deep gray sky. Even the rise and fall of the waves outside did not deter her, in her faith that Lizzie had the answer to her malady.

For two days, the gray sea collided with heavy clouds and rain beat upon the decks above them. On the third day, the sun rose, painting puffy white clouds with tinges of pink and lavender. They awoke to a mild swaying and gentle waves slapping against the sides of the ship.

The stewards removed the barrel every few hours and washed down the floors daily, for which they were profusely blessed. Lizzie dressed quickly, anxious to get up to the deck and sweet sea air. She didn't care if she missed breakfast as long as she could get outside. The air would be cold, the breeze stiff and unyielding, but she would breathe deep for the first time in days.

Eliza still had a grayish look and had not eaten during the ordeal, so Lizzie's first duty, after fresh air, was to get some food into her as soon as possible. Then, she would sit down and eat for herself. She knew she would have to be quick about getting herself outside, because breakfast was served at eight o'clock and promptly cleaned up at eight-thirty. No exceptions.

By the time she donned her coat, however, the breakfast bell had rung, and the steward had bawled out his announcement that breakfast was being served. Oatmeal, coffee, soft bread, and butter were served or rather slung into each passenger's containers. Every other day, Irish stew was added to the breakfast menu, and sometimes beans, though Lizzie opted for more simple fare. The coffee was bitter and not to her liking, but it was hot and comforting. The food was fair and plentiful. She noted that everyone was partaking after having missed several meals on the previous days.

Eliza sipped her coffee and ate the bread without butter. With Lizzie's urging, she tasted a few spoonfuls of oatmeal, gingerly and without enthusiasm.

26

Her breakfast seemed to perk her up and Eliza acqⁱ
a walk on the deck. Lizzie surmised her only motive was to see
James, whom they hadn't seen in two days.

"Dress warm as ye kin, Eliza. Ye've been feelin' poorly an'
ye will feel the cold more sharply. Here put my plaid o'er yer coat."
Eliza stood before her like a child and allowed Lizzie to dress her.
She was silent, defeated by her last few days. Although the food felt
good in her stomach, she felt weak as a newborn.

"Ye will feel better onct yer on deck," Lizzie said, hopefully.
*A few days o' fair weather would be helpful, Laird. We still have a
ways ta gae, an' sunshine would be a blessin' we'd lang remember.*

James was waiting for them on deck. He looked at Eliza,
then Lizzie, then back at Eliza again. "It's been a hard couple days
then, Eliza? Lizzie looks none the worse fer wear, but then, I figured
she'd no' let any rough sea git the best o' her. She's too ornery ta be
sick like the rest o' us, eh Eliza?"

Eliza smiled weakly. "Were ye bad off, James? Yer a
blessin' ta see fer these sore eyes. I tried ta do ever'thin' Lizzie tol'
me, but I still got sick."

"Ach, I'm all right, Eliza. I was a bit touchy fer a while
there, but I'm all right, nae. Come. Sit here on the bench in the sun."
James looked over Eliza's head at Lizzie, mouthing his unvoiced
question. *Is she all right? She's awful pale.*

Lizzie nodded her head. "Sit back an' enjoy the air, Eliza.
We can watch the other passengers and make up stories about them.
Look at that man in the tall hat. Where's he from? What d' ye think
he's about?" This was a game they played as children at
Castlewellan on Market Day, before they were old enough to mind
the tables.

Eliza smiled and picked out a candidate for her story. "He
used ta be a rich man, who's down on his luck. His clothes are worn,
but his head is high like he commands respect. He's goin' ta
America ta regain his fortune."

27

James joined in the game, "Lassies, I think ye have a gambling' man here. He pilfered the clothes a while back an' enjoys trottin' fancy, while he's lookin' fer new sheep ta fleece."

"I'm wit' James. I think he's had ta leave Queensland in a hurry, one step ahead o' the constable. Look, he's culled a lamb from the herd now," said Lizzie, as the man in question began a conversation with a young boy who dropped back from his companions. "Uh-oh, I dinna like the looks o' this."

Just then, one of the young men who had gone ahead returned and grabbed the boy by the ear. "What did I tell yer? If ye comin' wit' us, ye gotta keep up."

"I guess you two were right," said Eliza, perking up. After they played at their game for a while, James suggested they head for the other side of the ship as the wind grew stronger.

The next day was colder and their sojourn on deck shorter. They agreed to meet on deck in the afternoon, if the sea remained calm.

"I don't know what kind of meat they put in thet soup, but it was hot an' filled my belly," said James. "The bread was made of corn husks, I think, but it held up the butter jes' fine."

"I guess it pays no' ta be too curious about what they're makin' it wit'. Jes' fill ye belly when ye can, I was told," laughed Lizzie.

"Well, it was good, an' I was hungry fer a change, sae I'll no' complain," said Eliza. Turning to James, she revealed, "Lizzie's been writin' down our adventures on paper Maggie gave her."

"What d' ye find ta write about, Lizzie? We don' do anythin' but eat, sleep an' try keeping our food down," groused James.

"I find things ta write. I want ta tell Ma an' *Mórai* ever'thin' I see an' hear, so they'll knae what it's like. I skipped by the part about Eliza bein' sae sick, but I tol' them 'bout the bells an' our meals, an' the people we've seen on the ship," Lizzie revealed. "Ye knae how Ma loves books 'bout Africa an' India. Well, I kin tell her

28

'bout America. No' nae, but *someday*, maybe she'll come ta live wit' us."

"Well, we don't e'en knae what it's like yet, lassie. Yer cart's gittin' way ahead o' yer horse," warned James.

"I want ta tell the story from its beginnin', James."

"Well, don' leave out too much o' the bad parts, Lizzie. She'll think yer lyin'. Besides, from the look o' the clouds up ahead, we're ridin' right inta one o' the bad parts now! C'mon." James spotted the rain-heavy clouds as they were sailing into them. "Let's go!" James headed down the stairs helping the girls keep their footing, as the groups of passengers on the deck rushed down the hatchway.

That night, the ship pitched higher than it seemed possible. The ten women in the tiny quarters fought for space at the two portholes. The occupants of their quarters seemed to moan in unison, hanging onto the poles that supported their bunks to keep from being tossed out onto the floor. The women who were able to nurse the sick were buffeted about, banging into walls, beds and benches. The dinner bell went unanswered. One wee child, trying to help her sister was slammed against the door with such force Lizzie thought she surely was knocked senseless. She fought her way to her and found the child conscious, but brutally battered.

In the near darkness, Lizzie felt the child's arms and legs for breaks. There was already a knot on her head and she was frightened, but she would be all right. Lizzie found little to do but sit there on the floor and cry with her. She heard Eliza cry out, "Lizzie, are ye all right? Where are ye?"

"I'm fine, Eliza," she hollered back. "Just stay there. Moira is fine too. Ever'one please stay where ye are!" Lizzie held the girl and prayed for the storm to be over. Eventually, she slept. With her back to the door and the child in her arms, her prayers were answered.

"Lizzie," she heard someone calling. "Lizzie." The child had waked and was trying to rouse her. The blessed sun was shining through the portholes and someone was banging relentlessly on the door behind her head.

"Open this door!" a man roared behind her.

"Jes' a moment," Lizzie croaked, dragging her bruised body up off the floor. The child ran back to her sister and a shaky Lizzie opened the door. The young steward she met earlier stood staring at her.

"A-are you all right in here? We've come ta wash down the floors. Breakfast is served in yer dining room, Ladies. You have twenty minutes ta eat. Sorry, Miss." The young man backed away as Lizzie closed the door.

The women hurried for the wash room. Lizzie's curly hair was impossibly matted and her clothes filthy. On wobbly legs, she made her way to her bunk and tore through her bag to find something fresh to wear. She found a wrinkled blouse and skirt and donned them quickly. Her brush would not go through her wild bushy hair. "Lizzie, just tie it back in a knot an' I'll work on it after breakfast. Gae, wash yer face," said Eliza, taking charge for once.

"Aye, ma'am," teased Lizzie. "Oh, I mus' be a sight. I'll have ta clean my good dress, afore we land. How I'll do thet, I've no idea. If I wash it, it'll ne'er dry afore we git ta port."

"We'll figure som'thin', Lizzie. Let's git ta breakfast afore they shut it down." replied Eliza.

Toasted dark bread, jam and butter with terrible coffee and some cold lumpy oatmeal filled their empty bellies. "It's a good thing we're verra hungry, or this oatmeal wouldn't gae down," complained Lizzie. "Still, burnt bread an' jam is heaven after no supper last night. They canna ruin tea too badly."

Back at the women's quarters, Lizzie spread her ruined clothing out on the bed. "If I scrape the surface as best I kin, then scrub the stains only, perhaps I kin have it dry in a day or two. I

30

wonder if I could air it out on deck. If they won't allow thet, I'll wear it out on deck ta air it out," said Lizzie, thinking out loud. "I can't be meetin' my sponsor's family smellin' foul an' lookin' worse." Poking through her bag with the irons, she found her bag of rose petals. *If I use soft soap, I kin add some o' rose petals ta the suds. When I wash the spots, it should smell better. E'en when it dries, some o' the rose smell should stay on the dress.* Lizzie used the back edge of her comb to scrape the cloth of debris. In the wash room, she hung the soft wool dress on a hook and with careful attention to each stain, she scrubbed the garment thoroughly. When she was satisfied she had done her best, she held it up to the porthole in their room, looking for telltale signs of the storm's aftermath.

She lined up her irons on the heating pipes, hoping she could transfer enough heat to press her sopping dress. It would be several hours before the dress would be ready to press and the irons would be warm enough to smooth out the wrinkles, so Lizzie went to work on her disastrous hair.

Eliza made her sit on the floor while she sat behind her on the bunk. She separated one lock of hair and began to brush it gently. While she tackled each bundle of strands, she sang an old tune and Lizzie joined her. It was a peaceful endeavor and Eliza worked each lock with patience. *It's been a lang, lang while since she let me do this. Lizzie won't sit quiet enough fer it. Her hair is lovely, such a warm red-gold an' sae curly, hangin' beyond her waist. Most women would pray for hair this lovely, yet it's nothin' special ta her. If only life could be this simple. I could do this fore'er.* Impulsively, Eliza kissed the top of her sister's head and continued brushing.

Moira, the little girl Lizzie held the night before, sat down in front of Lizzie. "Yer hair is sae lang, Miss. I want my hair ta grow that lang, but Sissy say she'll keep cuttin' it if she has ta take care o' it. When I kin wash it myself an' keep it combed, I kin have lang hair. I'll ne'er cut it! No' 'til ferever an' a day," she declared.

31

"If Eliza didn't want ta straighten it out fer me, I'd have ta cut mine, too, Moira. I'm verra lucky ta have her fer a sister. Someday, she'll no' want ta do it, an' I'll have ta shave it like a man's whiskers. I'll no' have a hair on my head ta be counted." The little girl giggled at the thought.

"Well, I guess I'll have ta keep follerin' yer 'round ferever, brushin' yer unruly hair," said Eliza, winking at Moira. "I'm almos' done. What d' ye wan' me ta do with it? Shall I braid it, or d' ye want ta tie it in a bun?"

"I'll take care o' it nae, Eliza. Thank ye fer wadin' through it." Lizzie made three braids at each side of her head, pulling them back to the nape of her neck. There, she twisted the rest of it into a bun and secured it with combs.

"It's one o' the great pleasures o' my life, Lizzie," Eliza said cheerfully. Then her voice changed to one of concern. "Lizzie? With yer hair up lak' thet, I kin see how badly ye were tossed about las' night. Ye haf' a huge blue mark on the back o' yer neck. Does it hurt much, Lizzie? It looks verra painful."

"It'll be fine, Eliza. Should I wear my hair down ta cover it, then?"

"Perhaps ye should. James will worry if he sees it. Why don' yer jes' tie it back an' let it hang in a loose braid. Thet way, it won' git sae wild an' it'll still cover the bruise."

On deck, James was waiting for them anxiously. He was sporting a bluish lump on the side of his forehead, a memento of the previous evening. He touched it gingerly, and said sardonically, "I had a war with a heat pipe and fared the worst fer it. That was a wild one. Seemed like that first wave knocked us right outa bed. The top bunk fellers had the advantage o' havin' som'thin' soft ta land on. I'm hopin' we've somewhat fair weather 'til we land. I dinna think we kin stand the smell o' ourselves much langer."

"I wonder how the poor delicate first class is farin'?" speculated Lizzie. "At least they have spare clothing. My good dress

32

has seen far better days. I'm hopin' ta git it back inta respectable condition by the time we git there, 'cause it's all I've got, 'sides this 'un and a spare shirt."

"'Tis only two more days or so, an' we'll be in America, I hear. I kin las' until then, but nae more," said Eliza. "I canna imagine rich folk doin' this fer fun!"

"Well, first class passengers fair a wee bit better, an' on a bonnie day, it must feel a little like heav'n. I heard the salon passengers eat with silver spoons an' china an' crystal, an' dine on steak an' creamed potatoes. Someday, I'd like ta see that," mused Lizzie raising her little finger in a pantomime of drinking tea among the rich.

"Dinna worry, Lizzie. Steak an' potatoes ain't any better comin' up, than oatmeal and burnt toast. It's verra hard ta be elegant whilst yer losin' yer dinner, no matter how fer up the peerage ye go," laughed James. "Laird Annesley himself musta had a few rough moments wit' all the trottin' about he's done."

"Yer right, James, an' he said as much. But he musta had many wonderful moments, too," retorted Lizzie. "Otherwise, he wouldna kept goin', would he?"

The three were quiet then, each with their own thoughts. Lizzie was starting to feel nervous, with the aspect of America looming on the horizon. *What will it be like? What if...? Nae, I shall think only good things 'til they prove me wrong. Laird let me be up ta the task. An' let me be struck dumb afore my mouth gits me sent hame. I'll hafta watch my temper, too. Laird, I'm prayin' fer a forgivin' family, 'cause there's no' much hope fer my tongue an' my temper ta stay in check fer a whole year!*

Chapter Three

The next two days were fair with only a few scattered puffy white clouds to break the wide blue sky. In contrast to the peaceful weather, the ship was humming with tension born of impending landfall. Tempers flared among the men, homesick women grew weepy, and it seemed everyone was on edge but the children. The children ran unchecked about the deck, excited about the coming days. The card games were more intense, and erupted in violence, as desperate young men tried to win back their losings from craftier, professional gamblers.

Young people took to staying up late and walking the deck. They figured they would be lying awake staring in the darkness anyway. The air was very cold but fresh, certainly more pleasant than the confinement of the sleeping quarters. Eliza stayed inside, while James and Lizzie met on deck.

"I've got the shivers jes' thinkin' about workin' fer a minister's family, James. I'd pro'bly do better workin' in the shipyard wit' you," moaned Lizzie.

James laughed, "Ha! Ministers are jes' like other folk, an' they're only in charge come Sundays. They struggle with doubt an' anger like all o' us, an' their children oft behave like heathens in church. I knae, my bes' friend was one o' the worst. Besides, ye charmed thet stuffed shirt on the way ta Liverpool. He was ready ta purchase a ticket ta America, too!"

34

Lizzie blushed. "He was jes' coverin' up his uneasiness with gruffness."

"Ye may be right about workin' the shipyards, Lizzie. Ye're strong enough. Yer ears may be a little delicate fer the language though. I'd wager within a week, ye'd have the cussin' down pat, an' no one would take a poke at yer wit'out payin' the price."

Lizzie laughed at the thought of her working in the shipyard. "Yer right, imagine me takin' orders from a minister's wife, though. Eliza will have ta be on her guard ta keep me from gittin' sent back hame in disgrace."

"Lizzie, ye worry about *nothin'*. Ye took care o' yer ma, an' Maggie's practic'ly a lady herself. Jes' pretend she's an invalid, an' ye will be fine. Do ye knae wha' ye will be doin' fer this minister's wife?"

"Nae, I'm mostly a laundress, sae I've nae idea. I'm hopin' they'll keep the both o' us, but I've no fancy skills."

"One step at a time isn't thet wha' ye told Eliza? Yer gotta be strong fer her, Lizzie. Ye canna have her see yer trembling' o'er the prospects o' workin' fer this family. She's dependin' on yer ta be the brave one," James said, concern on his face.

"I *knae*, I'm jes' gittin' m'self worked up o'er nothin', aren't I?" Lizzie sighed. "It'll come soon enough, an' I'll do wha' I'm told ta do, an' thet's thet."

"Thet's right, Lizzie, I don' knae nothin' about a shipyard, but I'm figurin' all they need is a strong back thet'll take orders."

Changing the subject, she asked, "Does my dress look all right ta yer, James? Does it smell all right?"

"It looks fine, lass, but a 'course it *is* kinda dark out here. Ye smell strongly o' roses. Did ye dump a bottle o' rosewater on it?"

"Almos', it's too much, isn't it? I'm hopin' the sea air will air it out by the time we land. I don't knae how Eliza manages. She was much sicker than me, but her clothes did not suffer the damage thet mine did."

35

"Lizzie, she had only hersel' ta care fer. Ye were carin' fer the whole room, is wha' I heerd. Yer couldn't steer clear o' *ever*'one. It'll be fine."

"I'm sorry fer whinin' at yer, James. I shant complain ta Eliza. I shall be the epitome o' confidence."

"Epitome? Whate'er thet means, Mademoiselle Dictionaire. Yer talkin' ta a carpenter Lizzie, no' the Laird Mayor." He put his arm around her shoulders to soften his comment. "I'm gonna miss yer, Lizzie Heenan. E'en though yer a pain in my...." he stopped as Lizzie elbowed him in his side.

"Ye will miss the pain in yer *ribs*, if yer keep up thet talk, Mister James Heenan," laughed Lizzie. "I'm willin' ta miss yer, too. I'll write ta yer when I knae where yer stayin'. I'll be in Newton Lower Falls, Mass-a-chu-setts. I heerd o' Niagara Falls. I wonder if it's near thet."

"The sponsor is s'posed ta meet us at New York an' he'll be sure we're on the right train," said James. "Leastwise, thet's wha' Mister Coburn said. Since yer goin' wit' us mos' the way, he'll pro'bly give ye the address fer me. I'm no' much fer writin', but I wanna hear from yer, sae I'll send ye a note. Don't expect much from me, jes a page if thet, no' the volumes ye write ta Maggie."

"I'll be happy fer anythin' I git, an' I knae Eliza will, too. It's late. I think I'll gae in, James. I'm close ta freezin' out here."

"They say t'marra is the day. Right afta breakfast, I'll meet yer on deck, 'less they tell us different, g'night, Lizzie."

"G'night, Jamie-boy," she said using his childhood name. She took his hand down the hatchway stairs and he walked her to the women's quarters. Lizzie had been thinking all day, *this is the last time we'll do this on the ship. This is the last time we'll have supper, walk together on the deck, sit on these benches. It's been our hame fer eight days. It's hard ta believe we could miss it, but miss it, we will. All day, we've heard snatches o' conversations talkin' about the Lady in the Harbor, the statue holdin' a book an' a torch,*

36

welcomin' us ta America. T'marra, we'll see her. We'll see America!

Lizzie in her nightdress, slipped under the rough blanket, next to Eliza. In the dim moonlight shining from the porthole, she watched her sister in peaceful repose. Soon, she drifted into a fitful slumber, dreaming of the Lady in the water waving her hand, saying, "C'mon Lizzie, git off the ship. *America's* waitin' fer ye."

The next morning, when Lizzie and Eliza went up on deck, a crowd had already gathered at the prow of the ship. They edged their way toward the front along the railing. Their fellow passengers were chattering in a mix of Irish Gaelic and English. "Look!" someone shouted. "Over there!"

Straining their eyes and pointing, they could see a tiny slip of land along the far horizon. A great shout rose from all decks. They had seen hope. It was the *Promised Land*! The noise was deafening. It drowned out the crash of the waves against the bow. The spirit of the passengers was so elated, they broke into dancing and hugging the very strangers of whom they were so wary during the voyage. Women and old men wept for joy. Young men whooped and hollered, until at last they were spent.

The great ship's horn blew and the crowd settled into a quiet hum of anticipation. The stewards urged them to go to their quarters to prepare for landing. Since they were still a long way from shore, the passengers muttered angrily, questioning the order. Nonetheless, they followed the crowd down the hatchway to their quarters.

As Lizzie and Eliza gathered their belongings, the stammering boy-steward announced the reason for the return to quarters. "P-Please have your papers ready for d-debarkation, ladies. Keep them s-safely tucked away on deck. Anyone 'thout their papers when we land will be sent home forthwith. Bring yer baggage up to the deck in an orderly fashion.

"We will s-sail into the harbor and as you leave the ship, we will put yer name on the debarkation manifest list in order. You'll

37

have a number attached to yer clothing. Do *not* remove yer number. Once you're off the ship, you will board a ferry as directed. The ferry will bring yer to Ellis Island where you will be examined. If you pass inspection, you will be granted immigration status. Answer all questions." The young man took a breath then, resumed his speech.

"S-stay t'gether until directed otherwise. R-remain orderly. Do you understand? G-good."

Before opening the door to leave, he looked around at all the eager and frightened faces staring back at him and said with a grin, "Welcome to America, L-Ladies."

The women cheered their young steward and the nearest ones hugged him. His face turned red, but he was smiling as he hurried out the door. The women broke into noisy chatter that echoed through the cramped room that had been their home for so long.

Lizzie felt a shiver go through her as she thought of finally getting to America. She glanced over at her half-sister and found her grinning with excitement. "Let's git our bags an' go up top."

They made their way up to the deck, with the others. Climbing with their bags, bundles, and suitcases, they scrambled for a place near the rail.

The two girls edged their way to the front of the ship, so they would not miss a moment of the arrival. James waved them forward where he had saved a place at the rail. Off to the right, they could see forest lined shores with boats of every size bobbing in the water. Buildings peeked over the trees and in clearings. Seagulls swooped overhead crying raucously over the sound of the waves crashing against the ship.

"There she is! It's the lady with the torch. Look, isn't she *beautiful!*" Again a great roar went up from all decks. There were tears and shouts and dancing once again. Now it was real. Now was the moment for which they had waited. Lizzie squeezed Eliza's hand

and kissed her wet cheek. "We've made it, Eliza. We're here!" James grabbed them both in a great bear hug, and shouted, *"Hoorah!"*

The massive ocean liner pulled into the harbor and eased along a stretch of the wood planked dock. The steam engines thrummed and groaned, then shuttered to a halt. Lizzie could hear the sailors shouting as they called and answered orders far below the deck where she and her fellow steerage passengers stood.

Deep grinding noises vibrated in the belly of the ship, temporarily calling their attention. Shrugging in ignorance of the noise they heard, their companions turned once again to face Lady Liberty. On the gangplank, first class passengers began trickling onto the dock. Freed from their eight days of ocean captivity, they resembled drunken revelers once they hit the solid, unmoving dock. Lizzie recalled the warning that Laird Annesley had given her about the feet that would betray her on dry land. She could hear the steerage boys laughing rudely at the missteps of finely-clad passengers below. *Just wait yer turn, lads. We'll see how well you do then,* she chuckled.

"Come nae, m' lassies," urged James. "They're about ta gif' us our freedom from this queasy barge." He picked up his bundle and headed toward mid-ship where they were raising the second gangway. There was a clerk and a steward standing at the top, inspecting, and asking questions of the first of the steerage passengers.

Lizzie saw the steward attach the promised number to the jacket of the first man and point down to the dock, then off to the ferry which had docked just ahead of the liner. The ferry was pulling out as he reached the dock, but he went to the same area and stood there. Before long, she could see another ferry pull in, tie off, and open its belly to the gathering crowd of numbered passengers.

Lizzie stepped just in front of Eliza as the line grew smaller in front of them. Questions were fired at them: "Name", "Age", "Destination", "Born", "Number 4."

The young steward blushed, pinned a number on Lizzie's coat and said in a very official tone, "S-step lively, now. Go, down the gangway, to the left to that f-ferry there. It will t-take you to Ellis Island. Answer all questions. Good luck, M-miss."

"Thank yer, Steward Jameson. Good fortune ta yer, too," said Lizzie, her eyes dancing, taking one last delight in teasing the red-faced boy. Down the gangway she went, picking her way carefully, not wanting to be the object of mocking scorn of the boys watching from the deck above. Reaching the bottom, she noticed Eliza was not behind her. Another woman had taken her place. When she looked again, Eliza was at the top of the walkway, inching her way down, as others passed her.

"Ah, Number 4, step lively, nae," Lizzie teased. As Eliza reached her, she lurched dreadfully and Lizzie had to grab her quickly, else she would have slipped off the dock. "Whoops, better stick with me. Lucky fer us, I have a bag of irons ta keep us steady."

"Lizzie, where's James? Have y' seen him?" Panic lined Eliza's face.

"We'll meet up wit' him, if no' on the ferry, then at the registration center. Don't worry, Eliza. He's goin' ta Mass-a-chu-setts wit' us." Lizzie dragged out the name, hoping she pronounced it correctly. "It'll be all right. Let's git on the ferry. He's pro'bly waitin' on us. Look, Eliza, no' a cow in sight. Ferries in America are fer *people*," exclaimed Lizzie, trying to cheer her up.

"Lizzie, Eliza, o'er here!" shouted James from the back of the ferry.

"My word, James, ye sound like yer callin' the sheep hame." admonished Lizzie when she had fought her way to him with Eliza in tow.

"Beggin' yer pardon, m' lady, would yer rather no' find me at all?" he said tilting his head, mockingly. Lizzie took a very unladylike swat at his shoulder.

After about twenty minutes at the dock, the ferry shuttered and moved forward with a lurch. They were cruising to the island, going right by the Liberty statue. They stopped their chatter to stare at the giant woman holding the torch. The passengers were silent and stared gape-mouthed in awe of the sight.

Just beyond her, stood Ellis Island and the registration center. It was magnificent. Much like a wooden palace, its yellow-beige color glowed in the sunlight under a blue slate roof. The columned turrets, and surrounding colonnade, were breathtaking. The tree-lined walks, and expanse of well-maintained lawns, reminded Lizzie of the grounds at Castlewellan. A sudden pang of homesickness surprised her. *C'mon, Lizzie. This is the adventure yer wanted. Don' be faint o' heart, nae. This is America. This is where ye kin be anyone ye want ta be.*

"Attention passengers," a disembodied voice commanded. "You will disembark as directed, enter the building, and go to the aisle corresponding to your number. You will remain in *that* line only, until you are told to go to another station. Answer all questions. Conduct yourselves in an orderly fashion. Ladies and gentlemen," he said, pausing dramatically, "Welcome to America!" When the side rail was opened, the first passengers ran down the ferry walkway and into the building. There was much pushing and shoving, as men and women grabbed their bags and children, joining the tide of exiting passengers.

As Lizzie entered the building, her eyes were drawn up to the ceiling of the great hall. It was impossibly high, and flooded with light, from what seemed to be a hundred windows at the top. "This room alone must be almost an acre," exclaimed James over the babbling voices of hundreds of would be immigrants. "Here's number four." The aisle constructed of wooden rails was already

41

clogged with a long line of immigrants. There were twelve such aisles, James noted, and each one nearly full. He saw that some families were sitting on their bags and surmised they had been waiting a long time. "It looks like we'll be here awhile."

Now, Lizzie's assessment changed from "the last time we will sit on these benches..." to "the first time we rode on an American ferry...", "the first time we saw constables in America..." *There will be many 'first times' in America,* she mused. She tried to memorize what she was seeing, determined to describe it in full to her mother when she had the chance to write it down. Her eyes met another young woman's, two aisles over. Their lines seemed to move at the same rate. She noticed the disheveled girl was with child, and with a pang of sympathy, imagined how difficult her journey must have been. *She's barely more than a child herself,* thought Lizzie. *She's hangin' onto her husband's coat, fer fear o' losin' him. She looks sad, an' sae scairt. I wonder what drove them here. She's dressed all in black with her hair covered in a tight black kerchief, wit' nary a strand showin'. What language is she speakin' ta her husban'?*

"Lizzie!" Eliza's voice was sharp in her ear. "We're nearly ta the front. Gae ahead o' me, sae I kin hear what ye answer the man."

"Eliza, ye will be fine. Jes' answer the questions the bes' ye kin." Nevertheless, Lizzie stepped in front of her. James was already done and walking around the man at the desk, following the aisle to a man at another desk.

The inspector wore a black suit, tie and cap, with a white shirt. *His collar needs starchin' an' pressin',* Lizzie thought. She heard the questions and answered in the same mechanical voice he offered.

"Name?", "How did you pay for your passage?", "Do you have the promise of a job?" and "Are you an anarchist?" *An anarchist, nae, I don' plan ta overthrow the United States government!* "Are you going to join a relative or friend?", "What is

42

your destination?" *Newton Lower Falls, Mass-a-chu-setts, thets a mouthful.* "Are you traveling with family or alone?", "What is your occupation?" *Servant, a laundress really, but I'll do as I'm told.* "Where were you born?", "Where did you reside?", "How much is two and one?", "How much is two and two?" *I guess I don' hafta be too clever in mathematics, do I?* "How do you wash stairs; from the top down or from the bottom up?" *Seems reasonable ta start at the top, but I ne'er washt more than one step in m' life.* Can you draw a diamond?", "Copy this figure." *I ne'er saw but one diamond in m' whole life an' thet was in a man's hand. It didn't look much like thet, but if that's wha' yer wantin', here 'tis.* "Papers, Miss?"

"Good, Miss. Up the stairs to that gentleman in Aisle 4. Next?"

Lizzie lugged her bag up the stairs to the next station. Another room divided into the numbered aisles brought her to another inspector and assistant. She stood as tall as she could and answered more questions. He had a ship's medical inspection card in his hand, reading from it he said, "Name", "Last residence", "Diseases", "Infirmities", "Open mouth", "Bow your head", "Hold out your arms straight in front of you, that's fine", "No mark", "Follow the aisle", and at last, "Next?"

She moved on to another station, another inspection. He intoned, "Do you have a sponsor?", "A job?", "A place to live?", and "money?" *Aye, Aye, Aye and Aye.*

"Were you promised a job by anyone other than the clergy or the government?" *No.*

"What is your destination?" *Newton Lower Falls, Mass-a-chu-setts. Aye, I have a ticket. Aye, someone should be here ta meet me.*

"Go to that room, number five. Stay there until your sponsor arrives. If he is not here by four o'clock, you will be detained overnight. You will be fed and you will have a place to sleep. He

43

will be able to collect you in the morning." *Laird, is this it? Are we goin' ta be done wit' this? It's been hours.*

Lizzie entered room five, found a bench, sat down and waited for Eliza. She put her aching feet up on her bag, being careful to tuck her dress around her. *No' very lady-like perhaps, but I mus' rest m' poor hooves fer a bit. Here comes poor Eliza. She looks like she's been dragged through the streets, poor thing.* Lizzie patted the bench beside her. "Are ye all right, Eliza? Ye look a wee bit peaked."

"Thet was a load o' questions ta answer, wasn't it?"

Her half-sister offered no reply, but a weary stare and a stifled yawn. She put her feet beside Lizzie's and her head on her sister's shoulder. In the twenty by forty-foot room, *immigrants*, as they were now described, gathered in clumps waiting for their names to be called. Lizzie looked around the room, recognizing several passengers from the ship. Then she saw James at the far end, rising from his seat and walking toward them. She barely raised her hand to acknowledge him.

"I have ne'er been sae bone weary from standin' still an' answerin' questions," she said to him. "I suppose it was from worryin' if we were gonna be sent ta the other rooms for those who had no means o' support, a shakin' disease or were no' smart enough ta draw a diamond, or square. There was a little girl who had a sore on her chin an' they sent her ta the hospital."

"Aye, an' how about askin' us how ta wash stairs. I thought they were gonna make me demonstrate it. Did ye knae how many stairs they were? *Twenty-six!* An' they's watchin' all the ways up ta see if ye were gonna make it! I felt bad fer the little ones, sae I carried one. She weighed an unmerciful ton by the time I reached the top o' the stairs. I gladly handed her back, I'll tell ye."

"As much as m' bag o' irons I'll wager. The man asked how lang I had a limp, an' I tol' them only as lang as I been carryin' this bag. Then he came o'er and picked it up. 'Good Lord, woman,' he says, no wonda ye favor ye right leg. If ye kin carry thet thin' 'round, yer strong enough fer me."

"Elizabeth Heenan, James Heenan, come forward," shouted an official at the other end of the room. The three gathered their bags and walked toward the man who was calling several more names. "Papers." He looked over Lizzie and Eliza's papers carefully. He looked at the tall slender man in the black suit beside him. "Were you lookin' fer two Elizabeth Heenans?"

"One's Lizzie and the other Eliza?" asked the bearded gentleman of about thirty-five. "I received two sets of papers, but we were not sure if they were one with two sets of papers or two with one set of papers each. We paid for two and hoped that was right."

"Very well, I deliver them into your care, Mister Bachelor. Please sign here. James Heenan, Thomas O'Neill, Shamus Stewart, and Patrick Mahony, you will accompany this gentleman to Newton Lower Falls, Massachusetts. Once there, you men will continue on to Quincy. You have your tickets. Stay together."

The group of six awkwardly followed the man in the black suit. James grabbed Lizzie bag, and said, "Take Eliza's bag. It will be lighter, an' Eliza will need all her strength ta keep up. We're obviously in a hurry." Without regard for his shorter companions, Mister Bachelor loped purposely on long, lanky legs, through the corridor, and down the stairs. At the dock, he ushered them onto a ferry, and checked his watch for the fourth time since they laid eyes on him.

"Mister Bachelor, are we late?" asked Lizzie as sweetly as she could.

"We have to make the 5:15 if we are going to make the connection to Boston in Albany at 8:30," he answered impatiently. "You were expected to be through here an hour ago."

The group grumbled among themselves, wondering how they could have prevented their tardiness. Mister Bachelor added, "I realize you had no control over your situation, but it will be a tight

45

squeeze to get the train in time. When the ferry drops us, a wagon will be waiting to take us to the station, then we will have to hurry to get to track twelve before the train pulls out. Please step lively and stay together. We've a long night ahead of us."

Lizzie was tired, but excited by the bustling city. The buildings were taller than she thought possible. The noise and confusion both frightened, and exhilarated her. Nothing she had ever seen prepared her for the scope of New York City. As beautiful and impressive as the newly constructed Ellis Island Registration Center was, Grand Central Station seemed to overload her senses. The huge vaulted ceiling, the mass of people all scurrying from place to place, was overwhelming. The echoing cacophony of newsboys, and shop vendors, shouting over the train announcements, was deafening. The acrid smell of steam engines, mixed with the aroma of cooking food, made her stomach lurch. So many of the people were dressed in such colorful finery, that it was easy to believe that America was indeed the *Promised Land*. "Come, Lizzie!" demanded James. "We've no time ta waste."

At last, they boarded the train. Lizzie was amazed the boarding platform was at the same height as the train floor. She didn't have to lug her heavy bag up steps into the train. *Thank the Good Laird for small blessings! I'm sae tired I kin hardly put one foot in front o' the other. It's been a lang day. I kin no' believe I was on a ship from across the ocean this mornin', prodded all day, one way an' another, an' questioned o'er an' o'er. Nae, I'm on a train bound for who knaes where.*

Lizzie and Eliza settled into a seat near the front of the car and admired their surroundings. Mister Bachelor sat alone on the opposite side, while James and the other men sat behind. As the train lurched forward and gained speed, Lizzie stared out the window at the passing vistas. *Oh, this is interestin',* she thought. *It's the back o' the buildings an' hames. The laundry's strung out between the buildings, an' in the yards. How can they keep their*

46

linens clean wit' all this soot an' steam from the trains goin' by? There's a fire in a barrel sae close ta the laundry! These people are no' fancy dressers. I guess no' all the people in America are rich, then. How do they live all bunched up like thet? Thet one has four porches. What's it like ta hafta climb all those stairs at the end o' the day, jes' ta git hame? All we did was cross a threshold, ta be inside. Lizzie watched a group of children playing, and smiled. *Children are the same the world o'er, no matter what their circumstance. They don' knae different, sae they are happy wit' what they have.*

Eliza and Lizzie discussed the view, but the sound, and motion of the train, soon lulled them to sleep.

It seemed like no more than a minute, before James was jostling them awake. "Time ta change trains, lasses. We're in Albany."

Lizzie stifled a yawn and asked, "Wha's Albany?"

"Albany, m' lady, is the capitol city o' the state o' New York. Mister Bachelor says we will change trains there fer Massachusetts. We have a little time, sae we'll get somethin' ta eat, then board the next train."

Mister Bachelor said to the group gathered around him, "You'll each be allowed 15 cents for supper. I will take care of the tip. This will allow you a drink, a sandwich, and a slice of pie, if you wish. Come this way." He then led them to a small store just outside the train station, with a row of stools in front of a counter. The wall behind the counter announced their wares.

"Who's payin' fer dese Irishers?" demanded the man behind the counter.

"I am," said Mister Bachelor with an arched eyebrow. "These are hard-working, God-fearing folk who wish to have supper." With that, he reached in his pocket, and slapped two dollars down on the counter. He kept his hand over the bills, and added, "I expect the best service you can provide for them."

The man's angry face turned red and he replied, "Yes, sir. Beggin' yer pardon, but ye ne'er know wit' dis sort. Wha' kin I git cha?" The bald, mustached man in the dirty apron spoke only to Mister Bachelor.

If Mister Bachelor was angry, he did not allow it to show on his face. As each one of the group made their choices, he repeated them to the surly owner who wrote them down. When the orders were conveyed, the man went out to the kitchen.

"Mister Bachelor, have we done somethin' untoward?" asked Lizzie, nervously.

"No, Miss Heenan. It is a sad fact that some of the Irish who came before you have tainted this man's view of the entire race. You will find that some Americans follow his viewpoint, and others, thankfully, do not. Try not to let it bother you." He dropped his voice to a low whisper. "He is plagued with a very small mind."

Lizzie felt a sense of foreboding from the incident. *I've felt the stare o' people who thought I was less, because I owned less than they, but I have ne'er thought a whole country could be sae judged by virtue o' havin' been born ta it. Have I made a horrible mistake, comin' ta this country?* She looked back at their guide, and met his eyes.

He shook his head very slightly then, with a tight little smile, said, "We cannot dislodge the demons men wish to keep, Miss. We can only disprove their notions by demonstrating who we really are, with God's help."

The little man came back with their food in a better mood. He nodded at Mister Bachelor, perhaps hoping for a good tip. To Mister Bachelor, he said, "I hope dey enjoys da meals. It's all fresh an' da bes' in town." He smiled as if he hadn't exercised that part of his face in a long time. Mister Bachelor did not offer a reply, but simply nodded his head.

Lizzie had to admit, the food was delicious. The sandwich was made with a thick slice of ham, the whitest bread Lizzie had ever seen, and butter. Her tea was a bit different than she was used to, but strong and palatable, served with cream. They all selected the apple pie, served piping hot. The flavor of the food was aided substantially by the hunger of its consumers.

Mister Bachelor checked his watch again and announced, "It's time, ladies and gentlemen. We have another train to catch." Lizzie noticed he left eight cents on the counter.

Once they were on the Boston-bound train, she asked their guardian the significance of the eight cents. He replied, "The customary tip is one cent for each person. The eighth cent was for the next group of Irish immigrants that man serves. Perhaps he will acquire some manners, if encouraged to do so."

Lizzie smiled and mentally raised her appraisal of this man, sent to escort her group of 'Irishers' to their new home. *Next year, when he does this agin, will he gae back ta the selfsame place?* Answering her own question, she thought, *Aye, I'll wager he will. If only ta see if his experiment was a success.*

Chapter Four

The next nine hours were spent speeding through the dark, interrupted by few station stops. Lizzie slept fitfully. Waking in a start, she looked for Eliza, James, and Mister Bachelor. Having accounted for everyone, she noticed the dignified Mister Bachelor was sitting upright, and was wide awake.

"Mister Bachelor, what keeps ye awake?" she whispered.

"I am charged with bringing you safely to your destination, Miss Heenan. I will sleep tomorrow when that duty is done. Unfortunately, there are those who would take advantage of sleeping passengers, by stealing their possessions. So I will stand guard. You are safe, Miss. Get some sleep while you can."

Lizzie was moved by this affirmation of his protection. She hadn't thought she could be in danger. In her best speech, she replied, "Thank you, Mister Bachelor. I hope you're well paid for this."

"I receive expenses only, Miss. I do this for the man for whom you will work. I owe him much, and it is a small repayment on a very large debt."

"Can you tell me about him?"

"Only that he is a brave, Godly man who is a powerful inspiration to all who meet him. He is an educator, and a shepherd with a great heart."

"I only hope I can serve such a man without disappointing him. I'm told that I'm given to speaking my mind, and I'll have to practice not doing that."

Mister Bachelor chuckled. "As long as you're polite, you probably won't have to worry much on that account. He's a man of generous spirit and is known to be outspoken himself, on occasion.

50

Just do your best and you'll not go far wrong. Get some rest now, Miss. Tomorrow will be another long day for you."

Lizzie soon let the motion of the train lull her to sleep again. She dreamed of her new home, and the minister she would work for. She pictured him in the pulpit of a grand church, shouting about the Book of Revelation, telling her she would have to go home, she was not worthy of America. She was an "Irisher" who couldn't keep her tongue. She was being dragged in chains to a ship bound for Ireland when, startled by the stopping train, she woke again.

In her usual accounting, Lizzie noticed Mister Bachelor was gone! James, awake, answered her unasked question. "He's in the privy, Lizzie. He'll be back."

"There is a privy?" she asked.

"Aye, were ye no' listenin'? It's in the back o' the car the door on the left side."

The train threw Lizzie side to side down the aisle to the end of the car, just as Mister Bachelor was opening the narrow door.

"Be careful, Miss Heenan. The train is unpredictable in its motion." He pointed out the various features of the water closet and how it worked. *I never..!* Lizzie thought. *They's toilet papers comin' right out o' the wall; a chain to make water go through the bowl; e'en a towel on the back o' a door that circulates to a dry, clean area. They's no room fer a basket ta put dirty towels in, an' this one's always clean. They's a bowl inside the wall ta wash yer hands, by pushin' a button, fer heaven's sake!* A sudden lurch of the train brought Lizzie out of her state of wonder.

She left the room, sheepishly rubbing her elbow. Once she was in the corridor, she quickly assessed the arrangement of her clothing, thankful the others were asleep, and Mister Bachelor was facing forward. *There could be unfortunate consequences to using this privy in a full skirt,* she thought. She made her way to her seat, and asked quietly, "Mister Bachelor, how much longer?"

"Another hour or so, Miss. Just before dawn. The Newton Lower Falls Station is where you'll be met by the younger Reverend Twombly. I will continue to Quincy with the men, to the shipyard. I will see them settled, and then return to the falls. Is there anything I can do for you, Miss?"

Tired, she dropped her formal speech. "If it is no' too much trouble, could yer bring back the postal information where my cousin will be stayin', sae I kin write ta him? If I leave it ta him to write ta me first, it may ne'er happen, an' I'll lose him," said Lizzie.

"Of course, Miss. Oftentimes, young men don't think they need to write their families, to let them know they are well. Praise God, women are wise enough to keep those ties connected. Do you have other brothers and sisters at home?"

"Aye, I haf two half-brothers and a half-sister at hame. Eliza, here, is my half-sister. I am my mother's only child. When I kin save enough after this year, I'll bring her an' my grandmere here, too."

"Sounds like you have your plans all made. There are many twists and turns to the path of life."

"'Tis true enough, but a life should not happen only by chance. The Good Laird gave us a mind to use, did he not? We may face obstacles on our way, but shouldn't we follow the path o' the dreams He gives us?"

"You're a clever girl, Miss Heenan. I will think on that. I may have a dream to follow, myself," Mister Bachelor replied. Then, his thoughts turning inward, he faced the dark, misty window.

He has a lot on his mind, he does, thought Lizzie. Not for the first time, she wondered at his comments. *He owes the minister a great debt. He's at a crossroads in his life. Let him be, Lizzie. Ye may ne'er see him again, an' yer makin' up stories ta satisfy yer ain curious mind. Ye haf' enough ta keep yer worrisome brain occupied. We're almos' there, in Newton Lower Falls, an' ye will be wishin' ye slept this night.*

Before long, the braking wheels commenced their screeching, and the whistle signaled the train's approach to the station. The sky had lightened, and feathery trees took shape, as they slowed to a grinding halt. The last backward heave of the train woke Eliza. "Lizzie? We're here?" she asked in a tiny frightened voice.

"We're here, Eliza. The adventure continues!" Lizzie grinned at her sister, excitement creeping into her voice. "Let me straighten yer bonnet. James will get yer bag. Give him a hug."

James took both bags down the step to the platform where Mister Bachelor stood waiting to help the two women off the train. A hug for James from each of the girls, and he bounded up the step again. He turned to wave before he disappeared into the car.

Mister Bachelor shook hands with a pale and slender, but dignified man of about his same age.

"Miss Heenan and Miss Heenan, it is my pleasure to introduce you to the Reverend Mister Twombly. He will attend to your arrival at the parsonage. I regret I must take my leave so hastily. It was a great pleasure to have made your acquaintance. Miss Heenan, I will attend to your request upon my return."

The minister looked at Mister Bachelor with curiosity, and then dismissed it as if it were no consequence. He bowed slightly toward the two women, and abruptly turned on his heel, motioning for them to follow. Eliza and Lizzie looked at each other a little surprised, but quickly grabbed their bags, and scurried after him. At the side of the station platform, he led them to a small open carriage, indicated they should get in the back, and mounting the driver's seat, he waited for them to climb in.

Lizzie mulled over this odd behavior as she sat looking out the window. The spectacular view wiped the disturbing thoughts away, however. "Look, Eliza! We're riding right over the falls!"

There below them, was a great gushing of water, gleaming with the newly risen sun. Halfway across the rushing water was a brilliant rainbow. Lizzie caught her breath in the sheer beauty of it.

53

Deep green lawns painted the landscape before them. April morning dew made everything sparkle. The houses were grand with decorative trim at the rooftops, each one unique. The sky bore a deepening blue, now that the purple rays of dawn were gone.

She wanted this ride to go on forever. They turned a corner and houses were closer together, but still majestic. Until now, she had only seen the budding yellow-green willows and flowering hedges in pictures from Lord Annesley's botanical collection. *Ma would be sae excited ta see this! The Earl's trees an' flowers are everywhere.*

Lizzie gathered her courage to speak to the distant driver. "Reverend, it is kind of yer to drive us ta the parsonage. Ye are truly blessed ta live in sech a beautiful place."

The minister cleared his throat and abruptly answered, "Yes, Miss. We will be there shortly."

Again, Lizzie and Eliza looked at each other in wonder, and resumed admiring their surroundings. Within minutes, the carriage stopped and Mister Twombly stepped down. He held out his hand to assist them to the sidewalk, then folding his hands behind his back, he turned to lead them to the house. He walked briskly to the broad front porch, and then turned sharply to the side, following a pathway of flat stones toward the back of the house. The white clapboard house was three levels and much closer to the street than the previous, more lavish homes they had seen. The wide front porch lead to a massive double door with stained glass windows set in ornate carved frames. The tall narrow windows in the front made Lizzie think of the church at home, in a smaller, more intimate scale.

As they walked to the back of the house, the building became less decorated, but still interesting for Lizzie. There was a four-foot privet hedge near the back of the house with a decorative iron gate. Mister Twombly led them through a neat sunny yard to the back entrance of the house.

Four wide steps lead to a screened in wooden porch running two-thirds the back length of the house. The door opened suddenly as he approached.

"Come in, come in, and welcome," invited the tiny, energetic woman holding the door as they entered. For the first time, Lizzie saw Reverend Twombly smile. He kissed the diminutive older woman and said, "Hello Mother. How are you today?" He looked into her eyes, seemed to be satisfied that she was doing well and continued.

"May I present the Misses Heenan? This is my mother, Missus Twombly." Immediately turning back to his mother, he said, "I have a great deal to do to prepare for Sunday, Mother. If you'll forgive me, I will leave you to get acquainted."

"Of course, dear." Turning to her two new servants, she said, "You may hang your coats and bonnets on those pegs, for now. Come, sit. You must be tired from your long journey. I have tea and biscuits for you." Lizzie and Eliza, confused, sat as directed.

"Missus Twombly, please, I don' wish ta be ungracious, but please let me pour fer yer. We are no' here ta be served, but ta serve yer," said Lizzie.

"There will be time enough for that, my dear. Just indulge me for the moment, while I get to know you." She held out a tiny hand to keep Lizzie seated. *Indeed, this is strange. What is expected o' me? Keep yer tongue, Lizzie. Find out what's goin' on afore ye open yer mouth.*

For the next half hour, Missus Twombly asked questions about their experiences in household tasks, explained the family schedules, and talked about their social obligations. Lizzie felt that this warm and interesting woman would be demanding, but fair with them. *But, what am I ta do?*

"Now what I want," said Missus Twombly, "is to have a name to call you. You are both Elizabeth? What does your family call you?"

"I am Lizzie, and my half-sister is Eliza." *Oh, that sounds sae silly when I say it out loud. What mus' she think o' us?*

"Very well, then. Lizzie, you will be our cook and Eliza, you will be our maid. We have a lot of work to do to be ready for Sunday. For now, I will take you to your rooms so you can put your things away. Lizzie, your room is here off the kitchen, so you can tend the fires. Eliza, your room is on the top floor, to more efficiently tend to the rooms just below. You will find a list of duties and schedules in your rooms. I will personally show you how each task is to be completed, so if there is anything you do not understand, you will learn as we get through the week. You will find a clean uniform on the back of your door. Please put it on and we will make adjustments as needed."

Lizzie entered her room with great curiosity. She put her things away neatly and turned her attention to her uniform. There was a gray shift with slightly puffed sleeves, narrowing down to the wrist, a voluminous white apron that covered both front and back, and a ruffled cap that covered her hair completely. She had seen one such an outfit at the castle door in Castlewellen, but had never worn one. The apron had wide deep pockets that Lizzie tried to imagine filling. Poking through the drawers of the small bureau, she was relieved to find another uniform for a spare.

Dressed in her uniform and energized by the myriad of new things to learn, Lizzie was no longer tired from her train trip. She was anxious to get started. *How on earth do I cook here? I've always used a cook fire outside! I saw thet monstrous iron stove in the kitchen. Wha' do I do wit' it? Where's the fire? When Connie Morgan bought thet heatin' stove from America, he set it up outside an' all he could do is make smoke fer the first two weeks! He figured it out later, an' brought it inta the cottage, but it took a while. Oh my, how am I ever gonna do this?*

As Lizzie was inspecting her new work area, the door flew open with a bang and a dark haired woman of about thirty strode in,

56

carrying several dresses over her arm. "Where's Mother?" she demanded.

"I'm sorry, Miss. I think she went upstairs with the maid. May I help you?"

"Oh, she's not supposed to be climbing those stairs! Take these dresses and air them out." The woman turned on her heel, leaving Lizzie with a heap of clothes in her arms, staring at the closing door.

Thet was Miss Twombly? Well, I knae ta air clothin', let's see how they git it done here. She stepped out on the back porch looking around. Up under the roof of the porch, she found a pulley with a rope hanging down. *Well, that rope mus' gae somewheres. Look around. Ah, here 'tis. I'll tie it ta this hook on the other side.* That accomplished, Lizzie looked for pins or hangers and a sheet of some kind. Not finding any, she threw the dresses one at a time over the rope and fluffed out the skirts as best she could. They would need a little pressing, but the wind would air them nicely. They were conservatively cut frocks but very well made. Lizzie tried to imagine such beautiful dresses on her.

As she was turning to enter the house again, the door opened in her hand. "Oh, for pities' sake, Mother, when will we get some decent help in this house? She's put my dresses on the rope with no sheet under them, and nothing to secure them from blowing into the neighbor's yard. Honestly!"

"Isabella! Please do not be rude. We will fix your dresses. You go help your father." Turning to Lizzie, she said, "Please, forgive us, Lizzie. There is no way for you to have known."

Lizzie face grew red as she struggled to control her temper.

The fragile-looking woman smiled and patted her hand. "You did just fine. I will show you how to prepare the rope to receive my daughter's dresses and show you where the pins are. Do not concern yourself, Lizzie. I am remiss in that my daughter seems to have forgotten the virtues of humility and compassion."

57

Missus Twombly showed her a drawer near the door that held small clean sheets which she placed over the rope Lizzie had tied. In a box by the door on the porch were the elusive pins to secure the sheets. The dresses were thrown over the sheets and pinned. "You will have to watch the weather doesn't turn too damp while these garments are out here."

"Missus Twombly, ma'am, where would I press these fine dresses when I bring them in?" Lizzie asked as they were going inside.

"I will show you everything, Lizzie. First, Eliza will bring you the breakfast trays to clean, and then we will begin preparing lunch. Oh my, I think I will just sit here for a moment to catch my breath, if you don't mind. I can direct you from here." She sat slowly into a bentwood rocker in the corner of the gleaming kitchen. Smiling weakly, she continued to direct the activities of the morning.

Looking around quickly, Lizzie thought, *I will be fine workin' here. If I kin please this gracious woman, an' avoid her wrathful daughter, I may jes' be able ta last my time. I haven't met the Reverend's father yet, but 'twill happen soon enough. Ach, this woman has a list fer ever'thin'!*

In the next few weeks, Lizzie was caught in a whirlwind of new experiences. Mrs. Twombly explained the mechanics, vagaries, and what seemed the magical aspects of the *great iron beast* that dominated her realm in the kitchen. Missus Twombly for her part, kept her parties to an intimate size, having small groups of women for luncheons, and limiting her dinner parties to single guests while Lizzie was learning the complex duties of being the family cook of an important family.

Lizzie learned to cook from *Mrs. Lincoln's Boston Cook Book: What To Do and What Not To Do in Cooking.* It was the best of cookery, according to the tiny mistress of the household. Efficiency in cooking and the caring of her stove were paramount.

Nothing was to be wasted. On the back of her ever-engaged stove, were many small pots attesting to this 'waste not, want not' cooking. There was baked flour for darkening meat sauces; lightly dried crushed bread crumbs for dipping or frying fish and light meats; and darkened sugar to add to meat sauces and dark fruited breads. There were coarse salt, fine salt, and sea salt cellars.

There was an ever-cooking pot to catch the greens and ends of fresh vegetables. This broth was strained to add to gravies and "company soups" as needed. The rest of the broth, a little corn starch, left-over vegetables, and meat trimmings were added to a stewpot for "back-door" guests. Sugar or salt were added to balance the flavors.

Lizzie learned to maintain the fire in the stove for its best use. A low fire in the evening, best for raising bread dough overnight; high in the morning to bake the day's breads and cook breakfast; then a slower heat in the afternoon, for the more delicate dessert phase of her cooking.

Missus Twombly was an excellent teacher and Lizzie, a student equal to the task. Owing to finer flour and a cantankerous oven beaten into submission, light fluffy biscuits were the pride of Lizzie's early accomplishments.

Eliza was also adjusting well to her new surroundings. At first, she would sneak down in the night to Lizzie's room for comfort, but as her work became more exhausting, she stayed in her third floor attic room, too tired to move. The top floor windows at either end of the long narrow cell provided a refreshing breeze not found on the lower floors. Eliza also had the advantage of meeting the guests and the inhabitants of the house, from whom Lizzie was isolated.

Missus Twombly was not just generous with her help, Lizzie found. The various transients and workmen knew they could at any time of day or night count on a glass of tea and a bowl of stew from Missus Twombly's kitchen. "No one is ever to be turned away,

59

Lizzie," she said. "For in as much as you do this for the least of these my brethren..."

"Missus Twombly, ma'am," asked Lizzie one day, "Would it be wrong ta set a task fer one o' our gentlemen o' the back door, if he should ask ta do one?"

The old woman thought for a minute. "No, Lizzie. But, only if he volunteers, only if you can think of a task that *needs* doing and only if it would not upset our routine. They are still the Lord's guests. Let me think on it."

"Ma'am, old Jimmy seems ta knae about the herb garden, perhaps he could pull weeds. Captain Drebbs says he would trim the shrubbery fer his supper, if you'd be agreeable. Big John isn't much ta talk, sae I don' knae what he could do, but they seem ta like bein' useful. Sometimes it's hard fer them ta keep takin', if they can't gif' somethin' back."

"My goodness, Lizzie, how selfish of me. I hadn't thought of that." Lizzie grinned. *This woman hasn't a selfish hair on her head.* "Of course, Lizzie, whatever you can do for them is fine with me."

"Now, Lizzie. I have something to tell you. You have done so well, I have decided that we should have a real dinner party, Sunday evening, in two weeks time. That should give us plenty of time to send out invitations and plan our menu. We must have just the right mixture of company to keep the conversation lively. A couple from church, one couple from the literary league, one from the art council in town, a friend for William and one for Isabella. That would be twelve. A very nice group!

Yes, before I forget, Thursday of this week, you and Eliza will have a day off. You must prepare the food for Thursday on the day before. It will be all cold meals, so it can be put on ice. You will keep the stove going, so if it does turn out to be cool, we will have stew to warm us up. You must be getting luncheon ready for us, so I will sit over here and start planning. My word, I am all out of breath.

It's been so long since we've had a decent dinner party. How exciting it will be to have a party again!"

She watched as her mistress walked unsteadily to the familiar rocker and sat down. Lizzie picked up a small journal and a pencil and brought it to her. *Always the list,* she thought, amused.

She reached up to the peg for Missus Twombly's wrap and laid it across the older woman's lap. Within minutes, the tiny figure in the chair was asleep. *Poor dear, she's always moving, always planning. It's as if she's afraid if she slows down, she will fade away. Everyone depends on her — her husband, her children, all the groups she's a part o'. They all clamor for her attention.*

Lizzie turned her focus to the list on her stove, cold chicken salad, asparagus, and boiled eggs. Each plate had to be a work of art. Although this luncheon was only for the family, Missus Twombly said it was a 'dress rehearsal' for a larger luncheon to be held later in the summer.

She cubed the cold chicken, mixed it with celery and a small amount of French dressing. Each plate had four spears of cooked and cooled asparagus placed with the stalks in the center and tips to the edge of the plate. A ball of chicken salad was placed at the center of the plate, and then covered with a thin coat of mayonnaise sprinkled with parsley. She peeled hard-boiled eggs and separated the yolks from the whites. The shredded whites were made into nests, placed in the four spaces divided by the asparagus. Each nest contained one whole egg yolk. Carefully wrapping the plates, she placed them in the ice box until serving time.

Then Lizzie made a refreshing lemonade. Each tall glass had one teaspoon of raspberry syrup at the bottom, so that when Eliza poured the lemonade into each glass, the color would flow slowly upward just as each glass was served. Missus Twombly called this treat *sunrise lemonade.*

There was a great feeling of satisfaction for Lizzie in preparing these meals. It was not just the pride of accomplishment, but the dramatic presentation always brought ohs and ahs from the dining room. Missus Twombly said it was like putting a signature on the meal. Everyone remembered where they were when they had a meal this special. *If food translates to love, as she says, then their guests were indeed shown much love,* thought Lizzie.

She was excited at the prospect of having a day off with Eliza. It was their first time off since they started and she did not want to waste a moment of it. *James has every Sunday off,* she thought enviously. *He can afford ta be frivolous wit' his time off. He's got no excuse no' ta write ev'ry week. I hafta write when I am done wit' m' work, when I'm sae tired I kin hardly stay awake. First thin' I'll do, is fire up the stove then write ta Ma an' Mórai.*

Ma likes ta write, sae I have a time tryin' ta keep up wit' her. Good thin' I found those picture postal cards when I was shoppin' fer Missus Twombly. When I have some money, I will send one o' them, when I'm too tired ta write. At least she'll have somethin' from me. I hope James is writin' ta his mother more than he is ta me.

The other day, I finally got Big John ta talkin'. He tol' me 'bout a haunted house at Cook's Bridge. He say it's no' but a couple miles from here. The road goes right beside the river, an' he said it was a pretty walk. Eliza won' gae if I tell her about the haunted house, but if it's a fair day, she'll like the walk. I'll hafta git good directions from Big John when he comes ta the back door t'night.

Oh my, it's almos' time fer luncheon. I hate ta wake Missus Twombly when she's sleepin' sae fine.

The thought was chased from her mind as the kitchen door burst open. "Lizzie," the intruder demanded, "did you send this dress back to my room without attending to the wine stain on the bodice?"

"No, Miss Isabelle," Lizzie whispered, trying to show her that her mother was asleep in the kitchen. "I *would* not."

"Isabella? *What* is going on? Why are you castigating Lizzie so rudely? Is that any way to enter a room?"

"I'm so sorry, Mother. I didn't see you there. But look at this stain! Really! I put it on thinking it was fine, and then had to take it off again to wear something else. I had left it on my bed for Eliza to take down to Lizzie and it was back in my closet."

Missus Twombly said quietly in measured tones, "Isabella. It was not Eliza who put it in your closet. I found it in a heap on the floor and simply hung it up. Your clothing, stained or otherwise, does not belong on the floor. Please do refrain from jumping to conclusions. You may apologize to Lizzie, right now."

The still-angry red-faced woman turned abruptly back to Lizzie and said, "I do apologize for my misunderstanding. Please forgive me."

"Of course, Miss. If you would give me the dress, I will try makin' it right fer you," said Lizzie tightly. "How soon do you need it?"

"I *was* going to wear it today. Now, it doesn't matter when I wear it. Just have it ready by Monday." Looking at her mother's disapproving face, her tone softened as she added, "Thank you, Lizzie."

"That's better, Isabella. Lizzie, we will have luncheon in ten minutes. Will that be satisfactory?" asked the mistress of the house with a broad wink behind her daughter's fleeing back.

"Aye, ma'am," Lizzie answered, a smile playing around her lips.

That evening, when Lizzie was elbow-deep in sudsy dish water, the elder Reverend Doctor Twombly entered the kitchen door with a guest. "Lizzie, Missus Twombly is meeting with her garden club in the living room and this gentleman is waiting to take my daughter to a concert in town. I wonder if we could have a cup of your wonderful coffee, here in the kitchen, while we wait."

"Of course, Doctor Twombly, the coffee is still good from supper. I could bring it ta the dining room if ye like." Lizzie nervously dried her hands on her apron towel.

"No, we wanted to talk to you, so this will be fine. I hope you don't mind our curiosity?"

"No' a 'tall, sir, would ye care fer cream an' sugar?" She arranged everything on a tray at the counter and brought it to them.

"We were curious about your education in Ireland, the subjects you studied, and the level of education you've attained."

"Primary schoolin' gaes from first form to eighth, then secondary schoolin' gaes through ta college degrees, fer those who kin afford it, or have attained a scholar's grant. I studied through the eighth form: Grammar, penmanship, mathematics, Latin, French, some Classic Greek, literature and the sciences."

The gentleman in his mid-forties spoke, smiling, took her hand and said, "Quid vis faciam?" (What would you like to do?)

Returning his smile Lizzie answered brightly, "Te cum ambulare vellum (I would like to take a walk with you)."

Dr. Twombly laughed and slapped his knee, "Very good, Lizzie! She's got you there, Jason. Excellent! This is a delightful surprise. It flies in the face of the popular belief among locals that Ireland is a backward country full of ignorance and poverty.

"Begging your pardon, Lizzie, the locals are easily led, and not enamored of the *truth* when they decide their prejudices. I'm afraid the Irish have not had an easy time of late here in America."

Isabelle arrived in time to see Lizzie answer her gentleman caller in Latin, her hand still in his. Red-faced and struggling for control, she said coolly, "Mister Goodman, I believe we should be leaving now, if we are to meet the train."

Lizzie snatched her hand away. After they left, Doctor Twombly said, "I think, for a while at least, she won't keep her gentlemen callers waiting in the kitchen.

64

"This is excellent coffee, Lizzie. Don't let me stop you from your chores. Perhaps you can tell me about your family as you work."

The old man sat back in his chair sipping coffee, as Lizzie, with hands back in dishwater, told him about growing up in Legananny, just north of the Mournes, near Letrim, in the lower part of Upper Inveigh, County Down, Ulster. It felt good to share her stories of home with someone who seemed so interested.

Chapter Five

The first rays of light crept into Lizzie's window as she bustled about, getting dressed. It was Thursday, her first day off. Her head was swimming with things to do, places to go, with all day to do them in. As she brushed her wild red hair in the way she wore it at home, side pieces braided and tied in the back with all the rest wildly flowing down her back, she looked like the half grown child she felt herself to be.

Although she learned many things as a cook for the Twomblys, she felt like a pretender. She was not yet comfortable in her role as cook.

She was a laundress. Though Isabelle was difficult to please, Lizzie took pride in surprising her with her skills in caring for her clothing. *Fer a woman sae fussy about her dresses, she certainly wastes an unseemly amount of good food on them,* she thought uncharitably. She shook her head in self-admonishment. *Mind yer tongue, Lizzie Heenan, Missus Twombly would be ashamed o' yer thinkin' like thet. Perhaps Miss Isabelle's got a lot more on her mind than the food on her plate.*

She threw on her coverall apron to protect her only good clothes and headed for the kitchen to stoke up the fire in the stove.

Eliza, anxiously waiting, was dressed in her 'Sunday best,' complete with her flat straw hat and drawstring purse.

"Just give me a few minutes, Eliza. I want ever'thin' jes' perfect for Missus Twombly. Write her a note, if ye would, Eliza. Tell her there are pancakes in the warmer, maple syrup warmin' on the back o' the stove an' fresh fruit in the icebox. Her luncheon an' lemonade are in there, too.

66

"They're goin' out t'night ta dinner an' a concert, sae she won't need anythin' fer supper. There's cold meat an' potato salad, if they change their minds 'bout goin' out. She kin leave everythin' here an' I'll clean it up t'night. Thank her fer the day off an' tell her we'll be back by dusk."

Lizzie set out the plates on the side shelf of the stove to warm for breakfast. These chores done, she whipped off her apron, donning her hat, grabbing her purse and a book. She was ready. "Come Eliza, we're off ta our day o' freedom."

As they stepped out the door, it seemed the air never smelled so sweet. The birds were singing and the flowers seemed to waft their beautiful fragrance just for them.

She recalled Missus Twombly's words of caution the day before. "Lizzie, I know you and Eliza are very excited about your day tomorrow. You may do as you wish, but please bear in mind that the Misters Twombly are of the clergy and anything you do bears witness to this household. Your conduct must be exemplary at all times. You are both good girls and I'm sure you will use good judgment, but you may encounter others who are willing to lead you astray. So, please be cautious in your association with them. Mister Twombly and I want you to have a twenty-five cent piece each to spend or save as you wish. Enjoy a pleasant day. You have earned it."

She's sech a lovely lady. "Eliza, I've a surprise fer you. Here's a twenty-five cent piece from Missus Twombly ta spend as ye wish." Lizzie was rewarded by the light of excitement in Eliza's eyes.

"Oh, Lizzie this'll be the best day ever. Where are we goin'?"

"Well, Big John tol' me 'bout the most beautiful walk 'long the Charles. It gaes from the Lower Falls ta the Upper Falls. He said there's a walkway the whole distance. There's a grassy area all along it. We kin stop an' read fer a while, if we like. There's a place at the Upper Falls where we can have tea an' look at the pretty houses. It's a perfect day fer it, don' ye think? We kin pretend we're rich folk out fer a stroll."

It was full sunshine by the time they left the parsonage. Still early, there was no one about, so they kept their voices low. It was the first time they had been able to talk freely, without being keenly aware they may be heard by someone in the household. Even after the work was done and they were alone in Lizzie's room, they were sure someone could hear them. The open heat registers allowed them to hear the family talk among themselves. Usually, she was in the kitchen making more noise than the faint murmur she could hear from her bedroom. Although, it was usually nothing interesting to her, once in a while, she couldn't stop her curiosity.

"So tell me, Eliza. What're they really like? Ye get ta see 'em ever'day. I only see the Misters if they come in the kitchen or when they're in the pulpit on Sunday. Doctor Twombly comes in for coffee at night if Missus Twombly retires early, but young Mister Twombly ne'er does and Miss Isabella only comes in if I've committed a sin o' omission wit' one o' her dresses."

"It's no' right ta gossip, Lizzie, but I kin tell ye this, young Mister Twombly's sickly, like his Ma. He loses his wind climbing the stairs jes' like she does. I've seen her climb the stairs an' half way, she'll sit an' hafta rest afore she kin go on. Miss Isabella's real worried 'bout her. Fer all her gruffness, she has a good heart — fer her ma an' pa anyways."

"I've always heard her called Isabella," said Lizzie.

"Miss Twombly's parents call her Isabella, but she tells ever'one else, it's *Isabelle*. I guess it's more modern or somethin'. Young Mister Twombly calls her Isabelle, but wit' a kind o' sneer, like he's making fun o' her. They don' al'ays git along. Doctor Twombly put a stop ta their snipin' fer a while, though." Imitating the minister's deep resonant voice, she said, "the reason fer yer fine education was no' sae ye kin insult each other better. I suggest ye use it ta bring a little more kindness inta the world, startin' wit' each other." Eliza covered her mouth, holding in her giggle. "He was sorely angry."

"Oh my, I guess he was. He's sech an interestin' man. When he comes in fer coffee at night, he asks all kinds o' questions. Sae I ask him a question fer ev'ry one he asks.

"He educated himself fer the first twenty-six years o' his life, he said. He was a carpenter, a farmer, an' a teacher afore he was called by God ta be a preacher. He went ta two colleges and was ordained as a Methodist minister. He was e'en a teacher in a seminary. He held an office at Harvard an' was a sup'rintendant o' public schools on the other side o' Boston some'eres.

"Onct, he was e'en the president o' a university in Wis-con-sin. I don' knae where thet is, but nae he does mos' o' the preachin' at the church. Young Mister Twombly's supposed ta preach, but he can't always. The son does help him with accounts an' schedules an' other things. The elder mister is a great man, Eliza, an' he takes the time ta have coffee in *my* kitchen." Lizzie shook her head in wonder.

"The coffee mus' be good, Lizzie. We're verra lucky fer sure. He mus' learn sae much 'cause he asks sae many questions an' he don't care who he gits the answers from."

"He said thet. I wish Ma could meet him. She always said, 'ye kin learn somethin' from anybody. Don' waste a single opportunity ta learn. Oh Eliza, I miss her sae much!" Homesickness overwhelmed her for a moment. She saw the look in Eliza's eyes and pulled herself upright. *No sense in spendin' yer only day off weepin' fer home. Ye will git Eliza ta cryin' an' we won' have any pleasure at all t'day.*

"Look, Eliza, it's the Lower Falls. Nae, we jes' foller the river, cross Walnut Street ta Quinobequin Road, an' foller the water. There 'tis."

There were a few carriages pulling out onto the roadway now. The paved street was lined with puddles from the rain the night before, so the girls waited for the carriages to pass by, before they found a dry spot to step off the sidewalk.

The view was breathtaking. The river, widening after the falls, was lined with a grassy hill between the sidewalk and its shore. There was a second walk next to the river at the lower level. Across the river was a cluster of weeping willows stirring in the warm breeze and reflected in the current. Flowering shrubs and beds of riotous colors competed with each other on the far shore. Here and there, great white mansions peeked through the trees with pathways down to docks, surrounded by small boats and canoes bobbing gently in the water. The birds were singing, butterflies flitted aloft, and squirrels darted among them, chattering.

"Oh Lizzie, it's like a picture in a fairytale book. Here's a bench. Let's stop a while an' jes' breathe it all in."

The wrought iron bench with wooden slats was still damp with dew, but sit they did. Lizzie unconsciously began to swing her feet like a child. "Eliza, I've some biscuits. Would ye like one?"

They sat munching their breakfast as pigeons gathered around them, snatching the crumbs. "Look, Lizzie! O'er there by the dock on the other side, the swans! Aren't they beautiful? What a perfec' day."

After a while, they walked along the lower path next to the river. A gust of wind blew Lizzie's flat straw hat from her head and it sailed like a round kite with a ribbon tail on the breeze. The girls chased it to the river's edge, watching as it wafted toward a crew of rowers, intent on their practice. The girls shouted in dismay as it landed in the water out of reach. The coxswain shouted to his crew to snag the downed airship with an oar. The last oarsman managed to capture it and held it aloft like a prized fish. The coxswain once again seated, directed the boat to shore.

Close to the shore the rower proffered the sodden hat on the end of his oar to Lizzie. Laughing, Lizzie thanked him profusely and retrieved the dripping offering with thumb and forefinger. She curtsied deep and held her hat at arm's length, much to the delight of the oarsmen. One of them cried with his hands to his chest, "Oh, I am smitten. My heart is lost to the red-haired maid of the riverbank."

The young man behind him cuffed the back of his head and the coxswain directed them back to practice. The rower would not be silenced. "Farewell my lovely. Parting is such sweet sorrow."

"Thet I shall say good night, till it be morrow," replied Lizzie finishing the quote with a bow. He arched his eyebrow in surprise. The girls laughed and waved. "Thank you," they shouted, as the young men rowed away, now serious in their endeavor.

"I wish I could leave this here ta dry in the sun," moaned Lizzie.

"Verra likely, the birds an' squirrels would make a mess o' it afore ye git back. Shake the water off an' set it on the end o' the bench fer a while, if ye want."

"'Tis quite all right, let us continue our perambulation, Eliza." Lizzie said, with her pert little nose in the air. Eliza giggled at her imitation of Miss Isabelle's 'company voice. She bowed and offered her arm to Lizzie. Together, they skipped like children down the path, Lizzie holding her still-wet hat away from her skirt.

They passed the time chatting about home, the Twombly household, and James. Before they knew it, they were at the Upper Falls.

Lizzie hadn't told Eliza about her plan to see the haunted house Big John had talked about. When she asked him for directions, he said he'd meet her at Upper Falls at the Boylston Street Bridge, and he would take them there. Big John had been coming to the Twombly house for about two months for the 'back door' stew and had always worked for his supper. Missus Twombly said he had been a gardener and handyman for one of the mansions until he hurt his arm. He attended their church, standing in the back, then disappearing when the service was over. No one knew where he was living, but he was a good man, she said.

"Look Eliza, there's Big John!" said Lizzie as if it was a surprise to see him. At Eliza's anxious look, she added, "He's one of our 'back door' people, a friend of Missus Twombly's. He's a good man, and he'll be hurt if we don't speak ta him."

Big John waved his good arm and smiled. His size and his powerful physique made most men step aside, but he had a gentle nature and a sadness in his eyes. His clothes were neat, though well-worn and frayed. Just for the day, he had tamed down his black bushy hair, Lizzie thought amused. "Big John, I'd like ye ta meet Eliza, my sister. She works fer the Twomblys, too."

"It's a pleasure, miss."

Introductions over, Lizzie urged the mountainous man to walk with them to the bench by the falls. "Wha' kin ye tell us 'bout the village here?"

Big John knew this was his cue to launch into the story of the haunted house. "First, let's move to the next bench, to be in the shade, ye see." He wanted the angle to the bridge to be just right.

"Many, many years ago, thet house right there, the white one set back from the bank on the other side. Thet one." He pointed to an abandoned house with peeling paint and weeds growing up to the window sills. "Anyway, I heerd stories when I wus jes' a boy, thet the house there was *fiercely* haunted. It wus rumored thet there wus a baby less than a year old, wus *murdered* in thet very place. No one I knew ever found out if it wus true, but the house wus deemed haunted nonetheless. There were noises of a cradle rocking and a baby crying, that would disturb the sleep of even the bravest of souls."

Big John stroked his beard as he warmed up to his tale. "After a while, the house wus left empty, so distressful it wus. Later on, villagers claimed there wus a ghost baby that appeared on a rock in this very river just opposite the haunted house. Naked as the day

72

it was born, it wuz, an' about ten month old, they say. It would go from the rock into the water an' back, for about an hour, then disappear until the next day." Lizzie's eyes went from Big John to Eliza and back again. Eliza, rapt in the story, her face alternately expressed horror and awe as he spoke.

"Hundreds went ev'ry day to watch it. Everyone could see it pass back an' forth from the rock to the water. No one saw it go away, but it would al'ays disappear. They wus convinced there wus a devil's connection 'tween the ghost baby an' the child of the haunted house. For about a week, the crowds gathered about noon, excited to confirm the wonder. Even the bravest of boys would be home ev'ry night at dusk fer fear of being caught by the spirit of the ghost baby.

"One day, while they were gathered on the bank, one of the older boys dared to approach the rock to investigate." Big John stopped in his story and looked intently under the bridge. 'Oh, look!" The big man pointed to a spot under the bridge, where a bright light wavered back and forth. Eliza took in a great gulp of air and held it. Big John continued his story in a low voice.

"As I said, the boy climbed down to see the ghost baby up close. He *captured* it and brought it back to the crowd to see." He stopped again for effect then, grinned. "It wuz found to be a piece of glass. It wuz carried on the water to the rock an' left there at high water. When the water got to the right elevation, the sun would shine on it. The movement of the water struck the base of the rock, an' being reflected in the glass, produced the spectacle of the movin' ghost baby." Eliza let the air out of her lungs slowly, watching the light under the bridge dance on the water.

Lizzie laughed with glee. "Big John, thet was a won'erful story! Thank yer. Eliza, if yer coulda seen yer face!"

"Lizzie, it's no' funny! I nearly fainted dead away. Wha' is thet under the bridge, Big John?"

73

Big John looked apologetic. "Jes' another piece of glass, miss, I'm real sorry if it frightened you."

"Well, I forgive *you*. But I knae Lizzie had *somethin'* ta do wit' it, an' it may take a while fer me ta forgive *her*."

"Oh, Eliza, ye will hafta forgive me. I'm the one who knaes the way hame."

Eliza blushed. Grinning, she said, "I guess I will, 'cause I have truly no idea how ta git hame from here. Lizzie if ye weren't my ain kin…"

"But I am, an' love me ye do, fer all my teasin'." Then turning to her story-teller friend, she said, "I thank yer, Big John, fer the grand adventure. Nae, would yer like ta join us fer some tea?"

Suddenly shy, the big man said, "Thank you, but no. I couldn't spend your hard-earned money an' I have an appointment with a lady who needs her shrubs trimmed. You ladies have a lovely tea an' I'll see you tomorrow, for some of your fine stew an' some weed-pulling, Miss Lizzie. A pleasure, Miss Eliza." Big John rose to his full height, then bowed, turned on his heel and walked back toward the bridge.

"Come, Eliza. 'Cross the bridge is a butcher shop, maybe he'll knae where we kin git a cup o' tea."

The young butcher with his bloodied apron directed the girls down the street to a small tea shop. Once there, they had tea and sandwiches in a sunny window alcove. The proprietress took their twenty-five cent pieces and scrutinized each side before giving them change. "Is somethin' wrong, ma'am?"

The sour-faced woman made no reply, but muttered, "Damned foreigners" as they left the shop.

Eliza and Lizzie looked at each other, surprised at the cold parting words. "I concede ta being a foreigner, but no' ta bein' *damned*," sputtered Lizzie, ready to storm back into the shop.

"Lizzie, no, stop. Remember wha' Missus Twombly said. Our actions reflect on the Twomblys an' they've been verra good ta us."

Lizzie let a shiver of outrage run through her body. Though her face was still hot with emotion, she said quietly, "Yer right. What would I do wit'out ye, ta take the wind from my fury, Eliza?" Offended tears slipped from her eyes and she picked up the tempo of her steps as she headed back to the river.

Eliza, half-running beside her, pulled on Lizzie's arm to slow her pace. "Whoa Lizzie, I'm no' gonna make it hame, at this rate. Let's try making the best o' the afternoon."

Soon, Lizzie was back to her usual self. Although her volatile temper was akin to a summer storm, full of thunder and flashes, it rarely lasted long. When her sunny smile shone again, it was as if the tempest never occurred.

The danger was in her sword-sharp words when she was angry. They popped unbidden from her mouth and once loosed, though she was truly remorseful, they were hard to forgive. She had lost several prospective suitors for want of a captive tongue. The boys she grew up with often said being in her company was like "playing with fire, they's plenty o' warmth ta be had, but sooner or later, she'll burn yer."

Soon, they were back to the bench where Lizzie had lost her hat that morning. They sat for a while, reading and watching young mothers with their children. It's a perfect place for watching children at play. There were bonneted babies in ornate bentwood prams, chubby little yearlings in dresses, and older children in short pants with their shirts hanging out. Little girls in long frilly frocks chased elusive butterflies. Little boys, menacing them with wriggly worms in their outstretched hands, were rewarded by their girlish screeches.

"Lizzie, do ye ever wonder what kind o' man ye'd marry, or how many children ye'd have?" One look at Eliza's dreamy face and Lizzie knew Eliza had studied on this for a while.

"Tell me, Eliza. Who is the man ye dream about?"

"It seems ta change ever'day. Las' week, it was a farmer or a gardener; this week, a tailor, a shopkeeper, a man with a business in town. I want someone wit' enough money, thet I wouldn't ever be hungry. We'll have maybe six kids, enough ta be a help ta their da, but only enough ta be able ta feed. I want a house in town, sae I could walk ever'where, but wha' about yer?"

"I wan' a strong Scotsman wit' a business, who'll allow me a business o' my ain. He should be strong an' knae what's right, an' let me haf' my way in mos' things. I wanna raise my bairns in the country, sae they kin knae the land. I want lots o' babies, sae they'll ne'er be alone."

"He'll hafta be strong, ta handle the likes o' you, Lizzie Heenan," Eliza said, teasing her. "An' ye will probably git yer way in mos' things anyways, if he knaes what's *good* fer him," she added for good measure, ducking as she saw the twinkle in Lizzie's eye.

"Well, howe'er it turns out, promise me we'll al'ays be close by. I couldn't bear it if I lost yer, too," said Eliza, becoming unexpectedly serious. "Ye an' the boys are all I have, an' the boys are far away in Ireland."

"I'll stay as long as yer feet stay grounded, I solemnly pledge," said Lizzie, hugging her sister. "I'll no' move from yer side."

As they talked, the air freshened, dark clouds gathered and the children and mothers disappeared. "We'd better git hame, Eliza. It's gonna *rain!*" The girls grabbed their hats and started running for the manse. They had about a half mile to traverse before they could reach their destination and thunderous clouds chased them all the way. They were climbing the back steps just as the clouds loosed their torrent with great splats of rain. An earth-shattering clap of thunder hid the sound of the screen door slamming as the furious wind tore it out of Lizzie's hand. A series of lightning bolts, followed by the crack of a splitting tree and the continuous roll of thunder were fearsome. A flood of water poured through the open kitchen window as Lizzie ran to close it.

"Quick, Eliza, git the winders!" The girls ran from room to room, hurriedly shutting windows against the fury. Soon all they could hear was the water beating against the windows and the rattling of panes as the thunder withdrew to the distance. Lizzie ran back to the kitchen to gather rags for the puddles in each room. The rooms upstairs were the worst. The bedrooms were the last rooms attended. Lizzie felt the bedclothes and stripped those that were wet. Leaving the sodden heaps on the floor, they worked together to make the beds again. Eliza cleaned up the parlor and dining room, so Lizzie took the second floor. When she finished mopping the bedrooms, she piled all the wet bed linens in the hall and went to investigate the attic room.

The attic was divided by a wall the length of the house at the peak of the roof. One side was Eliza's room, the other side was storage. A quick look told Lizzie the storage side was not open to the elements. On Eliza's side, a window at each end had been opened to ventilate the room. Quickly closing the windows, Lizzie stripped the bed, mopped the floor, and flipped the mattress. *She'll hafta sleep wit' me 'til this dries. It may take days. Her uniform is only damp, so I'll press thet. If I close the windows at the bottom an' open them just an inch at the top, they should be all right. My word, I'll hae a lot o' wash t'marra. I'm glad there was no one hame. It surely makes this work a lot easier wit'out the family in the way, tellin' us how ta do it.*

Lizzie was glad for the narrow back stairs to take her mountainous wet load down to the kitchen. As she entered the kitchen, she heard, "Poor Lizzie! Is this how you spent your day off?"

77

"Missus Twombly, I didn' think ye were hame." She unceremoniously dropped the load in front of her, to see her mistress.

"Nor did I see you, Lizzie. Oh my dear, you're sopping wet," she replied, amused at the disheveled appearance of her cook. Her hat askew, her hair wildly plastered to her face and neck, and her dress completely sodden from her wet load. Lizzie was a sight.

"If ye will pardon me, ma'am, I'll put these out on the porch until t'marra when I kin wash them. Then I'll change. Eliza will be done cleaning up the rooms shortly. We came hame early 'cause o' the storm, ta find all the windows open."

"Oh dear, we hadn't given it a thought until the storm started. Then we were clear across town. By the time it was over and we could come home, the damage was done. I am so sorry. We could've prevented this extra work."

"It's understandable, Missus Twombly. Don' worry 'bout it. Ever'thin' will be back ta normal in jes' a moment or two. Ye look like ye could use some hot tea. I'll set the kettle ta boil and it'll be ready by the time I hang these."

"Don't trouble yourself, dear. I'll put the kettle on. You go hang those and change. You can join me when you're done."

"Thank yer, ma'am."

Lizzie humbly, hurried out the door. Soon Eliza was on the back porch with her, helping to lift the heavy linens over the lines.

"I did wha' I could with yer room, Eliza. I'll iron your uniform fer t'marra, but ye will hafta sleep in my room t'night. Yer papers are all wet, so ye will hafta start yer letter agin. I have some paper in my cupboard thet should be dry."

"Oh Lizzie, yer poor hat, it went swimming twict t'day! It's drooping like a wilted daisy."

"Ach, I guess it has seen better days, anyways."

Lizzie went straight to her room to change her clothes into her only other street clothes, a white blouse and a skirt. She tied her hair back as best she could without spending the time it would take to straighten it out. She threw on her coverall apron. *Missus Twombly is still waiting!*

When she emerged from her room, she was surprised to see three cups of tea and two places set for supper.

"It's the least I could do, after causing so much extra work on your day off," Missus Twombly said, raising her cup. "The family's supper is out and they've eaten already. Don't worry about them. Everything's set."

The girls were overwhelmed by her gesture. As they ate self-consciously, Missus Twombly gently put them at ease, talking about how well she thought they were doing. "Tomorrow, we'll talk about plans for the dinner party, but for now, I'd like to tell you about our trip to the Vineyard."

The vineyard? As far as I knae, the only drinkin' these folks do is Holy Communion on the first Sunday o' the month and thet were likely grape juice, thought Lizzie.

"It's an island called *Martha's Vineyard*. We will be going there in August and there is a great deal of preparation to be done for the trip. We will be in Cottage City for two weeks for the Methodist Tabernacle Revival. Doctor Twombly will be one of the speakers. A week before, I will go with you to open the house. Isabella and the men will remain here to fulfill their obligations, and give us a chance to make everything shipshape at the cottage before their arrival."

"What's the house like, ma'am? Does it hae a big stove like this one, wit' gas lights an' runnin' water?"

"Those are all good questions, Lizzie. It does not have all the amenities this house has, but this year, we'll have running water, an icebox, and hopefully, an indoor water closet. I'm trying to make arrangements to have that done before we get there. If not, perhaps it can be installed while we are there. It's all very exciting, but these things do take time to execute. We have dishes and linens there, but

79

we will have to bring clothing, some spices, and perishables with us. There is a greengrocer, fishmonger, and a butcher there. We'll have wood delivered. I haven't found my list from last year, Lizzie, so you'll have to make my new list. My writing has become so illegible, I can hardly read it myself."

"I will be happy ta do it, ma'am, honored, in fact."

"You are both very good girls. Now, if you'll excuse me, I think I will find out what my family is up to."

"Of course, ma'am," said Lizzie and Eliza, standing.

When she had gone, Eliza groaned, "An Island, Lizzie! I'll be sick all the way over an' all the way back. I thought I was done wit' boats! What am I ta do?"

"Eliza, ye will do wha' ye hafta. It may no' be sae bad as ye think. *Martha's Vineyard*, sounds pretty, don' ye think?"

That night, Lizzie dreamed of being tangled in grape vines on her way to the outhouse.

Chapter Six

Eliza and Lizzie sat in the servants' pew in their 'Sunday best,' anxiously waiting for the service to be over. Today, they would serve their first full-fledged dinner party. In her mind, Lizzie ticked off the items on Missus Twombly's list. *All linens pressed an' laid in the dining room. The turkey's in the oven. Potatoes an' squash are ready ta cook when we git hame. The onions are boiled. Cranberry sauce, crisp salad greens, cucumbers and tomatoes are in the icebox. Custard cups are in there too, waitin' fer the strawberry jam an' meringue. There's a pitcher o' lemonade, waitin' fer its 'sunrise.'*

As the congregation stood for the benediction, Lizzie and her half-sister slipped out and hurried back to the house. The Twomblys and their guests would be at the church for at least another hour, greeting and talking to the parishioners.

Lizzie and Eliza had to change into their uniforms, finish the cooking, take Missus Twombly's fresh flower centerpiece from the icebox to the table and have the first course ready to serve as soon as the guests arrived. Lizzie remembered Missus Twombly's words: "Make sure Eliza sits quietly away from the heat for at least five minutes before she serves the first course. It won't do to have her all flushed, damp and disheveled while serving. Whatever is going on in the kitchen, our guests must not hear any unseemly noise in the dining room. We will have two extra of every dish in the case of any mishap. Eliza, serve dishes from the left and remove them from the right side of each guest, serving guests of honor first and women before men, just like we practiced. Drinks, however, should be served and removed from the right," Missus Twombly said.

"If you should drop anything, I want you to simply pick up the dish and bring another as if nothing was amiss. You can clean up any spills after our guests have retired to the parlor. Place a napkin over anything that's spilled, so we can walk around it. If everything goes as perfectly as I expect it will, you may have the extra plates for your dinner. When you have served each course, Eliza, please wait by the door for instructions. I'm sure you will both do well."

"Lizzie," complained Eliza, "I can't 'member anythin'. I'm shakin'. How 'm I gonna serve all these fancy dishes wit'out droppin' them? Let alone whether it's on the right or the left?"

"You'll do fine, Eliza. Remember when we used to play at having grand tea when we were little? Jes' pretend they are children at our ain little tea party. Missus Twombly said they won't even notice you. As far as which hand, I have something fer that. Push up yer left sleeve." Lizzie took a ribbon from her pocket and tied it in a bow around Eliza's arm, just above the wrist.

"Now, the ribbon means serve from thet side. Everything else is done from the other side. Removing an' drinks have no ribbon. No one but you will know the ribbon is there. Will thet help?"

"Thank ye, Aye. I kin feel it through the sleeve. Ribbon means serve. I'm sorry I'm such a muddle."

"Ye will be fine, Eliza, I put yer extra uniform in my room wit' mine. Nae, lemme check the turkey." Eliza went to Lizzie's room as she was told, and Lizzie opened the oven to take out the turkey.

As Eliza came out of the little bedroom, the door swung open, hitting Lizzie full on her backside. With the impact, the turkey flew out of the pan scattering the drippings with it. Eliza, attempting to rescue the turkey, slipped in the hot fatty juices and slid across the ceramic tiled floor on her rump. The turkey bounced across the floor and finally halted under the rocker some eight feet from the stove.

82

Eliza's shocked face contorted, threatening to cry, but Lizzie's infectious laughter changed her sorrow to mirth. "Eliza," she sputtered, "Gae in my room an' change yer dress. I'll clean up out here. Be careful when ye come back out, 'case I have no' got it all up yet. Gae on, nae, gae!"

Lizzie looked the turkey over with a critical eye. It was salvageable. It was still trussed, so the legs and wings were still attached. There was a tear in the skin under one leg, but that would be hidden by the ruffle of the cabbage leaf bed on the serving platter. She rinsed it off with hot water, put it on a board and rubbed it with butter to bring back its shine then, salt and pepper. She set it aside to rest. She mopped up as much grease as possible with her kitchen rags, then filled a bucket with hot water and a little ammonia and borax. She mopped up the rest of the grease, and then wiped down the floor with a blanket from the laundry pile destined for Monday's wash. *This'll be a bonnie tale ta tell m' grandchildren one day, but right nae it's jes' a lot o' work in time I don' have!*

She turned her attention to the rest of her meal. *What 'm I gonna do fer gravy? I jes' mopped up near all m' drippin's. Mercy!*

She put the pan on the stove and inspected the crusty bottom. She added a little boiling water from her potatoes and a generous amount of butter. As it bubbled, she scraped the bottom of the pan until it yielded its bits of meat, then added salt, browned flour for color, and applesauce to sweeten the brew. A pinch of rosemary, parsley, and thyme completed the medley. *It mus' be a pound o' butter, fer sure. Missus Twombly will surely send me hame fer this. I paid 25¢ a pound for it. The way she doles it out by the scant teaspoon, it shoulda lasted us two weeks an' more! They's no help fer it nae. It's done.*

Eliza came in with her bundle of clothes held gingerly away from her fresh uniform. Lizzie threw them in with the rest of the greasy laundry she'd deal with the next day. Her sister sat in the rocker as instructed and went over Lizzie's list of dishes to complete the meal.

They were told to wait until Missus Twombly came to the kitchen before Lizzie started assembling the fruit course. The dishes would be set at each place setting with ice water and lemonade, then Eliza would announce dinner. Lizzie set the little pink compotes at the side board and heated the syrup as they heard the front door open. The ensuing bustle of the guests arriving together from church was their signal. *Here we gae*, thought Lizzie anxiously. *Please Laird, let the res' o' this endeavor gae well.* She resisted the urge to fill the dishes immediately, knowing Missus Twombly never gave her instructions lightly. It seemed an eternity before the little woman stepped into the kitchen.

"Lizzie, you may begin. Eliza, place the turkey on the buffet where it can be seen by everyone. When the first course dishes are on the table and the tray is set on the buffet, you may come to the parlor. Stand at the doorway with your hands clasped behind you until you see me nod, then you may announce dinner is served. Lead the way to the dining room and stand at the door to the kitchen. We will have grace and be seated. When the guests have all finished the first course, you may collect the dishes and return to the kitchen for the next course. Once the salad is served, you will take the turkey out to the kitchen once again for Lizzie to carve. Take your time and remain calm. Our guests are here to converse with each other, not just to eat."

"Aye, ma'am," Lizzie responded.

Lizzie was filling the dishes, first an iced tender pear half, then strawberry jam in its center, and a warmed apple-pear hard sauce poured over that. A fresh mint leaf garnish finished the ensemble. Lizzie crimped the leaf on each dish releasing its aroma to mix with the delicate pear. She marveled at the contrasts of texture, flavor and temperature. *No wonder people vie ta dine with the*

Twomblys. Ever'thin' she does is sae carefully prepared, sae perfectly done. Yet, she mus' be the kindest person I have e'er met.

Eliza took the lemonade and the glasses with the raspberry syrup into the dining room to prepare the 'sunrises', while Lizzie was still placing the compotes on her tray. Her potatoes were ready for mashing. The squash was almost done. The onions tender, ready for a white cream sauce. Together, it was a symphony of aromas, worthy of a king.

When Eliza returned, the cucumber and tomato salads were waiting for her to add French dressing and tiny toasted garlic croutons. Twelve plates delivered and served carefully, without incident. The turkey came back to the kitchen safely for carving. The main course would be served family style, so guests could choose their portions and their preferences for vegetables.

Lizzie carved the turkey, prepared three bowls each of the vegetables. She filled two gravy boats and two small bowls of cranberry sauce.

As instructed, Eliza brought all the trays to the buffet until they were all there then served each item to the opposing ends of the table. When all the dishes were served, she placed the platter of sliced turkey in front of Doctor Twombly who would serve his guests as they passed their plates to him.

Her service done for the moment, Eliza stood, watching the Twomblys interact with their guests. Dr. Twombly spoke to each one as he heaped their plates with the turkey. Missus Twombly engaged the others as the plates came back, offering the vegetables between snippets of conversation. "Mister Gardener, you may be interested to know Miss Manchester is a member of the Newton Garden club. She has a lovely rose garden, which I understand has won several prizes at the Flower Show in town. Mister Gardener has just bought a new home in town and informs me there is an extensively overgrown garden which he is attempting to revive. Perhaps you could advise him somehow?"

85

While an animated discussion about flowers ensued, Mrs. Twombly deftly turned her attention to any other dinner guests not actively talking. Eliza quickly made note of the bowls that were emptying. As soon as one was near empty, she removed it and went to the kitchen for a new one. Eliza recalled, *She said ta us, 'One must not let the guest think he is stealing the last bit of food from our mouths.' and 'Always have a fresh bowl at the ready to replace one that is less than a quarter full.'*

"Miss Davidson, your new article in the *Ladies Home Companion* is quite interesting. Where were you able to do your research?" Missus Twombly was rewarded with a brilliant smile from the otherwise shy woman in classic business attire.

"Thank you, Missus Twombly. The publisher sent me to a fashion house in Paris, to discover the newest trends in women's formal wear this year. It was so exciting! He's thinking of doing a regular series in the fall and spring on world fashion trends for women and how those trends may translate to the average American woman. Imagine *me*, a small town girl, in *Paris*. Never did I ever *dream*." The women at the table visibly leaned in her direction to hear about the trip. Even the men were somewhat taken by the young lady's enthusiasm for her subject. The conversation now in full swing, Missus Twombly looked at her husband at the end of the table and smiled. He returned the favor and nodded his head in awe of her skills as a hostess. Everyone was at ease, enjoying the food and conversation.

The main course was eaten leisurely. Each guest, including Isabella and William, was invited to share his or her special interest with the rest of the group. As they were encouraged to eat their fill, the guests expressed their appreciation of the individual dishes. The favorite was unanimous. The cook should be congratulated for its amazing rich and complex flavors.

"Eliza, dear, have Lizzie join us for a moment," Doctor Twombly asked.

"Aye, sir," she said.

Eliza stepped into the kitchen. "Lizzie, Doctor Twombly wants yer in the dining room."

Here's where I am found out! Lizzie hurried to her room to change her apron and fix her hair which had crept out from under her mob cap. Eliza led her back to the dining room with a worrisome look on her face. Lizzie stood beside her at the door waiting for someone to speak.

"Lizzie," Missus Twombly said, "Our guests would like to know how you made your wonderfully rich gravy. I have to admit my own recipe would never measure up to this *roux de dinde rôtie*. Would you tell us your secret?"

"Aye, ma'am, to the roasting pan, I added a large amount of salted creamery butter, browned flour, a small amount of applesauce, rosemary, thyme and a pinch of sage. Boil and stir to the right consistency then, strain into a bowl." Lizzie flushed deep red, which she hoped the dinner guests would attribute to working in the hot kitchen.

"Excellent, Lizzie, you can be sure I will add your recipe to my collection. Ladies and Gentlemen, I think we will retire to the parlor. Eliza, you may serve coffee, tea, and dessert from the tea cart in there, then return to clear."

"Aye, ma'am," the two servants replied, standing by the kitchen door. When their guests had left the room, the girls looked at each other trying to determine why the hostess had changed the venue without notice.

They hurried back to the kitchen to assemble the final course on the cart. The coffee urn and tea pot would fit on the parlor's side table with the cups, saucers, spoons, and napkins. To keep the cart from being overly burdened, Lizzie would follow with the caramel custard with jam and meringue topping. To fill out the large tray, Lizzie added a selection of sweet biscuits and candies. She clipped a couple of flowers from the floral centerpiece in the dining room, and

87

added them to the corners of the tray. This was in deference to Missus Twombly, who would probably have added this touch if she had prepared the tray herself.

She could still send me hame fer usin' a whole pound o' butter fer the gravy! She might as well send me hame for cuttin' her blossoms, too. I'm hopin' she'll like it though.

As soon as her guests were settled with their dessert and beverages, Eliza returned with her sister to the dining room to clear the dishes. Lizzie pushed the flowers around in the vase to hide the holes where the blossoms had been taken. As she removed the main course plates, she saw the reason for changing rooms. Under the remnants of the mashed potatoes and the creamed onions, was a very large brown puddle of gravy. The bowls had been oddly arranged at that end of the table to hide the disastrous spill. Lizzie smiled at the subterfuge Missus Twombly used to save her guest embarrassment.

In another of Missus Twombly's lectures on entertaining, Lizzie remembered, *'Etiquette is merely making certain your guests are as comfortable as possible in your presence.'* How can she be *sae perfect all the time? Seems like ever' time I say som'thin', I've hurt, angered or embarrassed somebody. Could I e'er be thet good?*

Lizzie finished clearing the table, put the flowers on the buffet and took the tablecloth to the kitchen. The stain was stiff now, so she scraped the gravy stain, soaked it in cold water then, put it on the still growing mountain of laundry. *It may tak' me a month o' Sundays ta wash an' press all thet. The 'backdoor guests' will hafta fight their way through a maze o' clothes lines ta find us t'marra afternoon.*

It was late when Lizzie finally finished the dishes, cleaned the stove, and set the fire for the night. Missus Twombly retired early, just after a light supper.

Doctor Twombly came for his coffee and was uncharacteristically quiet. He spoke of general things, more to himself than to her. She was busy enough, and having no desire to break into his thoughts, she let him ruminate on his own.

T'marra's another day, she thought. *I guess Eliza's sleepin' in her ain room, t'night. Her bed mus' be dry wit' the wind blowin' through fer a couple days now. Nae matter, I would pro'bly sleep through anythin' t'night. T'marra bein' laundry day, there will no rest fer the wicked, Lizzie.*

That night, her slumber was disturbed by a kaleidoscope of terrifying dreams. She was being dragged back home on a gravy ocean in a bouncing turkey boat. Doctor Twombly thundered condemnation from the pulpit, denouncing the sin of excess butter. Miss Isabelle screamed, "How dare she! Send her home this instant!" Just before she woke, she heard a crowd of disembodied voices shouting, "Hame? We don' wan' her back *here!*"

Lizzie awoke with her bed linens tightly wrapped around her, her pillow on the floor and her aching head pounding. The faint pounding was getting louder, faster. "Lizzie, open the door!"

She hastily pulled herself out of the tangled sheets and stood. Eliza was at the door. In Lizzie's thrashing, she had moved the edge of her headboard in front of the door, effectively locking her sister from her room. "Jes' a minute, Eliza, wha' time is it? Wha's goin' on?"

"It's jes' two o'clock. I was dreamin' an' got scairt, so I came down ta yer. I couldn't git the door open, an' thought somethin' happened ta yer. Why didn't the door open, Lizzie?"

"Sh! I was havin' a wild dream o' m' own, Eliza. When I woke, the bed was moved in front o' the door. Come in. We both need some comp'ny, I expec'. I hope we've no' woke the res' o' the house. I'll take m' punishmen' in the mornin', but I need some sleep t'night." Together, the girls straightened the covers, and climbed into bed. Almost instantly, they fell into a quiet slumber.

They were up again at five as usual and well into their Monday routines, when Missus Twombly came into the kitchen. She

89

sat in her rocker, fanning her face with her notebook, to cool the already climbing temperatures. "Lizzie, I noticed the biscuits were spread with jam and no butter. Just as a point of curiosity, why was that? Doctor Twombly *does* like his butter."

Tortured with guilt since the day before, Lizzie spilled out the story of the bouncing turkey, the drippings and the hasty gravy. "I've used all the butter, ma'am. I-I dinna knae wha' else ta *do!*"

Lizzie was astonished to see the elderly woman's shoulders begin to tremble then, shake with mirth. She threw her head back and laughed.

Struggling to come back to her usual calm demeanor, she said, "Lizzie, I don't know if I could have saved the day with such aplomb! It was fully worth the pound of butter to entertain my guests so graciously, completely unaware of the disasters going on in the kitchen! That was *excellent* work, Lizzie!"

She sat there smiling for a minute, and then pulled her attention to her menu plan for the week. "I *will* have to send you to the grocer to get more butter. The milkman won't be here until Wednesday. That's fine. I would also like some tomatoes and strawberries if they're in. How are we doing on potatoes, onions? Pick up some fresh mushrooms while you're there.

"Oh, adding the biscuits and candies to the tray of desserts was an excellent idea. I noticed the flowers too. Maybe we shouldn't have flowers on the tray with sweets, though. Mister Gardner was so distracted talking to Miss Davidson, he reached for one, and shoved a flower in his mouth instead. I thought we might have to call for a doctor for his coughing spell."

"Oh, dear, I hadn't thought o' thet. I'm sae sorry."

"It's all right, my dear. I believe Missus Gardener was about to put a stop to his conversation with Miss Davidson soon anyway." Missus Twombly replied, arching her eyebrow pointedly. "She encouraged her husband to make their regrets, and they left soon after that."

"Beggin' ye pardon, ma'am? I won't be able ta finish the laundry, if I gae ta the grocer t'day. It may take more than a day as it is."

"It won't matter if it takes three days to do it, Lizzie. You and Eliza will go to the grocer. Have the groceries delivered this afternoon. The fresh air will do you good. You'll have to go right after luncheon though, so we can have it delivered today."

Missus Twombly thought a moment, and then added, "You and Eliza can stop at the pharmacy for quart of ice cream, and buy a small dish for each of you to have there, if you like. It's a good day for it. Once you have the ice cream, hurry home. We still have some fresh cherries, so set out a bowl with the ice cream. You can serve it out on the side lawn. I had Big John set the summer chairs and table out there last week. There will be five of us. It should be shady there by then. Perhaps we can catch a breeze."

She went on with her menu for the week, writing her grocery list as she proceeded through the days. Lizzie listened to the hum of her mistress talking to herself. *She's awful pale t'day. The hot weather is wearin' on her. She's only a wisp o' a thing, an' she looks even frailer than before. She has endless meetin's ta attend. It's good Miss Isabelle ne'er leaves her side, 'ceptin' here in the house. Mister William does the same with Doctor Twombly, though it's Mister William, who's feeling poorly.*

"Ma'am, would you care fer a glass o' iced tea, with maybe a little sugar in it?" Missus Twombly looked at her blankly, and then smiling, she nodded.

Lizzie hurried. Missus Twombly took the glass with a shaky hand. "Whew! Thank you, child, I was a bit dizzy there for a minute." Lizzie helped her hold the glass steady as she encouraged her to drink more. Some of her color returned as the tea disappeared, but she was still shaky.

"Missus Twombly, why don't you lie down on my bed until ye've rested a bit? It's cooler in there."

91

"I-I'm fine," she said, swaying as she stood. "Well, maybe for just a moment." Lizzie put an arm around Missus Twombly, led her carefully to her room, and helped her into bed. The room was shaded that part of the day, so Lizzie opened the window wide and was rewarded with a fresh breeze.

"You lay there fer a while. Call me if you need me. I'll be right in the kitchen."

Lizzie left the door open a crack, and then sped through the house to find Isabelle. She found her sitting in the office with her father, reading.

"Miss, may I speak with you a moment, please?" Isabelle's eyes flashed at the interruption.

Stepping out to the hall, she demanded, "What is it? I'm helping my father with his sermon."

"It's yer ma, Miss Isabelle. She's restin' in my room. She's feeling a bit poorly an' nearly fainted. I thought ye should knae."

"Oh, my heavens," Isabelle exclaimed, running to her mother's side. She found her sleeping quietly. Isabelle put her head on her mother's chest and listened intently.

"Lizzie, go to my mother's room and on her night stand is a small brown envelope. Bring it to me with a glass of water, quickly!"

Lizzie ran up the stairs, meeting Eliza in the hall. "Which one is Missus Twombly's room?" she demanded. Voicelessly, Eliza pointed.

Lizzie snatched the envelope and ran back downstairs. Isabelle carefully poured a small amount of powder into a glass, and snapped, "Spoon, Lizzie."

Lizzie retrieved a spoon from the kitchen and thrust it into her hand. Stirring the concoction in the glass, she spoke softly to her mother. "Mother, take this." Isabelle spooned the liquid into her mother's mouth. As her mother rose to a sitting position, Isabelle gave her the glass. "Drink it all, Mother." Missus Twombly frowned, but obediently drank the liquid. "Rest, Mother."

In the kitchen, she said to Lizzie. "If she gets up, you let me know. Return this to her bed table, and then come down here to the kitchen. I want you to stay in the kitchen, until she gets up. If she has any trouble at all, you come get me. Do you understand?"

"Aye, Miss Isabelle. May I call upon Eliza to sit in the kitchen, sae I can hang the laundry?"

"Yes, yes, fine. Just until you get it hung, then get back in here."

Lizzie nodded, but thought, *what does she think I would do, go out there in the blistering sun fer a tea party? Hold yer tongue, Lizzie! She doesn't mean yer slackin' off. She's jes' worried about her ma.*

"Miss, you may want ta think about moving her to a cooler room this afternoon, when the sun comes 'round ta this side o' the house, if she's up ta it, o' course."

"Yes, you're right. I don't mean to snap at you. I'm glad you called me. She doesn't realize she's overdoing, until it's too late. Please forgive me. Call me if there's any change. I will be with my father."

"Aye, miss."

Lizzie went back to her washing on the back porch and checked on her mistress often. Soon, the elderly woman was feeling better, and surprised Lizzie at her wringer and tub.

"Lizzie, did we finish the shopping list? I've lost track of where we were," Missus Twombly said.

"I think sae, ma'am. Please sit down. Would you like another glass o' tea, or perhaps a cool glass o' lemonade?" Lizzie resisted the urge to run for Isabelle, until she could see for herself how Missus Twombly was faring.

"Plain lemonade, I think, if there is any already made."

Once Lizzie served the lemonade, she slipped out of the kitchen to tell Isabelle. Isabelle quickly went back to the kitchen to check on her mother. Satisfied that the *spell* was over, she kissed her mother, and warned her to be more considerate of her health. "Lizzie and I were very worried, Mother. You must be careful in this heat, not to exert yourself."

"Oh bother, child, I'm fine now. I *do* dislike being hovered over."

"Mother, it is unkind to dismiss our concern. We only want you to be well enough for you to engage in the activities you enjoy. You would do the same for us."

"Very well, Isabella. I'm fine now and will try not to worry you for the rest of the day. You may begin again tomorrow, if you wish." Missus Twombly hugged her daughter and smiled over her shoulder to Lizzie. "You're a good daughter. Now go tend to your father's needs."

Isabelle took one last careful look into her eyes, and satisfied her mother had returned to nearly normal, she left.

Lizzie changed her water-soaked apron, and began preparing lunch. It was already a half hour late, due to the worrisome events of the morning. The dining room was on the shady side of the house, so it should be still cool in there. Eliza could open the windows as they were just sitting down. *Where is Eliza? I haven't seen her all morning. She should have come down long before this to serve lunch.*

As if just thinking her name would conjure her up, Eliza materialized from the door at the back staircase. She had another huge armful of laundry and an apologetic look on her face. "Add it to the pile, Eliza. That much more will no' matter. You have jes' enough time ta change yer apron and cap afore this luncheon is ready." Eliza's apron was gray with dust and her cap was tossed askew from the efforts of her morning's work. She turned on her heel and ran back up the stairs.

94

"Poor child," said Missus Twombly. "Today, she's not only stripping the beds, but she's changing all the covers and curtains for the summer. The heavy winter curtains hide a lot of dust, and all the windows get washed at the same time. I had her hang the summer curtains straight from storage, so they will have to come down again to be pressed. There's no hurry. I'll be satisfied to air out the upstairs and let the light in there for now. We will wait until you can press the downstairs curtains before we hang those. We have put such a burden on you girls this week. We could send out the laundry, you know. Our neighbors would think little of it."

"Please, ma'am. I'd like ta do it, if ye don' mind. It's no' bein' done all ta onct, but I'd prefer ta do it m'self. I did it a' hame fer the Earl an' his guests."

"Well, if you have your heart set on it. So be it. You're very conscientious, Lizzie. I don't want people to think I'm working you too hard."

"No, ma'am, the wringer, the sink an' the lines haf' made it sae much easier, I can work faster than at hame. They's a great deal o' satisfaction fer me ta do it m'self."

Eliza returned and luncheon was served in the dining room. While the girls ate in the kitchen, Lizzie reviewed the grocery list. She checked the pantry and added salt to the list. When they heard the dining room empty, Eliza cleared the table, and Lizzie looked for Missus Twombly. She was in the office with her husband, so Lizzie waited at the open door, until she was noticed. She was given permission to add the salt to the list. "If you think you need anything else while you're there, please order that, too."

The girls left their aprons in the cook's room, neatened their hair, and donned their hats. Lizzie's hat dipped a little in the front since their excursion by the river.

Lizzie's face, still red from the rising steam of the rinse water, welcomed the refreshing breeze.

Dorothy MacNeill Dupont

Chapter Seven

The summer flew by like a runaway train, one day chasing the next, until suddenly it was the beginning of August. A heat wave threatened to smother the Twombly household. Dinner parties were curtailed and meetings cancelled. Mother and son took to napping in the afternoons.

Missus Twombly's lists became shorter and shorter. She had taken to writing them by lamplight on the back porch after sundown when the chance of a cool breeze made the chore more manageable.

The trip to Martha's Vineyard was approaching, and there was much to do to prepare. Lizzie had taken to asking Missus Twombly every afternoon, if she could pack a few linens, some dishes or perhaps add one or two items to the list. She couldn't pressure the heat-exhausted woman, but perhaps she could lift her spirits, by encouraging her to look forward to the trip.

Lizzie and Eliza put a small chaise on the back porch, so Missus Twombly could lay down in the afternoon shade, with a cool cloth on her forehead. Occasionally, she felt well enough to read a while before she napped. Lizzie put a small table by the chaise and placed her notebook and a pencil next to it, hoping for an addition to the list.

Lizzie didn't think about Martha's Vineyard, as much as she did the preparation for it. She tried to imagine what she would need to keep the family in the comfort to which they were accustomed. Eliza was able to pack all the clothes for the family, except the formal dresses and suits. Those would go in special boxes for

97

transport at the last minute. The travel clothes were hanging inside closet doors, covered with sheets to protect them from dust.

Lizzie's half-sister was getting more and more anxious as the date of the trip approached. Lizzie's anxiety was with other concerns.

It's been weeks between letters from James, who seems ta git along just as well wit'out us, Lizzie thought irritably. On Doctor Twombly's instructions, Lizzie wrote him that on their next day off, Lizzie and Eliza were planning to take the train to Quincy to meet him. James did tell her that he would arrange to be there. Eliza was sure they would be lost, and never see James at all. Lizzie however, was confident it would not be difficult.

Mister Twombly asked Mister Bachelor to go with them so they would arrive to their destination safely. *If he kin gae all the way ta New York an' back without mishap, surely he kin get us ta James at the shipyard safely. Then maybe James will tell us what's goin' on wit' him. His last letter hinted 'bout somethin' he's plannin', but he won' tell us wha' it is. He said it would haf' ta wait 'till he saw us.*

I hope he's not been caught up in some scheme like we heard about wit' those boy-os in Boston. Those sons o' Erin thought sure they were gonna be rich, but all the investors did was ta take wha' little money they had, an' make off wit' it. James is smarter than thet, I hope.

Doctor Twombly said, young immigrants had been tricked an' robbed in these parts, fer as lang as he could remember. Innocents in the hands of snake oil merchants, he called them.

The girls' day off would be Thursday, August 4th. They would be leaving for Martha's Vineyard the following Monday.

Lizzie hoped the blistering hot weather would break soon, so Missus Twombly could feel better. Eliza said Isabelle confided in her that her mother and brother suffered greatly in the hot weather, but once the weather turned cool, they were right as rain again.

Her father however, worked as if the heat had no effect on him at all. Even if it reached ninety or above, the only accommodation he would allow for the heavy humidity was to remove his suit jacket, and work in his shirt sleeves. The jacket went right back on if company came to the door. Isabelle and her mother changed to light cotton shifts, and did not encourage company.

The younger Mister Twombly stayed exclusively to his room. Once, when Eliza passed by, she heard a heavy thud, as if he had fallen. She reported it to Isabelle, who then went to check on him. She found he had fainted. She could not pick him up, so she enlisted Eliza's help. He woke as the women were trying to raise him to his bed and he chastised his sister severely for allowing Eliza to see him in his state of undress. He had removed his tie and unbuttoned his shirt, revealing his undershirt. Eliza ran from the room. Isabelle emerged a few minutes later, very angry.

"For pity's sake, next time remind me, and I will throw a sheet over his lordship where he lies, and then send for the doctor." She stomped down the hall, still muttering to herself.

Eliza's embarrassment was not for his state of clothing, but for the unseemly state of agitation between the otherwise distinguished brother and sister.

The passing days offered no relief, and Lizzie was worried about taking a day off while the Twombly mother and son were so ill. She broached the subject one night, when Doctor Twombly was sitting in the kitchen, reading the newspaper. He often read the paper aloud, while she cleaned up the supper dishes, so she waited until there was a pause between the articles he found interesting.

When she stated her concerns, he looked at her quizzically. "Lizzie, I am confident that Isabella and I will be able to take care of Missus Twombly and William. To be sure, however, I have asked one of the ladies from church to come in to lend a hand. She will be able to set out dinner and supper for us, and keep watch between times. She has been gracious enough to do that for several years

99

now, when any of the clergy is feeling under the weather, and the household help is away for the day. Please don't worry."

Then, his mood brightening, he said, "Mister Bachelor will tend to your journey and I know you've been looking forward to seeing your cousin for some time now. Mister Bachelor was quite complimentary toward the young man. I trust he is doing well?"

"I think so, sir. He doesn't reveal much in his letters. You talked 'bout how young impressionable immigrants haf' fallen fer some o' the land purchase schemes, you've been readin' 'bout in the papers? I'm hopin' that's no' the case with James. He desires havin' land sae badly, he'd do 'bout anythin' ta git some," Lizzie replied, a worried look creeping onto her usually calm face.

Dr. Twombly sighed heavily. "When something earthbound becomes so important to a man, he can be easily led to perdition by the devil who speaks its name."

"Yer right, o' course, he has a keen love fer the land, an' is a carpenter by trade. He came ta America ta haf' his ain hame. He's jes' an honest tradesman, sir, lookin' fer a way ta make a livin' an' haf a fam'ly."

"Well, I wish him well. Land is getting to be a smaller slice of the pie in this part of the country. The government is encouraging families to rush to the western territories and states to people the land out there. If I were a young man, I would be tempted to ply my trade out where the long arm of civilization hasn't spoiled the wild beauty of this country.

"However, farming prices have dropped considerably in the last twenty years. So much so, it costs as much to grow the corn, as the price the farmer can get for it. It's good he has a trade other than farming, to depend upon. If this country doesn't turn the economy around, I see a deep depression coming. Already in the northeast, there are fewer jobs than we have people to work them. We're going to have even more 'back door' guests next year, I fear."

"It's not a pretty picture yer paintin', Doctor Twombly. If it's as bad as yer think it's goin' ta be, will ye be takin' in another cook an' housekeeper from Ireland next year?"

"It's a very good question, Lizzie. It will be up to the deacons, I suppose. They finance it. It's still less money than hiring townspeople for the same jobs. It may come down to our obligation to support our own community, by hiring locally, though. I hadn't thought of it. We will have to consider it soon."

Thursday, after breakfast was served, the girls found Mister Bachelor waiting for them at the back door of the manse. His beard was neatly trimmed, his worn suit carefully pressed, Lizzie noted. As they walked to the station, the girls bubbled enthusiastically about the prospect of seeing James. "Mister Bachelor, it is sae good o' ye ta take us ta Quincy. Is it verra far? How lang do yer think 'twill take?" Eliza asked.

"I tol' James wha' time we were leavin' here, but no' when we'd git there. I hope he asked someone. Oh dear, I beg yer pardon. We've lost our manners an' haven't yet givin' yer a chanct ta speak."

The tall slender man laughed gently, "It should take about an hour and maybe fifteen minutes, I should think. This train is local, so it'll stop frequently. We'll have to wait until we're there, to see if James knows that, won't we?"

The girls laughed and hurried their steps to keep up with the lanky strides of their companion. The train station was less than a half mile from the Twombly house. Mister Bachelor bought their tickets, and they settled on a bench to wait. The girls could barely sit still, for the anticipation they felt.

"We'll go to Park Street Station, and then transfer to a trolley for Quincy. That should be interesting. Some of the trolleys are being changed over from horses to electricity. They think by next year the entire system will be electric."

"Isn' thet dangerous? What happens in a lightnin' storm?" asked Lizzie.

"Evidently, they know how to shield the electricity it uses, from the natural-occurring electricity in the sky. I don't know how it works, but with more and more electricity being used in street lights and public areas, they are even talking about putting trains and trolleys underground, so the streets above will be used for horses and carriages, maybe even those new motor cars. Maybe not, they scare the horses and make a lot of noise. They're more like a toy for grown men, than any practical use."

"Goodness, thet would take a lot o' people ta build, wouldn't it? With all those people workin', maybe the depression Doctor Twombly keeps talkin' about, won't have ta happen," said Lizzie.

"Well, Miss Lizzie. Your head is just chock-full of mechanical and political issues, isn't it? I am impressed," said Mister Bachelor, smiling at the growing pinkness of her cheeks.

"'Tis Doctor Twombly thet fills it, Mister Bachelor. He reads ta me ever' night, from the newspapers. All I do is listen an' keep doin' my work. I don' knae how his head holds all he knaes, I surely don'."

"She's al'ays been the smart one, Mister Bachelor," piped up Eliza, with a little envy in her voice. "When we were little, she's the one ever'body went ta fer book-learnin' answers."

Lizzie rejoined, "I ne'er sat still lang enough ta do fancy work, like Eliza, sae my mother gave me books an' my grandmere set me ta practical work. Someday, I'd like ta do some tattin' an' crochetin' like her." Lizzie looked at Eliza's face, and was rewarded with a smile tinged with pride. *Eliza hides her light under a bushel, an' people tak' her silence fer dullness, but I knae different. I'd be in trouble all the time, wit'out her by my side.*

The trio transferred at Park Street, as promised. The girls had but a moment to look at the tall buildings and the beautiful green park. "Perhaps, if we have time on the way home, you ladies would permit me to show you the Swan Boats of the Public Garden?"

"Oh, thet would be wonderful, Mister Bachelor! Oh Lizzie, please kin we?"

"If you'd like, Eliza, it's yer day off, too. It depends on how lang we spend wit' James."

"Oh dear, we can't be in two places at onct, an' we must see James fer as long as we can," said Eliza, torn between adventure, and her desire to see her cousin.

Her face looked so sad, Mister Bachelor said, "Perhaps another day? I could take you one day just for the Swan Boats. September weather should still be fair, I think, and not quite so warm."

As Eliza climbed into the trolley car, Lizzie caught their escort's eye, and thanked him for his kindness.

His smile crinkled the corners of his brilliant blue eyes. "Nonsense, it is as much pleasure for me to take you, as it is for you and Miss Eliza to see them."

Seated for the ride, Mister Bachelor leaned forward and spoke to the car man. When he sat back, he said, "Another twenty minutes and we'll be in Quincy."

"Mr. Bachelor, how are the plans ye spoke about, goin' fer yer?"

"Very well, Miss Lizzie. In the fall, I will commence my baccalaureate studies at Harvard University, by the grace of God, and the honorable word of Doctor Twombly. I owe so much to that man."

"And wha' will ye study?" asked Lizzie, her eye lighting up with interest.

"I am pursuing a life in the ministry, so first I must achieve a Bachelor of Arts degree. It's a long road, but one I am prepared to take, one step at a time."

103

"So ye'll be Mister Bachelor, Bachelor of Arts?" Immediately, she was ashamed of her words. "I'm sae sorry. I should nae make light o' yer ambition ta serve the Laird. My silly mouth runs before m' better sense takes o'er. Please forgive me."

"There's nothing to forgive, Miss Lizzie. 'Tis no more than I've said to myself, when the plan was first formed in my brain. It *is* amusing. When most men my age have already chosen a wife and are raising a family, I am at the beginning of my education. I am a bachelor who has not even earned his 'Bachelor' status yet. I figure to be about forty-two by the time I am ordained."

"Mister Bachelor," said Lizzie with an impish grin, "You are likely ta be forty-two some day, in any case. 'Twill be a wonderful thing ta be forty-two an' be an ordained minister, as well."

The serious but handsome man in the somber black suit threw his head back and laughed. "Misses Heenans, I don't know when I have had such a delightful day. I will remember this day when I get too serious in my studies, and full of ponderous thoughts. God willed us to laugh, and I must not forget that." Smiling, he looked out the window, and the little group grew silent watching beautiful scenes bathed in sunlight, follow one after the other.

While they were isolated by their own reveries, the car man broke through to say, "Yer stop, sir, Quincy Station. Step carefully. Next stop, shipyards."

Lizzie wondered if they were supposed to go to the next stop, but left the car at Mister Bachelor's urging. Her foot barely touched ground before she heard, "Lizzie, Eliza, over here!" It was James! He grabbed Eliza, then Lizzie in a big bear hug. When their feet touched down again, James grinned as if his face would split. He reached forward and shook Mister Bachelor's hand. "It is sae good ta see yer all!"

They stood talking excitedly, frozen in time. The little group stood oblivious to all but each other, while people swirled about them, busily rushing to and fro. When a young man brushed by

104

Lizzie, nearly knocking her over, Mister Bachelor held her arm, and said, "Is there somewhere we can go, where we'll be out of harm's way, Mister Heenan?"

"Aye, o' course, there's a park jes' beyond the station, where we kin sit. There's a street vendor there too, if yer hungry." Eliza took James' arm, and Mister Bachelor took Lizzie's elbow to cross the busy street to the park. In the lush green park, there was a small open octagonal structure that caught Lizzie's fancy.

"Mister Bachelor, what is thet used for? It's sae pretty."

"That is a band stand or gazebo. On summer nights and holidays, a band will be invited to play, or a speaker will make great oratories, from that platform. The people gather around it, and applaud, or boo whoever it is. Look there is someone there now."

As he spoke, the mournful melodic tune of a violin began to drift though the air.

"Come!" Lizzie called, impetuously grabbing Mister Bachelor's hand, pulling him up the long hill. Startled, but carried by her buoyancy, he followed her. With her other hand, she held her hat which threatened to fly off her head. Finally, she took it off, and waved it to James and Eliza, who were still far behind, talking. "C'mon!" she hollered.

Reaching the crest of the hill, she saw a boy of about twenty, passionately stroking the strings of his melodious instrument. She watched him intently as Mister Bachelor led her to a bench. As rapt as she was staring at the boy, so Mister Bachelor was, in watching her. Her red-gold hair wild and loose mesmerized him. Unconsciously, she still held his hand. He did not move, for fear she would come to her senses, and snatch it away. He let the music overwhelm his senses, as the presence of the pretty girl beside him, did. Everything seemed in sharp focus, colors more vibrant, sounds clearer than it seemed possible. Everything receded but the girl, the music, and the beauty of the day around him.

"Mister Bachelor." The sound of his name startled him back to reality.

"Er, yes?" Four sets of eyes were staring at him. Lizzie, Eliza, James, and the boy were looking at him expectantly.

"I'm sorry. The music was so lovely I was lost in my thoughts. Is there anything I can do for you?"

"Mr. Bachelor." Lizzie said gently, "We jes' wanted ta knae if ye'd care ta have a sausage with us from the vendor?"

"Oh," he replied too heartily, and turned red. "Yes, of course, here, young man, something for your music." Mister Bachelor tossed a penny in the violinist's hat. "Do you know any Strauss, *The Blue Danube,* perhaps?"

"Stay there, Mister Bachelor. I'll bring yer sausage to you," said James, smiling. *You're no' the first man I've seen caught in Lizzie's web. Nor will ye be the last, I'll wager,* he thought. *I doubt she even knaes it.*

"Mister Bachelor, are ye feelin' all right? Maybe ye should take yer jacket off?"

"I am quite all right, Miss Lizzie. I feel a little foolish, to be so deep in thought."

After their midday repast, the group moved on through the park, chatting continuously. Once again, Eliza was paired with James, Lizzie with Mister Bachelor. Finding a bench in a shady spot, the minister-to-be and the two girls, sat down. James plopped himself down on the ground in front of them. "Nae thet I have your attention, ladies an' gentleman, I have somethin' I want ta say ta yer," said James. "And, afore ye commence ta badgerin' m' sensibilities, hear me out." Eliza and Lizzie looked at each other knowingly, while Mister Bachelor's blank look showed he had no idea what was going on.

James pulled a piece of a newspaper page out of his pocket, and spread it on the ground ahead of him. He began to read. "White homesteaders wanted ta settle previously-restricted land, known as

106

the Cherokee Strip, Oklahoma. 6,500,000 acres o' land will be divided into 160 acre lots free fer the claiming. Claims must be made ta any o' the United States Land Offices on a first-come, first-served basis.

"The Land Run will commence at 12 o'clock noon, on September 16th, 1893. No person is allowed ta claim or enter the territory ta be settled afore thet time. Violators will be prohibited from claiming land in any part o' the territory. Claimants canna already own more than 160 acres in any other state or territory. They have ta be a citizen o' the United States of America, or have filed intentions ta become a citizen. They have ta be the head o' household an' over 21 years o' age.

"Ta *keep* the land, onct it's claimed, claimant must, within six months o' the claim, establish residence in a house upon the land, an' cultivate the land, continuously fer five year."

James looked at his sisters and said, "Thet's what I wan' ta do. I'm gonna git me some o' thet land. I have a year ta git there, file an intention o' citizenship, an' git a fast horse. Then, I'll stake my claim. Imagine, 160 acres, fer nothin'." He looked at the girls again. Still, they said nothing.

"It's the chance o' a lifetime, lasses!" He burst out. "Say *some*thin'!"

"James," Lizzie started slowly. "It sounds too good ta be true. Are ye sure 'bout this?"

"I've been askin' around an' they say they did a land run like this jes' last April. It's a whole territory thet's been opened up, an' not settled yet. It's the bloomin' government, wha's backin' it. How can it be wrong? We could have our own land, an' no one kin tell us ta pay rent on it."

"*We*, James?" said Eliza. "I don' think I want ta go out west. They's Indians out there."

"Indians sold the land ta the government. They've moved further west ta places called reservations."

107

"Eliza's right, James, I don' think I want ta gae traipsing' off ta the west. We don' knae what we'd be facin' there. I wan' ta be where my children will get a good education, an' I kin make a livin'. Yer talkin' about the middle o' *beyond*, James," Lizzie added plaintively.

"Well, it's wha' *I'm* settin' ta do, girls. Ye kin come wit' me or no'." James set his jaw, stubbornly. *Why can' they see wha' an opportunity this is? Farmland out here is way out o' reach o' most men's purses. I canna e'en git started here.*

"James, I no' wan' ta discourage ye from doin' what ye would, but ye canna be askin' me ta gae along wit' it. Eliza kin chose it if she wishes, but fer me, I don'." Lizzie's eyes were flashing with unspoken frustration. She knew how much he wanted land. She also knew she could ply her trade here. She was reading the papers too.

They's jobs in the paper fer laundresses, ev'ry night in the classified section. They's dressmaker shops too, where Eliza could do her sewin', tattin', and crochetin'.

She had it all thought out. They could all move to Boston when they were done with the Twomblys, and have a room, until they could move to a place where they could have land.

"I promise yer this, James, I *will* think on it. An' I'll talk ta the people I knae, too. Maybe I'll hear somethin' I like 'bout this scheme o' yers. In the meantime, put it in yer pocket, an' let's no' argue away the time we have left, this afternoon. Please, James? Mister Bachelor dinna bring us all this way, jes' ta hear us scrap like dogs o'er a bone." She smiled her prettiest smile, and hoped he would relent, at least for today.

"Very well, Lizzie, but this is no' the end o' it. Wit' or wit'out yer, I plan ta do this."

"I understand James, but fer nae tell me, are there any pretty lasses thet's caught yer eye?"

108

James smiled. Lizzie could always pull him out of his dark moods, and lighten his spirit, at just the right time. He saw Eliza was close to tears as she always was, when Lizzie was fightin' with anyone.

Mister Bachelor was drawn to Eliza now, James thought. *He canna make up his mind. First it's one, and then it's t'other. I'll wager, he spends too much time alone wit' his books, an' not enough time wit' the ladies,* he thought.

"Ah, there's Bridget, an' Colleen, an' Sally, an' Cherie, jes' too many ta count. I daren't chose one, fer fear the others are heartbroken. Wha' on earth shall I do? Poor me."

"Ach, yer shameless, James Heenan, Mister Bachelor will think yer spendin' all yer time wit' the lasses, 'stead o' workin'. Tell us what's it 's like ta be workin' in the shipyards?"

"Well, the loads are heavy, but ye build hard muscles. They have us bunked in rooms wit' hard beds an' noisy neighbors, but yer sae tired, ye hardly e'en notice. I start at dawn an' I'm done at supper, an' I have no time fer carousin'. The foreman likes m' work, which means no one else likes *me* verra much. They grumble 'cause I'm workin' too fast, an' makin' 'em look bad. I try ta keep out o' scuffles, but sometimes ye hafta teach 'em ta no' tangle with yer. S'all right, I guess, but I miss bein' alone, wit' the sun on my back an' a saw in my hands. Jes' makin' my ain livin', is wha' I'm langin' fer."

Lizzie watched James go from answering her questions, to drifting into memories of the Ulster life that was no more. *I miss it too, James, I do.*

Soon the sun was sinking behind the hill, peeking out between the darkening birches, telling them it was time to go. James kissed his cousins and held them tight, shook Mister Bachelor's hand and bid him farewell.

Mister Bachelor assisted them to the trolley seats and they settled in for the ride back to Boston, then back to the sleepy town of

Newton Lower Falls. Everyone was once again quiet, seeking to stay within their own thoughts, cloaked in the warm memories of the day.

Mister Bachelor was deep in the throes of self-doubt. *What on earth is wrong with me? Lizzie looks my way, and I am smitten. Eliza sheds a tear and I must protect her. They are little more than half my age, and I am a schoolboy in their presence. I am not only acting a fool over a child, but over two children.*

I am supposed to be someone they can trust. I think I had better find myself an appropriate wife and soon, or risk acting the biggest fool in the known world. But who would have a man who is just beginning his quest at my age. Who am I fooling? I have no time for courting a woman. I am just starting my studies. That's it; I'll have to throw myself into my studies so I don't have time to think of anything else.

Lizzie glanced at the man who chaperoned them all day and saw a man at war with himself.

Poor Mister Bachelor, whatever his battle is, he seems ta be losing. He has sech goodness in him. I hope he finds a woman worthy o' him. If he were already educated, Miss Isabelle would be a good match fer him. He'd soften her edges, an' she'd bolster his spine. Oh dear, she stifled a giggle, *what if it worked the other way 'round?*

Abandoning her match-making thoughts, she noticed with some regret, they were almost home, and their pleasant day nearly done. *Oh dear, Eliza's fallen asleep on Mister Bachelor's shoulder.*

Eliza was shocked and disoriented, when Lizzie woke her, as they pulled into the station.

The heat of the day had not retired with the sun. It was hot and humid. The crickets were protesting loudly, and Lizzie was anxious to get home. *Missus Twombly must be havin' a terrible time. I hope they gave her a cool bath with Epsom salts. It seems ta calm her in the heat.*

110

Mister Bachelor escorted them home and reluctantly it seemed, left them at the back door.

Everything seemed to be as she had left it that morning in the Twombly household. Eliza and Lizzie decided to bathe in Lizzie's room before going to bed. They dragged the galvanized tub into her tiny room, drew the shades and enjoyed the cool water. They washed each other's hair and worked at getting the knots out of Lizzie's red mop. Later, Lizzie threw on her robe, and checked the kitchen stove.

She noticed that Doctor Twombly uncharacteristically left the newspaper on the side table by the rocker. Sitting in the rocker, she thought she'd see what he would have read to her that evening.

Blazoned on the front page was a shocking headline. "Two Brutally Murdered in Fall River – Banker Andrew Borden, and his wife, Abby Borden were found murdered, bludgeoned by an axe, at noon today."

Shocked, Lizzie went on to read that the youngest daughter of the slain couple was also named Lizzie. She quickly read through the sensational account of the murder, then rearranged the paper neatly in the stack on the floor, as was Doctor Twombly's custom for all the papers for the week.

Horrified, she knew not to mention it to Eliza, or neither of them would sleep that night. Morbidly, she knew she would have to read about it in the paper the next day, to get any peace. *Imagine, the daughter's name is Lizzie!* She shivered. She found herself wondering what this Lizzie woman was like.

All day Friday, Lizzie anxiously awaited the reading of the paper by the elder minister. When the time came, Doctor Twombly did not read any articles about the murdered couple aloud.

Oh goodness, I'll ne'er sleep t'night! I hardly slept last night. I need to knae it was resolved, in some way. Having no satisfaction from Doctor Twombly, she waited until he went to bed, then frantically searched the paper for the Bordens. She still hadn't

111

mentioned it to Eliza, but she was beside herself in wanting to tell someone. *Ah, there it is.*

The article reiterated its previous information, plus it gave a timeline for when the bodies were discovered, who ran for help, who was in the house, who was away. It was a real mystery. She recalled the untimely death of an old woman back home when she was ten years old. *This was no' like poor Alice McCartan in Castlewellan, God rest her soul. This was no accident!*

She was relieved to read, that her namesake, Lizzie, was in the barn when it happened. *Oh the poor woman, what if she'd been in the house? She may have been murdered too, oh my!*

In the middle of the night, a rolling thunderstorm broke. The air freshened, and cooled quickly. The first clap woke the girls who were sleeping in Lizzie's room. The storm produced little rain, but the sudden cold wind drove them to shutting windows in the downstairs rooms. That accomplished, they ran upstairs to the banging window shutters. The curtains were flying inward, whipping violently, as if fleeing from the blinding flashes and house-rattling cracks of thunder. Lizzie pounded on the doors until the occupants of the rooms opened them, affirming they were all right, and could shut the windows against the impending rain.

All the time Lizzie was running to and fro in the darkened house with the violent storm outside, she was thinking of the Bordens.

Our windows were wide open, waitin' fer anyone ta climb in and murder us in our beds! She imagined the stark shadows caused by the flashing lights were nefarious creatures ready to pounce on her. Every door that yielded to her was a fiendish trap, every door that did not, was a blocked escape!

She prayed, and bargained with God, begging Him to deliver her from the storm, the lurking shadows, and her own imagination. Her hands were shaking, and once in the dark, she ran into Eliza. Lizzie let out a blood-curdling scream of fright and poor Eliza nearly fainted dead away. "What on earth is going on out here?" thundered the young minister, with Isabelle echoing his words.

"I-its fine, I just ran into Eliza in the dark. Nearly knocked her down, I did," Lizzie answered. Another heart-stopping clap of thunder crashed overhead, then finally the light show was over and the torrential rains came. Lizzie grabbed the lamp, put her arm around Eliza's shaking shoulders and led her downstairs.

As they started to descend the stairs to the front hall, the main entrance blew open. Her heart in her mouth, she handed the lamp to Eliza, and ran down the stairs. Lizzie pushed the door against the forceful wind, and slammed it shut. She locked the portal to secure it and headed back to her bedroom gingerly.

Was it the wind, or is som'one in the house? Be calm, Lizzie! Ye lookin' fer ghosties, an' heaven knaes, they've already heard yer screamin' like a banshee in this house t'night!

After a few restless moments, Eliza fell into a deep restful sleep as if the angels guarded her every breath. Lizzie envied her childlike slumber. She passed the night staring in the darkness, barely moving in her bed, listening for any sound that would support her fears.

Chapter Eight

Lizzie blessed the sun that rose, ending her night of terror. Missus Twombly was already in the kitchen in her rocker, working on her list, as if the last week of blast furnace heat had never occurred. The air was refreshingly cooler and dryer — a good day for last minute laundry, Lizzie thought.

She automatically began getting breakfast, saying "good morning" to Missus Twombly, and receiving a barely audible assent.

The mistress of the house was engrossed in her plans, furiously marking down items for her travel list. They only had two days to accomplish what she had planned a week to do. She was struggling to prioritize her list of tasks in preparation for the trip.

"Lizzie, I think the bed linens should be packed first, then the breakables and the dining linens and towels to protect them. The leather trunk from the attic will do nicely for that."

Lizzie pointed to the trunk in the corner of the kitchen. "I've done thet already hopin' thet would be the way you would do it. I put the towels around the breakables, and then lay the linens on top in rolls, so they wouldn't crease."

"Excellent, Lizzie, I should have known you'd have everything in hand. There's a metal box I use for toiletries, and medicinal items. Did Isabella show you? That can be set in the trunk, at the top, as well. There is a standing trunk for dresses and suits, with a place in the bottom for shoes. We can pack those tomorrow. We can buy our food there. Our dinner will be packed for the ferry. Our neighbor is willing to take what foodstuff that might spoil while we're gone, and she promises to set out supper for our 'back door' guests. I told her she could put it on our back porch, so

114

they won't be used to going to her house. She was very concerned about *that.*" Missus Twombly raised her eyebrows and smiled wryly.

"Are there any dresses you would like to prepare for the trip, that I don't already have, Missus Twombly? Your light shifts, perhaps? It could get very warm again." Lizzie wanted to take full advantage of Missus Twombly's return to good health to get her chores done, before they left on Monday morning.

"Perhaps just one shift each, for Isabella and me. It is much cooler on the Island than here, as a rule. We'll have company most days or we'll be invited elsewhere, so we may not even use the shifts.

William and Isabella have their bathing costumes and beach blankets at the Vineyard house. I'll have Isabella bring them to you there, to be aired out, and repaired if needed. We leave them at the cottage, so there is a modicum of sand to bring back with us. I don't suppose you and Eliza have swimming costumes? Well, no matter," she added, when she saw Lizzie shaking her head. "You can take off your shoes, and wriggle your toes in the water, if you like. The water's too cold for my taste, at any rate." She shivered.

"Isabella and I have paints at the cottage, and I hope to do some watercolor sketches, while I'm there. Isabella is the accomplished artist. I'm hoping she will teach again, someday. Perhaps we can sneak off on a deserted beach and paint in peace. William likes to paint on occasion, but he's mostly a writer of poetry. It would be nice to spend just a private afternoon with them, while we're there. I hope he's not too busy." At this point, she became quiet, perhaps thinking of breezy warm days with her children, exploring the quiet places of the island.

It mus' be wonderful ta make a picture of how beautiful a simple day o' sunshine is. In the paintin' upstairs, she caught the brilliance o' such a day shown within a clutch o' peonies. How kin one person have sae many talents, an' some o' us have sae few? She

115

writes poetry and hymns; paints pictures; an' finds the time ta be kind ta everyone.

Miss Isabelle says, she's on many committees, an' heads about half of them. She's even taught at a college in New Hampshire, she said. Her husband, a great preacher, is the first ta say she's an especially remarkable woman, in an age o' remarkable women. He's verra proud o' her. One day, I hope ta have a man who looks a' me in my old age as he does her.

Later that day, Lizzie found herself anxiously waiting for the evening paper, to see about the plight of poor Lizzie Borden, whose parents were dead and gone.

Last night's account stated the funeral would be that very day, and Emma Borden had hired a lawyer. Lizzie shivered. *The older sister must think she did it! But she couldn't have. She was out ta the barn, wasn't she? Git yer mind off it, Lizzie. Ye've got ta git yer work done.*

Lizzie's Saturday chores were multiplied by last minute travel preparations. All the laundry, pressing, and polishing would have to be done on Saturday, along with the usual chores.

The following day, Sunday services, light cooking, and light packing, would be all the quiet endeavors allowed on the Sabbath.

That night after supper, Doctor Twombly, sitting in the rocker, perused the day's events in the paper. Though she was sorely tempted, Lizzie didn't ask about the Borden case. She listened to him drone on about the storm damages and the predicted weather.

"I suppose you want to hear about the *other Lizzie*, Lizzie?" Seeing the flash of interest in her eyes, he went on, "There is an editorial, criticizing the police for inaction in the Borden case. That often happens in a murder case, Lizzie. The public thinks police work is simple, that somehow they, the public, know the real facts of the case."

He continued reading, "The funeral services for Andrew and Abby were held at the Borden home. There were understandably, no

116

bodies to view. Sorry, Lizzie, this is too gruesome, even for me. I shan't read the rest aloud. I will leave it here, if you must know the details. I should not have even begun reading it to you.

"It's amazing, how we are curiously drawn to the taste of evil. I will not deny you, since I was captivated by the scene myself, but don't spend too much time on it. It is shameful that newspapers print such salacious gossip, parading itself as fact. I don't know what this world is coming to. It makes me grateful to be old and not long bound to this earth."

"Are you no' feeling well, Doctor Twombly?" Lizzie asked, concerned by his statement.

"Oh, Lizzie, I am fine. Please don't be concerned. I am only ruminating about my advanced age, not about my health. This end of life goes quickly. One wonders if there will be time to do all one thinks to accomplish. It's God's will, not mine, that I am here even now. *We know not the hour...*"

His voice disappeared into thoughts beyond her. He was silent now, absently rocking. "Well, I guess I should retire now, Lizzie," he said, as if breaking through a fog. Hoisting his large frame out of the chair, he carefully refolded the paper, and left the kitchen.

Lizzie didn't quite know what to make of it. *He seems fit enough*, she thought. For a moment, she thought she might like to be here with this family for a long time. She knew it wouldn't happen. She would move on and another cook would take her place, but she recognized that she would miss these people, and this lovely house.

Eliza entered the kitchen, "I'm done fer t'day, Lizzie. Is there anythin' I kin do ta help ye finish?"

"Nay, Eliza. Why don' ye git ready fer bed, an' come out here fer a glass o' milk, while I finish up? We kin talk, an' it'll make the chore gae faster."

"Ye don' mind if I do? T'day's been a real bag o' nails and I wish ta tell ye, I am beat."

117

"Elizabeth Ann Heenan, what are yer *sayin'*?" Lizzie asked, shocked at her language.

Eliza giggled, devilishly. "I heard Big John say thet the other day. It means it's been a confusin' and frustratin' kind o' day, an' I'm verra tired. Miss Isabelle had me runnin' this way 'n thet, stoppin' me from doin' one thin', ta go on ta the next, all day."

"Well, I'm sure it's fun ta say, but don' be sayin' it in front o' the family, or anyone who knaes them. It's no' a seemly way ta express y'self." Lizzie could see Eliza was disappointed by her lecturing, so she added, laughing, "It *does* tell the truth o' it though, doesn' it? Now, gae off wit' ye."

When Eliza came down in her nightclothes, Lizzie was at the table reading the Borden article. Her eyes were wide, feverishly devouring the words before her.

"Tell me, Lizzie! What's it say?"

"Oh, just tells 'bout the Borden funeral. Everyone was gathered outside, but few went in the house. There were policemen guarding the house, an' there was no burial, 'cause the coroner still had the bodies."

Lizzie skipped over the part saying the coroner had taken the heads off, and sent to Boston to have them boiled, and run tests on the skulls. *Doctor Twombly was right. There's no need ta tell those kinds o' sordid details ta the public, or ta Eliza.*

She continued to read aloud, "Lizzie Borden will be questioned at the inquest on Monday mornin', as well as the maid, an' the visitin' uncle." It says, "Lizzie Borden went out to the store in the afternoon, all dressed in black with a heavy veil. A crowd followed her, an' one little boy shouted, 'Why d' ye kill yer Maw an' Pa, Lizzie?' Oh, how awful fer her, the poor woman. Well, thet's enough o' thet, let's gae ta bed."

"How could anyone think thet a woman coulda kill her mother an' father thet way?" asked Eliza, shaking her head.

"There're more things 'n heaven an' earth, Horatio, than are dreamt o' in yer philosophy," quoted Lizzie solemnly.

If she did do it, is she insane? Whoever did this horrific deed must truly be insane. In the same thought, Lizzie wondered if there were papers on the island, so she could follow the strange case of Lizzie Borden's parents.

She will be answerin' questions Monday mornin', while we journey ta the Vineyard. What will she say happened? Would I feel sae much sympathy fer this woman, if her name were no' Lizzie?

That night, as she had the last two nights, she prayed for the child of God, or the spawn of the devil, that was Lizzie Borden. No dreams disturbed her sleep.

Sunday morning's sermon was preached by the Reverend William Twombly on the evils of idle gossip and rumor-mongering. Lizzie was happy to hear, that at least these people were being reminded that they should not assume the worst in Lizzie Borden, based on rumors and innuendos, printed in the newspapers. She noted just that morning, that Big John was talking about the article in Saturday's paper. She was ashamed that she listened to his enthusiastic judgment of Lizzie Borden, with such interest.

She and Eliza were hurrying on their way home from church, when they heard a man calling them. "Misses Heenans, please wait."

"Mister Bachelor, what brings yer this way?"

"Let me first apologize for shouting at you. I don't mean to be rude, but I didn't think I would overtake you, before you arrived at the house. Do you mind, if I walk with you? I wanted to say goodbye, before you left for Martha's Vineyard." Red-faced and winded, he paused to catch his breath.

"Well, thet's verra good o' yer ta think o' us, Mister Bachelor. We'll only be gone two weeks," replied Lizzie confused by his anxious speech.

"'Tis true, you'll be gone only two weeks, but by the time you return, I'll be gone to the University, and I'll not be back this

119

way until Thanksgiving Day. I-I wanted to tell you, you've been a delight to know and I will miss you....both."

"Well, congratulations fer the commencement o' your studies, Mister Bachelor." Lizzie replied, smiling at the hesitation before he said 'both'. "We will miss you, too. You've been verra helpful and charming. Without you, we may have been hopelessly lost in Boston. Are ye sure ye will have no time fer us, afore Thanksgivin'?" she said impishly.

As if he had rehearsed it, he said carefully, "Alas no. I am not so clever to be able to neglect my studies, even for one day of pleasure. I cannot afford to be careless with this opportunity. I will look forward to Thanksgiving though, and to being reunited with... friends."

"I am sorry," replied Lizzie. "I should not tease you. I know how serious your studies are, and we too, will be lookin' forward ta the Thanksgiving. We wish ye well, an' ye have our prayers ta encourage ye, Mister Bachelor. I would love ta stay an' talk, but we must git hame afore the Twomblys. They are entertainin' company fer Sunday dinner an' we must be ready on time."

"Well, I for one won't mind. I am part o' the company. I won't detain you any longer now, but perhaps I could talk to you, after dinner?"

"I'm afraid the work gaes on, after dinner as well, Mister Bachelor. Unless Missus Twombly would allow yer ta visit in the kitchen, whilst I put things away an' do dishes. I've a great deal o' packin' ta finish this afternoon, sae it canna be fer long."

"Would it disturb you ladies, if I sat in the kitchen to wait for the Twomblys to come home? When they get to the front door, I'll slip out the back and *arrive* right after them."

"What d' ye think Eliza?" Her sister had not said a word since Lizzie and Mister Bachelor started talking.

Eliza replied with what was foremost on her mind, "What's this Thanksgivin'? Do the swan boats run at Thanksgivin'?"

120

"Thanksgiving Day is in November. I am so sorry, Miss Eliza. The Swan Boats stop in September, and don't run again until April of next year. At the time, I promised, I did not have a schedule. I should not have promised you, without knowing. I hope I can make it up to you."

"It's all right, Mister Bachelor. We're plannin' ta stay n Boston afta we're released from the Twomblys, sae maybe we'll go then. It jes' sounds *sae* wonderful."

"Here we are, Mister Bachelor. Come in the back door an' I'll get yer some lemonade. I'll be runnin' 'round half crazy, but ye kin talk ta us, whilst we work. Eliza, ye gae change, an' I'll git the table fixin's ready fer ye."

With Mister Bachelor ensconced in the rocker, and a glass of lemonade on the table beside him, Lizzie busied herself with her 'before dinner' chores. "Mister Bachelor, what day do yer classes start? You mus' be sae excited, nae thet yer fin'lly goin' ta the University."

"Harvard wants all freshmen on campus August 22nd. I believe you'll be back on Saturday, the 20th, but you probably won't have another day off until September 8th, unless they give you a day on the island. I am so sorry about the swan boats. I don't make promises, lightly. I admit to being beguiled by Eliza's enthusiasm."

"Please dismiss it from yer mind. If need be, I can find m' way ta the Public Garden an' the swan boats on our next day off."

"Miss Lizzie, I do hope you're not planning to go unescorted. You're very independent, but there are nefarious men who would take advantage of that, and of Miss Eliza's retiring nature. I would consider it entirely my fault if anything happened to you." The sincere concern in his voice made Lizzie look up from her work.

His face was openly fearful. "Mister Bachelor, I promise ta enlist the aid o' an escort ta gae ta Boston, should I gae. I felt sae safe as yer companion, that I didn't realize any danger. I kin take

121

care o' myself, but I canna put my sister in jeopardy. I will take yer advice, ye needn't worry."

"Thank you, Miss Lizzie. Do you know if Mister Baker and his wife will also be here for dinner?"

"Aye, I don't knae him, except as a man of the church. He's head o' the Sunday School an' one o' the trustees, isn't he?"

"Oh yes, but even more interesting, he's a carpenter, and he built this house. In fact, he owns it.

"He lives in another house, he built on Cornell Street, I believe. It's fascinating to me, that we know the man who made that door sill, that staircase, the very floors we're standing on. Mister Baker has strong, rough hands, but he is the very earthly foundation of our little local church. He's a very busy man, yet he ne'er shirks a responsibility to the church. He is a wonderful testament to our faith."

"He surely is, to hear yer tell it, Mister Bachelor." Lizzie was counting serving plates and water glasses anticipating Eliza's arrival. "Mister Bachelor, what is yer given name? When I read 'bout ye in the paper, I wan' ta know it's yer they're talkin' 'bout."

"In the paper? I hope it's for something good, Miss Lizzie. My name is Charles Bachelor, originally of Worcester, Massachusetts, son of a machinist."

"Thank you, Mister Bachelor. I shall put thet in my journal fer safe-keepin'." Eliza came in to collect the table fixings, smiled at the gentleman in the rocker and returned to the dining room.

"There's a lot o' toil an' turmoil back here, that yer ne'er see, if yer dinin' out there. Ever'thin' mus' look as effortless as possible, but be as complex as the fines' restaurant in Boston. Leastwise, thet's how Missus Twombly says it." Lizzie picked up a bowl of stew, and headed for the back door, before it was knocked by the first of her 'back door' guests. She returned, and brought two more, and set them outside on a small table. Just as she was coming back in, the front door latch snapped, signaling the arrival of the

122

Twomblys, and presumably the impressive Mister Baker and his wife. Mister Bachelor slipped out the back, as promised, and headed for the front door.

Dinner was served, without so much as a bobble. Lizzie hoped the molded sherbet dessert stayed recognizable as a rose seated on a thin orange slice, garnished with a pinched mint leaf. Since there were only seven for dinner, the delicate desserts were served on one tray. She could hear the 'ooh's and 'aah's, as Eliza placed each one before the diners, and raised the inverted frosted compote dish to reveal each perfect rose. Lizzie's biggest worry was averted.

Missus Twombly had maintained her reputation as supreme hostess of Newton Lower Falls. Not that it was her aim to be the best. It was her goal, to make each of her guests feel special, and to let them know she was honored to have them there.

Lizzie changed her apron, and fixed her mob cap, to be presentable when Missus Twombly asked her cook to come in, and receive her compliments for a fine meal. Eliza opened the door slightly, and said softly, "Lizzie, you can come in now."

She was surprised to see all the guests were standing raising their water glasses. Doctor Twombly said, "Lizzie and Eliza, we salute you for your hard work, and understanding the last few weeks. The meal was delicious as usual Lizzie, but both of you showed admirable steadfastness, kindness, and courage, during the heat wave, and the storms, when most of us were indisposed, and fell short of our own responsibilities. We are grateful for your presence in this house." The guests echoed his sentiments, and both girls were stunned with this acknowledgement of their efforts. Lizzie didn't know what to do, so she merely curtsied, and fled to the kitchen.

She was up to her elbows in dishwater when Mister Bachelor took his place in the kitchen once again. She was embarrassed that she'd been crying and she wouldn't look at him. "Lizzie, what's wrong?"

She wiped her hands on the towel, and wiped the tears from her face. "W-we were only doin' what we would have done fer anyone. It doesn't deserve all thet noise 'bout it. What we did, had ta be done, thet's all. They're family." As fresh tears threatened to flow, she covered her face and turned away.

"Lizzie, it's a sad world out there. Not everyone would have done what you've done for Missus Twombly, or Young Reverend Twombly. We have to recognize the generosity of spirit, when we find it. You deserve it, and so does Eliza."

She turned, and was surprised he was so close to her. His arms were around her, comforting her. She pulled herself back, but he held tight. "Sh-h, you're all right, Lizzie."

"Lizzie, wha's wrong? What's happened?" Eliza's voice broke. Mister Bachelor opened his arm, and drew Eliza in.

"I think she's just overtired and homesick, Eliza. Give her a minute. I know we're not used to seeing her without her suit of armor on, without the show of strength she girds herself with."
Finally, Lizzie stepped away, embarrassed by her show of emotion. Once again, she stuck her hands into the dish water and proceeded with her chore. "I dinna realize I was sae homesick.

Whew. I kin deny it seven ways 'til Sunday, but it's there. Takin' care o' Missus Twombly, an' young Mister Twombly, was like takin' care o' Maggie and *Moraí*. They seem ta be better t'night."

"It's a natural thing fer ye ta be takin' care o' ever'body, Lizzie," said Eliza. "Ye've been doin' it fer as lang as I kin remember. Ye took care o' me, all the way o'er in the ship. Ye don' think it special, cause ye al'ays do it. But it *is* special, Lizzie. Someday, ye will haf a whole brood o' bairns ta care fer, an' it'll still be special, how ye do it."

"Well put, Miss Eliza. When you're strong, ye think the whole world is strong. It's not true. We all have our Achilles' heel. Yours, Lizzie, is thinking you're not special enough."

Lizzie sighed. "Well, if ye two are finished, I'd like yer, Mister Bachelor, ta sit o'er there, an' yer, Eliza, git ta clearing the rest o' the dishes. I'm splashin' around in empty dishwater here." She smiled as she said it, showing there was no bite in her bark.

"Would yer like a cup a coffee, Mister Bachelor? An' would yer mind changin' the subject ta somethin' less affectin'? I think I've had enough tears fer t'day, thank yer."

"And how's the price of coffee these days?" he asked. In an exaggerated show of indifference, Charles Bachelor made a thorough study of the ceiling while speaking. He couldn't keep the smile from creeping onto his mouth, though.

"Humph, it's very *in*expensive if ye drink it here," Lizzie grinned, setting the cup and saucer on the side table.

"So, what do you think of this trip to Martha's Vineyard, Miss Lizzie?"

They lapsed into a light conversation about the coming journey, while Eliza went back and forth retrieving the linens and serving pieces. Soon, her sister left to see if their other guests needed anything more, then climbed the stairs to turn down the beds, and tend her other evening chores.

When Lizzie dried her last dish and put it away, she stood with her hip against the work table, still listening to her guest.

"I guess I'd better be thinking about leaving, before I completely outstay my welcome," he said seriously, reluctantly standing. He picked up his cup and saucer, to put it into the sink. Lizzie reached for it, and it clattered to the floor. Both of them stooped to retrieve it, and bumped their heads. Lizzie sat hard on the floor, and Mister Bachelor, trying to help her, stepped on the saucer, and nearly fell himself.

Maintaining his balance, he pulled her up by the waist. Again, in close proximity, they each risked a look at the other's eyes. Mister Bachelor kissed her forehead, and held her close to his chest. They stood that way, until Missus Twombly walked in.

"Say goodnight, Charles," the elderly woman said quietly.

"G-good night, Miss Lizzie…Thanksgiving," he said hoarsely. He turned on his heel and left by the back door.

"Missus Twombly…" Lizzie began to speak, her face on fire as she picked up the remains of the cup and saucer.

"Tut… No need to explain, child. He's a very lonely, very serious man, who is easily charmed by a lovely young thing like you. It's probably a good thing you are going away, and he is going to school. He has a long row to hoe, with an uncertainty at the end," Missus Twombly said with a dreamy look on her face. "Then again, so did my John, when I met him. Just be cautious, until you know what you want."

"Aye, ma'am, in truth, I find him fascinating, but I don' think I'm cut out o' the same kind o' cloth as he. I am too outspoken to be a minister's wife. I would be more a burden, than a helpmeet to him."

"I thought the same at your age. What I didn't know then was it helps a serious, dedicated man to be a better person if he plays hooky, once in a while."

"Hooky?" asked the red-haired cook.

"Yes, *hooky*… to play hide and seek, it means to run away or to skip school. Serious men need to have laughter and fun, amid their lofty and solemn endeavors," Missus Twombly said thoughtfully. "Sometimes these distinguished men of God have to remember, what it is to be human, with all our frailties."

Feeling conspiratorial, Lizzie blurted out, "Someday, I want a man thet looks at me, just the way Doctor Twombly looks at you."

"Then you must find a man at whom you want to look, the way I look at Doctor Twombly," she rejoined, with a faraway look.

126

She's rememberin' when they first met. Thet first look, the instant she knew, he was the man she wanted.

"Missus Twombly, is there anything else I should do t'night, ta be ready, tomorrow?"

"Just pack your bag and go to bed, dear. Tomorrow, you'll make breakfast, and then make sandwiches and lemonade for the trip. You'll have to bring the 'back door' food to Missus Manchester, put out the fire in the stove, and close up all the windows and doors. An' *then,* we'll be off!

"The list is on the table. If we forget to bring something, we will either get along without it, or we will buy it there. We wouldn't want to be *too* perfect. That would be dull, wouldn't it?"

"Aye, ma'am, I am sae glad ta be here, Missus Twombly, to work fer such a lovely person."

"Oh, go on with you. Go to bed."

Lizzie went to her room and found Eliza already asleep. She was physically tired, but not at all sleepy. *The letter! I'll write the letter ta Ma an' Moraí thet I promised. I kin put it on the mail box in the mornin',* she decided.

Dear Ma and Moraí,

I pray this letter finds you well. Eliza and I are going to Martha's Vineyard, with our sponsors, the Twomblys. I don't know if it is in your book of maps, but I will endeavor to tell you something about it.

It is an island. I am told it has wild grapes all over the island, but the vines were brought in from another place. Being an island, it has sandy beaches on all sides. There is a great church that brings worshipers from all over the world in August, for a week long service called a revival, held in a tabernacle. Doctor and Missus Twombly have a cottage there...

Lizzie wrote long into the night, her tiny cursive writing covering every square inch of paper. She folded, sealed, stamped, and placed the letter above the mailbox, by the front door.

Chapter Nine

If Lizzie dreamed at all that night, she didn't remember it in the morning. She bounded out of bed, put on her Sunday dress, her coverall apron, and cap. Eliza had slipped out of bed earlier, and was apparently on her morning rounds. The windows and doors in the kitchen were opened wide, hoping to catch some stirring of air, but to no avail. The fine cotton curtains hung limp, already saturated with moisture. Lizzie pulled them to the sides of the window and although the sun poured through, the longed-for breeze never came.

Throwing her hands up in mock defeat, Lizzie stirred up the fire, and put the coffee pot on. Moving to the side table, she set up the trays for her family. *Blueberry muffins, fresh fruit, an' coffee would do fer a warm day like today,* she thought. *I hope Missus an' son will be all right fer the trip. Perhaps the hope o' cold ocean water beneath their feet will be enough encouragement ta keep 'em goin'. We'd best leave afore the heat o'erwhelms 'em, an' we canna leave a' tall.*

As soon as the meager breakfast dishes were put away, Lizzie heard men talking in the front hall. The carriages were being loaded, one for the family and one for the baggage and the help. Peter Baker and Charles Bachelor were negotiating the best way to load a wagon. There was no shortage of advice from the two ministers and Isabelle as well. Missus Twombly came back to the kitchen to see how things were progressing in closing the downstairs rooms.

"Quickly, girls, bring your bags out to Mister Baker. Then come back here for the lunch makings. Keep that with you. We'll

129

eat on the ferry, *al fresco*." Missus Twombly smiled. "It's supposed to be all the rage in European circles. Only it seems just an excuse to drink wine out of doors, don't you think?" Lizzie and Eliza looked at each other, barely holding back their giggles.

In the last-minute activity, Lizzie turned quickly with the food hamper and found herself face to face with Mister Bachelor. "Miss Lizzie," he said taking the hamper from her and setting it on the floor. "I hoped to say a proper goodbye." He drew her close and kissed her full on her surprised lips.

"M-Mister Bachelor!" she stuttered.

"Miss Heenan, I beg your pardon. I've quite lost my head and with it my manners. While I cannot say I regret my action, I am sorry to have startled you, and taken advantage of your good nature."

Impetuously, she held both sides of his bewhiskered face and returned his kiss. "Mister Bachelor, if it is ta be goodbye, then there is nothing ta pardon yer fer."

At the sound of the kitchen door, they jumped apart. Eliza poked her head around the door.

"Ye two had better be gittin' out front," she warned. "Ever'body's waitin' on yer."

Red-faced and flustered, they stumbled, each one grabbing the basket, trying to get through the doorway at the same time. "Yer better collect yerselves. Ye look like two cats with their tails tied t'gether," said Eliza grinning.

Straightening herself up, Lizzie took the hamper from Mister Bachelor and with her nose slightly atilt, brushed by him, and out the front door. He held the door for Eliza and with an exaggerated bow, turned, and locked it securely. He slipped the key into his pocket and hurried to help the girls onto the loaded wagon. With a signal to Mister Baker, he flicked the reins over the backs of the two horses.

Lizzie grabbed her hat as the wagon lurched forward. Charles Bachelor looked down at her with a decided twinkle in his eye. He was remembering when he first met her at Ellis Island, the train ride, the trip to Quincy to see her cousin, and just a few minutes ago, in the kitchen. His impulsiveness surprised even himself. This was not like him at all. She didn't seem to mind though, not at all.

I dare not begin this! I have years of committed endeavors to perform. This was so very wrong of me, to indulge my feelings, when I cannot promise her anything but endless years of waiting. How arrogant of me to pretend I have any standing with this young woman! It is but the fascination of the flame that dances in her hair, and the fire in her eyes. As clouds of doubt shadowed his face, he grew more determined to get this journey done. *What a fool you are! You have nothing she could want.* Then the nagging thought crept into his musings, *yet, she seems to be everything I want.*

Confused by his withdrawal, Lizzie turned toward Eliza and engaged in some nonsensical prattle about their last shopping day for the family. Eliza gave her half sister a questioning look.

It's yer last chance ta talk ta him until Thanksgiving Day, Lizzie! What are ye goin' on about the butcher fer? Ask him about his studies! Ask if his parents are livin'. Ask him about anythin', but don't ignore him!

Looking around Lizzie, Eliza asked, "Mister Bachelor, do ye ken wha' yer studies will be this year?"

As if rehearsed until all feeling had evaporated from his speech, he answered her mechanically. With no animation, his words were economical, precise and devoid of the emotion he had shown discussing his schooling earlier. Disappointed with his reply, Eliza tried again. "It's all verra excitin' thet yer goin' ta college ta be a minister, isn't it?"

"Yes, it is, I suppose. From where I'm standing, being a minister seems like a long time to come."

"Tempus fugit when the mind an' soul are occupied in worthy endeavor, Mister Bachelor." Lizzie said, teasing.

"I'll have little time for anything else, ladies. I'll look to Thanksgiving for respite." His eyes danced again, noting her smile. "Perhaps you'll find some time for me, then?"

"I'll not hold yer ta promises, Mister Bachelor. Thanksgiving is a lang way from t'day. Ye will have a bonnie classmate or two ta spend ye time wit', I'm sure."

"Not at Harvard, Miss Lizzie, it's a man's institution, with nary a woman in sight. If Doctor Twombly had his way, half the students at Harvard would be women. I doubt the men would concentrate on their studies so well, in that case."

"Well, Mister Bachelor, I'll gae nowhere 'twixt now an' April, so ye could find me back here on yer Thanksgiving Day. I'll be elbow-deep in dishwater, cleanin' up after the holiday dinner party, if they haven't tired o' me by then."

The three chatted lightly for the next three and half hours to Woods Hole, where they boarded the ferry with their baggage. Arriving topside, Eliza and Lizzie spotted Mister Bachelor and Mister Baker on the dock and waved goodbye. Mister Bachelor waved enthusiastically, while Mister Baker merely touched his hat brim, turned on his heel and mounted his horse, waiting for his companion. The Twomblys would be met at the Oak Bluffs dock by two drivers who would handle the carriage and wagon for them.

Almost immediately after the ferry weighed anchor, Lizzie and Eliza were instructed to serve luncheon at the long tables of the dining area. Lizzie peeked around as grace was pronounced and realized the whole ship was likewise occupied. As soon as grace was done, passengers began making themselves known to the Twomblys. It was as if they owned the ferry. Family after family came to talk to them, welcoming them back to Martha's Vineyard — *before they even arrived. Does the whole world stop at Martha's Vineyard fer these two weeks in August, jes' ta see the Twomblys?*

Picking up the remnants of their simple meal, Lizzie glanced out the window at the water, then back at Eliza. *She seems ta be holdin' her own, sae far.*

She was gradually aware Missus Twombly was speaking to her. "When you're finished here, do go up topside to enjoy the air, girls. There's nothing like it to cleanse the spirit. I always feel like it's a fresh start, going to the Vineyard. Like we stepped into a new, yet familiar world, and the one we just left, never really existed at all."

"Like a dream, ma'am." *Though 'twas my whole life 'til I came here, Ireland is like a half-formed mem'ry nae. It's like this life in America is all there is. When I write ta my mother an' grandmere, I find it hard ta imagine them in the cottage wit'out a stove or the other things that are part o' my day's work here.*

"Exactly, things change, yet stay the same. When we go back to the Falls, it will be as we had never left. Take advantage of all the new experiences you are offered, children. These memories will keep you warm on a winter's night. Now finish up and don't miss the crossing."

When they finally went up to the rail, Lizzie and Eliza reveled in the constant cool breeze and brilliant sunshine. The sky was an intense blue, made more so by the few puffy, white clouds near the horizon. The air was salty and fresh with none of the city smells and noises of Newton. The sound of the engine, and the water lapping the sides of the ferry, reduced the voices of the excited passengers to a muffled indiscernible babble.

"Lizzie, it's wonderful! It's nothin' like the ship we came over on. Look, over there. Is thet it?"

"If it is, Martha's Vineyard seems a verra long island with a lot o' verra tiny docks." Lizzie could feel the ferry turn, and as it did, a town came into view. A village green, surrounded by houses of all colors trimmed in white, with a wide dock welcoming them into its arms.

It seemed to take a long time for the ferry to groan into place and shutter against the dock. The passengers swarmed to the exit doors, down the ramp and off the ship. Some passengers were met by friends, others gathered their belongings, and started trudging up the hill toward town. The carriage and wagon were waiting at the street, by the time the Twomblys disembarked with their servants.

Lizzie tried to take in everything she saw as she perched upon the wagon: the cobblestone street, the colorful shops and cafes, houses that looked like decorated cakes ready for Sunday tea. There was a carnival atmosphere that infected the people milling about on the sidewalks. Everywhere were frilly parasols, carried by ladies in pale yellows and blues, like the sunshine and clear skies they came to see. Lizzie was aware of the bouncy, joyful music of a calliope, but could not see where it came from.

Seeing her spin her head around looking for its source, the old wagon driver said, "It's them flying horses, Miss. A carousel, thet runs fum dawn ta midnight. Ye kin ride her fer a penny. Ye shud ride it least onct, while ye here."

Turning from the main street, the girls saw even more fanciful houses, all colors and trimmed with fancy carvings, looking like the icing on a mountain of tea cakes. Between some of the pretty houses were white tents, some as big as their neighboring wooden structures. In the center of all these homes was a large oak grove with a giant iron structure unlike anything Lizzie had ever seen. She looked again at her driver for answers.

"It's the Tabernacle, Miss, where the revival's held. They's services ev'ry morning an' evening, then Sunday aft'noons. The biggest service will be the Sunday mornin', afta the Illumination. But here we are, Misses, the green one there."

The two-story house had the same lacy trim as the others, a front porch and tall double door front entry. There was the familiar servant's walkway leading to the rear of the house. The carriage stood in the side yard waiting to discharge its passengers, while the wagon stood in front. "Wait here, Misses."

When the family had entered the house through the front, the carriage was removed, and the wagon drove to the rear of the house to unload its burden. Lizzie and Eliza hurried to the back door, just as Missus Twombly opened it. "Come in, girls. We've lots to do before bedtime.

"The family will be going out to supper tonight, at the Marlboroughs. That should give you enough time to clean up, make the beds, and put things away. We'll prepare a shopping list in the morning. We will require a change of clothes for supper, so do that first. My ecru suit will do. Eliza, ask Isabella what she wants to wear. See if you can freshen up the men's jackets, and put out a fresh shirt and tie for them. Open up the parlor first, so we will have a place to sit, and then do the clothes, the beds, and the kitchen.

"Once we are changed and gone to supper, have something to eat, and finish the bedrooms. Do what you can tonight, and the rest will have to wait for tomorrow morning. Have I forgotten anything? Well, no mind, we'll get to it as we need it, won't we?"

Lizzie and Eliza tackled the parlor first, as instructed. They carefully pulled the covers off the furniture so as not to dump the year's worth of dust on the carpet or into the air. Wrapping them with the dust inside, Lizzie brought them out to the back porch to take care of the next day. Once the windows were open, and the covers gone, the parlor looked relatively habitable.

Upstairs, they opened the windows, stripped the covers off the beds and retrieved the bed linens from the trunk. They inspected the beds for invading creatures and finding none, added the linens. They hung all the clothing for the evening's social activities in one bedroom and the curtains for that room were discretely closed.

Despite the long journey and close quarters of the ferry, Lizzie could hear a buzz of conversation floating up from the parlor. First one, then another stepped over each other's speech with something new to say. It was so unlike their usual quiet tones and businesslike conversations in the Falls house. Here, it was as if they let go their collective breaths, and were relaxed, laughing, and speaking spontaneously, without the careful regard of the clergy. They talked like old familiar friends, excited to see each other, delighted in the place they were, and the things they planned to do.

Hearing their voices, Lizzie was brought to a sudden awareness. *Thet's what was missing! All this time, I thought the Twombly of the Falls, were the real ones, sae careful in speech and manners. But nay, these are the true Twomblys, the real family. This is where they are themselves. No wonder they speak of Martha's Vineyard with such reverence and joy. It's not jes' the place, it's who they become, while they're here.*

Later, while the family was out, she and Eliza ate a cold supper in the still unfamiliar kitchen. They heard a thump at the back door, then someone running away. Startled, Lizzie jumped up and ran to see who it was. She saw a boy, no more than nine or ten, turning the corner out of the drive. She looked down, and there at her feet was a newspaper. At home, Mister or Doctor Twombly bought the paper at the little variety store in the village, during his morning walk. Here, apparently, it was brought right to the door.

She tore the string off the paper excitedly. Eliza put her hand on her arm to stop her, "Lizzie, thet's Doctor Twombly's paper. Shouldn't he get ta read it first?"

"I'll wrap it up again, don' ye worry. I hafta find out wha's goin' on with Lizzie Borden!"

"Lizzie..." Eliza started, but she knew it was no use.

"Listen ta this, Eliza! 'Mr. Borden was worth half a *million* dollars, an', though penurious as a rule, was inclined ta be generous ta his household. Lizzie resented his liberality toward her stepmother. Her own mother died givin' birth ta her an' she has been odd all her life. She grew up ta be a recluse. She is far from homely, though no' particularly handsome. She's never had a lover; she has avoided the company o' young men; an' has never been presented ta society. She has her defenders, who say she has an amiable disposition. Allegations ta the contrary may be mere ill-natured gossip.' It says this article was taken from *The New York Herald*.

"Sounds like idle gossip ta me. Why would they print sech awful things? An opinion o' whether she's pretty or no'? Wha's *thet* got ta do wit' her character? Poor, motherless child, no wonder she was a recluse an' wasn't sociable. Her sister pro'bly wasn't either."

"Lizzie, why do ye git yerself all worked up 'bout people ye knae nothin' of? Fold it up an' put it away. It gives me the creeps."

"The creeps? Ye seem ta pick up the oddest expressions, don' ye? Who told ye thet one?"

"I heard it from a boy talkin' ta the greengrocer a couple weeks ago. I'm trying ta learn some o' the expressions they use around here," Eliza said, grinning.

"Well, I hope yer sayin' it right. Ye could be sayin' somethin' ye don' e'en mean."

"Well, I only practice them on yer. When I hear it agin, I'll study on it."

"I don't think ye oughta use it on anyone else, in the meantime. I wouldn' wan' them ta think ye were talkin' like a dock worker, Eliza Heenan." She did, however, carefully fold the paper and retie the string around it. She found a rocker on the back porch and brought it into the kitchen. It seemed a good place to put the paper.

"Let's see if we can finish up the bedrooms, an' unpack the clothin' trunks," said Eliza. "I don' wan' ta hear Miss Isabelle askin' where all her clothes are."

"We'll do hers first. Bring me her dresses, an' I'll neaten up the pressin' on them. I put papers in the sleeves to hold them, but the skirts are longer than the trunk, so they pro'bly have some *beggar man pleats* in them. I'll clean up here, 'til ye kin git them fer me."

"They's no gas lightin' here, sae I'd best see ta the lamps afore darkness catches us. I found a spouted can on the back porch. This lamp's almos' empty."

The cook and the maid tended to the work at hand and barely spoke again until nightfall. The windows were opened and a fresh breeze blew throughout the little house. *I kin see why Missus Twombly wanted ta come down here a week early. I knae 'twas on her mind the whole time she was sick,* Lizzie thought.

As easy as it is ta git these things done while we're alone, no one sees it bein' done. I wonder if they think it was done by magic, rather than by hard work. Never mind, Lizzie. It jes' needs bein' done. Good work should be its ain reward. Nae, shake the dust out o' them sheets, they's a lot more ta do.

Lizzie looked around the kitchen. This house was similar to the house in Newton, but everything was smaller. The rooms were smaller, and there didn't seem to have a room off the kitchen for her to sleep. She had noticed earlier that the bedrooms all had sharp slanted ceilings, so there was unlikely an attic room. Where would they sleep? She wished the Twomblys were home, so she could ask them. They were usually home long before this. Lizzie's focus switched from her sleeping quarters to the mysterious whereabouts of the Twombly family.

She went to the front door and onto the porch. Looking around, she could see lights at the end of the little street and beyond to the grove. There were gas lights on the street surrounding the grove and the tabernacle was lit up like a New Year's log. People were milling about, greeting each other, carrying lamps or candles. Children were running through the clusters of walkers. Small children rode on their fathers' shoulders or slept in their arms. *Isn't thet a lovely sight! No wonder they love it here.*

"Eliza," she called softly. "Come see." As she turned, she was surprised to see her half-sister right behind her, watching the same tableau, awestruck, and smiling wistfully.

"Isn't it beautiful? It's no wonder they're no' hame yet."

The girls went back into the house, checking the downstairs rooms as they made their way to the kitchen. "We'll hafta tackle the dining room, first thin' in the mornin', Lizzie. "Tis the only room we haven't touched."

"Right after breakfast dishes, Eliza. I haven't found where we're sleepin' yet, an' I'll be needin' my bed shortly. It's been a lang day." Lizzie yawned, her mouth gaping. "How about a cup o' tea, while we wait?"

Eliza nodded, and sat down at the metal topped work table. Lizzie could see she could barely keep her eyes open. "Eliza, why don' ye sit in the rocker, while I git the tea."

Wondering if the effort was worth it, she did as she was told. By the time the water was hot, Eliza was softly snoring, her head hanging to her chest. Smiling, Lizzie thought, *they say the sea air will sap yer strength. I don' think they're half wrong. Sleep, sister. I'll write a note ta James.*

Just then, Lizzie heard the latch at the front door. The Twomblys came in still chatting happily, oblivious to the quiet house. "Welcome home," Lizzie whispered, as Missus Twombly came into the kitchen.

"Oh, I am so sorry. We came barging in here, as if there were no one else home." The tiny woman grimaced at her imaginary faux pas. "I haven't told you yet where you are to sleep, have I?"

"No, ma'am."

"Mister Twombly, my son, has his own little house around the corner. He prefers his privacy at the Vineyard. Even while we are all at the Falls, he sometimes will take a sabbatical here for a few days, to relax and work in solitude.

"So you see dear, the room you set up for him, is yours and Eliza's. You'll notice there are a few of his clothes here, but most of them are at his house. You may move your things in there, and keep his things in our room. I'm very sorry. I did not tell you about the

139

arrangements. I'm afraid my memory is poorer than I'd care to admit."

"Thank yer, ma'am. We'll try not to disturb you, when we get up in the morning."

"We tend to rise earlier here. You may serve breakfast on the side porch, if it's fair weather. If not, we'll eat in the dining room. If we are not up, leave the tray in the upstairs hall in front of our doors."

Lizzie was thinking quickly. *The porch an' the dining room are no' cleaned yet. We thought we would have time t'marra. Well, I'll remove the covers from the dinin' area t'night, then do wha' I kin in the mornin'.*"

Bone weary, she cleaned up the dining room as best she could. She added the dusty sheets to the pile on the back porch. She noticed the curtains in all the windows were light cotton or crocheted linens as suited the summer cottage. *They should be easy enough ta clean an' press, afore puttin' back up. The windows needed washin'. Perhaps I kin git Eliza ta do thet, while I'm washin' the curtains an' cover sheets. Maybe no', she's got the side porch ta wash down, an' those pillows ta freshen'.* Again, she thought of how wise Missus Twombly was, to try to get here a week before the rest of the family. *It's not her fault she was sick an' couldn't travel.*

She washed her hands again, wondering if she would ever get the dust and grit dirt out of her hair. *Maybe t'marra night, we'll have time fer a bath. By then, I may hafta take a rake ta my hair.* She smiled at the thought of pulling a garden rake through the knotted curls.

In the meantime, I'll hafta git Eliza upstairs ta bed wit'out her wakin' up sae much, she won' gae back ta sleep. C'mon girl, up one stair, then the next. Ye kin do it. I could easily sleep on a bed o' nails t'night.

Lizzie sat in the window of the front bedroom and peered out into the grove. Most of the families were gone, leaving only the lovers, walking arm in arm. She saw them emerging from the dark, into the light of the street lamps, then fading back into the shadows again. She envied them, their attention wrapped up in each other, to the exclusion of all others. *I'm probably not the only one watching, wishing to be among them.*

She remembered Mister Bachelor's arms around her, his rough coat scratching her cheek. It was not him she longed for, so much as anyone who would hold her, and think she was special. Someday, there would be someone whom she loved to abandon, she was sure. She would not be alone like poor Lizzie Borden.

Lizzie woke in the night, still at the window with a crick in her back and a dream of searching for someone, or something she could not identify. She crawled into bed, beside Eliza, vaguely realizing she was still in her Sunday clothes. She went right to sleep.

Eliza woke her before dawn. "Ye better git up, Lizzie! I kin hear someone up already." She was dressed in her uniform and apron, ready for the day.

Lizzie sat up, bewildered, until it came back to her where she was. She quickly dressed and rushed down to the kitchen. Missus Twombly was stirring the fire. "Oh, there you are. I wanted to be up to see the sunrise. It's spectacular here. For a cup of coffee and the sunrise, the front porch is the best place to sit, except of course, the beach itself. Here, you take over, I will be out front."

Lizzie shook her head in wonder. Gone was the sickly, pale, and quiet Missus Twombly. The ocean and the fresh air seemed to have rejuvenated her body, spirit, and soul. The coffee was perking and Lizzie started gathering breakfast for the trays. Missus Twombly came back in with bottles in her hands. "The milkman's been here already. There's fresh cream for the coffee, and fresh eggs for breakfast."

Lizzie readjusted her menu and took the items from her mistress's arms. "Ye gae see yer sunrise, ma'am, an' I'll have yer breakfast, afore the coffee's done. Her pan already hot, she threw in

141

the butter and mixed up the eggs to scramble. Biscuits were almost ready to come out of the oven, and jellies were on the tray. She knew Doctor Twombly would not be far behind.

"Eliza," she softly called out the window to the side porch. "Come git breakfast."

"Fix your hat an' change yer apron. Missus Twombly is out on the front porch, waitin' fer the sunrise, an' this breakfast. She's fit as a fiddle this mornin'."

Eliza did as she was told, grabbed the tray, and set out for her first breakfast. Missus Twombly, knowing the side porch wasn't done yet, sat on the front steps to enjoy her repast. Doctor Twombly joined her, as Eliza was returning to the kitchen. The second tray was ready for delivery. As soon as she heard Miss Isabelle's footfall on the stairs, her eggs went into the pan.

"Hello Mother, Father, isn't this a glorious day?" Isabelle said uncharacteristically. *Oh, I love this place! Whatever brings joy to Miss Isabelle in the mornin', must have been wrought by heaven itself,* Lizzie thought, ungraciously.

"Oh thank you, Eliza. Look, the sun's just coming up. Praise God, what a blessing!"

"Aye, miss." Eliza fled inside, but stepped into the dining room to watch the blues, pinks, and grays splash over the sky. "Lizzie, come see."

Lizzie left her stove to stand beside Eliza and watch the unfolding of a new day. "Lovely, isn't it? There is something *verra* special about this place," Eliza whispered. "I think the faeries have bewitched them all."

"You may be right, Eliza. I feel exceptionally happy here, myself."

"Are ye sure it's the faeries an' no' Mister Bachelor thet has ye feelin' thet way?" teased Eliza.

Lizzie gasped, and swatted her sister's backside with her dishtowel playfully. "Is thet ye, Eliza, or ye green eyes talkin' fer ye?"

"I dinna ken wha' yer talkin' 'bout, Lizzie Heenan. My eyes are brown as dirt," answered Eliza, the light in her eyes dancing.

The show over and breakfast done, they were soon back to scrubbing and cleaning, pressing and dusting, to make the little house ready for company.

Missus Twombly told Lizzie that the first week they would be out for most dinners, then the second week, it would be the Twomblys turn to reciprocate. They would take picnic luncheons for painting and beach excursions. Rainy days, they would arrange informal visits or have visitors for very informal lunches. "Some days will include William, as he chooses."

She gave Lizzie a shopping list for the first week and a menu to look over for the next. She asked Lizzie to look in the *Boston School of Cooking Cook Book* for some new and interesting recipes for the whirlwind of dinner parties they were facing. Hopefully, she said, there would be some things they could prepare well ahead, that would not spoil in the coming week. Illumination Night celebration would be a pot luck supper held on the Village Green. She would give her more instructions before Monday of the next week. *I jes' hope she's up to all this,* Lizzie thought. *I hope she doesn't overdo. It's sae good ta see her in her element as grand hostess again.*

Chapter Ten

Most days that first week, after the chores were done, Lizzie and Eliza had time to explore the little town, and the beaches beyond. Their presence would only be required at the Friday night and Sunday morning services. Due to the relaxed atmosphere at the campground, they were told they could sit anywhere, but they were welcome to sit with the family if they wished.

On one of their first excursions, Lizzie and Eliza set out to find the 'Flying Horses', the driver had mentioned. They put on their practical and sturdy blue-gray cotton dresses, their straw hats, and drawstring purses.

Lizzie wistfully thought someday she would like to have just one dress of fine pale yellow cotton with a gossamer bow and puffy sleeves like the chatty young women who walked about town with their flowery parasols and white lace gloves. It wasn't like her to be envious, but they looked like they belonged in this beautiful place, like the flowers that graced the pretty houses.

Lizzie felt the fine beads of perspiration already dampening the red curls around her face. The ever-present breeze blew her hat off to her shoulders. Tied loosely beneath her chin with a ribbon, she let the annoying hat stay where it fell. She had braided her errant locks down to the nape of her neck, and then let the rest hang free to blow in the wind. Eliza kept hers in the required servant's knot and kept her hat securely in place, but Lizzie wanted to be anything but a servant that afternoon.

The girls left the campground, as the Tabernacle area was called, by an alleyway to the shops lining Circuit Avenue. They headed down the hill, stopping to peek in the windows of the candy store, a millenary, and a pottery shop. As they made their way down the hill and around the corner, they were jostled carelessly aside, by well-dressed young men intent on impressing the pretty young girls, in even prettier dresses.

"Come Lizzie, let's go," said Eliza, watching her half-sister's face grow dark. "Ne'er mind them, we're almos' there. Accordin' ta the driver, it's jes' around this corner. Ah, look." The sign over the door of this big green barn-like structure did, indeed, say "Flying Horses", and there was no denying the music of the calliope, pouring out of this place.

They paid their pennies and waited at a little gate, while they watched in wonder. Exquisitely painted, and trimmed with real horse hair, miniature horses frozen in mid-stride, seemed to race around a wide circle platform. There were decorated carriages, placed between the horses, for more sedate riders. The riot of colors and sounds assaulted the eyes and ears, to everyone's apparent delight. The laughter and shouts of children comingled with the onslaught of noise.

Lizzie turned her head, and the smells of popcorn, fried clams, and fish flooded her already loaded senses. Over the din, she heard, "Only a penny a ride, Ladies and Gents. Catch the brass ring, and get a free ride on the Flying Horses." At the corner of the building, a little man, with his cane raised, loudly exhorted the crowd to come in, in an abrasive, jaded voice.

The carousel slowly came to a complete stop and a young man blocked the little gate in front of Lizzie and Eliza. "Exit to the right please. Exit to the right. Redeem your brass ring where you buy the tickets. Exit to the right." The youth's bored, mechanical speech bespoke his months of service to the Flying Horses.

"C'mon, open the gate. M' boy here wants a ride," shouted a man, as the growing crowd behind the girls pushed forward, pinning them against the gate.

145

Quickly assessing the situation, the young man told the girls to step to one side while he let the others through. "Don't worry ladies; I'll get you a good place." As he led the way to the other side of the carousel, he asked, "Ye wanna horse 'r a carriage?"

"Horse" "Carriage" Lizzie and Eliza spoke simultaneously.

"One horse, and one carriage, comin' right up." He took Eliza's hand, and led her to a brilliant rainbow-painted seat. Then, he took Lizzie's hand, and led her to a bridled white stallion. "If you'll allow me, m' lady," he took her by the waist and set her up side-saddle onto the polished leather saddle. "Enjoy yer ride an' see me afta."

The young man jumped off the carousel and back to his post. Lizzie looked back at Eliza and waved joyously. Eliza looked a little worried, but smiled back. Lizzie spotted the young man slouched against the wall. When she waved at him, he lazily waved back and smiled.

At the end of the ride, they went back to the young man as instructed. Reaching into his pocket, he handed them two brass rings. "Yez kin ride agin on the house. Jes' turn these here in at the ticket booth. Try not ta be first in line this time. Ye kin ride as long as yez want, as long as ye see me, before ye git on. They allays gif' me a few brass rings ta give out as I want."

They rode twice more until Eliza admitted she was getting a bit queasy after the last ride. They thanked their benefactor and walked further down the street. Lizzie soon discovered the joyful carnival atmosphere had changed. There were fewer shops and the buildings were run down. The people walking around them were rough and unfriendly.

"Eliza, we're goin' back."

"To the carousel?" asked Eliza, warily.

"No, Eliza, back to the main street, where the pretty shops are." Lizzie could see Eliza hadn't noticed the seedy shops, the children in ragged clothes, the men with bottles in their pockets. The

146

language in the passing conversations had become coarser, more confrontational.

"All right, Lizzie, I jes' thought there might be another candy shop down there."

"We'll see one on the main street, Eliza. Would ye mind walkin' a little faster?" She saw someone walking behind them, following them.

Eliza was quiet now, wondering why Lizzie seemed so angry. When they were at the Flying Horses again, Lizzie grabbed Eliza's hand and ducked inside. She went right to the head of the line and spoke to the young man they had seen earlier. "Excuse me, sir," Lizzie asked, "Is there another way out of here?" Then she whispered, "Thet man at the door is following us."

"Very well, miss, step this way." He opened the gate carefully, allowing only the two girls to come through. "The carousel is still movin', so be careful. If y' git hurt, it'll mean my hide. This way," he said. They went to the back side of the carousel as they had before, but through a little door hidden from view. He brought them through another door and down a long corridor. When he opened the last door, it was on an alleyway, leading to the main street. "This should get y' far enough away. Are y' from the campground?"

"Aye, thank ye sae much. What is yer name, sir?"

"I've never been *sir* t' anyone, miss. I'm jes' plain Garrett. Look, I have ta go. The music's slowing down."

"Goodbye, an' thank ye, 'Jes' Plain Garrett." The young man disappeared into the corridor, waving as he went.

"Well, that's an adventure we never need ta have agin, thank yer verra much," Lizzie said under her breath.

"Lizzie, what's goin' on?" asked Eliza, worry forming on her brow.

"Nothin' nae, Eliza, ye know how my imagination gits goin', we're fine. Let's find thet candy store." Lizzie hoped whatever that

147

mysterious man wanted, would not see the light of day on the "pretty" side of town. *From nae on, we'll gae as fer as the carousel, an' no' one step more.*

As they turned for the campground, Lizzie stopped to buy another paper for Doctor Twombly. He had said although the *Herald* was delivered, he'd much prefer *The Globe.* The newsboy was shouting the headlines at passersby. "Lizzie Borden arrested! The Fall River spinsta, trown in jail! Read all about it in the *Boston Globe.*"

"Oh my, Lizzie, do ye think she really did it?"

"Never! Look a' thet sweet face. How could anyone think she hacked her mother an' father up like thet? It would take a monster ta do thet." Lizzie was incensed at the thought of the world thinking this gentlewoman had killed her parents. She wanted to read the article, to find some error in its reporting, that would show Miss Borden could not have done this terrible thing.

"Lizzie," Eliza hissed through gritted teeth. "Ye hafta wait ta git hame ta read the article. Ye canna be seen readin' a paper in the street. Someone will see ye, an' it'll git back ta the Twomblys!"

"Oh, bother!" Lizzie tucked the paper under her arm and strode purposely toward the Tabernacle with a struggling Eliza trailing behind. "They'd make up etiquette rules fer a tempest, if it were willing." Lizzie sincerely hoped there would be no one home when they got there. She had to read that article.

Don't ye worry, Lizzie Borden. They'll find they have no' a haepenny's worth o' reason ta keep yer there. What on earth is the world comin' to, when they hafta put a woman in jail, fer a crime it would take a man ta do!

Deeper in her heart, Lizzie was hoping the woman had neither the will nor the strength to commit such an act.

Heaven knaes, I git angry enough by times, but ta kill yer ain parents? I'll be prayin' fer yer, Miss Borden, thet yer will hae a superlative judge ta show yer innocence. Barrin' thet, ye'll be needin' God himself ta save yer.

Bursting through the back entrance, Lizzie was dismayed to find the family home. "Missus Twombly, I dinna knae ye'd be here this afternoon. Is there something I kin git yer a lemonade perhaps? Will ye be here fer supper?"

The frail woman headed for her rocker, sat looking around for a moment, and satisfied everything was in order, spoke, "Nothing for now, dear. We'll have supper with the Thompsons tonight, and we'll be at the meeting after that.

"Tomorrow, we'll need a picnic basket for eight. It should be ready by ten o'clock sharp. Isabella and I will take a group to the dunes on the other side for a painting holiday. You can use two baskets, so they won't be too heavy. There will be Doctor Twombly, William, and Mister Sanders." Counting on her fingers, she named the rest of the party, "Isabella and me, Miss Meadows, Miss French, and Mrs. Sanders. Put together some crackers and brie, sliced cold meats, sliced cheese, rolls, condiments, cucumber salad, and lemonade. Some cherries, I think. Maybe add a plate of tea cakes and cookies for dessert. Wrap everything well to keep it as cold as you can. We'll also need…"

"Plates, tumblers, napkins, a cotton table cloth, silver service for eight," added Lizzie, automatically.

"I'm sorry, Lizzie. Better make that for nine. Things are so informal here. One never knows when we'll have an additional guest, pop into the equation."

"Very well, nine. Shall I add the "sunrise" in a separate jar?" she asked.

"What a lovely thought! Yes, even if I don't use it, it would be nice to have it available, wouldn't it?" Missus Twombly smiled.

"I am so lucky to have you, Lizzie. I don't remember these things as well as I used to, and it's not important enough for the rest

149

of them to even consider. But it's those things that guests remember about a luncheon."

"*That*, an' how special ye make everyone feel, Missus Twombly," Lizzie said, reciting the "Litany of Fine Dining Etiquette," according to her thoughtful mistress. She was proud to be a cook for this gracious woman.

Ma would be sae pleased ta knae Missus Twombly. The highest-ranking nobility or the lowliest drunkard receives her kindness in equal measure. Ma would stay a 'lady' all the time in her presence. I kin do it fer a while, but I lapse into my tenant brogue within a minute or two.

"That's right. If the Good Lord puts someone in your path, it's for a reason. Every man is a child of God, and should be treated as such," the diminutive woman said.

Then, taking a breath, she continued, "Lizzie, I want you to be very careful when you go outside the campground. There are rumors about some very unsavory characters looking for young ladies having an accent of any kind. I am told these men are kidnapping foreign women and selling them as slaves.

"Do be very aware of your surroundings. Do not talk to strangers. Keep to yourselves and stay where it is well lit and populated." Missus Twombly shivered. "These men are extremely dangerous." She slowly turned her head, staring sightlessly out the window, deep in thought. There on the side table near the rocker, was the newspaper, its headline blazoned at the top of the page, calling to Lizzie. If Missus Twombly saw it, she did not acknowledge its existence. The tiny woman sat for a moment, picked up the paper and left the room.

Forgive me, Laird. Thet paper has far too much importance fer me than it should have.

Disappointed at the loss of the paper, Lizzie started laying out the items needed for the picnic the following day. She thought about the events of that day and how close they had come to an encounter with the man who followed them.

I hope no one takes it upon themselves ta tell Eliza 'bout the men who steal young ladies off ta who knows where. It'll take all I have, ta git her ta leave this house. Even if I do, I don't knae if I would be able ta get her out o' the campground again.

Just then, Doctor Twombly entered the kitchen, paper in hand. "Lizzie, the family and I are leaving for the Thompson's tent now. I thought you might like to have the paper. Just leave it on the side table when you're done. It's a shame about your namesake, isn't it? Well, time will tell. I hope for her sake, she didn't do it. We must pray for her in any case."

It took all of Lizzie's control not to snatch the paper out of his hand. She stood with it behind her back, caressing it in her hands until he left the room. She barely heard him saying goodbye, her mind was so drawn to the Lizzie Borden tale of distress.

I kin hardly think o' her as a real person! This is a story out o' a dime-store novel. But who coulda conjured up such a tale, full o' dastardly murders, a damsel accused, an' nefarious creatures, lurkin' in th' background.

Lizzie plunked herself into the rocker so quickly she had to straighten the chair before she could read.

Voraciously, she devoured the story. At the end of the column, she wanted more. She tried to picture Lizzie Borden in a court room, questioned under siege by the district attorney for hours. No wonder she confused what she had said earlier, while trying to recall the exact events before, during and after the murder of her parents.

Four hours! How could she be expected ta remember all thet. She was in shock an' sedated wit' morphine b'sides. Her parents were dead. Nae, she's thrown in jail.

Drawing from her own experience, she pictured Lizzie Borden in the Castlewellan gaol, with dirt floors, pitted iron bars, stone walls.

Well, at least it will be cooler there. She's practically a prisoner in her ain hame as 'tis, wit' all the reporters an' lookers-on surroundin' it. I wonder if Dr. Twombly has the Herald *paper in the front room.*

The days at Martha's Vineyard seemed to fly by, and the nights went even faster. Religious music from the Tabernacle was almost constant, from nine o'clock in the morning, until almost ten at night. There seemed to be services and meetings, with people filing in and out, at all hours. On Saturday, the dinners for the next week were planned. Missus Twombly prepared a list for Sunday's entertaining.

"At noon tomorrow will be the Thompsons and Marlboroughs. That will be eight total. Monday evening, will be the Germains. That will also be eight: three of us, William will be going elsewhere, Mister and Missus Germain, and their three children. We should do something fun for the children. Tuesday, is a picnic on the beach at sunset, I won't know 'til the last minute how many. I'll make a chart for the week, so we can keep it straight.

"By Wednesday, I'm sure I won't know what day it is. Ah, yes. Wednesday is a luncheon for the Ladies Missionary Council, twelve in all. Then, we have the Reverend Jacobs and his wife that night.

Thursday night, is the Illumination, and a supper in the grove, so we need something special for that night, one dish that serves eight and lemonade for about twenty. We'll have to remember to sit with the Boothbys and their brood, that day for luncheon. We'll sit with the Chambers, that night. So that puts Reverend Johnson and his wife and children on Friday, at sunset. Doctor Twombly and I thought we'd demonstrate a Seder for them.

"Saturday, we'll be going home, so we have to pack in between times for that. Whew! It's a heavy schedule, but not one we can't handle."

"Beggin' yer pardon, Missus Twombly, ye will have ta take some time ta rest ever'day, ta keep thet schedule. I knae ye won't wanna disappoint yer guests," Lizzie said gently.

"My goodness, I think you and Isabella are in collusion. She said the same to me this morning. The Vineyard lightens my spirit, and lets me forget I am an old woman. Thank you for your concern, I promise, I will nap every day. Doctor Twombly and William will be the next ones to tell me, I suppose."

Each day went as planned. Missus Twombly's social calendar was now sporting Xs through the obligations fulfilled. Wednesday was the most difficult, with twelve chatty women at noon to two o'clock, then a sit-down dinner with Reverend Jacobs that night. Although there were only four for dinner, the two men were engaged in philosophical and religious debate, for hours. The women at first engaged in social banter of little consequence, but they too were drawn into the loftier discussion.

Eliza offered to serve them coffee and cakes on the porch at sunset, but they seemed to enjoy sitting at the dining table for their dialogue. She had never seen them so animated in their speech. At times, she said to Lizzie, they seemed to be arguing and other times, they were nodding their heads in complete agreement. Hot coffee became cold, abandoned without a thought. The cakes sat, looking tired, untouched. Still the game went on and on.

Eliza stood in the corner as was her station until Missus Twombly looked up at her. "Oh dear, I'm afraid we owe Eliza an apology. We have taken advantage of her good nature, and kept her standing there, needlessly. We are truly sorry, dear. You may clear, and we will remove ourselves to the porch." The other members of the group murmured their embarrassed apologies.

153

Doctor Twombly said, "Eliza, we *are* terribly sorry. It is unlikely we will solve all the ills of the world in this one night, but we can certainly do it out of your way. Terrance, Millicent, let me walk you home. I'm afraid we have kept Betsy up far too long. Dear, you need your rest."

Missus Twombly made a weak show of protest, but acquiesced in the end. Doctor Twombly escorted the Johnsons on the short walk to their tent. The two men continued their debate quietly on the park bench nearby. The Tabernacle bell rang its ten o'clock curfew for young people, before he returned to the little green house at 8 Central Park.

The next morning, Doctor Twombly seemed unusually chipper. Lizzie surmised his step was lighter because he finally had a worthy adversary for his fertile mind.

It mus' be frustratin' ta have no one who kin challenge a man as brilliant as he. From wha' Eliza says, Mister Jacobs gave as good as he got, in the talk they had. I wisht I coulda heard it. Preachin' is much like teachin', but ta exercise yer mind in a fair exchange, thets like teachin' each other. Ye both learn somethin'.

After cleaning up breakfast dishes, Lizzie could hear a commotion on the Tabernacle green. She went out the back door and to the street. There on the green were about a dozen men setting up long tables in the grove and covering them with bed sheets. They were shouting at each other good-naturedly and laughing.

Lizzie was impressed by the number of people that they were expecting at the supper. In the center of the tables, they had set up a round platform, about two feet tall and eight feet across. The tables were arranged between the trees, like the broken spokes of a wheel.

In the kitchen, Lizzie was boiling a big pot of potatoes, and making her French cream dressing. She had chopped celery, parsley, boiled eggs, and left-over ham, diced fine. She calculated it would amount to three large bowls of potato salad.

Missus Twombly had suggested that she add the ham to her potato salad, in case someone forgot the meat dish. She said in large suppers like this, there was always someone who was confused about what they should bring. The supper wasn't until about five o'clock, so she hoped the air would be cool by then.

The Twomblys were going out for lunch, so Lizzie had plenty of time to make the salad and get it cool before supper. It should be in the ice box a full three hours before serving. She figured it would be in there for at least that long. That time would give her a chance to pack clothes, and the items they would not be using Friday and Saturday.

Lizzie was very interested in the Seder foods she would be preparing. Missus Twombly had written down the recipes for unleavened bread, the sweet punch they would substitute for wine, apples and cinnamon, then lamb roast and potatoes, with no dairy products, with a parve carrot kugel dish. The meal would end with a fruit meringue and honey.

The lamb had to be salted and set for a half hour, to draw the blood out, then soaked in clear water for an hour before roasting. Missus Twombly said it would traditionally be roasted over an open fire, but was not necessary for a "pretend" Seder. Lizzie replied it would be no problem if she wanted to, she had always cooked on an open fire. When her mistress pointed out the potential of the wind spreading the flames through the grove, Lizzie agreed to roast it in the oven. Still, it would be very interesting to see.

"Missus Twombly, if it would no' be too impertinent ta ask, d' ye think I could watch the Seder with Eliza? I kin tend my kitchen as well."

"Of course, Lizzie, I'd forgotten how much you miss seeing, when you're back there. When ye see Eliza pick up the plates, you can step back into the kitchen for the next course. As long as you can tend your work, it would please me for you to see the Seder."

"Missus Twombly, why are we having a Seder dinner?"

155

"It is well you should ask, Lizzie. Doctor Twombly and I think it's good to remind ourselves where our religious roots are. Our Lord did not turn away from His people. He brought us to a greater awareness of our relationship with God. We have grown away from our traditions, but it is good we remember them. It is a part of the rich heritage we have as Christians."

It was as if another great truth had been revealed to her. She knew tomorrow night would be very special indeed.

Just before they were to go to the grove, Lizzie applied the finishing touches to her three bowls. Asparagus spears, deviled eggs and Spanish olives formed a summer flower on the top of each of the salads. Gathering the basket of napkins and dinnerware, Lizzie looked for Eliza to help her carry the bowls.

Eliza was in the front yard holding a ladder for William. Lizzie was astonished and more than curious about this tableau.

Wha' on earth, Mister William is no' accustomed to doin' manual labor.

"Hand me the next lantern, Eliza," said William almost cheerfully.

"Now William, be careful." his mother admonished, anxiously. "Don't reach too far. Oh, goodness, I won't be calm until you're down from there."

"We only have one more, Mother, and then we're done. Eliza is holding the ladder. You've nothing to be concerned about. I'm coming down to move the ladder, Eliza. Then, if you would steady it once again, we'll be done."

Lizzie could see Eliza was trying unsuccessfully to hide the smirk creeping onto her determinedly serious face. She stood to one side as William approached the bottom rung. Missing it, his foot went through the space between the rungs while the other slid down the face of the ladder, scraping the full length of his shin. Eliza had a firm hold on the ladder, but that did not prevent the distinguish Reverend Mister William L. D. Twombly from landing

156

unceremoniously on his backside. His hand flew immediately to cover his mouth, lest any unseemly words should slip out.

"Come now, Mother, your son is just fine," chuckled Doctor Twombly. "He's just had a labor lesson in humility. You may want to change those elegant trousers, son. You seem to have created a new pocket in them."

William's face was a deep red, but he laughed good-naturedly. "If you'll permit me, I will heed my father's advice. I'll be just a moment." He edged his body discretely away from the women, and ducked into the house and up the stairs.

Eliza looked at the one lantern left in her hand questioningly.

"I'll get it up there, Eliza," said Lizzie, already climbing the ladder. Answering the shocked, and worried looks of those still on the round, she said, grinning, "I used to be the best climber in County Down. They sent me up to fix the roof every spring." She placed the final lantern on its hook and scurried down again.

"Well, you never cease to amaze us, Lizzie. When William comes down, we can go to the grove."

"What are the lanterns for, Doctor Twombly?" asked Lizzie impulsively.

"You will see, Lizzie. The Illumination is tonight. William will not need a ladder for that." Doctor leaned a pole with a wick at one end, against the porch, with a box of wooden matches on the railing next to it.

Lizzie motioned for Eliza to follow her into the house for the forgotten basket and potato salads. Tonight, they would sit with the Twomblys at supper. Missus Twombly was trying to encourage the other families to have their servants eat with their families, on this one night. This night was very special, she explained. This was a community night. Servants and families were all part of the Christian community.

Lizzie and Eliza followed the Twomblys to a table near the platform. The table was already beginning to fill up with heaping

157

platters and bowls of food. Children were running back and forth through the trees, and neighbors were waving across the tables in shouts of recognition.

"Ah, there are the Chambers now. I was afraid we would have to give their seats to someone else," said Missus Twombly. "Eliza, Lizzie, you may serve the lemonade now. When everything is set up, you may sit on this side with Doctor Twombly and I. Isabella and William will sit with the Chambers. You may join the conversation, politely and non-controversially."

"Aye, ma'am," said Lizzie quietly, thinking, *the likelihood the Chambers or the Twombly children could find a mutual conversation with servants, is as sure as my kissin' the moon.* Still, they took their seats with the Twomblys and wondered what the evening would bring.

"Mister and Missus Chambers, my children are accustomed to indulging their mother, but I wonder if you, too, could indulge a whim of mine this evening? I want to conduct a social experiment. Isabella, I'd like you to sit on Mister Chamber's right, William, on Missus Chamber's left. Lizzie, if you would sit on Doctor Twombly's left, and Eliza, on my right. Isabelle rolled her eyes as she crossed behind the Chambers, and mouthed "Mother?" showing obvious disapproval. William just smiled endearingly at his mother, having played this game before.

"Before the festivities start, let's take turns, starting with Isabella. Tell us to how many countries you've been."

"I have lived in this country my whole life, Mother," Isabelle said quietly.

"As a matter of fact, Isabella, you've been to two countries. But I will wait until my turn to explain that," replied Missus Twombly. Hearing this news, Isabelle was intrigued and drawn deftly into the game.

Mister Chambers said, "I've been ...." He paused as he counted, "Four times to Canada, twice to England, here, of course, and Texas. That makes four countries."

"Texas is in the United States. That's three countries," said William, challenging him.

"No. I was born in Texas in 1844. It wasn't a state yet. Four," retorted Mister Chambers.

"Oh, I beg your pardon. When did it become a state?" asked William.

"1845. That's when we moved back East. Don't remember any of it, but it's the truth," said Mister Chambers.

"Just two, for me, I was born in Nice, France. I've been here twenty-five years," broke in Missus Chambers. "I married Mister Chambers the year I arrived." *That's why she has that pretty music in her voice*, thought Lizzie.

"Mother, if what you were saying earlier applies to me, then two," said William.

"For me, I think it's three countries, isn't it, Lizzie? Ulster, England, and America?" asked Eliza. Lizzie peeked around Doctor and Missus Twombly and nodded.

Missus Twombly sat up straighter in her seat and said, "Isabella and I have been to two countries. When we were in Wisconsin, we crossed over the border to Canada by ship on Lake Superior. We did not land, but made a great circle and returned to the same shore from whence we commenced the journey. So, Isabella, we have been to two countries. William, you were not yet born, so I believe you have only been to this one country."

Doctor Twombly stated, "When I was a young man, a carpenter, I chanced to ride with my uncle on a long journey north. We were already high up in New Hampshire, and he claimed we went to Canada on that trip. I don't remember much of it, except I was with my uncle and we were forever surrounded by thousands of tall trees. He said I asked more questions than any three people he knew. How about you, Lizzie?"

"Ulster, England, an' America. We came within sight of Greenland, Newfoundland and Nova Scotia, but we thought they were all part of America," said Lizzie.

Doctor Twombly said, "Nova Scotia and Newfoundland are part of Canada, and while Canada is part of America, it is not part of the United States. They are a separate country. So is Greenland. I guess if you came within fifteen miles, you could count them as countries you've been to. If we count Missus Twombly's visit to Canada, then you should count those two. On the other hand, Mister Chambers probably went the same route. He could add two to his four. Depending where Missus Chambers came into this country, she could add those two as well."

Mister Chambers laughed. "If I did go to those countries, I must have slept through it. I don't recall having even been told I was near them and I've been across twice! Who would have thought such a simple question could bring up all these ramifications?"

"Sh-h, Reverend Keyes is about to speak," said Missus Twombly. Whatever the outcome of the number of countries, the group was much more relaxed and enthusiastically engaged in conversation with all the participants at the table that evening. Whether or not Missus Twombly's social experiment was a success, she didn't say. *It did even the footing twixt servants and families, however,* thought Lizzie.

After the meal, a contented hush seemed to fall over the crowd. The sun was just beginning to set. "Ladies and Gentlemen, please rise." The Reverend Mister Keyes raised his hands in benediction over the gathering.

The prayer finished, the crowd was still silent and no one moved. "Gentlemen?" he said. One man from each family group walked to the outside of the grove. Then in the waning light, there was a collective "ah-h-h" from all over the campground. Lizzie stretched her neck to see thousands of colored lanterns surround the little grove. "It's beautiful!" Lizzie whispered to no one in particular.

"Yes, it is," murmured Missus Chambers with her charming French inflection. "It surely is."

The congregation stood for a while in silent awe. Then, one by one, the families gathered their belongings and walked through the trees in a reverent procession. Lizzie watched, her eyes sparkling, as the families walked, not to their homes as she had expected, but arm in arm around the perimeter of the grove. Someone started singing a low mournful hymn, *"Abide with me, fast falls the eventide..."* Little by little, the families joined in singing.

Suddenly, completely overwhelmed, Lizzie began to cry. At first, she furiously wiped the tears away. Then, the flow was too copious to manage, and she gave in to it. *Fer heaven's sake, git a holt o' yersel'. You're a spectacle! Stop it.*

The memory of everything she ever regretted in her life seemed to wash over her. She broke away from the crowd, and into the darkened grove. Stumbling, half-blind with tears, she ran into roots; scraped her arm on the bark of a tree; and hit her head on a low branch. Finally, she just sat in the shadows, the twigs in her hair and dirt on her dress unheeded. She placed her face in her hands, and cried like a child. Big, gulping sobs gripped her lungs. Slowly the storm subsided. She sat quietly. She knew her face was red and blotchy.

"Lizzie, where are you?" she heard, then a thud. "Damnation, Lizzie!"

"Over here, sir," Lizzie started to laugh. "I am sae sorry, Mister William," she giggled. *Lizzie stop! He'll think you've lost your mind.*

"Lizzie, my mother is worried sick about you. Are you all right? Are you hurt?"

He sounded so sincerely worried, it sobered her demeanor instantly. "I'm fine, Mister William. The singing and lights made me homesick, is all. Please forgive my outburst."

William cleared his throat, and said. "Very well, then. You'd better get along home." He cleared his throat again. "Take my hand, I'll guide you. It is treacherous walking in these trees."

"I know I am a sight. Maybe, you'd better let me go first. People may think terrible thoughts, if we are seen together. I've leaves in my hair, and I'm afraid I've torn my dress on a branch."

Again, he cleared his throat. "You're right. Goodness, thank you, as long as you're all right, Lizzie."

"I am. And I am sae sorry to have caused you any bother."

She eased her way out of the grove and toward the Central Park cottage. When she looked back, she saw him watching her retreat before heading for his cottage across the way. *No danger o' scandal, nae. Funny, all the time I wus talkin' ta him, I wus talkin' lak' a lady. I haven' done thet since I saw Laird Annesley! Wha' are yer thinkin'? He's no laird. An' he swore too.*

Stop laughin' at yer betters, Lizzie. They will think yer have gone entirely mad!

Chapter Eleven

Calm now, Lizzie hoped there would be no one in the kitchen when she entered. She was destined to be disappointed. Not only was Eliza waiting for her, but the rest of the Twombly family. Either by curiosity or concern, even Isabelle was waiting for her. Eliza jumped forward and wrapped her arms around her. Missus Twombly took her daughter's and her husband's hands and drew them quietly out of the room. "We can see she is home safely. Let's leave her be a moment, shall we?"

Lizzie knew she looked a sight. She gently peeled Eliza off her and headed for the bedroom upstairs. "Eliza, please help me with this hair, or it will take me all night."

Eliza followed her obediently, anxious for any hint of what had happened. If Lizzie was to reveal anything, Eliza thought, she would have to pry it out of her. She was horrified at the aberration before her. It was as if Lizzie had gone wild and went to live in the woods. "What happened, Lizzie, did thet man from beyond the carrousel try ta get you? Are ye goin' ta *tell* me?"

"Eliza. I'm fine. I'm embarrassed it's come ta this. I wus sae overwhelmed by the singin', thet I wus cryin'. I guess I wus homesick, but I couldn't bear havin' all those folk seein' me like thet, sae I went into the grove ta git away. "Twus light enough ta see the trees, but I tripped on the roots, scraped m' face on the branches an' tore m' dress ta boot. Mister William found me. He wus none too pleased, either. He hit his shin on *somethin'*. The selfsame shin

163

he scraped this afternoon, poor man!" The memory of the tall, reserved minister swearing in the grove, made Lizzie burst into giggles again.

"Oh, no!" said Eliza, her eyes shining, her mouth quivering with simmering mirth. They both clapped their hands over their mouths to silence the escaping giggles. Eliza slid to the floor with her other hand holding her stomach, shaking her head. As one girl's spasms would subside, the other one would resume, so they remained in paroxysms of hilarity for some time.

Finally, Lizzie gave the brush to Eliza, put on a falsely serious face, and said, "We've gotta git back ta the kitchen, Eliza. I still hae work ta do."

Still smiling, Eliza went to work unsnarling the curly red mane and removing its clinging debris, a chore that was both satisfying and nostalgic. When Eliza was still a small child, Maggie allowed her to brush Lizzie's hair because she was so gentle with it. As the years went by, it became apparent that her fiery hair and her matching temper were the only chinks in Lizzie's well forged armor, *and* the only vulnerabilities wherein Eliza would be allowed to come to her aid. She hummed to herself as she worked.

Hearing the old Irish tune Eliza hummed, threatened to undo all the attempts Lizzie had made to overcome her homesickness. Yet, it was pleasant and she could not bear to stop her half-sister's music.

The music here seems harsh and thunderous, joyful, but heavy. An Irish tune is light as the mist it sings about. When e'er I hear it, I think of the sun o'er the Mournes, the fresh air, the river, and a hawk in flight. Móraí talked about Scotland thet way. She felt the same about the mournful wail of the bagpipes. I guess it's the same fer ever'one that has moved from his homeland.

Eliza finally finished and bound Lizzie's hair in a respectable bun. Lizzie changed her dress, and washed her face. All signs of her emotional collapse were erased, except for the sadness in her eyes, the scratch on her face, and the uncharacteristic slump of her shoulders which she tried to erase.

In the kitchen, Lizzie was surprised to see the dishes washed and put away. The breakfast trays were laid out, the floors swept and the stove cleaned. Lizzie checked the larder and the icebox for supplies needed, and found a list on the worktable. She added one item, checked the oil in the lamp, and left the room.

They must've done ever'thin' while they were waitin' fer me. If yer teachin' me humility, Laird, I have taken the lesson. I indulged my emotions lak' a child, an' they punish me by doing my work!

Upstairs, Lizzie undressed quietly, seeing Eliza already asleep. She slipped in beside her. Laying awake in the dark, she prayed to be worthy of the kindness of those who watch over her. Somewhere in midst of her heartfelt prayer, she fell into a deep restful sleep.

The next morning, Lizzie opened her eyes to a room bathed in pink, and the chattering of Twomblys rising from the front porch. She ran to the window to see the brilliant sunrise. Dressing quickly, she tied up her hair, donned her cap, and went down to the kitchen. There, she saw the coffee was brewed, and Eliza was pouring. "Good morning, sister," she said so joyously, Lizzie couldn't help but grin.

Lizzie pulled out dessert glasses, and filled them with cut up fruit. Toast was browning on the stove top, and pots of marmalade and jam were ensconced on the trays. She had hardboiled eggs in their respective egg cups, and bacon frying in the pan. When the bacon was cooked and drained, she expertly drizzled bacon fat on the eggs. As Eliza came back for the first tray, Lizzie took the second, and they marched out to the porch. The ladies were served, and as Lizzie turned to get the third tray, Missus Twombly put her hand on her arm. She nodded at Eliza who went for Doctor Twombly's breakfast tray.

"Lizzie, dear, are you all right?"

165

"Aye, ma'am, I apologize for any distress I may have caused you all. It won't happen again."

"Lizzie! There is no apology necessary. These things happen. Goodness knows you've seen us at our worst. We just want you to know you can come to us, if ever you need help. When William didn't come back with you, we didn't know what to think."

"Mister William went back ta his cottage at my ain urgin', ma'am. My dress was ripped by a branch an' I didn't want Mister Williams ta be seen wit' me an' cause undue scandal. Even amongst the fines' people, tongues do wag, ma'am."

"Oh, my goodness, I see what you mean. That was very considerate of you. I still think he should have seen to your safety first, *then* to his own reputation."

"Beggin' yer pardon, ma'am, I *did* insist, an' he did see me ta the edge o' the grove, an' watched as I went ta the house. I was entirely safe, an' under his watchful eye."

"Very well then, it was a frightful scare when you disappeared. But all's well that ends well, I suppose. Isabella, before the Seder tonight, perhaps you'd be kind enough to lend Lizzie some powder for her cheek. That scratch is dreadful looking. "

"Yes, Mother." Isabelle smiled mischievously. "We mustn't let our guests think we've been beating her. I'm glad you're all right, Lizzie," she added.

"Thank you, Miss Isabelle. I am fine. Please enjoy your breakfast."

Lizzie was glad to get that over with. Now, she could get on with her preparations for the Seder tonight. Missus Twombly had written the order of the Seder and what should be on the table first, what would follow, and how dessert would be handled. It would be exciting to see it unfold.

Laird, please let me do this rightly in yer sight, fer the Twomblys, the Johnsons, an' fer me. Amen.

166

Missus Twombly came into the kitchen at about ten o'clock and sat at one end of the work table. "I hope I'm not disturbing you, Lizzie. It helps me to remember, if I see what you're making, so I can write out the Seder service. We won't sing all the songs, and the Johnsons probably won't know if we miss anything, but I want it to be a wonderful experience for them. Each person will have a part to play in the presentation, so I want to include everything I can remember. I have a *Haggadah*, a book that tells the order of the traditions, but I don't want to make this too long for the children," she said.

"Oh, tonight before the Seder, I want you and Eliza to wear these kerchiefs to cover your hair instead of your mob caps. Isabella, Missus Johnson, and I will be wearing them, too. Doctor Twombly or William, whoever wishes to lead the Seder, will wear the white robe I had you press. The robe does not have to be packed in the things for Newton, but put in a drawer for next year." Missus Twombly seemed to run out of breath at the end of her long speech. "Oh dear, I think I will just sit for a minute, and be quiet."

Lizzie smiled and returned to her baking. *Sae many things ta remember! The table setting is simple fer the Seder part. Two bowls o' water an' two towels fer washin' hands will be brought around by Eliza an' me. Enough fruit punch fer everyone at the table ta have four small cups. The Seder plate is set with horseradish, romaine lettuce, a paste of fruit an' nuts; then celery, the roasted lamb bone; an' a roasted egg. I guess I can throw it in with the lamb to roast?*

Candles on the table, thet matzos I made yesterday, an' a small bowl o' salted water; a bowl o' candies fer the side table.

The main meal will be the lamb, sliced boiled potatoes, an' fresh peas. I'll use the lamb drippings on the potatoes, if there are any, after all thet soakin' an' drainin'. The kugel looks delicious. I canna imagine how these things gae together. I'll jes' hafta wait an' see.

167

The afternoon flew by. Soon, there was a commotion at the front door announcing the arrival of the young minster's family. William was there with them. After a short discussion in the parlor, William entered the dining room wearing the white robe that designated the leader of the Seder. "You'll correct me if I'm wrong, Father? I'm doing this mostly from memory... and the book, of course."

"It's time you took over, and yes, I'll let you know when you go astray."

"At any rate, William, we are not likely to know the difference now, are we?" joined in the Reverend Mister Johnson. Mister Johnson was about thirty, average height, had thinning light brown hair, the rich tanned complexion of a man who labored in the summer sun, and had a cheerful disposition. His wife was well-suited to him, with the same dove color hair, round and short, with a sweet face and temperament. The three children were well-mannered and bore varying degrees of likenesses to their mother and father.

All the men and the two male children wore *Yarmulkes*, and the women and the girl wore kerchiefs on their heads. William took his place at the head of the table and waited for everyone to sit down. "Let us first ask God's blessing on this evening's enterprise.

"Merciful Father, it is with humble hearts, we come to You. Bless, oh Lord, this gathering of friends for fellowship and prayer. We come to You with open hearts and minds, to partake of the bounty You have so graciously bestowed upon us.

"Bless our recreation of the Seder, that we may show Your everlasting love for all Your people. Help us to demonstrate the traditions that Jesus observed when He walked among us. In His Holy Name, we ask it. Amen." Then he nodded to his mother.

Missus Twombly said, "At least eighteen minutes before sunset, the Shabat candles are lit. Isabella?"

168

Isabelle stood at the center of the table and lit one candle then the other, moving her hands together in the smoke drawing it toward herself, she said, "The smoke is drawn in circular motion, invoking the Shabbat, or Sabbath to come to us. This is done three times."

"Thank you Isabelle," said William. "In Jewish tradition, Passover occurs on the 15th of Nissan, just as the moon waxes for 15 days. The Seder fulfills itself in fifteen steps. These represent fifteen steps toward freedom. The first is the blessing of the first cup of wine. For which we have substituted a red punch. The unleavened bread is covered. The blessing is a special one for Passover. We thank God for the deliverance of the Jews from Egypt, for water in the desert, and for the unleavened bread they took with them."

Eliza stepped forward and filled William's cup. Then William took the pitcher from her hands and walked around the table and filled all the other cups. He made a short prayer and drank until the punch was gone. The room was nearly dark now and the candle glow seemed to warm the room.

Eliza and Lizzie entered the room with small bowls of water and towels over their forearms. Starting with William, each person dunked their hands into the water and dried them with the towel. Missus Johnson helped the youngest child with this task.

At this point, William held up a piece of celery, dipped it into a small bowl of salted water and took a bite. "The celery is indicative of spring and the salted water is representative of the tears shed by the Jews as slaves in Egypt."

Next, he turned to the three matzos stacked upon a plate. He removed the top one. The middle one, he broke in half. Taking the larger of the two pieces, he wrapped it in a napkin. He said, "Eliza, I want you to take this and hide it in the parlor. After supper, the children will search for it. Whoever finds it first, will receive a small prize." If they had grown a bit sleepy, the children's eyes were wide awake now.

169

"Billy, do you remember your question?"

Billy sat up straight, now the attention was on him, and answered brightly, "Why is this night different than all other nights?"

At this point, William told the story of the Passover. He told a simplified and animated version, entertaining the children. He then took the Seder plate, and raised it over the heads of all at the table, saying, "In haste, we went out of Egypt, with our bread of affliction, now we are free people."

William, warming to his role as teacher, explained the significance of items on the Seder plate, the cups on the table, and the steps of the Seder.

He told the story of the Exodus, then signaled for the bowls of water again. They washed their hands as before. William said a blessing. The matzos were broken and passed around for everyone to eat.

"It's a cracker!" exclaimed Billy. The startled group laughed.

William had explained the bitter herbs represented the bitter years of slavery and the apples and cinnamon represented the building blocks they had to make as slaves for the storage houses. He dipped the bitter end of romaine lettuce into the apples and cinnamon and bit off a small piece. William made a dramatically sour face to the children's delight. "Would anyone else like to try it?" The children shook their heads emphatically.

He said a small blessing, then took two small bits of the matzos and a little of the romaine, made a sandwich and ate that.

Again he took the punch and filled their cups. With another short blessing, they drank their 'wine'. He looked up at his guests and said, "Well, now that we have eaten, do you think you have room for a little more?"

"Yes," was the resounding cry from the children. Then Sarah piped up, "But no more bitter herbs, please." Again the group burst into laughter.

Eliza withdrew to the kitchen. Lizzie and Eliza both returned with platters laden with succulent lamb, potatoes, and peas.

William said, "Let us say grace for the Lord's bounty. Reverend Johnson?"

Lizzie and Eliza stood at their station by the door. While grace was pronounced, Lizzie peeked at the faces of the Twombly family and their guests, bathed in candle light.

How beautiful an' sweet this night is! The Seder's strangely unfamiliar, yet familiar at the same time. The children are sae wrapped up in the story. I dinna think they'll e'er fergit it, nor will I.

The family and guests were noisy and chatting as in a usual supper, full of questions and comments concerning the Seder. Following the kugel, almond meringues with honey finished the meal. William stood and said, "Children you may be dismissed to find the *afikoman*, the matzos, hidden in the parlor. The first one to find it will receive a prize." Eliza followed the children to keep a modicum of decorum as they frantically looked for the napkin.

"I have it!" said Robert excitedly. His announcement was greeted with the disappointed groans of his siblings.

Back in the dining room, William took four candies from the dish on the side table and presented them to Robert. He took two candies in each hand to give Sarah and Billy, saying, "Next year, perhaps you will be the one who finds it."

William opened the napkin, broke the matzos on a plate, and said, "Take an olive-sized piece of matzos and eat it. It is to remind us of the bread of affliction and to never take for granted this freedom we have."

He then took the pitcher and again poured the red punch for his guests. "We drink this cup and thank God for our redemption."

The cup being empty, he asked Robert to open the front doors of the house. When Robert returned, William poured the rest of the 'wine' into a silver cup in front of the Seder plate. He recited the verses of Psalms 79:6-7 and said, "This is the cup of Elijah. The

171

Children of Israel await his return to announce the coming of the Messiah. The door is opened in preparation for his arrival." William drank the cup, and said, "Next year in Jerusalem." The lamps were again turned down, so that only the candles on the table lit the room. William indicated they should join hands, and said, "The Seder is ended except for the singing of songs. Let us sing one familiar to ourselves, the Doxology. *Praise God, from Whom all blessings flow; Praise Him, all creatures here below; Praise Him above, ye Heavenly Host; Praise Father, Son, and Holy Ghost. Amen.*"

The room was silent. William stepped away from the table, walked to his mother and kissed her cheek.

"This night was truly a blessing for me, Mother. Father, thank you." William shook his father's hand, then Mister Johnson's. He made his way around the table and acknowledged all the participants.

Lizzie and Eliza remained at the door until the room emptied. The group was very quiet. Even the children were silently moving toward the open door. At the door, William turned, and strode back to the dining room. Standing in front of Eliza, he nodded and said, "Eliza, bless you." He turned to Lizzie and said. "Bless you, Lizzie." He raised one hand to the scratch on her cheek, gently touching it. She looked up at his eyes and saw how moved he was.

"You're most welcome, Mister William. It was sae beautiful." As if coming out of a fog, he straightened, turned quickly and left the room.

Eliza and Lizzie worked without talking. Lizzie wanted to savor the last moments of reverence and peace she felt during the singing. She wanted to remember this night in all its detail to tell her mother and *Mórai*.

To see Mister William so moved, felt like she was eavesdropping on a private moment. She could still feel his hand touch her cheek. It was so unlike him. She had never seen more than a half-smile or a shadow come over his eyes to betray his emotion.

172

He's forty, I heard them say. Why did he ne'er take a wife? He's been verra ill fer much o' his life, his father said. Still not ever'one who marries has good health. Well, time ta stop daydreamin'. You've plenty ta do afore tamarra. We're goin' back ta Newton Lower Falls. I wonder if Isabelle and William will return to their usual 'out-of-sorts' selves when they git there.

After the dishes were put away, Eliza put the ghostly white shrouds over the furniture for another year. They drew the shades and under curtains in the parlor and dining room, then the main drapes in the parlor. The fireplace flues were shut. The fire in the kitchen was low. The lamps were emptied except for the least amount of oil. The trunks were at one end of the kitchen, ready for the driver tomorrow morning. The clothes they wore for supper would have to do for the journey home.

After a peaceful rest, Lizzie bounded out of bed the next morning. She had a myriad of tasks to accomplish before the driver was due to arrive. Breakfast was simply fruit, biscuits and jam with coffee and tea. As soon as the last coffee was poured, the fire was put out, its remains scraped into a hod, and cast into the garden.

The summer dishes were wrapped and packed on the shelves. The beds were made and the sheets pulled over to cover them. The small rugs were rolled and put in a corner. Candles were put away and lamps emptied, clothes lines removed. When at last everything was in order, Lizzie sat down for a moment while Missus Twombly went through her list. "The parlor curtains...?"

"Aye, ma'am, closed an' covered. The parlor stove wasn't used this year, sae I jes' covered it."

"Well, we've done our best then. Whatever we didn't think of will have to wait until next year, won't it, Lizzie?"

"Aye, ma'am, I'll walk aroun' once more upstairs an' down, ta see if there's else ta do."

"Thank you, Lizzie, the family and I will be on the front porch saying our goodbyes to the neighbors."

Lizzie climbed the stairs thinking of the last two weeks, and all that had happened in them. She would miss this summer paradise. Visions of the Flying Horses, the main street shops, the grove, and the people she met, flowed through her mind as she checked the rooms.

In her own room, she found one of the drawers slightly ajar. She checked to see if anything was left in it. She found nothing. There was a scraping sound as she was closing it. Again, she opened it, and found a yellowed curled up paper stuck in the back. She pulled it out and unrolling it, she read, "Miss Millicent Bakersfield requests the honor of your presence, Saturday, August 14th, 1887 at a Garden Cotillion at her home...."

"Well, I guess Mister William had his opportunities, at least." Lizzie let the paper roll up in her hands, and tucked it far back in the drawer again. She glanced in the mirror, turning her face to see the scratch, now less angry-looking. She touched her cheek as he had, and smiled. *Lizzie, you are a silly romantic goose.*

"Lizzie!" The sound of her name being called so close shocked her out of her daydream.

"The driver is here, hurry." Standing in the doorway, Eliza had Lizzie's straw bonnet in her hand, beckoning her to come.

"I'm ready, Eliza. Let's go." Together, they scurried down the stairs to the waiting wagon.

It seemed strange to be taking the trip in reverse, packing the wagon, going down the hill to the dock, boarding the ferry and sailing away again. It was as if they were erasing the last two weeks by turning it around to the point where it began. The same luncheon was served, the same party atmosphere, only this time they were more subdued, saying sad goodbyes. As she was cleaning up the last of the luncheon scraps, she heard her name, "Miss Lizzie?"

"*Jes' Plain Garrett!* Eliza, it's the young man from the carousel! What brings yer here?"

His eyes twinkling, his carriage straight, he hardly seemed like the laconic, bored boy they had encountered. "I've quit the carousel, an' I'm goin' t' seek my way on the mainland."

"But what will ye do? Where will ye go?" asked the girls.

"I'm not sure, but I'm trained in carpentry. I'll find somethin', somewheres."

"Perhaps ye kin git a ride wit' us. There's a man drivin' us hame, who's a master carpenter in Newton Lower Falls," Lizzie said impulsively.

"Lizzie! It's not our place…" Eliza said, worried.

"Nonsense, he should be able ta ride wit' us at least. Then, we kin introduce him ta Mister Baker. If he has no place ta go, Newton Lower Falls is as good a place as any, ta be, eh? I will ask Missus Twombly, if it'll take the worry off yer face."

Lizzie left them there, while she looked for the family outside. She found them surrounded by campground dwellers who were reminiscing about the events of the past weeks. She stood patiently waiting while they were engaged in conversation. She saw Mister William edge to the back of the crowd surrounding his parents. Circling around to her, he asked, "Miss Lizzie, is there something you need?" She hadn't counted on this. She knew she could ask Missus Twombly anything, but Mister William was a whole other matter.

"Well, sir, I-I happened to encounter a young man on the ship who was very helpful to us on the island. He is seeking carpentry work. S-sir, I wondered if it would be permissible to allow him a ride to Newton Lower Falls and, er, to meet Mister Baker?" She was sure he could see her shaking, her former bravado broken.

William, having bowed his head to hear her words over the crowd and the ocean waves, now drew himself up to his full height. Staring off to the horizon, he said, "You want us to give a perfect stranger a ride to our home, and introduce him to our dearest friend, for the sole purpose of getting him a job with Mister Baker."

175

"I-Isn't that what the Lord would want us to do, s-sir?" Lizzie's reddened face now looked more worried than Eliza's had.

He thought a moment, frowning. "Keenly put, Miss Lizzie. Have you ever played your hand at chess? I believe you have checkmate. If I say yes, I stand to lose a good friend, and be saddled with a young man whose true intentions, we do not know. If I say no, I am not worthy of my profession, and am an abomination to my faith. I will err on the side of the Lord, Miss Lizzie. I hope this young man is worthy of your help. I will explain it to the family."

"Thank yer sae much, Mister William! Thank yer."

"There it is. I've wondered where your Irish tongue goes when you speak with me. Do you turn it off and on at will, Miss Lizzie?" His countenance amused, there seemed to be no sting in his words.

"I don't mean to, Mister William. I was trained to speak well, but when I am with those of my own station, I drift back to the tongue of my family in the North o' Ireland." Lizzie reddened again, embarrassed at his observation.

"It's interesting. I've not encountered it before." He turned back to the family, who were staring at him now. "Tell the young man he is welcome to the ride and the introduction, but he will have to ask for the job on his own." With a wave of his hand, he dismissed her, walking back toward his family.

Lizzie fairly raced back to the inside table to Eliza and Garrett. "Young Mister Twombly said, 'Aye!' Garrett kin have a ride ta the Falls and he will be introduced ta Mister Baker."

Turning to Garrett, she said, "You will have to ask fer yer ain job and find a place ta live."

"Fair enough," said Garrett. "Lizzie, you sure are somethin'!"

"We haven't figured out *what* yet, but she surely is *somethin'*," teased Eliza. "I canna believe ye asked Mister William."

Lizzie grinned and shrugged her shoulders. *I hope he's as good a carpenter as he is a rescuer o' damsels in distress. He seems ta have good character. I shoulda thought o' thet afore I got mysel' involved. Will I ne'er stop ta think, afore I jump in?*

While Garrett and Eliza were talking, Lizzie looked out at the ocean, lost in the blue that melded water into sky at the horizon.

It wasn't long before they were debarking at Woods Hole. Mister Baker and another man stood by their respective rigs waiting on shore. Lizzie expected there would be someone else in place of Mister Bachelor.

Upon closer look, it *was* Mister Bachelor. He had shaved his beard and sported a mustache and trim side burns instead. He looked so much younger. *And e'en more handsome,* she thought.

At the wagon, she introduced Garrett Johannson to Mister Bachelor. Eliza volunteered to sit in the back with Garrett, leaving Lizzie alone up front with Mister Bachelor. "You may want to fold the blanket back there for your seats, Garrett Johannson. These roads are rather rough for riding in the back of the wagon." Turning to Lizzie, he said, "Your sister may regret her generosity in sitting back there, but I, for one, am happy she did."

"Why Mister Bachelor, whatever do yer mean...?" Lizzie asked coyly.

"Call me Charles, Lizzie, please."

"Very well, Charles. I thought ye would be in school this week."

"I've been to campus and found my lodging, but I don't have classes until Tuesday, so I came back to see you...." He hesitated, then continued, "...*And* Eliza, of course. I have a surprise for you. I've made all the arrangements and I hope you will agree."

"But M-Mister... Charles, I don't understand," said Lizzie.

"I have cleared it with Missus Twombly to take you and Eliza to the swan boats tomorrow afternoon. She says they are going out to the Bakers for Sunday dinner, and if you wish, you may accompany me after church. I'm to bring you home by sundown."

"Oh, Charles, how nice, I'd be honored ta go wit' you." Then lowering her voice, she added, "I'll tell Eliza tonight, when we're alone. She is goin' ta be sae excited."

"Then it's settled. We'll leave straight from church in the morning. After the swan boat ride, we can take a stroll on the Common. I hope you won't mind eating from the street carts."

"Not at all M-Charles, when did you have time ta arrange all this?"

"I talked to Missus Twombly before we left for Martha's Vineyard, and she said if I could arrange my schooling obligations, then you had her permission to go. I see she did not betray my trust and spoil the surprise. I must thank her for that."

They chatted for a while, until Lizzie became mesmerized by the steady hoof steps of the horses and nodded off to sleep. She awoke with a start when the wagon rode over a rock. Her head was resting on the rough wool of Mister Bachelor's jacket and his arm was around her waist.

"Oh my goodness, Mister Bachelor, er, Charles, I am sae embarrassed. How rude o' me."

"Not at all, Lizzie, it was my pleasure, indeed," he said, his eyes alive with delight.

"Tell me, Charles what prompted you ta shave yer beard? I like it, ye understand, but why, after all this time?"

"It's the fashion of the students to be clean shaven, so this is my compromise between fashion and tradition. The youngsters have taken to calling me 'old man,' not that I minded, but I didn't want to be *that* old."

"I do like it, Charles, it's distinguished. I think it quite handsome, if ye will forgive me fer being sae bold."

"Not at all, if you do not think me rude to ask how you came by the scratch on your face?"

"Oh dear, there is a grove at the Tabernacle, an' I tripped, scratchin' my face on a branch. It was the night of the Illumination, an' we had a picnic in the grove."

"As long as you were safe, my dear," he sighed, and said seriously, "I've missed you so very much these two weeks. Even though I've been very busy, my thoughts kept drifting back to you. It will be such a long, long time until Thanksgiving, and I don't know if I can bear it." He looked at her intently.

"Mister Bachelor," she said gently, "we are in sech different circumstances, I canna see what Thanksgiving will bring. I hope I have no' encouraged ye ta think in thet direction. I do enjoy yer company, but I hesitate ta allow sech thoughts. Ye need ta be concentratin' on yer studyin'. Ye have a great mission ta accomplish. I do no' want ta stand in the way o' thet. When my time is done wit' the Twombly family, I'll be movin' on, an' I don' knae where I'll be."

Keeping his voice low, he said, "Lizzie, let's just take it a day at a time. I've no right to put a claim on you. I have only the pleasure of your company for tomorrow. Let's not plan further than that. I will be home Thanksgiving Day. If you are willing to see me then, I will arrange to be where you are. Should I find the time, I will write you and you can choose or not, to reply. Indulge me this one day, Lizzie, and I'll not demand another. It is your ship to steer, Lizzie, yours alone."

They rode silently for a while. The air felt charged with unspoken thoughts. Finally, she felt compelled to speak. "Charles, you shall have yer day, an' we will delight in it. We mus' no' be serious though. I should like ta hear from yer occasionally, fer I do care about yer, dear friend. Please dinna ask fer promises though, fer I shall no' make them lightly."

"Very well, then, Lizzie. If it is one day, we shall make it a *memorable* one," he said, with forced cheerfulness.

Lizzie looked behind her to Eliza and Garrett, wondering if they heard anything of their conversation. She smiled, seeing their animated talk and laughter. She envied the lightness of their banter.

Chapter Twelve

Sunday morning's winged choir burst into chirping at first light. Lizzie shook her head at sudden recognition of her room. Missus Twombly was right. It was as if they had never gone to Martha's Vineyard. Except for the half empty household trunk in the kitchen and Eliza's golden tan, it seemed all evidence of their journey had evaporated with the morning dew. Even the scratch on her cheek had faded to a pale pink line.

Lizzie let Eliza sleep. They had both worked until late in the night, unpacking and straightening the clothing, for the family. The sheets that covered the furniture in their absence, added to the great piles of laundry for Monday's wash on the back porch.

Big John welcomed them back when he came for his 'back door' supper alone, his friends having gone to work down river. He said he didn't want to seem ungrateful for free food, but he was very glad Lizzie would be making the stew again.

Lizzie wondered if Missus Twombly could get him work cleaning up the church. It would at least be steady. *She probably thought o' thet when John first hurt his arm. It won't hurt ta ask though.* She wondered too, if Garrett got along with the Bakers the previous night. *I hope sae, It'd be nice ta repay his kindness wit' another. Eliza seemed ta have a pleasant ride hame,* she thought, smiling. Lizzie peeked in the bedroom off the kitchen and saw Eliza was dressed and just fixing her hair.

As a special Sunday treat, Lizzie made French pancakes, rolled with blueberries inside and served with lemon syrup. A few rashers of crisp bacon and coffee completed the meal.

Breakfast was served on the side porch in the summertime. It was easier for Eliza, because she didn't have to run the breakfast trays up and down stairs. The flowers, which usually adorned the trays, were gathered into one bouquet for the table. It was gratifying that even though the men and Isabelle seemed to think these little details were frivolous and took them for granted, Missus Twombly knew the work that had to be done to accomplish it, and how special it was. That was satisfaction enough for Lizzie.

After breakfast, Missus Twombly gave Eliza and Lizzie fifteen cents apiece. Lizzie protested, "But Missus Twombly, Mister Bachelor says he's taken care o' everything."

"That is true. And a finer man than Mister Bachelor would be hard to find. But, Doctor Twombly and I agreed, when going out with a gentleman, no matter how fine, a young lady should always have carfare home should an emergency arise. Always be prepared, so you may have the option to strike out on your own, if you deem it necessary. If you don't use it, then you may save it for another day. Now, do have a lovely time. I understand Mister Bachelor will be escorting you after church, and he will bring you home by sundown. Please give Mister Bachelor my regards."

The girls thanked her, and wished her well at her dinner party. *She thinks o' ever'thin',* thought Lizzie. *She's lookin' a little paler than yesterday, though. I hope she's all right. Maybe I should say something ta Miss Isabelle, though I don' think it's too worrisome.*

Later, when the family was going out to the carriage for the ride to church, Lizzie separated Isabelle from the rest of the group.

"Beggin' your pardon, Miss Isabelle, I notice Missus Twombly's lookin' a might more peaked t'day. I thought ye should knae."

"Thank you, Lizzie. I'll keep a close eye on her. I think the trip yesterday wore her out. If I think she's not up to it, I'll give our regrets to the Bakers and take her home to rest. I'm glad to have someone else's eye watching her, as I do, Lizzie."

"If ye think Eliza an' I shouldn't gae ta Boston, please let me knae," said Lizzie.

"Nonsense, I can make a sandwich, if it comes to that. She ate her breakfast and she may even perk up during church. We'll be fine."

"Very well, I'll check wit' ye afta church, should ye change yer mind," said Lizzie.

"That's very kind of you, Lizzie, but we'll be fine."

The church service seemed an eternity. Lizzie stretched to see Missus Twombly from the servants' pew. She couldn't really see her. She stopped looking for Missus Twombly, when she saw Charles Bachelor wave surreptitiously at her from the seat behind the Twomblys, perhaps thinking she was stretching to see him. She caught Eliza grinning, and glared at her in frustration.

Mister William also looked tired and pale as he took the pulpit for his sermon. He kept the sermon shorter than usual, as he seemed to be out of breath through most of it. *They both do sae much better on Martha's Vineyard.*

After the last 'amen', Lizzie made her way to Isabelle, with Eliza in tow.

"It's like I thought, girls. She's perked up during the sermon," said Isabelle. Lowering her voice, she added, "Truthfully, she nodded off a bit, but that's not unusual. I think we're fine. You have your afternoon with Mister Bachelor, and we'll see you tonight."

Lizzie was a little disappointed. She realized part of her wanted to stay home and miss the trip to Boston.

Am I crazy? Eliza wants ta gae, an' I wanted ta gae. Why am I resistin'? Mister Bachelor is a fine man! I don't feel 'bout him as

183

he does 'bout me, but it's only one afternoon. She knew it was the emotional encounter she did not want to face. *Maybe I'm makin' too much o' this. He said what he wanted ta say, as did I. Gae, Lizzie. Have a pleasant afternoon.*

Arm in arm, Mister Bachelor and the two servant girls walked to the train station. Eliza chatted without stop. Quiet and introspective, Lizzie and Charles pretended to listen. While Lizzie was serious, Charles' demeanor was light and excited, as if he had a secret he was bursting to reveal.

Distracted from her worry for Missus Twombly, and her talk with Charles the previous day, Lizzie stole a glance at Charles' beaming face. *What could he be thinkin'?* On the train, the two women sat together and Charles sat across facing them. *I hope Eliza ne'er runs down from her incessant chatter, 'cause I haven't the slightest idea how ta make conversation today.*

At South Station, they took a trolley to Park Street at the Common. Lizzie was surprised at the number of people strolling on the street and through the park. Standing on the sidewalk, Charles was looking around purposefully. Then a look of recognition came over him. He offered his arm to each woman, and began to walk into the park.

There by a park bench waving frantically was James! Eliza broke with Charles and ran to greet her cousin. Lizzie hung back with Charles, and said, "This jes' may be a perfect day, Thank yer, Charles. Ye're amazing'. Ye arranged all this?"

"It's what I wanted, to have a day where you and I, with Eliza and James, could be together, just as before. I learned many things about myself that day, and since. I owe that all to you, Lizzie. I had quite forgotten how much I missed the love of family, and the freedom of having a day to do nothing but play."

"Do ye have family here, Charles?"

"Sadly, no, my parents are gone. I had a sister, but she died of measles as a child. My aunts and my uncle went west when I was

184

very young, and I've lost touch with them. I have no regrets, except that I didn't realize how much I missed my family. Do you mind sharing yours with me?"

"Not at all, Charles, how did ye find James?"

"While your letter to him was in the hall, waiting for the mailman, Missus Twombly wrote down the address for me. While you were at the Vineyard, I went to Quincy and sought him out. We conspired to meet here and ride the swan boats."

"It's sech a wonderful surprise. I'll give him a fierce hug, then I may have ta wring his neck for no' writin' back ta me. I'll wait until after the swan boat ride, however," she said with a twinkle in her eyes. She broke from Charles to hug her cousin tightly. He lifted her off her feet and spun her around.

Laughing, James said, "I don't knae how Mister Bachelor kept his secret from yer, Fireball. Thet was all he could talk 'bout, how he dinna wanna be spillin' the beans."

"Well, if you want to ride the swan boats, we'll have to move along," said Charles. He offered his arm to Lizzie again. "Don't fret, my dear," he said quietly, "I ask no promises, and make none in return. Today, we'll just have some fun. You are safe from serious thoughts and endeavors."

"Very well, I'm sorry fer broodin'," she said. "I'm worried 'bout Missus Twombly. She dinna look good this morning. I think she may be gettin' sick again."

"Well, see if you can let that thought go for now, and we will check on her upon our return. We cannot know what is true or not, while we are here, so we may just as well enjoy ourselves."

"I knae yer right, Charles, I'll no' cast a pall on our day. If ye see me lookin' sad agin, remind me o' thet." Lizzie made an effort to smile, and in smiling, she did feel better.

"Indeed I will, Miss Heenan. Now, take my hand and we'll catch up with your sister and James." Weaving their way through bicycles and baby prams, Lizzie and Charles were at a near run.

185

Eliza and James were still up ahead, but they were closing in fast. Lizzie's hat flew off and bounced on her shoulders, her cheeks were rosy and she was grinning like a child. To Charles, she had never looked so beautiful. *If only...* he thought. *No 'if onlys' today, let her have a day of carefree fun. No promises, no maybes, no somedays, just today.*

Together again, the four crossed Charles Street to the Public Garden. "Oh look, Eliza, sea asters! But they're sae lush, an' sae many colors!"

"We just call those asters, they may be a different species than you're used to seeing. Here's a sign, *Aster Novae Angliae."* Charles read, *"New England Aster.* Well, it's slightly different, I'd say."

"Oh my, signs ta tell ye what ever'thin' is. What's this one?"

Oh, wouldn't Mother love this! This mus' be what Laird Annesley is doin' wit' his arboretum. With all the years he's been collectin' his plants, It mus' be huge by nae.

Lizzie hadn't thought of how an arboretum would be designed, just that the plants would be there. *The catalogues with all the Latin names are used on the signs fer each plant.* It was as if a door had been opened and she could see the future.

"Wouldn't Maggie *love* this place? This is wha' Laird Annesley is doin' in Castlewellan. All these years, I ne'er knew." Lizzie spoke with such passion, that the others just stared at her.

"Who is this Maggie," asked Charles, "And Lord Annesley?"

"I, fer one, ne'er cared much wha' Laird Annesley was about," said James darkly.

Eliza just looked from one to the other and reminded her cousin, "Laird Hugh Annesley was verra good ta us, James. He coulda jes' taken our land, but he forgave us the rent fer nearly two years, sae we could pay the taxes on it. Even if your Da bought the

186

land when he had the' chanct, then the laird still coulda foreclosed, but he didn't, fer a lot o folks. He's a *good* man, James."

"Oh, I'm sorry, Charles" Lizzie explained, "Maggie is my mother, Eliza's step-mother. She works fer Laird Annsley, cataloguin' the plants he brings hame for the arboretum he's building."

"That's an amazing undertaking, and he's doing it *himself*?"

"He and my mother, and his gardeners have been working on it fer years. I dinna knae how it would all come together, 'cause I only saw the plants come in, and my mother cataloguing them, then they went to Castlewellan. I've ne'er seen the arboretum itself, just the castle."

"So, it's like seeing the tail of an elephant and never seeing the head and trunk. This Lord Annsley is a landlord of sorts? I guess you'll have to tell me about it later, after we're on the swan boats. The line is long, and we must be in it to go on the boats. Come, this way, Heenans."

"C'mon, Ladies, there's no time to waste." James didn't want to talk about his family's farm and what he considered his failure as a son. Eliza and Lizzie exchanged glances, knowing they should avoid the subject if it advanced itself again in James' presence. The look that passed between them assured Charles Bachelor, he was decidedly out of his depth in the dynamics and history of the family Heenan. *I will have to ask my questions of Lizzie alone,* he thought.

After a short while in line, they climbed aboard the swan boat. Charles hung back to see if Lizzie would choose to sit with him or maneuver one of her siblings to take her place. She chose a seat and looked to Charles to sit by her. She was gratified to see the look of delight on his face. *He's sae thoughtful, an' I'm thankful, yet I dare no' let him hope for more.*

She lowered her voice, so the others would not hear. "I've only seen Laird Annesley about a dozen times in my life, but I usta

187

make up stories as a child 'bout him an' my ma. When I was older, I was introduced ta him by my mother. I had no idea they knew each other thet well. I always saw her work wit' his gardener, ne'er wit' him.

"As far as James was concerned, he was the absentee landlord. James resented the fact that the Laird forgave his father's rent, 'cause he couldn't get a fair price fer his crops. He felt 'twas the Laird's duty ta keep the prices up sae his Da an' his fellow farmers could make an honest wage. Truth is, the Laird fought fer it in the gov'ment, an' lost. James didn't think he tried hard enough.

"The English bought their goods elsewhere an' Ulster was left with its crops in the fields. Bad weather followed, an' the farm failed. Charles, I don't think he woulda come ta America, except fer the promise o' new land. Maggie says James' father has magic in his hands. He could grow corn from a rock, if needed. James wanted ta be a carpenter instead. Nae he feels bad, that he didn't stay ta help him."

"Well then," said Charles, "I hope James finds his land. A man is blessed who has a passion for his work. Sometimes a man's work chooses him, and his worth is measured only by what he brings to it. It sounds like James has passion enough for several men. I will pray that he finds the land he seeks, and that he can ply his trade, as well. Please pray, that I become worthy of the work I seek."

Charles and Lizzie, lulled by the smooth glide of the swan boat, fell silent, drifting along with their thoughts. "Look, Lizzie!" Eliza called from the front, "Swans, *real* swans."

There among the myriad of green hues reflected in the barely rippled water, were stark white swans with their grayish offspring behind them. Awestruck by their beauty, Lizzie stared contentedly as they floated by. She turned to Charles and was startled to see his eyes were solely on her. She caught her breath. "We are all transfixed by beauty, dear. Each man's heart chooses to define what beauty is to him," he whispered, smiling.

The swan boat bumped gently against its dock, to Lizzie's relief and regret, ending the ride. She stood up abruptly, and then scrambled to regain her footing and her composure at the same time. She was deeply moved by his last words. *No' his words,* she corrected herself, *his intensity.* Determined to lighten the mood, she said, "Would it be terribly rude ta tell yer, I'm verra hungry? There mus' be a street cart here somewhere." Charles laughed at her deflection.

"Back to Charles Street then, there will be plenty of carts there with sausage rolls, popcorn, fruit, chestnuts, roast potatoes, soup, root beer, tea, and coffee carts, if we're lucky. They are usually not all there at once, but there will be at least some of them there. If they've been cleared out, as sometimes happens, we can take a walk over to Scollay Square. It's less than a mile."

Someday, Lizzie thought, *this'll all be familiar ta me. But nae, the tall buildings, the noise an' all these people are a wee bit o'erwhelmin'. Charles takes it all in stride. I kin see the pride he takes in showin' us his Boston.* She thought wistfully, *Maggie, yer children are far from hame, an' we're seein' things o' the likes, ye'd ne'er dream.*

They ate at a bench on Charles Street, facing the Common. The food tasted so exotic and satisfying, it was a mere memory in no time.

The endless stream of carriages, with their horses decorated with ribbon rosettes, brass fittings, and polished leather bridles, were fascinating. The whole of Boston was on parade in their Sunday best, each one saying, 'Look at me, I am more beautiful than all the others.'

After eating, Charles stood, offered his arm, and said, "Shall we leisurely stroll the Common, my dear?" Lizzie smiled contentedly, and took his arm. Regretfully, she noticed the shadows were growing longer before them, and they would have to leave soon. In a low voice, Charles said, "Would you prefer to walk with James for a while? You haven't seen him since May."

"Thank yer, Charles, thet's very kind o' you, but I'll surely see him again, afore I see yer at Thanksgivin'." Her small sacrifice was richly rewarded by his beaming smile. He put his other hand over hers, nestled in the crook of his arm. *He is sae handsome, nae I can see his face.*

"Charles, tell me 'bout yer classes. What's university like? Ye have a room there?" Lizzie wanted to know enough to picture him in that place.

Charles answered each of her questions with such enthusiasm; she could see every detail, the tall brick buildings, the heavy text books and the young students rushing back and forth, with youthful exuberance. He described the library near the dormitory, with its vaulted ceilings, the long oak tables, tall spindled-backed chairs, and long rows of green-shaded lamps.

She pictured rows upon rows of books from the most brilliant minds in the world. He would be able to absorb all those works, and create his own philosophies to share with the world. Charles would do well there. He had no need of an ungrateful Irish country girl, green as grass, and devoid of manners or charm.

He saw the shadow cross her face. "What troubles you, Lizzie? Have I offended you?"

"No' a 'tall, Charles. It's been sech a perfect day, I'm sad ta see it end. Thank yer, Charles, fer keepin' a promise we'd no right ta expect, an' fer bringin' us James, fer the day. We're entirely in yer debt."

"In that case," he said his eyes bright with humor, "I have a request of my own. I know, I know, no promises. Will you write to me, Lizzie Heenan? Just a few lines, to keep my hope alive, that I'll see you again, at least at Thanksgiving?"

"I'll see yer on Thanksgivin' Day, but 'twill be a verra busy day fer me. I'll answer yer letters, should ye write, but no' too often. I want yer mind on your studies, an' the new friends ye will make. Ye will be sae hard at work, you won't haf' time ta think o' me, an' that's as it should be, Charles. Ye've the chanct ta be a minister. Every moment mus' be devoted toward yer goal," she answered. *Oh my, how self-righteous an' full o' yer ain conceit ye are, Lizzie Heenan!*

"Lizzie, Thanksgiving Day allows us a four day holiday. When students go home for a reprieve from their studies, I'll be coming home to you. You will have at least one afternoon off that week, with Missus Twombly's blessing. Surely, you could find some time for me." He was smiling, but a fear and sadness crept into his demeanor, so heartbreaking, she could not be stern with him.

"O' course, Charles, ye deserve more than I kin give, but I kin surely give ye the time I have," she said, shyly, humbled by the restrained emotion in his voice.

"Thank you, Lizzie, I am sorry to push you. I'm sad, too, that this day is nearly done. I am greedy to have you near me again. You have me feeling like a schoolboy, pulling pigtails for a girl's attention. Forgive me, if I don't want to be without you." His voice dropped to a whisper, hoarse and weighed with emotion.

She realized they had stopped walking, facing each other, talking so intently, they were attracting attention. Suddenly, coming to her senses, she looked up to see Eliza and James standing twenty feet ahead, staring at them. Her face turned red, and she silently cursed its betrayal of her deep emotion.

"Oh my, Charles, come. They are waiting fer us." She ran forward, pulling him behind her.

Laughing, Charles said, "Whoa, Lizzie! There are plenty of trolleys to catch. You'll want to take a little time to give James a proper goodbye." They were near the Park Street entrance of the Common. Trolleys of various destinations were arriving at curbside.

191

"James, ye knae I love ye as fierce as a cousin kin love, sae I need yer ta answer my letters. I want ta knae wha' yer thinkin' an' wha' yer plans are. It's cruel ta leave yer cousins waitin'." Lizzie growled at the man with the sheepish grin. She hugged him tightly, and then punched his shoulder.

"Yay-*ess*, *Mother*, I'll write me cousins onct in a while, ta tell them I'm still livin', an' haven't run off ta join the circus," James laughed, and winked broadly at Charles. "Why is it that Eliza here is content ta talk ta me all day. An' you come ta me late in the day, beggin' epistles o' my comin's, and goin's at ev'ry turn?"

"I have been occupying her time, I'll admit," Charles laughed good-naturedly. "Maybe if I *ignore* her charms, she'll deign to write to me, too, eh, James."

"I think she looks at you, with a lot more interes' than she has fer her poor cousin, Charlie, m' boy." Lizzie's face flushed again, and she punched James' shoulder again.

"Ouch! I caint imagine wha' ye see in her. She's a wild child, wit' a vicious manner about her." James danced out of reach of her next blow, laughing.

"It is precisely her charm, James. It was good to have your company again, my friend. Perhaps I'll see you again around Thanksgiving Day?" asked Charles, shaking his hand.

"An' when, exactly, would that be, Charles?"

"Oh dear, of *course*, how would you know?" he said. "Thanksgiving Day is the fourth Thursday of November. Since Lizzie and Eliza both will be working that day, I am hoping to convince Missus Twombly to let them have one day of that weekend off, to celebrate it on their own. I am also hoping they will include me in their holiday. And, of course, if you could be there, it would make the festivities complete," said Charles.

"Thets a whole shipload o' hopin', Charles. I wish ye some fine Irish luck ta gae wit' it. Lizzie will write ta tell me which day, I'm sure, if she hasn't disowned me, by then. I'll be there, ere die

192

tryin'." He planted a quick kiss on Lizzie's cheek to show her he meant no harm with his teasing.

James looked down the line of conveyances, gave Eliza a quick hug, and then loped off to board the Quincy trolley. The three stood there for a minute staring at the trolley that was pulling out of line. James reappeared in the window, waving. They watched waving until the trolley rounded the corner.

Charles took each girl by the elbow, and steered them toward the South Station trolley. "Alas, Ladies, it's time to go. I promised to have you home before dark, and I think we'll be just a little beyond last light. Missus Twombly will have my hide, if I cause a scandal bringing her girls home at an unseemly hour. What would the neighbors say?"

The train ride was short, but Eliza succumbed to slumber. The car was empty, except for the three, and Charles saw it as an opportunity. Lizzie stared out the window, lulled by the clacking of the wheels and the swaying of the car. "Lizzie." Charles whispered. As she turned to face him, he kissed her gently. Startled, she drew back, then surprising herself, she kissed him back. His nearness was heady. She smelled the starch in his collar, his shaving soap, saw the curl of the hair in his sideburns. She broke away. "Oh Charles, this is crazy."

"I know. Don't you think I've had that conversation with myself? She's a child with her whole life ahead of her. What would she want with me? God help me. I am completely infatuated, and have naught to do about it. I have nothing to offer and will have nothing for years. It *is* crazy and foolish and unforgivable, to want a future with someone so young. But, I feel like I am at the new beginning of my life, and I want to share it with you. I have never felt so free. I won't ask you to wait for me. I won't ask you to love me. Let me enjoy this feeling for now, and don't turn me away, just yet. When and if you give your heart away, I'll not ask for more than I've already had."

193

"Dear Charles. I'm afraid ta let ye hope. I am sae likely ta betray ye, an' I would hate myself fer it. I care fer you, Charles," she replied, her head down.

"Sh-h, this has been a wonderful day. Let's not spoil it with 'shouldn'ts' and 'maybes'. My heart is not your responsibility. So, let's enjoy the remaining moments, and not think about tomorrow." He sat back and smiled contentedly. Lizzie could not deny the pang of emotion deep in her core, and the light-headed euphoria the kiss had caused. *My goodness, I am near ta faintin'.* She was surprised at the whirl of emotions flooding her mind. *This is foolish! I've kissed a boy before. Why am I sae befuddled? Ah, that's jes' it. Charles is no boy that ye kin play wit' an' say 'no' ta. It'll be harder ta say 'no' ta this man than ye planned. Nae, you're fightin' against sayin' no.*

Just then, Eliza woke. *Oh my,* she thought, *something's happened. Charles is smilin' from ear ta ear. Lizzie has her head down with no smart repartee for him.* Eliza smiled in wonder. *Lizzie doesn't have the upper hand. Hail the conquerin' hero, Charles! Poor Lizzie, she's sae usta havin' control o' ev'ry situation.*

The three alit from the train and strolled home with almost no conversation. Charles was on the street side, then Lizzie, then Eliza. "Thank you, fer today, Charles. A lovelier day I've ne'er seen," said Eliza quietly, not wanting to break the reflective mood.

Charles nodded in agreement, meeting her eyes. Lizzie walked between them not hearing, her head still bowed in thought. Except for holding Charles' arm, she would have stumbled aimlessly, not knowing where she was.

Soon, they were in the yard, approaching the back door. "Good night, Charles, thank yer." Eliza stretched to her tiptoes and kissed his cheek.

"You're welcome, Eliza. She'll be in shortly." He stopped short of the light from the window.

In the gathering shadows he held Lizzie close. After a long moment, he raised her chin, and kissed her deeply. There was no resistance, and then slowly, the passion built. When she kissed him back, it shook him. He broke the kiss, and cradled her gently. He kissed her forehead, and said hoarsely, "You should go in now, Lizzie, go. Write to me." He led her to the back door, opened it, and gently pushed her in. She looked back at him, confusion in her blue eyes, so fragile, and tender.

He watched her go in, and then bounded off the porch, to the front yard, and down the street. God and the devil would fight for his soul that night. Charles fought for the heart of a red-haired girl and won. *Or, did he?*

Chapter Thirteen

The next few months slipped into a routine, interrupted only by the intermittent signal of the post man, letting Lizzie know she had mail. She had confided in him one day, that she was anticipating letters from some very special people. When he delivered the mail on most days, he just dropped them in the slot. If there was a letter for Lizzie, however, he would knock on the door three times.

Of course, she couldn't just drop what she was doing to get the mail, but it was a thrill to hear the three knocks, just the same. She knew Eliza would bring the mail in to the family, and get her mail to her as soon as she could. Lizzie wrote letters to her mother and Móraí, to James, and to Charles. She had received one letter from James, several from her mother, but none from Charles.

She was surprised how the absence of letters from Charles disappointed her. After inventing several excuses for him, she decided perhaps she should be grateful. After all, she had professed to wanting just that, little or no attention, where there was so little hope. Then, the memory of the last few moments with him, rekindled the heat of her imagination. Her frustration seemed boundless. *Ye don' want it, 'til ye canna have it! Yer such a stupid child, Lizzie Heenan!*

196

Knock, Knock, Knock. There it was. The leap of anticipation rising in her chest would only be met with probable disenchantment, again. *It's ridiculous ta get sae excited after sae many days o' disappointment,* she thought. *Here 'tis the end o' October an' no' a word from him, an' you want ta run fer the door in the hope o' a letter. It's pro'bly mother, tellin' me the news o' the village.*

Lizzie thrust her hands into the ever-present dishwater, willing herself not to care.

"Lizzie! Lizzie!" Eliza burst into the kitchen, looking around. She spoke in a low, but excited voice, "It's from *Charles!*"

Lizzie dried her hands, trying to keep them from shaking. She tore open the envelope and read:

Dearest Lizzie,

I hope this letter finds you well. I pray too, that the Twomblys and Eliza are well also.

My studies are overwhelming, but I am keeping my head above water, as they say. It is thanks in part to my new study partner and tutor, Millicent Palmer. I would like you to meet her. She is bright and accomplished, has received her Bachelor degree from Wellesley, and has been granted special permission to use the Harvard library for her theological research studies.

I have so much to learn, but Millie reminds me that my years of living to this ripe old age, have taught me to respect the teaching I receive, and I am more receptive to it, than my junior colleagues.

I miss all the Heenans, and hope you are still willing to see me during the Thanksgiving break. Your letters have been most welcome, and I apologize for not attending to them, before now. I plead weariness, from the arduous and unfamiliar journey I am taking. I seem to be climbing mountains of Latin, science and literature books, only to reveal even more mountains to scale.

In the wee hours of the morning, I have had time to reflect upon our last meeting, and I am appalled at my behavior. Overcome

197

by the aspect of not seeing you for months, I must have taken complete leave of my senses. I have taken advantage of your innocence, and for that I should be flogged. You are a beautiful, charming young lady, and I have accosted you in a most shameful manner. I hope you can forgive me. I will understand, if you do not wish to see me again.

May the Lord bless you, and keep you safe from harm, until we meet again.

Ever your friend,
Charles Titus Bachelor

Lizzie's head was spinning with angry, fearful questions. Who's this Millie person? Is he tryin' ta spurn me in a gentle way? Am I jes' a child ta him, nae thet he's surrounded by educated people? He misses the Heenans, no' me?

Seeing her half sister face contort into anger, sadness, and worry while she read the long-anticipated letter, Eliza asked, "Lizzie, wha' is it? Is he ill? Wha's wrong, Lizzie?"

"He's fine, Eliza. I'll read the letter, agin later. Maybe I'm readin' it wrong. I'll read it ta ye, an' see wha ye think. I have work ta do nae, an' sae do you."

Lizzie attacked the dishes with such fury, Eliza backed out of the room. For the rest of the day, Lizzie was a whirlwind of activity born of anger, frustration, and hurt.

Later, in her room, she and Eliza read the letter again. "Lizzie, please don' assume the wors'. Wha' he said, doesn't necessarily mean any o' the things you're thinkin'. He met an' respects a woman who's helpin' him. It doesn' necessarily mean he has those kinds o' feelin's fer her, like he does fer you. He thinks he's overstepped his bounds wit' ye, an' is contrite. He misses all o' us. Remember, you dinna want him ta single you out, thet you dinna feel about him the way he feels about you. You wanted ta let him gae gently. Maybe ye've succeeded. He still wan's ta see yer. How do ye feel about him, nae?"

"I don' knae, I hafta admit I liked it better when he wanted ta be wit' me, no' her. I knae, I don' wanna spend my whole life tryin' ta be a minister's wife, an' failin' ever'day. He confuses my senses, Eliza. How kin I be sae selfish? I don' want ta spend my life wit' him, but I don' wan' someone else ta take him from me. I'm a terrible person, Eliza."

"I think he's awakened somethin' in yer, thet yer afraid o' knowin'. Ye love the attention he's given yer, an' yer reluctant ta give it up. Maybe yer a little jealous, thet someone could take thet attention away. If ye've made up yer mind about no' wantin' ta spend ye life wit' him, ye've got ta let him knae, Lizzie. If ye hafta hurt him, do it soon, don' dance aroun' it. If ye think ye might wan' him, tell him thet, then. He's no' a boy. Wha' ye mus' no' do, is play wit' his heart. Wha' will it be, Lizzie?"

"Oh, Eliza, I knae yer right, I jes' don' knae if *I'm* right. I've waited sae long ta git a letter from him, nae I don't knae how ta answer it."

"Well, before ye start, take each line he writes fer wha' it says, wit'out tryin' ta change its meanin'. Be sure ye say wha' yer want ta say, wit' no regrets. When ye've thought it all through, write ye letter from yer heart."

When Eliza went to bed, Lizzie struggled over the letter she was to write. After the third attempt, she wrote:

Dear Charles,

I hope you remain well. I truly miss you, and am looking forward to seeing you, at Thanksgiving time. Eliza and I talk about it from time to time. I've written James to let him know we expect him here.

I'm happy you found someone with whom you can study, and share your interests. I am sure you will do well with your studies with her help. I pray every night for your success.

Doctor and Missus Twombly are very proud of you, with regard to your pursuit of the study program for the ministry. They often ask, if I have heard from you. They are eager to hear any news of you.

Please do not concern yourself about your actions, when last we met. Nothing you have done causes me any consternation. I have no regrets, nor should you. I hold you in the highest regard, as I will continue to do so, when you reach your goal as minister. On that day, I will proudly say, "I am honored to know this man."

God bless you and keep you in the palm of His hand.

Ever your humble servant,

Lizzie Heenan

Slowly, she read her letter through, hoping she set the right tone. Satisfied, she quickly folded it, sealed it and addressed it, before she could change her mind in the wording. She placed a penny with the letter to give the postman in the morning. That night, alone with her thoughts, she recalled the kiss that almost convinced her to become a minister's wife.

The next morning, she heard the three sharp knocks again. Who could that be? Surely not James, sae it must be from mother. I hope everything is all right…

It was late that night before Lizzie could read her letter from Maggie. She opened it with a trepidation she did not understand. She had received many letters from Maggie and Móraí, none of which were anything but newsy missiles of the village. She read aloud to Eliza as they huddled on Lizzie's bed in their nightgowns.

Darling Lizzie,

I pray every night for your well being, and for that of Eliza and James. It is difficult for me to write this letter to you. Mórai, God rest her soul, passed away peacefully in her sleep, five nights ago. I wish I could be there to hold you, as you read these words. She's at peace now, Lizzie. Her last words were of you. She said to me, "Do not fret about Lizzie. She will take care of Eliza and James. She will always stand strong. She knows her own mind."

I am writing this epistle from Castlewellan. Laird Annesley arranged a room for me at the castle, after Mórai's funeral. My room is far away from him and his family, but he has seen to my every need.

His wife has been very gracious about my being here, and sometimes comes to visit me. She is very young, and is with child. She seeks my advice and I freely give as much as I can. She is a lady, but treats me as if I were of noble blood, as well. I don't know what Laird Annesley has told her about me, but she shows no animosity toward me. Against her husband's wishes, she will go to London for the rest of her confinement to be with her mother.

Laird Annesley is making arrangements for me to leave here November 31st, to arrive in New York, December 10th. He thinks this is the best course of action for me. I cannot stay here, and I long to see my children. I hope to be living near you, by Christmas. I will have enough money to pay my room and board for about six months.

Your uncle John is still at the farm. He seems to do best alone. There is a woman from the village, who comes to clean, and make him supper, for a small fee. Lord Annesley says he will send the assistant gardener, to make sure John has all he needs.

My dear children, I am so sad to bring you this news, but I do look forward to seeing you again. God bless you, my dear children.

Your Loving Mother

As she handed the letter to Eliza, who was watching her face as she read, her eyes were filled with tears. Eliza leaned toward her sister to hold her. Lizzie stared straight ahead, stone-faced, and unmovable. Her eyes were bright with questions, and frustrations unspoken.

Oh Laird, what am I going ta do? How will I take care o' her? Maggie canna cook on a stove. I dinna even knae if they will let her stay! She's an invalid. They could put her in the hospital and send her home, wit'out even steppin' foot on shore. We saw thet at Ellis Island. If she even survives the trip, she may no' be allowed into this country.

Lizzie remembered the long nights of misery during the storm at sea. What kin ye be thinkin', Maggie? An' Laird Annesley, how could ye advise her ta do this? She has no sponsor, no job, and no residence here.

After turning and tossing half the night, Lizzie finally fell asleep. She heard the church bells ring, heralding the new day almost immediately after her eyes closed. She woke with tears on her cheeks, and heaviness in her heart. When she left home, she knew she would never see Móraí again, but knowing her grandmother was with Maggie was comforting. Now, she was gone, and there was an emptiness she knew she could never fill.

Her immediate concern was Maggie, though. Today, she would seek advice from Doctor Twombly. He would know what to do, wouldn't he?

Eliza was pale and sad as she entered the kitchen for the breakfast trays. *Poor Eliza, Maggie's as much her mother as mine. She's known no other. Móraí was so like her own grandmother and she misses her dearly. It looks like she dinna sleep, either.*

Lizzie said to her, "It'll be all right, Eliza. I'll talk to Doctor Twombly to see what he can tell us about a place fer Maggie ta live, how ta git her here, an' whether he thinks she'll be able ta stay.

We'll take one step at a time, an' figure it out. There's nothin' else we kin do, is there?"

"Ye think so? Maybe the Earl will put her in first class? They would take care o' her there, wouldn't they? Ye think they'll quarantine her?" asked Eliza.

"Well, we dinna knae anythin' at this point, do we?" Lizzie replied, exasperated. Seeing Eliza was close to tears, she softened her tone. "It's been a big week fer both of us hasn't it? We'll git through it."

The girls went through their routines, keeping their thoughts on the tasks at hand. Finally, after supper, Doctor Twombly sat in the rocker to read the paper.

"Doctor Twombly, sir? May I seek yer advice on a matter?" Lizzie asked nervously.

"Of course, Lizzie, what's troubling you?" answered the robust old man.

Lizzie presented the letter to him, without explanation. He looked over his glasses, then down at the letter, reading slowly with concern. "Lizzie, I am so sorry. Who is this Móraí, of whom she speaks?"

"She is my grandmother, Doctor Twombly. She was very old and frail. Sixty, I think."

The seventy-seven year old minister cleared his throat, "Sixty. My goodness, I'm sure she is at peace now, with our Lord. I'm truly sorry for your sadness, child. How may I help you?"

Lizzie poured out all her concerns about her mother's trip to America to him, as she sat at the kitchen table.

"Well, Lizzie, first, I think you should write to your mother, or perhaps this Lord Annesley, to find out what the problems really are. Perhaps they have solved some of them already between them. If she sails first class as Eliza was thinking she may, her trip would be much more comfortable, wouldn't it? Also, she would be treated as a guest, when she reached Ellis Island too, I suspect. First class passengers are processed aboard ship, and after going through customs at Ellis Island, are free to enter the United States. Depending on her arrival date, perhaps we could entreat Mister Bachelor to collect her at New York, and bring her to Newton Lower Falls? Of course, we must line up our schedules to arrange that, won't we? I assume you and he are still on friendly terms?"

Lizzie turned deep red. "I think so, but I don't hear from him often, sir."

"Very well, he will be here at Thanksgiving, at any rate." He smiled knowingly and raised an eyebrow. "Sometimes, Missus Twombly confides the household intrigues to me."

He continued, "We have a few very respectable boarding houses in the area, where she could be comfortable, I think. This would allow her room and meals, for a reasonable weekly stipend. If we investigate the ones closest, perhaps we can find one that would have a room, water closet, and dining room, all on the same floor. If it had a porch on the same level, she could even take fresh air as she wanted. It may take a little doing, but it's possible. When your time with us is up, then you can find a situation that is suitable wherever you find employment. What do you think so far?"

"Oh Doctor Twombly, I knew you'd knae wha' ta do! Thank yer, I will write ta them t'night. An' on our next day off, Eliza an' I will look fer boarding houses, fit fer Maggie's chair, thank ye sae much!"

"You are very welcome, my dear. I'm glad I could shed some light on the problem," he said. "Now, would you like to hear the latest news about Lizzie Borden?"

"Oh aye, sir, have the journalists been cruel ta her again?" Lizzie asked eagerly.

Doctor Twombly smiled, and read from a short column on the second page. *At least it wasn't in the headlines on the front,* he thought. *They never seem to run out of something to say, about this poor, unfortunate woman. A person is supposed to be presumed innocent, until proven guilty. Even if the court finds her not guilty, she will never be shown to be innocent.*

Like our Lizzie, I am much too eager to see what the newspapers will find to say about this notorious woman.

Later, in her room, Lizzie looked out her window at the cold night sky. As she always did, she pictured Maggie in Ireland, staring at the same stars, wondering what she was doing, or thinking. This time, the vision of Móraí came, unbidden. She was in her familiar chair by the fire, huddled in her tartan, praying. Lizzie picked out the North Star from the pattern of tiny lights in the sky. This was her portal to those whom she lost: her father, her brother, Little James, who died from measles; Eliza's grandmother; even the people she didn't know, but for the stories her family told her. The star faded from her sight, and she realized she was crying.

Oh Maggie, how do I say goodbye? My father, and nae my grandmother, are gone wit'out a word. I still have sae much ta say ta them. Can they hear me? Do they knae I still love them? In that moment, she stopped worrying how to get her mother to America. She knew it had to happen. *Come, Maggie, come ta us. We need you.*

In Castlewellan:

Maggie heard a knock on her door. "Enter." she said carelessly, thinking it was the kitchen boy with her afternoon tea.

"Maggie? I hope I'm not intruding. I need to talk to you." Lord Annesley spoke barely above a whisper. His carriage bowed, his demeanor somber, the Earl stepped into the room.

"Hugh? You shouldn't be here. You know she visits me in the afternoon. Why are you here?" Maggie asked anxiously.

"She's gone, Maggie. She's gone to London. I didn't want to let her go, but I cannot deny her. She wants to be with her mother. I'll follow her, after you've sailed. She's insisting I stay, while you're here." He arched his eyebrow wryly, and mimicking his young wife, he said, "After all, we have a guest in our home." Then, seriously, he said, "Lady Priscilla begs me to give you her regrets, that she did not say goodbye."

He hung his head. "We argued before she left. She is embarrassed I housed my dear friend and confidant, so far away from our living quarters. She finds you most endearing." He looked up at last and met Maggie's eyes. "God help me, so do I."

"Please sit down, Hugh. Have tea with me." Maggie gestured toward the French brocade settee. "Why are you so agitated?"

"Why? That enchanting creature I married to be mother to my children, and ensure an heir to the estate, *hates* Castlewellan, *hates* the North of Ireland, and after only four months of marriage is running home to her mother."

"Oh poor Hugh, she is but a child herself. She is frightened to distraction, in a strange place, with children who lost their mother not so long ago. No wonder she's homesick. Are the children with her, or did she leave them with you?"

"She left them with me. I am to take them to London, when I go there. Before we married, she loved everything, but now nothing interests her but the new clothes on her back, and how fast she can get back to that filthy, God-forsaken City of London!" He ground the last words through his teeth, with obvious distain. "I swear I would get an annulment, if she were not already with child."

"Hugh, stop, just listen to yourself. You'll work yourself into apoplexy. It took a while for Mabel to adapt to your life here, and it wasn't overnight, Hugh. Priscilla will come around. She misses all the attention an unmarried young lady receives at court. She's lonely, scared, and sick every morning. She will do better, once she has a few familiar faces around her. Perhaps, after the bairn is born, she could bring someone back to Castlewellan with her, in the spring. She will certainly not be amenable, if you go to London, growling like a bear!"

Hugh smiled. He was a little ashamed of himself. "I suppose you're right. But then, you usually are, Maggie."

"Give her some time. Show her you want her happiness, as well as her children, and perhaps she will want your happiness, too," laughed Maggie.

"Maggie, I am so sorry. I am so full of me and mine; I never asked how you were. Is this room adequate? I cannot imagine the consternation of my wife coming here to visit with you. You are a wonder, Maggie. How do you manage to be just whom everyone needs, at a moment's notice?" His eyes softened, and he touched her cheek.

"It's easy, Hugh. All anyone needs who comes to see me is someone to listen to them. No one expects an invalid to act on a problem, or cast judgments like an able-bodied person. I just open my ears, and close my mouth."

There was a knock on the door once again. This time, Hugh said, "Enter."

The kitchen boy came in, set the tea on the table and asked nervously, "Lord Annesley, shall I bring tea for you as well?"

"Yes, Jeremy. That would be fine, just another setting, however. There is enough here to share," the Earl said. When the boy had gone, he added, "I see you have made an impression on the kitchen staff, Maggie. They seem to think you need more nourishment, than you're getting." His hand swept over the tray piled high with sandwiches and tea cakes. "…unless you were expecting a party of four? Ah, but, I see there is only one cup."

Maggie laughed. "The kitchen boy, Jeremy, confided in me that the cook thinks I am much too thin, and has promised to fatten me up."

There was another discrete knock, and another tea setting. After the boy left, Hugh poured tea, sat at her feet and ate ravenously. Maggie rested her hand on his silver hair, as she sipped her tea. "Maggie, you're not eating. Are you well? I am so inconsiderate. I keep rambling on about my own troubles, without a thought of all you've been through."

"I'll be fine, Hugh. I am sad, and that's to be expected. I miss mother in so many ways, but especially so, since Lizzie, Eliza, and James are gone. Young Joseph and Johnnie spend all their time at the farm, and I cannot bear to be isolated like John. This trip to America will be just what I need."

"I will arrange it so you will travel in comfort in first class, and there should be no difficulty for you entering the country. First class passengers are not subject to the same processing as are the steerage passengers. Since you have employed relatives in the United States, you are not considered a risk for becoming a public charge. I will send a letter to your children, so they will be assured you are taken care of properly."

"Hugh, surely not first class, you have done so much for me, I ...." Hugh raised his hand to stop her plaintive speech.

"It is the very least I can do. I have had cause to regret many things in my life, but I will never regret anything I do for you. You owe me nothing, my love." He spoke quickly, as if he were afraid it would not leave his mouth. He kissed her forehead and she leaned into it.

The simple gesture was so charged with emotion, she said, "Please Hugh, you must go. I will not betray that dear, sweet child, who thinks I am merely an old friend. I will not be a party to broken vows between a man and his wife. We have never broken a marital trust, and I will not commence now."

Hugh stood, saw her sudden tears and took out his handkerchief. They both laughed softly, at the unspoken memories it brought. "I will go, though it is not my honor I would save, but yours," he said, sadly.

"From now on, Maggie, we will meet in my quarters in the company of others. I promise this. We will not be alone, if I have to drag my gardener in to dine with us. I know you are right, though I dare not trust my heart to obey your rules. My heart is a rogue, or it never would have found you, my love." He stood, kissed her hand as he would any lady, and turned in military posture to leave the room.

Maggie bowed her head and let the tears flow, tears as yet unshed for her mother, again for her father, and her husband. She wept, too, for love barred from fulfillment.

Newton Lower Falls:

Drawing away from the window, Lizzie wrote her letter, trying to choose the words that would not be discouraging, yet asking the questions to which she needed answers.

In her heart, she prayed, *Heavenly Father, Please help us find a way to bring her here without suffering the agonies we endured. Laird, bring her to us safely, and in good health. Help us to find a way to care for her. In Christ's holy name, I ask it, Amen.*

Her conversation with Doctor Twombly had calmed her fears to a manageable worry. She remembered Móraí saying, *ye do all the things ye kin do yersel' first, then ye pray o'er the things ye canna do, twixt God an' the fairies, the things b'tween will take care o' themsel's.*

She sealed her letter, took out yet another penny, and put it on the table for the morning. Seems like a lot o' letters comin' in an' out o' the Twombly's house this week. Yawning, she gently pushed Eliza aside, and climbed into bed. *She doesn' sleep upstairs much anymore, does she?* Lizzie thought. *There must be ghosties up there. Or, more likely, the branch thet rubs on the roof o'er her room. I'll hafta git Big John ta look at it in the mornin'.*

The rest of the week was uneventful, and then on Sunday, October 30th, Missus Twombly planned a special menu for the next night, Halloween.

"The emphasis is on the children, Lizzie. We should have beef stew, mulled cider, plenty of apples for bobbing, divinity fudge, little pumpkin cakes with orange icing, and a smiling jack-o-lantern

209

with a candle in it for the table. We're having a little party for the Bakers, their children, and Garrett, if he's willing. Missus Baker will sneak over here early, to help decorate, and set up for games. She'll have the baby with her. Mister William will go to the Baker's house, for a special Halloween treat they have planned for the children. Oh, this will be such fun!"

Lizzie and Eliza smiled at the surprising glee Missus Twombly was taking in her narrative.

The following night, a small wash tub was placed in the kitchen with about 6 inches clear water in the bottom and a dozen apples floating in it. That afternoon, Lizzie watched the improbable scene of Mister William, sitting on the back porch, in a heavy leather apron, carving a ghastly, leering face in a pumpkin. He looked up at her, smiled, and said, "Don't tell, but it's always been my favorite time of year! It's not very dignified, or churchlike, but all in good fun. The solemnity of tomorrow's All Hallows Day will come soon enough. There, what do you think?"

"I think it's very scary, Mister William," said Lizzie, watching him beam with pride. *I ne'er woulda guessed the Twomblys would be sae excited about Halloween. They're like children. It's nice ta see them like this. It's almost like bein' back at Martha's Vineyard!*

"Oh, Lizzie, can you get me a length of rope about six feet long? I need it for the ghost walk."

"I think there's one here, in the basket for the clothes lines. I wondered why it was sae short. It doesn't fit the porch lines or the post lines."

"Perfect, we'll tie a knot in each end, and we'll blindfold the children and lead them all over the yard, ending up at the kitchen door. I'll hold one end, while Eulah holds the rope next to my hand, Frank holds the rope next to Garrett's hand and Mister Baker is last, with little Laura, so he can pick her up, if the little one gets too scared. The children think we are blindfolded too, and they are guiding us, so we bump into them once in a while for effect. We'll go between the bushes, around a tree, up the porch steps, and down the other steps." Lizzie could see Mister William was taking fiendish delight in his role as leader. "I'd better get started, if the darkness catches us, we might as well be all blindfolded. It's good, it's not raining."

Lizzie marveled at this new insight of the younger minister's character. *Who would have thought Mister William would enjoy scrambling around in the dark, with the children? There is sae much hidden in the people, we think we knae.*

Later, she could hear the group in the yard, the children, squealing, and yelping with delight at each new sound, and bump of unseen ghosties. The men were making howling noises, rustling through the trees. The cold, crisp air blew in ahead of them, as they came in the backdoor, their blindfolds discarded. The children's cheeks rosy, and their eyes bright with excitement, rushed to their mother, talking all at once, reporting their Halloween adventures. Missus Baker took off their coats and hats, and hung them on the cellar door, ushering them to the dining room, where their hot apple cider was waiting.

As the group followed them, Garrett lingered back to talk to Lizzie. She was busy at the stove, but asked him how he was, and how the work was going. He seemed content enough to sit in the rocker for a moment, and talk. Lizzie tried not to be distracted from her menu. Everything had to come together at the same time.

"Garrett, perhaps you'd better git ta the dining room. This is about ta be set on the table."

"Yes, ma'am," he said with a sarcastic edge to his voice. Eliza swung the door open to start service, and hit him square on the nose. The next few minutes were occupied by getting Garrett back down in the rocker, with a towel to his blood-gushing nose, and Eliza apologizing profusely for having injured him. Missus Twombly came in, wondering what the commotion was.

211

"My goodness, there is more noise in here than in the dining room with the children. What is going on?"

""Everything is under control nae, ma'am. Mister Johannson has bloodied his nose, an' we were trying ta help stop it."

"I'll not ask how this came to be, but you young ladies could start serving. Mister Johannson, I trust you are not mortally injured? Lizzie, give him one of Mister William's shirts. All that blood will add too much authenticity to the children's Halloween imagination. When you are presentable, young man, you may join us in the dining room." Missus Twombly nodded and left the kitchen.

"Da...er... Good heavens." Garrett struggled to correct his speech. "I hope yer not in trouble because of me. I'm such an ox."

"Yer fine, jes' take this shirt to the water closet, an' change. I'll soak yers, an' git it back to ye tamarra." Lizzie gently pushed him. "Gae now, afore we're all in trouble, fer delayin' the meal."

"Yes, Lizzie," he said, in a not so sarcastic tone, this time.

Within a minute, everything was back to normal. After supper, the children came back to the kitchen to bob for apples. Lizzie had sticks to put their apples on and caramel heated on the stove to coat them. "I'll bring them inta the dining room, in jes' a minute." When the children left, Lizzie took the apples and coated them. Taking the Indian pudding from the oven, she drizzled a vanilla hard sauce upon it and set the desserts on a tray.

Once the table was cleared, all the lamps, but one, were extinguished. The jack-o-lantern was put in the kitchen. Doctor Twombly, using hand shadows and simple paper silhouettes on sticks, began the story of *The Boy Who Cried Wolf*. His voice was slow and deep as the narrator, high and scared for the boy, and angry for the villagers. He adopted menacing animal sounds as needed to complete the dramatic effect.

The children were fascinated by all the animals the minister could make, just using his hands, casting shadows on the wall. There was a barking dog, a howling wolf, a bear, and an old man.

No less amazed was Eliza, who stood at her station by the door, watching.

When the children were very tired, the Bakers bundled them up, and carried them home. Garrett took the oldest, with a promise to return the minister's shirt the next day.

Lizzie washed the homespun shirt in cold water, poured hydrogen peroxide on it, rinsed it and hung it on the porch to dry. Although the air was cool, she was confident it would not freeze overnight. In the morning, she would hang it in the kitchen away from the stove.

Although Lizzie would have a hard time admitting it, the idea of hanging the shirt on the porch was Móraí's superstition, that blood spilled on Halloween night, could be purified by the early morning sun of All Hallows Day. *It canna hurt, an' might do the trick,* she thought.

That night, she reflected on how nice it was to see Garrett after two month's time. She wished she had time to talk to him about his job with Mister Baker. *It mus' be workin' out, since he's still livin' there. I wonder what he thinks o' wearing Mister William's fine shirt. He's probably ne'er wore one like thet before. Nor would he need ta, I suppose, bein' a carpenter. O' course, we really don' knae anything' 'bout him, an' what he's used ta, do we?* She smiled, when she remembered his near slip of the tongue when he thought he caused the girls to be in trouble with Missus Twombly. *He mus' constantly have ta mind his language at the Bakers. I've heard Mister Baker fired a man once, fer usin' bad language on the job.* In Garrett's recent history at least, he was used to a lot rougher company than the religious Baker family.

I'll hafta bring Garrett's shirt ta the Bakers myself. I'm sure he'll be workin' 'til Saturday afternoon, an' I should git Mister William's shirt washed, an' back ta him afore then. Maybe I should send Eliza with the shirt...

Lizzie went to bed dreaming of children, Halloween, and her friend, the mysterious Garrett Johansson.

Chapter Fourteen

November blew in with an air of excitement. Lizzie woke one morning, to see snow dancing in the air, and the trees glistening with frost, in the morning sun. Gray clouds soon moved over the sky, smothering the sparkling lights, but not before Lizzie had made it a dazzling memory.

This place has sae many kinds o' weather, she thought in wonder. *I've seen sunshine, snow, rain, drizzle, frost and mist, all in a single week. An' the temperature seems ta go up an' down at a whim.*

The morning seemed to disappear, covered in a dull gray fog and Lizzie's bright spirits along with it. She hadn't heard from anyone to whom she had written, for what felt like a long time.

She had searched out the boarding houses as Doctor Twombly suggested, and found two that seemed suitable, but without more information, she dare not make any arrangements for her mother. She had no money to secure a deposit, so it was a moot point, she supposed. She stopped short of thinking, *what if....* She would not venture a guess as to what could happen if she was not prepared for her mother's arrival. Also weighing on her mind, was Charles Bachelor. He was also among the unresolved problems plaguing her thoughts. James, too, had not replied one word. The

215

suspense of waiting for the mail was almost unbearable. *Was thet a knock?*

Did she really hear it? She opened the kitchen door to see if Eliza stopped to get the mail. She didn't see anyone, but she thought sure there was a knock on the front door. She could see the shadow of the mailman in the lace-covered window of the front door. Just as she stepped a foot into the hallway, she heard Eliza rushing down the stairs. Lizzie retreated to her kitchen, knowing Eliza would bring her the mail as soon as she could, if indeed, there was anything that belonged to her. She checked the oven and saw the unbaked cheese biscuits were still on the counter, forgotten in her anxiety.

As she slipped the biscuits into the oven, she heard Eliza hiss, "Lizzie!"

"Aye, what?" she answered, closing the oven door with a clatter.

"It's a letter… from Laird Annesley!" Eliza's excited voice whispered, as she held the envelope out to her. "Hurry, Lizzie. Open it!"

Lizzie turned the envelope over in her hands. There was the red seal with Hugh Annesley's ring stamped in it. The careful swash of the writing made her name look elegant, even regal. The fine textured paper was the color of rich cream. "Open it, Lizzie," begged Eliza.

Not breaking the seal, Lizzie sliced the top of the envelope with a sharp knife and slipped the letter out. She read:

My dear Miss Elizabeth Jane Heenan,
    Lizzie, if you would permit me,
    I hope this letter finds you well. I was pleased to have met you before your trip to the United States, and I trust you have fared well in both your journey, and your current situation.
    I have talked to your mother at length about her impending trip to America. I want you to be assured her passage is arranged in

216

full. She has refused first class, but she will travel second class to avoid any undue discomfort during her sail. I am assured that there will be no difficult interrogation at The Port of New York. Her papers will be in order, and there should be no problem with her entering the United States, for a duration to be determined by the current laws of the United States for foreign visitors.

If you would arrange at your end, to have her met by your envoy, and transported comfortably to Newton, I would be most grateful. Your mother and your envoy will have sufficient funds to pay for her transport from the Port of New York to Newton Lower Falls, in addition to six months' lodging and board. If you have any reason to believe it is not sufficient, please inform me immediately, and allow me to address the situation.

It will be my honour to see your mother safely aboard the City of Chester, *at Liverpool, England, November 30th, to arrive at the Port of New York, December 10th. If your envoy will make himself known, the Master of the Ship, Frederick Passow, will transfer responsibility of your mother's wellbeing to him.*

Master Passow is a personal friend from my days in service to the Queen. He will see to it that your mother is well cared for in my absence. I regret I must pass this duty off to him, but circumstances and my duties, make it impossible for me to travel at this time.

It is with great reluctance that I send your mother to you. However, her longing for her children is greater than my ability to deny her. When I met you, I was impressed with your independent spirit, your practical nature, and your apparent strength of character. I believe you will use all of those qualities to care for your mother. Should she desire to return to Castlewellan, it will be my honoured duty to make that possible for her.

Please accept the bank note enclosed, to secure a place for your mother's stay. If you, together with your sponsor (or a citizen of United States of your choosing), present it to a Federal bank along with your papers, you will be able to have the funds released to you. The funds are to be used for the first three months of your mother's room and board, in a suitable establishment of your choosing. May I humbly suggest you pay the establishment in advance, for one month's stay, and then open a bank account to deposit the balance for safe-keeping. Your mother will have a similar amount for an additional three months, with her.

God bless you, and keep you. God keep your mother safe, and in good health, until we meet again.

Most cordially, Hugh Annesley

She looked at the letterhead again. The Honourable Hugh Annesley, Fifth Earl Annesley, of Castlewellan in the County of Down, and Viscount Glerawly, in the County of Fermanagh. *Ma, this 'friend' o' yours, is more than 'friend.' What other tenant could wield this power over the Fifth Earl of Annesley, of Castlewellan, County of Down?* Lizzie shoved the envelope into the pocket of her coverall apron, as Missus Twombly entered the kitchen.

"Lizzie, those biscuits smell heavenly."

Lizzie spun around to retrieve the biscuits from the oven. They were just browning lightly on the top. "Aye, ma'am, may I help you?"

"Yes. Did the mail come today?"

"Oh dear, it did, ma'am, said Eliza. I'm sorry, Lizzie received a letter, and I stopped to hear it. Here are the letters, Missus Twombly. I'll set up for dinner, ma'am." Eliza was so flustered, she handed the letters to her mistress, but let go before Missus Twombly had them in her hand. The letters spilled onto the floor, and Eliza scrambled to pick them up.

"Just set them on the table, Eliza. Lizzie, we have soup and biscuits for our luncheon today? We are going out tonight, if this fog lifts by five. If we do not, be prepared to bake those chops for supper. We will defer to eat at seven, to give you enough time."

"For luncheon I have split pea soup, cheese biscuits, stuffed eggs, and some apple crisp fer 'afters', ma'am."

"Excellent, Lizzie, good news from home, I trust?"

"Aye, ma'am, arrangements for my mother's arrival," Lizzie answered.

"Very good, I am looking forward to meeting her." Missus Twombly scooped the mail from the table, and left the room.

That night, Lizzie showed the letter to Doctor Twombly. "I am impressed by the width of your social circle, Lizzie. Is it usual for an earl to have such close ties with his tenants?"

"Indeed no, sir, he's a friend o' my mother's, since she was a child. I've only met him recently, an' have only seen him wit' my ain eyes but a few times. He appeared in the background o' 'most ev'ry funeral an' christenin' in our family, but I ne'er knew he was my mother's friend, 'til this year. She said 'twas to avoid gossip among the other tenants."

"He seems to have great regard for her. He's attended to every detail of her crossing, her safety, and her comfort. Have you heard from Charles? I wrote him as well, enquiring about his ability to meet your mother at New York. This letter will make it much easier for him to collect her. Oh look, there is another paper in the envelope. Ah, this is the note of introduction to the Master of the Vessel. We merely have to fill in the name of the person who will take charge of her safety, and have him present it to the master. When we hear from Charles, and if he agrees to the task, he can put his name on this document."

Lizzie smiled nervously. "It sounds like it's really goin' ta happen, Doctor Twombly."

"How do you feel about that, Lizzie?" he asked, noting her demeanor.

"I am betwixt being sae happy I kin hardly contain myself, an' afraid I canna take care o' her properly, sir. Although she's strong o' spirit, an' is ne'er sickly, when I leave here ta work on my ain, I won't be able ta arrange fer her comfort. There're sae many things ta consider. I canna leave her alone all day amongst strangers an' the chair will no' fit ev'rywhere she may want ta be."

"Lizzie, if she is as strong in spirit as you say, perhaps she will figure out some of these things herself. You will adapt to your challenges, my child. You are practical and strong-minded enough for the task. I have every confidence in you." He barely got his words out before he began to cough in deep spasms.

Lizzie thumped him on his back, trying to clear his airway. Finally, with a great intake of air, he stopped. His face was florid, tears fell from his eyes, and he gasped for air for several minutes.

"Goodness me, where did *that* come from? I'm all right now, Lizzie. If Missus Twombly didn't come running, that means she's already asleep. You needn't inform her of this little incident. You know how she worries over the least little thing. I will be right as rain tomorrow."

"Aye, sir, I'll no' say anythin' if *as ye say,* ye are right as rain' t'marra. But if yer not, I'll hafta tell Miss Isabella."

"You *do* know how things work in this house, don't you, Lizzie?" he laughed. "Isabella would have my head before I complained of anything to Missus Twombly. She's a good girl, she is. She has her hands full, caring for the missus and her brother, especially in this damp, cold weather."

"Aye, sir, if you'll excuse me, I'll be settin' up fer breakfas', checkin' the oven, an' trimmin' the lamps, afore I gae ta bed. Is there anythin' I kin git fer ye, Doctor Twombly?"

"I think maybe another cup of good, strong coffee would be just the ticket, Lizzie." He sat back in the rocker, and for the first time in her memory, he seemed physically defeated. Every one of his seventy-seven years was etched sharply on his haggard face.

She had never seen him less than robust, energetic, and sharp-witted, his eyes and his color, bright. Now he was a pale, sad replica of the vital man she knew. *I give ye 'til t'marra, Doctor*

Twombly, ta work out wha'ever 'tis, thet's ailin' ye. Then, I'll hafta tell Miss Isabelle.

Lizzie went about her late night chores with one eye on her employer. When he said 'good night', she collected his cup, and noted he had never even looked at the paper. *I'll hafta wait 'til the mornin', then.*

Later that week, another letter came from her mother. Lizzie could sense Maggie's excitement for her impending journey and felt her stomach clench up with apprehension. *We don't knae if Charles will be able ta fetch her from New York. I should write her an enthusiastic letter, telling her all the wonderful things she'll encounter on her trip, but I'd rather knae thet everything is in place, first.*

That night, Doctor Twombly took his place in the kitchen, looking tired, but much better than earlier in the week. The newspaper lay in his lap while he extracted a letter from his suit jacket.

"I have heard from Charles, Lizzie. He says he would be honored to receive your mother from the *City of Chester* when it lands in New York. He has worked out his schedule so that Friday, he will stay overnight in New York, and sees no problem meeting your mother on Saturday, December 10th. Depending when the ship arrives, he could even hire a Pullman berth for your mother, so she can rest on the train. It will depend on how she fares on her journey, and if a berth is available of course."

"Thank you, Doctor Twombly! Everyone has been sae kind in helpin' wit' her arrival. I hope Charles will no' lose any study time on account o' me an' my mother. He's been working sae hard on his studies."

"That he has, I'm sure. But, speaking from experience, he must be sure to take some time to relax as well. The brain works better, if one lets it work on other activities, then go back to one's academic studies. That is why Martha's Vineyard, is such a pleasant respite for us. It rejuvenates the spirit, to be engaged in a variety of unfamiliar activities." The elderly man seemed to slip into a reverie of pleasant times. He leaned back in the rocker with a smile, and a faraway look in his eye, calling back his younger, stronger days.

Lizzie fell silent as well, not wanting to disturb what appeared to be amiable memories.

I hope Charles still thinks ta reply ta my letter. Even though he is agreeable ta my needs, I want him ta tell me fer himself. Immediately, she saw the contradiction in her thoughts. *Ah, Lizzie, yer sae selfish. Ye've gotten what ye want an' yer lookin' fer still more. This, from a man who ye swore ye dinna want his attentions. Kin ye no' make up yer mind?*

Several days passed, with Lizzie watching the door willing it to produce a knock from the postman. Unsuccessful in this venture, she went through her daily routine with a feeling of dissatisfaction nagging at her. Missus Twombly was planning her Thanksgiving dinner to the minutest detail. Just after supper each night, she would ensconce herself in her rocker and make her lists of preparation. Not surprisingly, her mistress had invited the elusive Mister Bachelor to Thanksgiving dinner. Lizzie found this an awkward, but understandable arrangement. *Oh my, what if he brings this tutor thet he spoke o' in his letter?*

She pictured him with the young lady sitting at the table carrying on polite conversation, while Lizzie labored over her hot oven, her face flushed with the heat, and the effort of providing them with a lavish meal, at which she would not be welcome.

"Missus Twombly, if I may be sae bold to ask, would ye be givin' Eliza an' I a day off followin' Thanksgivin' Day? We were hopin' ta see my cousin James, an' I have some business at a Federal bank."

"Oh dear, did Mister Bachelor not write to tell you? He did request that very thing of me, some days ago. Now where did I put that letter?" Smiling, she reached into her pocket and handed a sealed letter to her. "This came in this morning's mail, my dear. Do read it, Lizzie."

"Oh!" It was all Lizzie could do, not to snatch the long awaited letter out of her hand. It was one page, which she read quickly. "Saturday," she said in wonder. "We will gae ta Boston ta meet James. Oh, Missus Twombly. Thank you." Lizzie's eyes blurred with sudden tears, betraying how much she missed her cousin, and how much she had wanted the long-awaited word from Charles Bachelor.

Missus Twombly smiled at her kindly. "Mister Bachelor is an honorable man, Lizzie. But then, I remember how hard it is to wait for a letter from someone special." She seemed to look out the darkened window at a memory of Doctor Twombly and herself, in days long ago. "I should have given it to you immediately, Lizzie. Please forgive me. I had quite forgotten it was in my pocket," she said quietly, staring at the window pane. "Letters delayed are most distressful."

"Are you feeling all right, Missus Twombly?" Lizzie asked, concerned.

"Oh yes," she said snapping out of her reverie. "I am right as rain. Now, we have the matter of your day off settled, shall we continue? Tomorrow, I want you to go up in the attic to the linen trunk. There are some holiday place settings and decorations for Thanksgiving. We must freshen them up and make them presentable for this year's table. There are two dolls. A man in black with a tall hat and a woman with an apron and a white cap. These will represent our Pilgrims. Let's see, there are orange and brown candles, and the extra-large serving platter for the turkey."

Missus Twombly continued her list until Lizzie noticed her nodding off. When Lizzie gently asked if she would like more tea, she declined, and left the room. A few minutes later, Lizzie heard Doctor Twombly helping her up the stairs. The sound of their conversation was low and sweet as they took one step, then another.

One day, I will have a love like theirs. One that grows richer wit' time, until we're verra old, Lizzie thought wistfully.

That night, she wrote a letter to Charles explaining the errand she had to complete at the bank, and how much she anticipated seeing James. She asked that he let her know how much it would cost for him to take the train, and stay overnight in New York, when he escorted her mother. She also wrote that she was looking forward to seeing Charles himself, aside from all he was doing for her. A weight seem to roll off her shoulders in the writing of the letter, as she realized how many problems she worried about, had been solved between Charles, the Earl, and Doctor Twombly. Her heart lighter, she went to bed, and slept soundly for the first time in several weeks.

The days flew by until Thanksgiving morning. Missus Twombly was in her best spirits, issuing orders to all who were in the house. Lizzie smiled to herself as she busily prepared breakfast.

This is her finest talent an' her guests have nae idea how she orchestrates the most comfortable, effortless dinner fer them.

The guests were from all walks of her life. Big John, one of the 'back door guests', Charles Bachelor, student of theology, Miss Minnie Littlefield, the church organist, Garrett Johansson, apprentice carpenter, the new primary school teacher, Constance Merriweather, and Mary Brown, an elderly spinster. Isabelle, William, and the Twombly elders completed the list of diners for the Thanksgiving feast. Lizzie wondered if her chief aim was to make love matches among the single guests, or to prevent anyone from dining alone on the holiday. Either way, Missus Twombly could claim success. Lizzie was happy to know a certain tutor was not on the list, and wondered if Charles was content about the exclusion.

She's prob'ly a lovely, sweet an' endearin' thing. She's surely better suited fer Charles. But let me have this holiday, wit'out having ta serve this rival fer Charles' affection. I'll be gone from here, soon enough, then he kin choose whome'er he wishes, but no' nae, no' t'day.

Lizzie sent Eliza off to deliver breakfast trays, and started checking off the list of dinner items to be prepared. Breads, pies, petit fours, and meringues were all prepared the day before. Vegetables were cut and ready for cooking the night before.

The main object of her culinary skills was the turkey with cornbread dressing, giblet gravy. The kitchen was steaming up with the smells of roast turkey, boiled turnip, braised parsnips, onions and carrots, potatoes and butternut squash, ready to mash, and cranberry and apple sauces. Any frugality was banished from Thanksgiving dinner. It was to be a feast for all the senses.

The table was set with deep red candles, dark cranberry punch in sparkling wine glasses, crisp orange napkins, and the finest china service pieces. Any pieces that did not match the table setting were tied with orange and brown ribbons to coordinate with the napkins and tablecloth. The Pilgrim dolls and the orange and brown candles flanked the buffet awaiting the presentation of the main course.

The guests were due at one o'clock and would be entertained in the parlor until dinner was announced at one-thirty. Plates of nuts and fruits were scattered in the parlor, ostensibly to stave off the hunger pangs created by the rich odors of more substantial foods, wafting through the house.

Lizzie was thinking of her first turkey last spring, chuckling to herself at the vision of Eliza bumping into her, the turkey flying, and her half-sister sliding across the floor in greasy pan drippings. Looking toward the ceiling, she folded her hands in a silent prayer that she not repeat that scene for this meal. *Lovely gravy, though.*

At last, with everything in order, Eliza stepped in cautiously to enquire about the timing for dinner. Lizzie ticked through the order of service on her fingers. "Start by bringin' in those fruit compotes, an' I'll have the turkey presentable by the time you're done an' have announced dinner. As they're bein' seated, come git the turkey. Place it on the buffet ta be admired an' wait fer grace ta be said. Then, brin' it ta me, an' I'll carve. I'll make two platters. One fer whoever is at the head o' the table, an' one fer the buffet." By way of explanation, she added, "William may elect ta be *'father'* fer t'day. The doctor has been feelin' jes' a little poorly o' late. Nae scoot."

Lizzie's heart swelled with pride as she was rewarded with the 'oohs' and 'ahs' coming from the dining room. "Oh Laird, the gravy is still here!" Just as she opened the door a crack to get Eliza's attention, she heard her name.

"Lizzie, please come out here." She took one gravy bowl with her as she entered. "This is the finest feast we have ever laid eyes on." The younger minister raised his glass of cranberry cider, and urged his guests to do the same. "To Lizzie, surely, the finest cook from the Emerald Isle. We thank you for your talents."

Lizzie blushed and nodded. She said, "It is Missus Twombly who deserves the credit, Mister William, but thank you." She scurried back to the kitchen and opened the back door to cool her heated face.

As she was about to close the door, she saw three of the Baker children standing on the back porch. "Oh dear, come in, come in. Is there anything wrong? Eulah, what is it?"

Eulah, as the oldest, said her prepared speech. "These loaves of cranberry-nut bread are for Doctor and Missus Twombly from Mister and Missus Baker. It is a small token of our affection for them and the family." She turned and looked at her younger siblings, and they all shouted, "Happy Thanksgiving!"

"Would you like to give your present to them yourself, Eulah? I'm sure they would love to see you and hear your lovely speech," Lizzie urged her gently.

"Mamma said we were to gif them to you, and not 'sturb their dinner, Miss. Could you jes' give it to them, and tell 'em what I said? Mamma would be very angry if we made a fuss."

"Very well, Eulah. I will tell them. I'm sure they will be very grateful for these delicious breads."

Young Frank spoke up, "How d' you know they're d'licious? You ain't tasted 'em, haf ya?"

Lizzie laughed as Eulah glared at her brother. "I'm sure they are as sweet as your mother's smile," she answered.

The two younger children rushed out the door under Eulah's command, and the littlest looked back with a brilliant grin. "'appy Fangsgiffin'," she said shyly.

Oh Laird, I wanna dozen o' them, jes' lak' her. Send me a man who could put up wit' me, an' I'll give him two dozen children. No child o' mine will be alone. Immediately, she felt ashamed of her thoughts. *Joseph, Johnnie, Anne, an' Eliza are my brothers and sisters. I am no' entirely alone. I am only 'half' a sister, but Eliza is more than 'half' ta me. Nae we're in America, I kin see her ever'day. No one kin govern how one is born, an' who he shares his life with in their childhood. But, by the angels in heaven, and the luck o' the faeries, I kin choose how I spend the rest o' my life, an' wit' whom I spend it.*

Lizzie was chagrined at the impromptu argument she waged in her mind. She hadn't thought their strange family had affected how she viewed the world, but evidently it did. She thought of a phrase she overheard at the market fair when two old women gossiped about her. "She's an only child, o' an only child, that one. Hand-raised, like a glasshouse plant." She was only twelve then, and the villagers had pronounced her fate. "She may be fair o' face, but they'll have ta tame her harsh tongue, an' high spirits, or no man will have her." The echo of the mean-spirited cackles still rang in her head, even at twenty years old.

227

*Why should ye care about the idle prattle o' two old biddies?
Ye will make yer ain way in this land, an' in this life. Laird, make
me worthy o' the man who'd put up wit' me. Amen.*

"Lizzie? Lizzie," Eliza's voice broke into her thoughts. "Are
the desserts ready? They will take dessert in the parlor, sae I kin
clear the table on my ain."

"Aye, Eliza. I have them on the cart with the dishes. The pies
are cut, they can select their ain, an' ye will serve. I'll clear the table,
since ye will be busy servin'. Missus Twombly thought she'd like ta
try it this way. She has a dinner party next week, too. If this works
well, she'll serve dessert this way then, too."

Eliza nodded, checking the cart for serving pieces, napkins,
dishes and desserts. "Is there another pum'kin pie? Missus Twombly
said they may all want pum'kin pie."

"I've one in here an' another squash pie, too. If ye serve the
guests first, the Twomblys will *suddenly* have a taste fer one o' the
other desserts, rather than deny their guests another piece o'
pum'kin. If ye git a chanct, ye kin let her knae discretely, there's
more pum'kin."

As her sister left the kitchen, Lizzie quickly cut half the
remaining pies and covered them with parchment paper. She made
up two plates for Eliza and her, covered them and set them on the
back of the stove to stay warm. She checked the back step for 'back
door guests,' and having none, she began packing away the remains
of the meal. She made a sandwich of turkey, cranberry sauce,
stuffing and a little mashed potato. She wrapped it in parchment and
put it in a small brown bag for Big John to take back to the church
basement where he was staying. Having done that, she thought
again, and made a second sandwich for him. *Maybe he has a friend.
If no', it'll keep till t'marra on the window ledge.*

Later, when Eliza returned to the kitchen, Lizzie heard the
guests leaving the house. "Is everyone leavin'?" She did not dare
say Charles' name.

"Aye, Lizzie. Missus Twombly asked Garrett and Charles to take the ladies home. Big John is still talking ta William, but I asked him ta stop into the kitchen. Is that his sandwich?"

"Aye," Lizzie answered disappointed. She had hoped Charles would stop in the kitchen before he left. "I made two." She turned toward the stove and steeled herself against the tears of disappointment that threatened to fall. Taking the two warm plates, she set them on the table.

"Thank you, Lizzie. After seeing all that food, I could barely keep my hands off it. It smells heavenly, hmm."

Lizzie picked at her food, listlessly. Big John came in, took his sandwiches, and Lizzie barely acknowledged his presence. He chatted with Eliza, making sidelong glances at Lizzie, his expression quizzical. Eliza just shook her head, hoping John wouldn't give voice to his questions.

"Lizzie? Charles said he would be back ta see you, after he took the ladies home, if that's all right wit' you."

"Thank you, John. I'm sorry he had ta make yer his messenger." She rose and quietly went to her room, leaving John and Eliza to stare at her, then each other. Eliza shrugged her shoulders and continued eating.

"'Twill be fine, John. She's just tired from all her work today. She'll be happy ta see Charles when he gets here. She doesn't mean ta be unpleasant." She smiled weakly at John. "Happy Thanksgivin', John."

"And to you, Miss." Big John went to the back door, glancing at the door to Lizzie's room as he left.

Lizzie sat on her bed for a moment, and then stood up to see the small mirror. Her cook's cap askew, a few red curls escaped, framing her red face. She hated the way her emotions were uncharacteristically displayed across her face. She took a deep breath, straightened her cap, and blinked her eyes fiercely. He *did* say he was coming back. In a fit of pique, she wished she didn't have to be here when he came.

Lizzie you can't blame him fer bein' a gentleman! O' course, he had ta take the ladies hame. Ye wouldn't be happy if he didn't. Just take wha' comes. Don't ruin it by bein' unreasonable.

When Lizzie realized she was talking out loud to her mirror, she thought wryly, *Eliza will think I've los' my mind.* She brushed furiously at her apron, and seeing the flour and squash stuck to it, finally decided to change into a fresh one.

Back in the kitchen, Lizzie resumed pushing her Thanksgiving dinner around her plate. Eliza quietly rinsed her plate, and started doing the dishes that were piled high on the side board.

"Thank you, Eliza, leave the pots and the roaster fer me. I have ta break down the turkey an' make a stew, so whatever is left in the pots will gae inta that. Maybe ye kin take a nap afore late tea."

"I'm fine, Lizzie. Ye take yer time, an' I'll git these done."

The dishes done, Eliza went into Lizzie's room, changed her apron, fixed her little maid's cap and sat down at the kitchen table. She watched Lizzie strip the turkey carcass. She packed away the large slices, scraped the small pieces off and piled them onto a plate. Having stripped the bones, she put the skeleton into a cheesecloth bag breaking the bones as she stuffed it into the pot. She covered the bones with water and set it to boil on the stove.

The first step of her turkey stew on its way, Lizzie thrust her hands into the dishwater, to clean the fat and grease off them. She kept her apron almost spotless, but her cap was off to one side again, and her nose itched. She raised her arm out of the water and tried to scratch her nose with her fore arm. It was in this inelegant pose that Charles found her.

"Hello, Lizzie." He smiled, and his eyes were sparkling, teasing her. "Garrett, why don't you ask Miss Eliza, if she would take a walk with you? It's such a lovely day and warm for Thanksgiving."

"I'll get my coat," said Eliza, as if it were prearranged, which it was, of course. Charles had mentioned it to Eliza while she was serving his pie and to Garrett on their ride to the house. Lizzie was the only one he hadn't told. She stood looking from one to the other, her face flushed, not knowing whether to be angry or happy about the arrangement.

As Garrett and Eliza left, Charles took the towel from her, and began wiping her arms with it. It was both sensual, and endearing. Trying to feel back in control, she snatched the towel from him, threw it on the side board, and turned back to the sink. He slipped his arms around her waist and nuzzled her neck. "Mister Bachelor," she protested half-heartedly.

She turned in his embrace, and he answered, "Yes?" He kissed her responding lips.

"Ch-charles, please, the Twomblys could come in any minute," she whispered.

"Missus Twombly is my co-conspirator. She's keeping everyone out of the kitchen today," he answered hoarsely.

"Why, that's scandalous, Mister Bachelor! Ye've arranged this wit' everyone, but me," she said, the light in her eyes dancing now. "What would they say about yer behavior?"

"That I am a man who has too little time to plead his case," he grinned. "And, that you are a woman who does not respond to pretty words and polite gestures."

"Charles, please sit down. I will be a disgrace in the very house I serve." She sat primly on the edge of a chair and gestured to the one at the far end of the kitchen table.

As he passed her chair, he playfully took the cap from her head. He moved his chair close to her, dropping the cap out of her reach. "It's a shame to hide that fire under a cap." He cupped the side of her face tenderly, and her head leaned into his hand. He took her open palm, kissing its center. A sweet mystical pang deep in her body, leaped at his touch.

"Talk ta me Charles. Tell me this is right. I am sae confused."

"I cannot tell you, if it is right for you. I feel like the most blessed man in the world, that you will even see me. I am hopelessly addled, in love with you."

"Charles, I don't know what ta say. What do you want from me? Ye said ye have at least four years o' school, afore ye are a free man. I don't know where I'll be, or what I'll be doin' in four years."

"Lizzie, you're right. I am in love, and for me four years is a short time to wait for what is my greatest hope. But you are young and four years seems forever, I know. All I ask is that you let me know where you are, and let me love you for as long as you are not promised to another. For that, I will be content. Well, if not content, then I will be hopeful that one day, you will love me too." His speech finished, he drew her up and kissed her so deeply, she thought she was drowning.

When he released her, she became aware of tears streaming down her face. "Lizzie, you're crying. Tell me I've not hurt you with my stumbling, clumsy words."

"No, Charles. I wish I could be the person ye seem ta think I am. Ye deserve *thet* person. How can I tell ye how much I want ta be thet person?"

"Perhaps in these four years, if you let me stay in your life, you will learn that I *know* who you are. I don't need you to be anyone else. You are a spirited, fiery-tempered girl, who talks to God every day, and is as strong and opinionated as He made her. You are a daring, endearing girl who drives me insane, and is exactly who I need."

"Charles, I will write ta yer, an' see ye fer as lang as there is no one else. Promise me, if I find another man who is more suited ta me, you will seek another more suited ta you."

232

"Very well, if all hope is gone, if you love him, *and* marry him, I will look elsewhere. But for the present, there is no one who owns my heart, but you."

"No' even a certain tutor," Lizzie, teased.

"Ah, there is hope. My little Lizzie is jealous. You *do* care! You can't deny it now." Charles hugged her tight and kissed her joyfully. Lizzie looked at the kitchen door almost willing someone to enter. Her wishes answered, Eliza and Garrett returned from their walk.

Chapter Fifteen

The next morning, Lizzie danced through her work with a carefree abandon. Although there were mounds of stained linens to clean, and numerous pies to bake, she was calm and industrious. She had a smile for everyone, and everyone assumed it was the visit from one Charles Bachelor that set Lizzie in her euphoric mood.

Some of that assumption was true. But her secondary intoxication was monetary. Saturday, she was going to the bank to cash Laird Annesley's check, open an account, give Charles the money for his trip to New York, and make a deposit at the boarding house for her mother. The weeks of worry about how to care for her mother upon her arrival, was lifted by the Earl's generosity. Now, she could look forward to seeing her mother with complete joy. By the time Maggie's money ran out, Lizzie would be released from her debt to the Twomblys, and would be earning a wage.

B'twixt James, Eliza an' I, we should be able ta take care o' Maggie. Ach, I dinna think we kin count on James, though. He's bound ta be off ta somewhere in the west o' this land, ta make his fortune. I hope he finds wha' he's seekin', but it would surely be helpful fer him ta stay. Right nae, he's the only o' us makin' a wage, as little as it is.

Lizzie shook her head as if to clear her mind of worries. She had a Sunday dinner to prepare. She could have the linens ready, shop for food, and still complete the list of items Missus Twombly gave her. Her turkey stew, began the night before, filled the house with a most delicious aroma. For lunch, she added cranberry biscuits, plain cider or cinnamon tea. For supper, at Missus Twombly's request, a small beef roast would provide some variety. Saturday, they would have more turkey stew, or sliced roast beef for lunch, if needed. The Twomblys were invited out for supper, so Lizzie did not have to prepare for that.

By noontime, half the kitchen was filled with pies cooling for the church. Lizzie was way ahead of the schedule she set for herself. One corner of the kitchen had ministers' white shirts drying on wooden hangers ready for pressing. The side board held trays of food ready for lunch, waiting only for Eliza to breeze in, and deliver them to the dining room. Satisfied with her progress, she took a bowl of soup for herself, and sat at the corner of the table already laden with baked goods. As she was about to take her first sip, a knocking at the door drew her attention. Through the window she saw Big John.

"John, would you like some turkey stew? Is it warm enough out there?" asked Lizzie.

"I've come to deliver these pie crates for you," he said. "They're for carryin' yer pies to the church tomorrow. See, each shelf just big enough for one pie, and there are six shelves in each crate, so they can carry a dozen pies without breakin' them. There a handle on top and this wide canvas strap to hold them in. It attaches at the top like this. I made them crates myself for Missus Twombly," he said proudly.

"John, these are wonderful. Since the shelves are open, I can use them for cooling the pies, too! What a wonderful invention! You should sell these at holiday time."

"I got the scrap wood from Mister Baker an' he lemme have the brads. He helped me with the measurin', too. I sanded them down and shellacked them so's there'd be no splinters."

"Come in, John. Put one in this chair and I'll put the pies in it. Then we can put the other one on the table, while I put the other pies in it. I'll have room on the table ta eat, nae. How would yer like some turkey stew, John?"

"Smells like heaven in here, Miss Lizzie. I kin eat the stew outside, as usual. I don' wanna be in the way."

"What is the commotion in here, Lizzie?" said Missus Twombly as she entered the kitchen.

Lizzie explained the pie crates to her and how John made them for her.

"My goodness, what a clever idea this is, John! Come join us for lunch. Lizzie, Eliza will be in for the trays in just a minute. Come into the dining room, John. We'd love to hear all about your pie crates."

Lizzie grinned at John's bewildered look. She understood his confusion. Thanksgiving dinner, he figured was charity. But lunch the next day in the dining room, felt like part of the family. They had done so much for him. This was the kind of people the Twomblys were. Lizzie marveled at the fortune that brought her to this generous and God-loving family.

Their faith is strong, and they live it day by day. I wish I were one-tenth as saintly, as they. Not for the first time, she prayed, *Thank ye God, fer bringin' me ta the Twomblys. Amen.*

Now that her pies were in the crates, she had much more room for her lunch. She set out a place for Eliza, with a plate of biscuits. Her activity of the morning whetting her appetite, she devoured her stew and biscuits. By the time Eliza was finished with service and John had left, Lizzie was back to work, pressing shirts. Eliza was talking between sips of stew, excited about where they would go the next day.

Lizzie was barely listening, engrossed in her favorite chore, the one for which she had the most pride of accomplishment. Sunday morning, she would check the men of the Twombly family for their starched white shirts, judging how much whiter and smoother they were than the rest of the congregation. The handkerchiefs were at sharp attention in their breast pockets. The sin of pride was undeniably her hardest to conquer, and humility was far from her reach when it came to her laundry skills.

She saw Eliza get up and rinse her plate, before she realized she hadn't heard a word she said. "Eliza?" she said, ashamed of herself.

Eliza said not a word, but left the room.

I've hurt her feelin's agin. How she puts up with me, I swear, I'll never knae. She ne'er stays angry, jes' hurt. Laird, teach me ta be a better, more attentive person. Amen.

The rest of her day was spent making up for her transgressions. She made batches of oatcakes and hermits. The oatcakes she learned from her grandmother and the hermits came from *Mrs. Lincoln's Boston Cook Book*, Missus Twombly's pinnacle of Cookery. Stored in a crock, the tasty oatcake bites would last for months. She knew Eliza had a fondness for the Scottish oatcakes of her childhood, and Missus Twombly intimated her weakness for thick molasses hermits at Martha's Vineyard. Lizzie hoped the presentation of hermits would soften her reprimand for using household ingredients in making oatcakes for Eliza.

Later that night, after Eliza had retired to Lizzie's room, she wrapped some oatcakes in a napkin and brought them to her. "Eliza, I'm sorry I was sae distracted today that I didn't listen as I should have. I made these as a token of my contrite heart."

"Oh Lizzie, thank you, I've missed these sae much. Ye knae I kin ne'er stay angry at ye, but thank ye all the same," she said, tearfully. Lizzie gave her a hug, and snatched one of the oatcakes for herself.

237

"T'marra after breakfast, we'll have an adventure. I wonder where Charles will take us this time. I hope we gae inside, it's gettin' cold again. Well, eat yer oatcakes an' dream o' hame, Eliza."

The next morning, Lizzie was grateful the sky was clear, and the ground was free of snow. It was still dark, but not far from sunrise. She stoked up the fire, and soon the kitchen was filled with the aroma of apple pancakes. The pancakes were set to the back of the stove to keep warm until the first stirrings upstairs. Today, she willed them to rise early, and be done with breakfast, so she and Eliza could leave.

Charles probably won't be here afore nine, sae all yer wishin' won't make it gae faster. Ye might as well have a cup a tea.

She sat with her tea and biscuit, ticking off in her mind her tasks for the morning.

Eliza breezed in happily from feeding the furnace in the cellar. Slipping off the great coverall apron she used for this dirty task, she said, "I think I heard Miss Isabelle rise. I'll take her tray first. She'll wake the rest."

"Whoops, jes' a minute there, Miss Eliza," Lizzie grabbed her washcloth and wiped Eliza's brow of soot. "Ye had a mighty streak of coal dust on yer lovely visage, deary."

"Why is it when yer hands are completely occupied wit' the dirtiest of dirt, yer face itches?" laughed Eliza. "Thank ye, am I all right, nae?" she grinned and tipped her head coquettishly. She washed her hands and went off to deliver her first tray.

Soon, Lizzie was too busy to worry about how long it would take to be on her way. She gave biscuits and coffee to her 'back door guests', milk to the neighborhood cat, collected the milk, eggs, and cheese from the dairy man, and set out the lunch trays. Before she knew it, Charles was at the back door.

She sat him at the kitchen table with coffee and a biscuit, then went to her room to get rid of her apron, and straighten her hair. She picked up her coat, checked the pocket for her papers, took her purse, and went back to the kitchen. "What could be keepin' Eliza, I wonder?" she said to Charles, who just smiled at her.

Leaving her coat in the chair, Lizzie went in search for Eliza. Not finding her downstairs, she cautiously went upstairs. "Eliza?" she called softly.

"Lizzie, can you help me?" Eliza was standing in an alcove with a pair of men's trousers in her hand. She was trying to button leather suspender togs onto the back of them. "I can't get the last one and Doctor Twombly is waiting for them."

Lizzie grabbed the trousers and fastened the elusive button for her. "There." Eliza laid the garment over her arm and knocked softly on the bedroom door.

"Missus Twombly, I have his trousers ready." Missus Twombly in her night cap, stretched her arm through the barely open door, and retrieved them, without a word. "Is everything satisfactory, Missus Twombly?"

"Yes, yes. It is all as it should be, Eliza. You may go now."

Lizzie and Eliza looked at each other, and fled down stairs to the kitchen. "Thank you, Lizzie, I think I would be there all day, trying to button thet blasted thing," said Eliza.

"Eliza! What will Mister Bachelor think?" cried Lizzie.

"Oh dear, I didn't see ye. I am sae sorry fer my rude language, Mister Bachelor!" Eliza blushed, curtsied, and ran into the bedroom.

"We should be on our way in jes' a moment, Charles," Lizzie said, laughing.

"I wondered how she could have such perfect manners all the time," said Charles. "I'm afraid that is my Achilles' heel. When I am all alone, I fear I no longer control my tongue as well as a divinity student should. I have a long way to travel, before I am a godly man like Doctor Twombly."

Recalling when young Mister Twombly barked his shins on the tree trunk at Martha's Vineyard, Lizzie dropped her voice to a

239

whisper, "Even Mister William has his moments, Charles. '*For all have sinned, and fall short of the glory of God*'."

"You quote the Scriptures, and you say you are afraid to become a minister's wife?" teased Charles, his eyes twinkling. He stood, and kissed her forehead.

Eliza entered the kitchen wearing her coat and hat. "I am ready. Thank yer, fer yer patience. We can leave, if I'm no' interruptin' anythin'," she said, grinning.

It was Lizzie's turn to blush. She reached the door handle before Charles could react and went out the door unassisted. Charles and Eliza hurried to catch up with her.

The weather was unseasonably mild. They boarded the train to the Boston & Albany Terminal on Kneeland Street, then a trolley to The Common at Park Street to meet James. They looked around for his familiar jaunty cap and waving hand, but did not see him. To the girls' surprise, they did see young Garrett Johansson who was running toward them. The girls both turned to Charles questioningly.

"I hope you don't mind, Mister Baker released him for today, and I asked if he could join us. I hope I haven't been too forward in assuming you would enjoy his company?" Eliza and Lizzie assured him that Garrett was a most welcome guest to their party. *My goodness! I wish I had thought ta ask him mysel'*, Lizzie thought.

"Oh look," Eliza said. "There's James. He has someone wit' him!"

Indeed, there was a young lady of their age with flaxen hair, glowing in the bright sunshine, and pretty blue eyes that were fastened on James. *She holds his arm as if he might fly away*, Lizzie thought.

"We seem to have accumulated quite a crowd. Does anyone here know how to get to Copely Square on your own?"

"I do," said the little yellow-haired beauty. "We can take the trolley over here."

240

"May I present Miss Marianna Peterson, folks. This is Lizzie, Eliza, and Charles. I'm sorry, I dinna knae yer young gentleman, Eliza," said James.

Eliza turned a pretty bright rose, and pushed James' shoulder. "He *is* a gentleman, no' mine, however. May I present Mister Garrett Johansson? Or, as he likes ta say, 'Jes' Plain Garrett'," she said, with her eyes sparkling. "James is our cousin, an' keeper of secrets, it appears. Verra nice ta meet yer, Marianna."

This was the most James and Lizzie had ever heard Eliza say in front of a stranger. *Perhaps she was more willin' for Garrett ta be 'her gentleman, than she would admit,* Lizzie thought.

"Let me propose a plan," said Charles. "If Marianna would be so kind, she could bring you to Copley Square to the Boston Museum of Fine Arts there, whilst I take Lizzie to the First National Bank of Boston. It's in the opposite direction, but we could meet you at the museum in, say, about an hour and a half. Is that acceptable to everyone? Does everyone have the fare? I have your fare for the museum. James, would you be in charge?" The two couples speaking all at once, agreed to the proposal.

James added with a wicked smile, "Do have a lovely trip ta the bank, Charles. Are ye sure ye don't need a chaperone, Lizzie?"

"James, I swear ye are in the devil's hold!" Lizzie pulled an angry face, but she couldn't hold it, and laughed. She cuffed his arm in play.

"Now Lizzie," said Charles, teasing her. "We mustn't resort to fisticuffs. James needs at least one arm to escort his lovely guest. Now, let us be off."

"Lizzie, dear," he said, after the others had boarded their trolley, "The bank is on Franklin Street, about a half mile from here. Do you wish to walk it, or take a trolley?"

"It's sech a lovely day, let's walk. We kin take a trolley back if we're runnin' late, can't we?"

241

"Of course," he answered. They fell silent as they walked. Lizzie admired the tall buildings and bustling traffic.

Ahead of them, there was a small group of walkers stopping to stare in a window. "Wha's goin' on over there?" Lizzie asked.

"I'm sure I don't know, Lizzie. It seems to be a carriage of some sort," said Charles.

A man near them said, "It's a *horse-less* carriage from Europe. I'd heard of 'em, but never seed one up close before. Says it's a Bentz. Funny name, don't ye think? There's a motor inside."

"Interesting, I suppose we'll have them by the dozens, pretty soon," said another man.

"If it has a motor, it'll probably scare the horses. I can't see it being practical, can you?" said a third.

Lizzie and Charles left them to their speculations, and walked on. "This area is called the Financial District. The bank is in the next block." They crossed a side street then stood in front of the First Federal Bank of Boston. A nervous shiver went through her as she climbed the steps to the massive door. Charles opened it, and she stepped through to a huge vaulted room with gilded-cage windows, long tables, and people rushing from one place to another.

Lizzie looked at Charles and asked, "What should I do?"

"Let's ask this gentleman over here," he said, guiding her to a man standing at attention in front of the first table facing the outside door. "Sir, this young lady wishes to open an account, and cash a foreign check. To whom should she go?"

The man seemed to take stock of them both, and directed Charles to a desk near the back of the great hall. Charles thanked him, and lead Lizzie to a spindly young man with glasses perched on his nose. He looked over his glasses, and looking at Charles, said, "Please have a seat. How may we help you today?"

"This young lady has a check from Ireland she wishes to cash, and she wishes to open an account."

The thin man smiled rather gruesomely, and said, "Very well, Miss. I'll need some identification of course."

Lizzie took out her papers. He perused them for a moment, murmuring, "Ah, immigrant, Irish, servant." He looked up without raising his head, and said, "I'm sorry, we cannot help you."

"W-what, I don't understand. My papers are in order," Lizzie looked from the disapproving clerk to Charles."

"I'm sorry, Sir. I don't know how you found her, but we deal with this sort often, and whatever foreign check she may have is likely counterfeited. I must ask you to leave."

"Now see here—," Charles protested.

"Please, sir, you don't want me to summon the police." The young man's eyes turned menacing.

"I demand to see your supervisor, sir!" Charles' voice rose up a notch as he stood over him.

"Please sir, we don't want to create a scene," said the man behind the desk.

"I certainly do, if it will bring your supervisor." Charles' face was turning crimson, his neck pressing against his collar. Several men came running. He turned to one of them, and said, "Get me this man's supervisor, immediately."

Quietly, Lizzie and Charles were ushered into an empty anteroom. There was a desk, a wall of books and no identifying desk plaque. "Do you suppose they'll call the constabulary, and have us arrested?" Lizzie whispered in a frightened voice.

There was an argument going on outside the slightly open door. Lizzie couldn't hear what was being said, but it seemed like there were three or four voices, each clamoring over the others in angry, but hushed tones. "I will handle this," said one voice. An elderly man stepped into the room and took his place behind the desk.

"Let's see what is going on here. I'm afraid my clerk was hasty in his judgment, and reacted without enough evidence to support his assumptions. You will have my apology, if indeed that is the case. Miss Hemming, is it?"

"No, sir. My name is Heenan. Elizabeth Jane Heenan. Here are my papers, and here is the letter I received with the cheque from Laird Annesley."

"I see." The man patted his pockets and discovered his glasses were perched upon his balding pate. He looked up, smiled, and said, "I'm always misplacing them. Now where was I?"

Lizzie and Charles sat silently as the man looked carefully at Lizzie's papers and the letter from the Earl. Finished, he sat back, and folded his hands across his wide vest. He seemed to think for a moment, then he said, "I will have to verify the check, but it should not take too long. If he is on the estate, I should hear back in about an hour or two, provided the cable is still intact. Would it surprise you to know I have been to Castlewellan? I was there about four years ago, on a trip to Northern Ireland. I did not meet Lord Annesley, but I did see the castle there. I understand he's quite an accomplished man."

"Aye, sir, he is. I've only met him a few times myself, but my mother is a good friend. The money he sent is for her lodging while she visits here," Lizzie abruptly stopped talking. She felt she was prattling on about things he didn't need to know.

"Go on dear, what *else* do you know of Lord Annesley?"

"He's well-educated, fought in the Crimea, and was injured in the face. He wears a black mask all the time. He's an amateur photographer, and he is creating an arboretum. My mother kept the records of all his plants from around the world. I didn't fully understand what an arboretum was, until Charles took me to the Public Garden, and I saw the Latin names for the flowers and trees there. I understand the Earl has a new wife who is with child and has gone to London."

She continued at his urging, "My grandmother passed away, and that's why Lord Annesley is sending my mother to me. She is an invalid, and I will take care of her.

"Lord Annesley has been most generous, but I cannot take care of her, until I have this money. I work for a minister and his family who paid for my passage here, but my mother's passage is paid for by the Earl. I need enough money to pay the deposit for her room in a boarding house near me. When I am through with my indenture, I will be able to earn enough to care for my mother. I need this money today, sir," she concluded.

"Hmm, it is obvious you know your benefactor. I think we can go ahead, open an account, and allow you enough for the deposit to hold a room for her. The rest, we will hold in the account until we can verify the check. The cost of the telegram will be deducted from the account, when verified. You understand if it cannot be verified, I will have to report it to the authorities."

He spoke softly, "I do apologize for my over-zealous clerk. I hope you can forgive this institution for his faulty assumptions. He will be reprimanded, and taught to more thoroughly ascertain the facts of a matter, before acting.

"Now, we will fill out these forms, endorse the check, and set up your account, Missus..." He looked down at her papers, "...Heenan, And *Mister* Heenan?"

Charles smiled for the first time since entering the bank. "I'm afraid not, sir. I am Charles Bachelor. I am her devoted friend, not yet husband of Miss Heenan." Lizzie blushed at his self-assured statement.

"Well, perhaps you'd like to witness her signature on the account, Mister Bachelor? Is that agreeable, Miss Heenan?"

"Aye, if there are no further obligations to Mister Bachelor." She bowed her head and looked up at Charles.

"It is only to affirm that you were in no way coerced to open this account, and that you are the only one who may withdraw its moneys," the banker asserted. "This is a savings account and you will be issued a passbook. You must keep your passbook in a safe place and when you wish to withdraw money, you must have it and your papers with you. If you change your address, you must notify us in writing. The money will earn interest for as long as it remains in the account. Do you understand?"

"Aye, thank you," she replied. The banker led them to one of the gilt-barred windows and completed the transaction, giving her the deposit money she needed.

After the money was securely in her purse and tucked into the hidden inside pocket of her coat, Lizzie couldn't stop grinning. Such a weight flowed off her shoulders that she fairly skipped to the trolley, and into the Art Museum, to meet the rest of the group.

Charles marveled at the change in her demeanor and reveled in her beautiful smile. He hardly noticed the other people or the great works of art surrounding them. He saw only this charming red-haired girl. He heard only her voice, which changed when she saw her sister and cousin, back to the tenant brogue she had easily discarded while talking to the banker.

Fascinating, like a chameleon, she changes as needed, to hide from those who would disparage her country speech, he thought.

There was a commotion at the entrance of the next room. James came back to where Lizzie and Charles were lagging behind. "The next room is not suitable for ladies, Charles," he said.

""What could it be?" said Lizzie, curiously.

"Statuary of naked men," James whispered.

"Are they Greek or Roman?" asked Lizzie, her eyes dancing.

"What does it matter? They're naked," he hissed.

"Is the statue of David less beautiful, because he is unclothed?" she said in mock innocence.

"Lizzie, yer sister and Marianna are no' sae worldly as ye are, an' should no' be lookin' at sech nakedness. Why can't ye jes'

246

be more lak' them? *That's* what comes o' reading all them books. Charles, help me. I have no control over her."

"She's just teasing you. Aren't you, Lizzie?" Charles turned to James and said, "As far as my having control over Lizzie, heaven help the man who thinks he does. You take your group to the paintings in that room over there, and I'll take Lizzie, if she feels she needs to see this one."

Charles took her by the elbow and bravely steered her toward the statuary room. "Oh look, it's Roman," she said. "Charles, you're uncomfortable. We don't have ta gae in here. Ye kin tell them I was overcome with the 'vapors', if you like." Charles stared at her in disbelief as she pretended to faint.

"Lizzie, you are unlike anyone else I have ever known. What are you thinking?"

Lizzie bit her lower lip, "Truthfully, I don't really want ta gae in there. They are much larger than life an' I find them o'erwhelmin', regardless o' their lack o' attire. I'm sorry, if I embarrassed you. I have seen many o' them in my mother's books. For the most part, they were positioned very discretely, but I wanted ta see jes' one all the way around. I *am* a very curious girl."

"Very curious and intriguing, I *am* very uncomfortable in this room, so if you don't mind, I would like us to leave. I think if someone I knew from school came in; I would have to hide in a closet until they left. However, since no one can see us..." His voice tapered off and looking around, he stole a kiss.

"Why, Mister Bachelor! I do believe this room has a devilish effect on you." Lizzie teased, as she ducked out of his reach and out of the room. Charles, smiling, chased after her, and they joined the rest of their group in a salon they called a 'picture room.'

Eliza saw them breathless and blushing. She promised herself to question Lizzie that night. In the meantime, she was quite content holding Garrett's arm. She noticed too, that Marianna rarely took her eyes from James' face as they walked around the room.

247

The three couples bought lunch on the street as before, and sat in the sunlit park to eat. When the sun dipped below the massive construction of the new Boston Public Library, Charles said to Lizzie, "Someday soon, you will be able to borrow thousands of books to read in that building, more than we've ever dreamed of in our lives. And the best part, it will be free, and open to everyone, rich or poor. Imagine. You'll be able to see all of Michaelangelo's sculptures and paintings as often as you come here."

"Is everything in this country brand new? It seems like everythin' is just been built or is bein' built."

"We have a few old things. Maybe not as old as your old things, there are some dating back to about 1680." Charles laughed. "It is still considered a new country, and it has a long way to grow, but it has its own history, too. The Financial District is so new because twenty years ago, it burned to the ground, sixty-five acres up in flames. I was just a boy in Newton at the time. We could see the smoke for days."

"That must have been terrible," Lizzie said.

Charles gathered the group together to go home. The air had cooled noticeably, and the electric trolley's steam heater was a welcomed surprise to the chilled passengers. The heat, the busy day, and the sun in her eyes made Lizzie sleepy, but content. She was startled when Charles shook her shoulder gently, announcing they were back at Park Street for their transfer.

Waiting for their next trolley, the group exchanged farewells and chatted. "James, I'm sae glad ye brought Marianna wit' ye. Fer one thing, she's a lot prettier an' quieter than you. Maybe she'll tame yer, too!" Lizzie said as she poked James in the ribs. As she kissed Marianna's cheek, she whispered, "Take good care o' him, he's verra special."

"I know," the tiny blond whispered back, "And I will, for as long as he'll have me."

I hope he's as smitten wit' her, as she is wit' him, Lizzie thought. *An' I hope she's stronger than she looks, if he's thinkin' o' takin' her west.*

"Write ta me," she called as they ran for the trolley car. Her eyes filled with tears at the prospect of not seeing him until Christmas. *I spent hardly any time wit' him, an' nae he's gone.* Part of her was jealous of the time Marianna would have with him until next month.

It wan' be lang an' mother will be here. What a lovely Christmas it'll be! Lizzie brushed away an errant tear, hoping no one took notice, but Charles watched her with concern.

Silently, they boarded their trolley for Newton Lower Falls. In the seat in front of them, Garrett and Eliza spoke softly to each other. Charles and Lizzie said hardly a word. He held her gloved hand in both of his and watched as conflicting thoughts crossed her face. "Talk to me, Lizzie," he whispered. "Tell me what troubles you."

"I dinna knae if I kin even put it in ta words, Charles. The clerk in the bank was sure I was a bad person an' dinna even knae who I was. I'm from the North o' Ireland. Does that make me a person of ill repute? Why did he look at me wit' sech hatred? Would he hate a Scot, too? For I am thet, too."

"It has naught to do with you. It has everything to do with his own ignorance and perhaps a bad experience, of which we will never know. Who knows what formed his opinion, or how many people it encompasses? He is not worthy of your concern, Lizzie. He is like a flea on the back of a mighty horse. The horse *knows* he is mighty and the flea will blow away."

"That's fine for the mighty horse, Charles, but what if this flea is but one o' many? I am an Irisher in America, an' I will have ta find work an' a place ta live in a few short months. I've seen the signs that say, 'No Irish need apply'! Should I gae west, as James plans ta do?" Lizzie looked plaintively at Charles.

"Oh gracious, don't even think it. You will find work. You will have Missus Twombly's recommendation. Please Lizzie, don't let one stupid man drive you from this place. If I could marry you today, I would. You must have faith that God has a plan for you... for *us*, Lizzie. I believe that, Lizzie." The panic on his face startled her and she blamed herself for putting it there.

"Oh Charles, I dinna mean ta upset ye. I was confused by his anger. I could no' understand it. I have no desire ta leave this place, nor do I have the wherewithal ta do it."

Charles' face calmed, but still showed new worry etched on his smooth shaven face.

"Charles," she asked, "Do ye think we'll be home in time ta gae ta the boarding house ta make the deposit, or should I wait until Monday afternoon?"

"Hm, if it is still light out by the time we get there, perhaps. Ye won't want ta interrupt her evening meal wit' business, though. Monday would probably be best. How close is it ta the Twombly house?" he asked.

"It's two blocks nearer the station, Charles. I'd rather get it done today, wit' you if I can," said Lizzie, hopefully.

"Very well, if it's still light when we get to the street, I'll be glad to go with you. I'm sure Garrett will be delighted to take Eliza home by himself," he said, arching his eyebrow.

Lizzie giggled. *I dinna think she'd object either.*

Charles put one finger to her lips to hush her mirth. His blue eyes were dancing once again, as he looked back at her.

Chapter Sixteen

"That's gonna be two dollars a week for rent, starting on December 11th, first floor, with board. There are three weeks until the end of the month, totaling $6.

"She will have no gentlemen callers in her room. The water closet is adjacent. Use of the porch is permitted during daylight hours. Use of the living room is permitted only when I am present in the house and downstairs.

"Meals are at specific times and boarders will be seated five minutes prior. Boarders may be evicted for unseemly behavior of any kind. Do you understand?" The plump middle-aged woman with the stern face jutted her lower jaw out, as if looking for an argument.

Seeing none, she continued. "The door will be locked promptly at ten o'clock. There will be no noise after that time. Permission must be granted prior to an event, if a tenant wishes to stay out after that time.

"Very well then, here is your receipt. I look forward to meeting your mother." If she was, indeed, looking forward to meeting Maggie, it was not evident on her face.

Lizzie tried to pay attention to every word, but had no idea when her mind began to drift away. Her mother's face floated before

251

her, smiling, eager to see her. It was the Maggie she saw when Lizzie came running home from school.

Bringing herself back to the present, she said, "Until the 11th of December then, Missus Stanhope. Thank you for your time." Lizzie shook the older woman's hand and with a nod, turned on her heel and left. Charles followed, a little concerned.

After they were well out of earshot, Charles said, "Are you sure your mother will be comfortable here?"

"She'll have everythin' she needs. I'll be able ta see her late afternoons on Saturdays an' those days when the Twomblys gae out ta friends fer supper. An' she'll have Missus Stanhope eatin' peas from her hand by the week's end," said Lizzie saucily.

"Your mother would have to be most charming, to get more than 'good morning' from that bitter, angry, old woman," said Charles.

"I have faith that Maggie will have Missus Stanhope turning cartwheels for her pleasure in no time," laughed Lizzie. "She may be in a wheelchair, but she is not without considerable strengths. Besides, no one who is that angry all the time, would no' have a reason o' two, ta be thet way. Maggie will be good fer her."

"It'd be a pleasure just to see that woman smile, but I do not have your faith," said Charles a little doubtful.

"If I were a bettin' woman, an' ye were a bettin' man, *that* would be a wager I'd take," Lizzie said.

"The room looks nice, don't ye think? Windows ta give her sunlight in the morning. I hope the doorways are wide enough. I saw a piano in the parlor. I wonder if anyone plays. She'd like thet." Lizzie prattled most of the way home from the boarding house, while Charles fell silent. "Is there anythin' wrong, Charles?"

"Not at all, my dear, you seem to have everything under control. I wish I could have taken the trip and brought your mother back from Liverpool on my own, is all. That's just my sin of pride talking. I have no money and the Earl has provided that

252

convenience, so I shouldn't be wishing for things I cannot do. One day, my love, I will be able to give you those comforts and I'll ask the Good Lord to help me be patient 'til then."

"Charles, let's jes' be grateful, God has given us a way ta make it possible."

"Watch your step here, Lizzie." The dark had reached the Twombly house and skirting the front porch to the side path to the back was a tricky walk. "Allow me ta go first, Lizzie." Going around her, he stumbled, but regained his balance.

Once in front and out of range of the light from the windows, he stopped and pulled her into his arms. He kissed her slowly, intently. Smiling and releasing her, he led her to the back step, into the light from the back porch. Before stepping up, they both looked into the kitchen.

There in the light of the kitchen were Garrett and Eliza talking near the back door. Charles put a finger up to his lips to keep Lizzie quiet. Garrett pecked Eliza on her forehead and opened the door. "Oh, Eliza, here they are now," he said.

They didn't realize how cold they were, until they were greeted with an almost smothering blanket of warmth from the kitchen stove. "Is the family home, Eliza?"

"Nay, would ye an' Garrett like ta come in fer tea, Charles?" Eliza asked shyly.

"Perhaps we shouldn't. I wouldn't want to cause a problem for you girls, should the family come home. I should be getting back to the dorms at any rate. They lock up at ten and I have to stop at the library for a book. But thank you, Eliza." Turning to Lizzie, he said, "I will leave on Thursday night, December 9th, and sleep on the train. The next day, I will meet the ship and bring your mother back to you."

"Charles, I had intended ye ta stay o'er night afore the ship arrived. Ye will be exhausted sleepin' on the train. Ye didn't sleep 'tall when ye brought us here," protested Lizzie.

253

"Lizzie, dear, I have classes until afternoon, so I'll not have time to leave earlier, but I will sleep while I have no charge for whom I am responsible. I will stay awake while your mother is aboard the train on Saturday, don't worry, dear. Have you checked with the Twomblys about allowing your mother to sleep here, the night of the tenth?"

"Oh dear, I hadn't thought o' that! I'll ask Missus Twombly t'marra. She should be able ta sleep in my room, if they permit it. Eliza, I hope yer won' mind sleepin' upstairs thet night? I'll gae up wit' yer, if you like. Thank yer for sayin' somethin', Charles. I had quite fergot her room will be ready on the 11th, but no' the night o' the tenth."

"Not at all, Lizzie, now I really do have to leave, if I am to meet my curfew. I never thought I would ever say that as a grown man, but there it is. I am pursuing a young man's challenge, and I will just have to abide by the rules set for him, won't I?" said Charles, sheepishly.

"It is the goal ye have to look at, Charles, not the little details. When ye've earned the prize, ye wan' hafta think about the little niggles thet plagued ye alang yer way."

Fully aware of the other two watching their every move, Charles kissed Lizzie's hand, and staring deep into her eyes, said, "Good-night, my sweet. I will see you on the night of the tenth and I will be here early Sunday morning to bring your mother to her new home. God be with you until then." He kissed her forehead and left abruptly.

Garrett stared after him, and as if awakening from a dream, he said, "I'd better git, too, I guess. Mister Baker said he'd have my hide if I came in late and woke up the kiddies. They have a new puppy that raises a ruckus ever' time I come in the house. I'll see you agin, Miss Eliza, Miss Lizzie."

"Goodbye, Mister jes' Plain Garrett." Eliza teased as she opened the door. He quickly kissed her cheek, fled down the steps, and ran off to the Baker's house.

"Seems like ye had a lovely day wit' young Mister Garrett, Miss Eliza," Lizzie said with her hands on her hips and a smile on her face.

"'Twas verra nice, Miss Lizzie." Eliza curtsied in bright-eyed fun. "*He's* verra nice, too."

"I'm glad ye had someone while Charles an' I were off at the bank. James' Marianna seems a bonnie girl. She's completely swept up wit' him, isn't she? Maybe he'll take her west wit' him."

"Do ye think so? I thought she was more interested in *him*, than James was in *her*, though."

"He'd have a hard time livin' wit' himself, if he was breakin' her heart, Eliza. She looks like a porcelain doll."

"James says she's stronger than she looks. She has a whole passel o' younger brothers an' sisters ta care fer. He says she has two or three in her arms or on her back all the time."

"Really? It jes' goes ta show ye, ye can't tell a book by its cover, kin yer? Oh, the paper's here. There's another article about Lizzie Borden. 'ALICE RUSSELL TELLS THE GRAND JURY ABOUT THE VISIT SHE RECEIVED FROM LIZZIE THE NIGHT BEFORE THE MURDERS,' it says." Lizzie scanned the article. "My goodness, she's bein' bound over fer trial. This was only the Grand Jury an' they only present the part o' the case that will decide if she is ta be held fer the full trial. I don't understand. How many times do they hafta try a person? Anyways, she's goin' back ta jail, poor thing."

"How kin you read about thet awful stuff, Lizzie? I would think it would give yer nightmares," said Eliza. "It would *me!*"

"It's fascinatin' ta me. It doesn't seem real, but I like ta 'magine 'twas me. What would I do? I think I would stay as calm as I could, and no' give anyone any more information than they demanded o' me. Jes' like Lizzie Borden. Poor woman! Havin' ta

255

stay in a dirty ol' jail this whole time." Lizzie tried to picture what jail would be like for Lizzie Borden. Her mind drifted to Castlewellan Gaol, the only jail she knew. It was dark, dirty, dank, and *bone*-chilling cold, this time of year. *I haven't seen a jail in America, but it's pro'bly no' sae different. Pro'bly bigger, seems ever' thin's bigger an' newer in this country.*

The next day after Sunday dinner, Missus Twombly sat in her rocker in the kitchen, going over last minute changes to the menu for the following week. There were no guests for today, which meant there were several meetings during the week. Lizzie waited patiently for the schedule of events and menus to be finalized. Tuesday, a ladies' brunch for the Christmas Pageant Committee was planned. The women would arrive at ten o'clock. A buffet would be set up at the end of the dining room, with chafing dishes of French toast, coddled eggs, home-fried potatoes, hot syrup, and fruit compote. Thursday, there would be the Men's Prayer Meeting and Church Planning Group at six o'clock. Isabelle and Missus Twombly would eat in their rooms. There would be no Sunday Dinner guests.

As Missus Twombly closed her social journal, Lizzie seized her chance to speak. "Missus Twombly, my mother is arrivin' on the evening of December 10th. Would ye be willing ta have her sleep in my room thet night? Eliza an' I could sleep in the attic, if that is satisfactory. I would be able ta take my mother ta her boarding house early Sunday."

"Oh Lizzie, I should have known you would need to do that. Of course, it would be our pleasure. Will she be joining us for Church in the morning, do you think?"

"I don't know. If she fairs well on the trip an' the train ride, then perhaps she will. I think she should probably rest as much as possible on her first day here."

"Well, then let's plan to have her here for Sunday Dinner. We are most anxious to meet her. Perhaps we can persuade Mister

Bachelor to join us as well. Would you like that, Lizzie?" Missus Twombly said, smiling mischievously.

"Oh, I would no' like ta impose, ma'am. Ye have been sae kind in accommodatin' us already," said Lizzie, blushing.

"Nonsense, we want your mother to feel welcome in her new home, don't we? Anything we can do to make things comfortable for her, we'd consider our privilege to do. Will there be any problem getting her into the house, Lizzie?"

"I'm sure we kin manage. If Charles brings her in first, then gaes back fer the chair, it should be fine. Any other problems, we will figure out as we come ta them."

"Well, I'm sure William would be glad to lend a hand if needed."

"Aye, ma'am," Lizzie kept her silence, as the amusing thought of frail Mister William struggling to carry her mother became almost overwhelming.

Dinna laugh, Lizzie! It was kind o' her ta offer his services e'en though 'twould be easier fer me *ta carry my mother wit' all her luggage, than ta imagine William delicately managin' her all by himsel'.*

"You are mos' kind, ma'am. You will hardly knae she's here, afore she's gone agin," Lizzie said.

"Please do not worry about it. We welcome a little change in our routine every once in a while. It keeps us from getting stuck in our ways, as it were. You must be so excited to see her."

"I am, but I will be happier when she's finally settled here, I guess." Lizzie confessed.

"These things have a way of working out for the best, dear. Before I forget, in the New Year, we will have many meetings in town for the national church organizations. You will have less responsibilities at home, while we go into Boston, two or three times a week. Since we will be having chicken dinners for luncheon almost every meeting day, we request the meals we have at home, be anything *but chicken*."

Seeing Lizzie's amused reaction, Missus Twombly laughed. "Our chicken-less meal regimen lasts through until March, about the time our chicken dinner meetings run out." She laughed again. "This is the time our girls usually look for the work they will do when their time with us is up. You will also want to find a place to live, probably for the beginning of April. The church will start enquiring about new servants commencing January."

"Aye, ma'am, Eliza and I've become sae comfortable here, we hadn't thought much about the end o' our stay. It's good ye mentioned it. There's sae much fer us ta prepare. Thank yer, I canna imagine a more congenial fam'ly fer whom ta have worked." Lizzie was surprised how the prospect of leaving moved her so.

"That's very kind of you to say. If it were up to us, we would continue as it is. You and Eliza are very worthy students of your work. Alas, we are none of us in control of our destinies. We are servants ourselves, at the mercy of the church's dictates. But we adjust our sails to follow the stars, as it were." She cleared her throat and continued, "I'm sure you will find work in whatever endeavor you pursue. We will happily give you recommendations of your good character and excellent work.

"I really must lie down for a while. We may have callers this evening, and I should be in attendance. They will be here for only a short time, so tea or coffee and dessert will be sufficient. Thank you, Lizzie."

Lizzie checked her remaining pie and tea cakes, deciding she had enough for about eight people. She could fill in with hermits, if necessary. She set out eight dessert plates, one footed dessert plate on which she stacked the remaining hermits and eight dessert forks for the dessert cart. She checked her stew for supper and laid out her ingredients for twin rolls. She had been challenging herself by making a different kind of rolls for supper each day of the week.

Crescents, Parker House, bread sticks, hot cross buns, cheese biscuits, and on Sunday she planned to make a braided wreath with currants and raisins.

The week flew. *Next Saturday, Maggie will be here,* thought Lizzie. She tried to think of everything that could make her coming to America more comfortable.

It canna be easy fer her ta leave Ireland an' travel alone ta this place. She's not young, nor able-bodied. But, if there's anythin' she kin do better than us, it's adapt ta whate'er life has in store fer her. If she canna adapt, she'll charm the beasties who dare stand in her way.

Eliza had been working on an afghan for Maggie. Not for the first time, Lizzie wished she had a talent for fine work, something that lasts. Something she could give as a gift.

Lizzie sought out Missus Twombly's copy of <u>Mrs. Lincoln's Boston School of Cooking</u>. Perhaps candies. Nothing. Missus Lincoln did not approve of sweets. She tried to remember the peppermint drops that Mórai used to make. *I'll have ta ask Missus Twombly's leave ta make them anyways.* She knew she could buy some of the ingredients, but not all. She had a few pennies from her last day off, but the rest of the money in her purse belonged to Maggie.

The next time Missus Twombly sat in her rocker, she broached the subject carefully. "Missus Twombly, wit' Christmas comin', an' the Baker children sure ta visit, do ye think we should have some Christmas candies fer our guests? I haven't bin able ta find any recipes in Missus Lincoln's book. *Mórai* usta make peppermint drops, but I dinna ken the proportion o' peppermint oil ta sugar she used."

"My goodness, Lizzie, we will have to research that, won't we? My mother used to make popcorn balls with molasses taffy," Missus Twombly said.

"Imagine a world without confections! Last year, Dora had a recipe of her mother's for pecan brittle, but it made so much we were eating it for months.

"I will send Isabella to the library to see if there are any recipes for confections there. When you go to the grocer's, see if he has any printed recipes there. He sometimes has Greta, his wife, write out a recipe so he can sell more of one ingredient or another. If he doesn't, you may want to suggest it to him. What a wonderful thought, Lizzie! The children will love it."

"Missus Twombly, if you'd allow me, I'd like ta add my pennies ta pay fer makin' a few extra candies fer my mother, too. I've bin tryin' ta fin' somethin' I could give her as a present."

"Nonsense! You had the idea, and you're doing all the work, I think you've earned a bit of candy fer your mother. This is a good week to make candy. I don't have any meetings. We're going out Tuesday, for supper with the Johnson's and Wednesday, for the Christmas supper at the Church and the Pageant." Missus Twombly smiled and added, "Eula Baker will be Mary."

"Oh, Missus Twombly, she will be a wonderful Mary! Do you think Eliza and I could gae, jes' ta the pageant? We'll have all our work done by then."

"Of course, Lizzie, I would hate for you to miss our little angel as the mother of the Baby Jesus. I have no doubt about you getting your work done. You always do."

She thought a moment, and added, "Oh yes, and either Tuesday or Wednesday, I'd like you to help Eliza take the heavy drapes in the parlor down and freshen them up. The parlor stove just covers them in soot. Eliza does her best, I know, but they really need to be taken down, beat on the back porch, then brushed to bring the nap back. That room will have a lot of company in the next two weeks, so I want it to look its best. The under curtains can be washed the day before and hung while the heavy draping is being cleaned."

Lizzie thanked her profusely. *Eliza will be sae pleased. We've served at the meetings an' heard sae much about this pageant, we hardly dared ta dream we'd see it fer ourselves.*

As far as the drapes are concerned, Eliza mentioned how much they needed refreshing ta me jes' las' week. She probably said as much ta Missus Twombly. I hope this weather stays fair. I'll clean the under curtains Monday, jes' in case.

Lizzie mentally went through her schedule for the week, and was satisfied that they would be done in time for the pageant, and still have some time to make sweets for all the children, even the full grown ones. She chuckled as she pictured Doctor Twombly seated in the rocker, sipping coffee with one hand and reaching for a plate of peanut brittle with his other.

Lizzie was grateful she was busy enough not to think of her mother on the ship during the day. At night, when she was snug in her bed however, her fears of her mother's discomfort crept into her dreams.

Aboard the Steamship, City of Chester:
Maggie sat by the porthole watching the moonlight dance on the water. She could not discern the meeting of sky and water, so black were they, except where the moon and the lights from the ship bounced on the waves. The thrum of the engines and faint sounds of music in the salon overhead soothed her thoughts.

Laird, it does not content me to do what is right for the protection of my soul. Hugh thinks I am righteous and better than he. He dreams that I am strong in my protection of his young wife's honor. I am not. Running away from his arms, I yearn for them no less. Ease this sad empty longing, Laird. It is right for me to leave him, but it contents me not.

Lord Annesley was true to his word at Castlewellan. He dined or had tea with her only in the company of either or both of his children, visiting colleagues, or even the gardener as he

261

promised, to keep all rumors and innuendos at bay, while she resided at the castle.

The servants adored her and squelched any careless word from passing the lips of any of the house staff. They observed the congenial demeanor of their master and credited her with the uncharacteristic lightness of his step.

The trip from Castlewellan to Liverpool was taken with the coach curtains closed. Passersby may have thought it was to keep out the cold north wind, but the driver closed them to shield Hugh and Maggie from onlookers. It was not the cold that drove them together on that long, sad ride to Liverpool. They did not leave the coach even on the ferry. The driver stood guard against curious ferry passengers.

At first, they tried to talk as if this was just another sojourn of many, but neither could sustain the pointless chatter and they fell silent. Her hand in his, she watched his sad face seem to grow more forlorn with each mile. "Do you remember..." she began softly, then hesitated.

"Yes," he said. "I do."

"But..."

"I remember every moment," he said, almost inaudibly. Hugh shifted his body to face her. "I remember when you were a mere child, not more than ten, with a scratch across your nose because Joseph Heenan pushed your chair over a stone in the school yard and you toppled out. It was before I was in love with you, but it nearly broke my heart to see you cry. Then, when he tried to help you back into the chair, you hit him and called him a clumsy oaf. I thought to myself, Maggie will be strong. I was unforgivably delighted to see the boy so upset to be the object of your fury." Hugh smiled, wistfully.

"I remember thanking God when you fell into my arms, instead of down the mountainside on Blaeberry Sunday. I fell in love that day. I remember a thousand times since, when I held my breath, and said, 'Thank you, God, for this moment with Maggie'."

He closed his eyes, as if against physical pain. The rough road rocked the carriage throwing Maggie even closer to him. They sat silently for a long time, listening to their comingled heartbeats, breathing in each other's breath.

"If I come home..." Again, he stopped her speech. He put a finger on her lips gently.

"Don't let me hope, sweet Maggie. I will wither and die of loneliness every day, if I have hope. I will be able to live my life, if I have no hope of seeing you again. Let me be selfish in this one thing. Let my family, my tenants, and my country have all of me, or none of me. If I look for your return, I will lose all sense of who I am to them."

"Of course, my love, we mustn't torture each other with promises to break. Just hold me now and once I board the ship, let there be no more reminders of this day. Do not ask that I forget you, however. Hugh, you are the best part of who I am."

The fleeting miles seemed to fall behind them and they were keenly aware, the hour of her departure was upon them.

She cried, silently shaking as he held her ever tighter. He kissed her, and she held her breath, hoping time and earth would stand still.

As time relentlessly passed, her heart seemed to beat faster, ever faster. She stared at him, memorizing every aspect of his face.

The carriage stopped. A discrete knock on the door brought them out of their trance. It was time to complete their physical separation. The Earl of Annesley wondered if he could order his legs to move, or if his arms would let her go.

With a protesting groan, he left the carriage and walked around to lift her to her chair. The driver took her bag and Hugh pushed her chair to the walkway. There, a man in uniform turned the chair around and dragged it up after him. Hugh followed empty-handed, his eyes locked on Maggie's.

Hugh met the captain, shook hands with his old friend and answered the questions required for Maggie to complete her boarding. The captain drew the uniformed man aside, and spoke sternly at length, while he darted glances at Maggie. The man saluted and returned. "I must bring her to her cabin before we depart, sir," he said.

Hugh stooped down to Maggie. He put her papers in her hand and said, "Goodbye, my love. I will pray for you every night that you are safe and happy. May you feel my arms around you whenever you need comfort, hear my voice in your joyous moments, let my shoulder be your pillow as you rest, and I will be happy all of my days." He kissed her gently on her lips, smiled sadly into her eyes, stood, and walked quickly away.

Maggie's hand flew to her trembling mouth as if to make his parting kiss linger there. In her hand, without her realizing how it got there, was his handkerchief. She smiled through falling tears, and felt the chair move. Far below, she saw him walking purposefully to the carriage. He did not raise his head to look at her.

Then, as her eyes followed the carriage down the pier, the curtain moved and his face slid into view. She caught her breath and whispered, "Goodbye, Hugh."

Once in her cabin, she cried like a child, howling, with her mouth wide open, gulping great sobs, bending in half in emotional pain. When she was just short of being physically ill, she stopped. She washed her face, wetting his handkerchief in the basin left on her dresser. She wheeled herself to the port hole and stared at the ocean for a long time.

Soon, the alien life aboard ship began to develop a rhythm for Maggie. The steward assigned to her needs was a congenial young man who fell under her charming spell. With his help, she was able to explore the ship, dine where she liked, and sit on the deck with or without company. He saw her sadness and encouraged her to seek the company of other passengers at least in part of her day. Captain Passow invited her to join him for dinner every day, but she declined most of the time. She often dined with other second class passengers or alone in her cabin.

Neither adverse weather, nor the motion of the ship, seemed to affect her comfort. Though the young steward tried his best, neither the exceptional amenities of the *City of Chester,* nor the special attention accorded her, could erase the pervasive sadness in Maggie's eyes.

In Newton Lower Falls:

Lizzie woke early Wednesday morning planning her day, and to attend the Christmas Pageant that night. All they had to get done was hang the drapes they had cleaned the day before and make Christmas sweets between breakfast and luncheon. With no guests, the meals were easy to prepare and serve. Even if they had "drop in" guests in the afternoon, they would not be there long, because of the Christmas supper at the church before the pageant.

The drapes were not so much difficult, as awkward. Lizzie climbed the step stool while Eliza handed her the rods with the drapes to hang. After a bit of wiggling and waiting to hear a solid click as the heavy rod slipped into the brace under the cornice, Lizzie was able to climb down and attack the next window. The massive bay window had four tall sections to cover. Only the side windows had heavy drapes all the way to the floor. Each of the center windows had a matching swag that draped below the cornice. Within an hour, the windows were draped and the curtains arranged satisfactorily.

Lizzie helped Eliza straighten up the parlor until it was perfect. Her half-sister asked Missus Twombly to view the room with a critical eye. With nothing left to change, Missus Twombly returned Doctor Twombly's current reading material to the book shelves, and pronounced the room ready for Christmas.

"Will you have a Christmas Tree, Missus Twombly?"

"Oh yes, but not until Christmas Eve, or perhaps the day before that. We'll want it fresh for Christmas. I think we'll place it in the dining room, and take out a leaf or two from the table. At Christmas, we have small, intimate dinners. Those who have larger families have guests to their homes during the season.

"We like to have just those who have nowhere else to go at Christmastime. Christmas Day, most everyone finds some family with whom to have dinner. It's usually just us that day. Maybe we'll add Charles and your mother. No more than that."

"And Big John?" asked Lizzie.

"John usually goes to the Mission in Boston and serves Christmas dinner there. Garrett will probably be with the Bakers. He's become one of the family over there."

Missus Twombly checked the clock. "Well, thank you ladies. The pageant is at 7 o'clock sharp, so plan your time accordingly. We will be leaving here at about 4 o'clock for the supper. We are not expected to bring anything for that. Missus Baker and the Ladies Group are there now, preparing the meal."

"Very well, shall we have soup and biscuits for luncheon, with cider, ma'am?"

"That will be fine, Lizzie. We don't want to be full and not be able to complement every woman at the supper on her wonderful cooking, do we?" Missus Twombly laughed, conspiratorially.

"No, ma'am," said Lizzie, smiling. "I'll get started on the sweets."

Lizzie hummed to herself as she made fudge and toffee, hard candy drops and honey chews rolled in powdered sugar. When the fudge was set, she cut it into small pieces and decorated them with tiny rosettes. She set aside three pieces of each kind of candy and placed them in a small tin Missus Twombly gave her. She wrapped the tin in butcher paper and tied it with a ribbon she bought on market day. With a satisfied smile, she tucked it in her dresser for Christmas.

She bought an extra ribbon for Eliza's summer hat. *I'm glad I saw her hat ribbon was all in strings. I will replace the ribbon, poke the straw back in place, and that will be my present to her. I hope she doesn't realize her hat is gone from her room.* Lizzie pictured the hat in its hiding place under the dresser. *She almost caught me putting it there!*

She liked that America seemed to make much more of Christmas presents than they did at home. For the Scots and Northern Irish, New Year's Day was more of a celebration, than Christmas. Although it was celebrated in church on the nearest Sunday, it was just another work day at home. In America, it was a true holiday. They went to church on Christmas Day and celebrated all day long. Lizzie was especially excited about the Christmas Pageant.

That evening, Lizzie and Eliza slipped into the crowded church and went up to the balcony. They were surprised to see it nearly full. They sat in the side pew near the front and had a wonderful view of the whole front of the church. The choir marched in singing, *Oh Come, All Ye Faithful.* The lights were dimmed, the crowd hushed, and the reader began, "And it came to pass in those days, that there went out a decree from Caesar Augustus that all the world should be taxed."

As he went on, the lights came up on the stage revealing Joseph, played by Tommy Perkins in an obviously itchy robe belonging to his father; Mary, sweet Eulah Baker in a beautiful blue robe sitting beside the manger; and the baby Jesus, played by the newest congregant of the church, who was sleeping peacefully. The audience murmured a collective "aw…"

Next was the entrance of the shepherds. Three little boys in robes, holding their awkward crooks, thudded onto the stage. Mary turned with an angry "Shhush!" which made the first shepherd stop in his tracks and the other two banged into him. The second shepherd was clunked on the head with the third one's crook. This altercation woke the baby, who began to wail. Mary bent to pick up the baby, when Joseph shouted, "You're not supposed to touch the baby! Let her mother get her quiet."

The incensed Mary replied, "I *am* the mother. Baby Jesus is *mine*. I'll take care of her!" Eulah picked up the baby, laying her head carefully upon her shoulder. Then, to the astonishment of everyone in the church but Eulah's, the baby went back to sleep. Eulah held the baby for the rest of the play. Except for a small squabble among the three kings, as to who should carry the gold, the rest of play went smoothly.

The thunderous applause at the end woke the baby. Mary stood, dignifiedly walked to the side of the stage, and handed the screaming baby to her mother. "She's not Jesus any more, Mrs. Babcock," explained Eulah.

"Thank you, Eulah. You're a very good mother," Mrs. Babcock replied, with an irrepressible grin.

Eulah found her own mother, shook her head, and said succinctly, "Boys! I *told* them to behave."

Lizzie and Eliza were giggling in the balcony, when Garrett walked over to them. "I wonder what Jesus thinks of our play," he mused.

"I'm sure He looks at it with a kind heart, Garrett," answered Eliza, wiping the tears from her eyes. "I'm very happy to have seen it. Will you walk with us, Garrett? We have to get home before the Twomblys."

"I would be delighted, ladies," he said, with a twinkle in his eye. He led the way to the outside of the throng, then offered his arm to each of the girls when they reached the sidewalk. Most of the audience paused to shake hands with the ministers and comment on the pageant. This allowed the three to walk leisurely home by themselves.

"I don't think they will be home for a long while," commented Garrett. "Say, Lizzie, when's yer ma gittin' here? Should be soon, right?"

"She'll be here by Sat'day night, won't she, Lizzie?" said Eliza. "I kin hardly wait."

"Aye, Sat'day," said Lizzie thoughtfully. "I canna believe she's almost here."

"Lizzie! Don't worry. It'll be wonderful ta have her here. Wait 'til you meet her, Garrett! She's beautiful, an' charming, an' sweet," gushed Eliza. "She's no' my real mother, but the only one I've known."

"Aye, she is lovely," said Lizzie quietly.

C'mon, Lizzie, show some enthusiasm fer seein' yer ma. Why are ye sae scared o' her bein' here? She'll be happy here. Ye will find work enough ta take care o' her. This is the land o' milk n' honey, isn't it?

"Well, I'm sure she's all o' those things, an' more, but wha's *botherin'* you, Liz?" asked Garrett.

"She's jes' worried we won' be able ta take good care o' her. Maggie's an invalid, ye ken, an' takes more care than most," said Eliza. "But we kin do it, Lizzie. Yer the best laundress in all the North o' Ireland. An' I'll find maid work or somethin' ta do. 'Tween you and me, we'll take care o' Maggie."

Still Lizzie was quiet. Eliza went on, talking to Garrett about the wonderful Maggie, naming all her talents and charms. Garrett watched the two sisters in their disparate reactions to the impending arrival of Margaret Heenan. He could draw no conclusions with the evidence presented to him. *I'll jes' have to wait an' see*, he thought.

269

Chapter Seventeen

"Please don't worry, Missus Heenan. Your escort should be here shortly," said the captain to the nervously fidgeting passenger in the wheelchair. "We arrived a bit early, so he was probably told the expected time of arrival was noon. It is now just half ten. Are you comfortable? Shall I get you another blanket?"

"I am just fine, Captain Passow. I understand you are an acquaintance of the Earl of Annesley," she said, trying to change the conversation away from herself.

"Ah yes, Lieutenant Hugh Annsley and I served in Kafir when we were not much more than beardless boys. He saved my life and was shot for his reward. He brought me to the medical tent in time for an attack on it. Blasted heathens," he growled under his breath.

Then, as if just realizing his inappropriate speech, he softened his tone and said, "Oh, I do beg your pardon, Missus Heenan. It's not a very savory topic for casual conversation. Needless to say, I've been in his debt for forty years. It is gracious of him to allow me to repay him this way. You have my deepest respect for your association with him and his high regard for your comfort, ma'am."

270

"You have mine, as well, Captain. He speaks highly of your sense of duty and trustworthiness, sir. I thank you for your many kindnesses on this voyage. The young man you assigned to me was most attentive and helpful. Please let him know I appreciate his efforts, won't you?"

Pausing to survey her surroundings, she said, "You have a magnificent ship, Captain Passow. I have visited the ship near its entirety, and I am pleased to hear the care of your steerage passengers far exceed what I have been told of other ships. Although plainer than second or first class accommodations, it is comfortable, and the food is plentiful and varied. You should be very proud."

"I am at that, Missus Heenan. I run a tight ship, but I pride myself on taking care of *all* of my passengers. There has been a great deal of political talk of improving the lot of steerage and second class passengers, but not much done about it. I hope to change that even more so. It is easier on a voyage like this, however, when none of the passengers have immigrant status. The boarding and debarking are easier when all the passengers have families waiting for them. Although our steerage travelers are poor, they have ties to this country, and are reasonably well behaved. They respond well to good accommodations."

Maggie saw him swell with pride as he spoke. Spying a tall, somber man climbing the gangway, she asked, "Could this be the gentleman we are waiting for, Captain Passow?"

"We shall see what his papers say, Missus Heenan. I'll not hand you over to just anyone, without the proper documentation."

The man stood at his full height and handed a paper to the captain. "Mister Bachelor, from whom did you receive this document?"

"F-from Lizzie Heenan, sir," he replied nervously. "I am to escort her mother, Margaret Heenan, to Newton Lower Falls, Massachusetts."

"Very good, Mister Bachelor, this is Missus Heenan. I put you in charge of her comfort and safety, until such time as she is rejoined with her daughter, Lizzie Heenan. If there should be any mishap, you are charged to wire the Honorable Hugh Annesley, of Castlewellan, County Down, Northern Ireland immediately. Is that clear?"

"Y-yes, sir," Charles answered with an automatic salute. Blushing at his blunder, he extended his hand to the Captain and said, "Excuse me sir, I served for several years in the Revenue Marine. Old habits die hard. Captain, I accept this task with honor. I am pleased to meet you both. Missus Heenan, are you ready to see your daughters?"

Smiling broadly, the captain turned to Maggie and said, "You will be in good hands, Missus Heenan. Bon voyage. Good luck in your new country and God bless you."

Maggie nodded. "I will tell the Earl you fulfilled your promise with honor, Captain Passow. Bon voyage to you, as well. I am pleased to have met you." She turned to Charles Bachelor, and smiling, said, "Shall we, Mister Bachelor?"

Later, as he was taking her to the train, Charles Bachelor was notably careful in his speech, gently guiding her chair, and keeping an eye on her luggage.

She is as beautiful as I imagine Lizzie will be at her age. She seems comfortable with everyone, no matter what their station, and gracious in acknowledging everyone who helps her in any small way. The young porter is completely enamored of her. He keeps looking back as if she may disappear at any moment.

Boarding the train, the porter lead them to a private compartment, stowed her luggage, and stood gazing at her. Charles said, "Thank you, son, that will be all." Charles nudged the boy, dropped a coin in his hand, and gestured toward the door.

"It was a pleasure, ma'am, and safe trip." The boy, not taking his eyes off Maggie, slammed his shoulder against the doorway. "Excuse me, sir," he said.

Charles raised his eyebrow and smiled wryly at Lizzie's mother. "You seem to have had a powerful effect on our young friend, Missus Heenan."

"Perhaps it was just the motion of the train that threw him off balance, Mister Bachelor," she said, her eyes dancing.

"Oh dear, I didn't realize we were moving. I am so sorry, Missus Heenan. Would you allow me to get you out of that chair and into a seat near the window?"

"That would be nice. If we could move the chair a little closer to the seat, I'm sure I could manage it myself," she said. Charles moved the chair parallel to the rose velvet bench and held it steady as Maggie slid from one surface to the other. "Do you think there is a place outside this room for the chair, Mister Bachelor?"

"I will find one, Missus Heenan." Charles went in search for a secure place for the chair. Maggie scooted toward the window and pulled her skirt straight.

It was still early, and traveling north, the east window was bright, but away from the sun. As the train moved slowly through the city, the sooty backs of tall tenement buildings revealed dirty children playing in small fenced yards and balconies. Between the buildings, there was a strange network of clotheslines, full of flapping sheets, from the first to the very top floors. She watched housewives, their heads bound in kerchiefs, precariously leaning out windows, alternately hollering the day's news to their neighbors, and screaming at their wayward children below.

Her companion came back and settled down on the bench opposite her. "Mister Bachelor, I would like it if you would call me, Maggie. I am sure we will be friends before long, and it would please me."

"Then you must call me Charles," he said tentatively, not knowing what else to say.

"Lizzie has written to me about you, Charles. You must be a remarkable man to have caught her attention."

"I am very fond of Lizzie, but I fear I am fonder of her, than she is of me. I am a student of divinity and as such, I can have no claim on her affections."

"Oh my, are you to become a *monk*, then?"

"Oh dear, no," Charles replied, flushing deeply. "I misspoke. I merely meant that I have a great deal of schooling to complete before I could possibly declare my intentions toward any woman. I cannot ask anyone to wait that long, no matter how I feel toward her."

"Charles, one thing you must learn about me, is that I have a teasing nature. I apologize for my silly question. I knew you were studying to become a minister and that it is a long, arduous road. I can see you care for her. I am looking forward to getting to know the man for whom my daughter holds such regard."

"Thank you, Missus uh, Maggie. I have heard many nice things about you. Please ask me anything you'd like to know."

"Firstly, one of a practical nature: How long will it take to get to this Lower Falls of Newton?"

"Oh, of course, it's about eight hours. We will not have to change trains for this trip, so we will make rather good time," answered Charles.

"Eight hours. Well, that brings us to a second question, and I apologize for having to ask. Is there a place where I could freshen up in this car?"

"It is I, who needs to apologize, Maggie. There is a water closet at the end of the car. Although I confess, I do not know how to accommodate you," Again, he flushed deeply.

"We will figure it out together, Charles. Although I cannot walk, I can stand if I am holding onto two solid posts or walls, so perhaps it will not be as difficult as first thought. Shall we try it?" she asked gently. "If you bring me to the water closet, and open the door, perhaps I can manage the rest."

"Yes, ma'am," said Charles. He was terrified that the motion of the train would send them toppling down the passageway before their arrival at her destination, but there was no help for it. He had to do it.

Try to have some modicum of dignity, man! It cannot be comfortable for her to ask such a thing. Gently, carefully, get in a rhythm with the train. Don't drop her! Charles talked to himself during the entire trip down the passageway.

He tried not to think of her alarming physical closeness against him and the warm feel of her breath on his ear.

Don't be such a child! This is Lizzie's mother! What are you, evil run amok?

Charles desperately tried the door. It was locked. *Step back, lean against the wall, as you wait. It's a good thing she doesn't weigh much. Put one foot in front of you, so you can balance, when the train lurches,* he thought as the train seemed to thwart his attempt to keep his stance calm and secure. *Please Lord, don't let me drop her!*

"Charles, you're doing very well. It will be over soon," said Maggie, hoping she spoke the truth.

The door opened to a man startled by the couple just outside the tiny room. He squeezed passed them, then turned to watch the strange event of two people trying to enter the small space at the same time.

Charles gently set her down to a standing position, and still grasping her waist, waited for her to get her bearings. Maggie grabbed a post just inside the door and leaned heavily on the edge of the tiny sink. Over her shoulder, she said, "You may close the door, Charles. I'm quite all right."

He did as he was told, dropping his arms to get the blood flowing back into them. He listened for a dreaded thud that would force him into the little room to rescue her, but it never came. Shortly, he saw the door open and Maggie was standing there, shaky and pale, but upright.

"We seemed to have managed without incident." She grinned weakly. "Let's go back home, Charles."

"Yes, Missus Heenan." Charles felt his natural color would never return.

She doesn't even seem self-conscious. She must have to depend on people doing this all the time. I can see why Lizzie has such a practical nature. Dealing with her mother's difficulties must make her think she can do anything. It cannot have been an easy life for either of them, always having to find an alternate way to do all the things we take for granted, and do it with grace and dignity. I can see why Lizzie's so nervous about having her mother to care for again, as well.

"Maggie, you have taught me a practical and humble lesson this day," he said when he finally had her settled in the compartment. "Next time, we will do this with a little more grace."

It was Maggie's turn to blush. "Charles, I am sure we will. I am sorry to involve you, a virtual stranger. You are a very special man. Lizzie is blessed to have you in her life. Now that we have solved this little problem, tell me about yourself, Charles. What has made you this remarkably adaptable man?"

"The accolades you bestow upon me Maggie, belong to the two remarkable and adaptable women I have so recently met. Through them, I have found in myself new talents to bring to the tasks put before me. I now know a deeper meaning of something I heard once from a great man: 'Do not pray for tasks equal to your powers. Pray for powers equal to your tasks.' It was an Episcopal minister, I heard a few years ago. You and Lizzie put those words into practice every day." Charles shook his head in wonder.

Humbled by his words, Maggie said, "I believe every person is given a set of tasks to fulfill in this life. We must each rise up to them. God gives us strength as we need it. I think you will be a good minister, Charles."

"I hope you're right, Maggie. It is my fervent wish to serve Him in that way. My doubts so often confound me. I struggle through my studies. I study things in which I find no connection to the service of God. I plow through passages that seem to have no meaning for me. Yet, I pray someday I will understand and make use of it all."

"Ah, God doesn't tell us everything. Even when we pray and plan and prepare, we don't know where His path will lead us. Would we take the path, if we knew? Perhaps not, I do believe if we pursue a particular goal, God will lead us to where we are supposed to be according to His plan, but not necessarily according to *our* plan. Learning is never wasted. We need to educate ourselves, so we can be prepared for whatever His plan is for us."

Charles fell silent for a while, pondering her words. "I guess I shouldn't question my courses, just study until I understand them."

He sounded so morose, Maggie laughed. "Question *everything*, Charles! Study hard, but joyously, all of these disciplines are part of God's world. Learn about His world, and you'll rejoice in it. If you would be a minister, open your mind and your heart to His creation. Enjoy the journey, Charles."

He was thoughtful and silent for a moment, and then said, "I confess, I have never met anyone quite like you. I think you may have changed the way I look at my studies. Thank you, Maggie Heenan." Charles looked as if a great weight had fallen off his shoulders. "Would you excuse me if I do some reading for a while?"

"Of course, do you have more than one book with you? I would love to read also."

277

"Yes, I do. I have *The History of Western Civilization* or ..." he said wrinkling his nose, "*Principles of Advanced Algebra*. Which would you like?"

"You choose. It is more important that you study, than which one I choose to read for pleasure," said Maggie.

"I will take the Algebra for now, then. It is my weakest subject," said Charles wryly. "I will try to read it... *joyously*." She grinned, when she saw him laughing at himself.

"Do try, if you have a point you'd like to discuss, please don't hesitate. In the meantime, *Western Civilization*, it is."

Adjusting their positions to read by the window light, they were silent. Only the sound of the chugging engine accompanied their thoughts.

After about an hour, Charles stood to stretch his limbs and said, "I didn't realize it was so late, Maggie. Did you have an early luncheon on the ship?"

"No, Charles. What do you suggest?"

"Well, we could try to get you to the dining car, or I could summon the porter and order us some food for the cabin. Which would you like me to do?"

"Maybe we should limit our excursions to ones that are absolutely necessary, such as to the water closet, and order the food for here, if we can," she said, smiling.

"That is very practical, Maggie, and I think you're right. I would like to take you to the dining car for supper, though. I think you should get to see it. It's quite an elegant experience. Lizzie thought you would enjoy it."

"Well, I think I would like that. I hope you don't regret having to do it, though. Perhaps after our luncheon, I will go back to the water closet, then we can both rest before we take the trip for dinner. I wish my chair folded up, so we could use it on the train. I've heard of one that is designed to do just that. Mine was made by

278

a friend many years ago," she said wistfully. "Now, how do we alert the porter?"

"There is a knob here that calls the porter. All we have to do is pull it. Don't pull the red one however. The red knob indicates emergency. We don't want that."

Shortly after Charles summoned him, the white jacketed porter knocked softly on the door. When asked about the dining car offerings, he produced a card from his pocket. He read a list of items that included full meals and small luncheon items. "We also have a variety of tea, coffee and aperitifs for your pleasure, sir. Tonight, the menu will be similar, but the portions will be larger and the tariff a bit higher in proportion. The dessert tonight will be Apple Brown Betty. Brandies and whiskies are served after seven."

"With your permission, Missus Heenan, I'll order." At her assenting nod, he turned again to the porter and ordered a small tray of finger sandwiches and tea for them both. When the porter left, they resumed their reading in silence.

Soon they heard the tinkle of dishes on a rolling cart, stop at their compartment door. Charles opened the door before the porter could knock again.

"Please sit, sir," the porter instructed. Charles obeyed, and was surprised when the porter pushed the cart between them to the wall. A leather strap attached to the cart fastened the cart to the wall. The cart now stable, the porter laid cloth napkins across each lap, and poured tea into delicate translucent china cups nestled in matching saucers. "Bon appétit! Ma'am. Sir."

"This is very elegant, Charles. I have seen this only at Castlewellan, and in the first class dining room aboard ship."

"Castlewellan, ma'am?"

"Yes, at the castle where Lord Annesley lives."

"Ah, I knew I had heard the name before, but not in context. Lizzie mentioned it, when she read his letter. I understand this Lord Annesley is a wealthy and powerful man in Ireland." Curiosity outweighed his nagging sense of propriety, in bringing the subject to light. "He is a friend?"

"You may well wonder how a woman of my meager means could count herself a friend of Lord Annesley. I have had a nodding acquaintance with him since I was a small child, just arriving in Ireland from Scotland." She measured her words carefully. "He knew my mother and father."

When she grew silent again, he did not press her. She had a wistful look he feared would dissolve into tears, as she spoke of him. *I do not need to know, if it hurts her to tell me.* He silently admonished himself for asking. *There is more to this than I have any right to know. Find a subject worthy of idle conversation, fool.*

"After luncheon and our trip down the hall, perhaps you'd like to take a nap? I can study in the parlor car, so you may have some privacy," said Charles. "I'll leave a note outside the door, so you will not be disturbed."

"You're very thoughtful, Charles. I've been up since before dawn and I think a nap would be lovely. Thank you."

They finished their meal silently. Charles unhooked the cart, rolled it out to the hallway were he found a similar latch mechanism to secure it. Maggie and Charles took their trip down the hall without incident and returned to the compartment. He found an afghan and a pillow for her, stowed in a cabinet under the seats. Attaching the promised note to the door, he left.

After a few moments, Maggie was resting peacefully on the bench, rocking gently back and forth to the sway of the train.

The December light waned early. Before Maggie was aware of her surroundings, it was dark. In the overcast, moonless night, she sat up, but could not reach the lamp whose location she only vaguely remembered. Using her arms for support, she slid to the door side of the compartment and reaching for the handle, it flew open. Trapped behind the door that banged against her knees, she yelped.

Charles quickly shut the door and asked if she was hurt.

"Only my pride, I was almost to the door handle, when it opened. If you open it again slowly, we'll be able to find the lamp."

"Maggie, I am so sorry. One moment please. There, that's better. Are you sure you're not hurt?" he asked.

"I'm fine. What time is it?"

"It's five-thirty. Time to take our supper, I'm afraid. I had the porter reserve a seat near this end of the dining car, so I won't knock everyone's meal off their tables taking you through. I'm afraid by the time I get the hang of this, our journey will be over," he said, chagrined.

Maggie smiled at the expression 'five-thirty' used instead of half five. She wondered if Lizzie and Eliza had adopted this Americanism. Or, perhaps she was simply behind in the modernizing of phrases. *I'm sure there will be many phrases I will have to learn in this change of locale.*

"Should we leave a light burning here? Oh, dear, my hair must be torn apart. If you would allow me to fix it, I will be much more pleasant company for you."

Please do, Maggie, if only to keep evil tongues from wagging, imagining how your hair became disheveled. Charles grew red again, ashamed of his own thoughts. Aloud, he said, "I'll step into the hall, while you prepare yourself. Is there anything I can get you?"

"Charles. If you could just hand me that purse, I will have all I need. I will only be a moment." She took the small bag and retrieved her comb. Removing the pins from her dark red hair, she combed it out and refastened the bun at the back of her head. She replaced the combs securely.

She knocked on the door and was gratified to note Charles opened the door very cautiously this time.

They managed to maneuver the shifting floor between cars and reach the table without mishap. Charles set her down facing

281

most of the dining car, and then settled her shawl around her shoulders, warding the draft from the sliding door behind her.

Maggie took in the vision of elegance, memorizing it, to savor at a later time. Soft gas-lit sconces made the crystal goblets sparkle with dancing lights on spotless white table cloths. Ornate French provincial chairs with velvet cushions, and the silk brocade covered walls seemed outrageously incongruent to the heavy iron monster driving them through the night. Even the noise of the wheels against rails seemed to dim with the music of the single violinist roaming through the car. *No wonder Hugh loves to travel. There is no discomfort here. Not for men who can pay the price, that is. Oh Hugh...* Maggie snapped herself out of her reverie. *Don't torture yourself. Be content with your memories.*

"Surely this is not the way all Americans travel? Lizzie did not travel in this manner. She would have told me."

"No, of course not, we traveled by coach, passenger car. We are permitted this because our compartment ticket includes these luxuries. Lord Annesley insisted that you have as much comfort as you would allow on your voyage. Enjoy it at his pleasure, Maggie. It is his gift to you," Charles spoke softly, not wanting the wonder to disappear from her eyes.

"He should *not* have done this. It is such a waste of money." The gesture humbled her and slightly angered her for reasons she could not articulate.

"You must be very dear to him, Maggie. Enjoy it, for his sake. He could not come with you to see to your comfort, so he planned as much as he could and charged his friend, Captain Passow, and Lizzie to see it fulfilled. I'm sorry to be such a clumsy escort." While he spoke, Maggie stared out the black windows, as if they held the key to her sadness. Charles became silent, keenly aware of her fragile state.

After a moment, he said, "Are you warm enough?"

As if rising out of a heavy fog, Maggie shook her head, saying, "I apologize for what must appear as shocking ingratitude,

Charles. You are not at fault for my moody lack of composure. How rude of me. Of course, we should enjoy this repast, and share each other's company, in the Earl's name. Please order some wine, and we will salute our benefactor." Maggie smiled broadly, but her eyes, Charles noted, showed only melancholy.

Perhaps if she makes a pretense of happiness, she can will it true, thought Charles. He spoke to the wine steward, asking him to choose a modest wine.

When it arrived with a plate of cheese and fruit, Maggie raised her glass, as did Charles. "To Hugh Annesley, a man of determined nature, honorable and loyal. To my new friend, Charles, may he fulfill his mission, please God, and confound his enemies."

"Here, here," said Charles, being at a loss for other words.

The rest of their meal was accompanied by Maggie's polite and charming chatter. Charles watched the light behind her eyes change several times, not quite all the way to happiness, but a fair imitation of it, at least.

Maggie, your words say you hide from nothing, but your eyes betray the truth. Who are you, Maggie Heenan? Your daughter does not hide. How long did it take to perfect your pretty mouth to hide what you want to say? Lizzie is always exactly who she says she is. She does not charm or beguile. She has no need.

At that moment, seated opposite the most beautiful, charming woman in the room, Charles Bachelor, almost painfully, longed to see Lizzie.

After a long, leisurely supper, Charles took Maggie back to the compartment. He took her baggage down from its perch and waited for the end of the ride.

"Another half hour, Maggie, and you'll see your girls again. Lizzie says you'll stay in her room tonight, then tomorrow after Sunday dinner, you'll settle into your new home. Are you tired?"

"No, Charles, just a little apprehensive, I suppose. It will take a little time to adjust to my new surroundings. Lizzie worries

283

about me, needlessly, at times. I know I came earlier than she would have wanted, but circumstances force change. I'm sure everything will work out for the best, won't it?"

"With hard work and God's will, Maggie," said Charles quietly.

"That's right. Even algebra can be conquered with hard work and God's will, eh, Charles?" she said brightly. She smiled, hoping to lighten the mood.

Charles, deep in thought, gave no indication he heard her. He was counting the minutes until the Newton Lower Falls Station.

Maggie sensed Charles' distance from her. Something's shifted in him. He's wary of me. Well, perhaps he'll come around again. Don't give up on me, Charles. Lizzie, you've got a good man here.

The conductor rushed through the passageway shouting an unintelligible station. Charles jumped up, opened the door and called out, "Newton Lower Falls?"

Hearing a sound of assent, he stepped out of the compartment, turning back to say, "I'll just get your chair, Maggie."

Fastening her hat upon her head, a feeling of gloom fell over her.

What is the matter wit' me! I should be happier than I'd any right ta be, but I'm ready ta weep! C'mon, straighten up, pinch your cheeks an' look alive, Maggie! You're goin' ta see yer girls agin. She uttered a hollow laugh as she realized the tenant speech had returned to her thoughts.

Suddenly, Hugh's face floated in front of her. Her stomach clenched, and it was all she could manage not to burst into tears.

Hang on, Maggie. Yer made o' sterner stuff than this. She took a deep breath, and let it out slowly. *Here's yer chance ta git ta knae yer daughters again. Leave the past in the past. Sit up, smile an' face the devil, if ye have ta. Yer girls are wantin' ta see ye.*

"Are you ready, Maggie?" Charles was at the door with the chair. He'd fastened it to the wall, as he'd seen the porter do with the luncheon cart. Stepping into the compartment, he picked her up, just as the train lurched forward, then back. Fortunately, he landed on the seat with Maggie in his lap. They looked at each other and burst out laughing, breaking the tension that had been building for the last two hours.

"Oh my, that was fortunate! I think we should take our leave of this train, before anything else happens, Maggie."

"Yes. I think you're quite right." Maggie put her gloved hand over her mouth to stifle her percolating laughter.

"Can you carry your bag until we get to the door, Maggie?" Charles asked. At her nod, he set it gently in her lap, and pushed the chair to the exit. The conductor ran to meet them, taking the bag while Charles took Maggie. He brought her to a bench, and went back to help the conductor with the baggage laden chair. Once the chair was on the platform, Charles looked around for a familiar face. He visibly relaxed when he saw William Twombly standing there.

"Reverend Twombly, how good it is to see you," Charles said a little too enthusiastically. Clearing his throat, he introduced him to Maggie Heenan.

William took Maggie's bag. Charles put Maggie in her chair, and rolled it to the horse and carriage next to the platform. He would have carried Maggie to the carriage, but he would have had to leave the chair on the platform. With several unknown young toughs hanging around, he didn't think the chair would be safe there. With a sigh, he noted that William was already in the driver's seat waiting for him to deposit Maggie inside the carriage and put the chair onto the back luggage tie-on. He promised himself, when he became a minister he would help out wherever it was possible, rather than hold himself aloof from manual labor.

Even if William Twombly couldn't do it on his own, it would have been nice if he could at least tie the ropes while I held the weight of the chair!

Charles was embarrassed that Maggie saw his minister refrain from even the least amount of work. Frustrated, and feeling mean-spirited, he sat in the carriage with Maggie, instead of climbing up to sit with William, as he would have in a better frame of mind.

"Well Maggie, our luxury is over now. We're 'back door' people again. I'll bring you into the kitchen, then go back out to get your chair and baggage. I hope you don't mind."

"No' at all, Charles. I only knew one 'front door man' in my whole life. All my other friends an' family would probably be counted as 'back door' people. O' course, when ye come right down ta it, we only had two front doors on the cottage fer many, many years. We didn't have a back door ta use," she said, laughing. "I knew an' worked wit' the Earl, but I didn't live wit' him."

"Maggie, your speech is different now."

"I knae, I seem ta adapt ta the ones I talk to, an' I'm gettin' close ta talkin' ta my girls, sae I start talkin' like them. I was at Castlewellan, after my mother died, then I was on the ship with English an' gentry, so I talked like them. You, Charles, are well-spoken, so I continued until nae. How I do miss my girls."

"Lizzie does that too, changes her speech patterns to suit her surroundings, that is. Here we are, Maggie. He'll pull around back and we'll get you into the house."

As they stopped at the back, Lizzie stuck her head out the door. "Eliza, she's here!" She grabbed her shawl, bounded down the steps and set to work on the ties that held Maggie's chair.

When they were all in the kitchen, with her bag and her chair, Maggie looked around her. "Come, children, let me look at ye! I would hardly knae yer, yer sae grown up. I've missed yer both, fiercely."

The girls hugged Maggie from both sides of her chair. She accepted their kisses and looked Charles in the eye, as if to say, *these are my girls, together we are whole again.*

Just for a moment, the façade of sophisticated charm and clever wit slipped away, and Charles saw a woman whose whole world comprised of these two young women, and their only aim was to please her.

Chapter Eighteen

Lizzie woke up with a smile on her face, but in strange surroundings. After a brief moment of confusion she remembered climbing the stairs to the attic with Eliza the night before. She hurried to get dressed, trying to outdistance the enveloping cold, threatening to invade her bones. Her breath creating vapor from her effort, she understood why Eliza liked to snuggle in the downstairs room, where it was toasty warm from the kitchen fire. They had taken to leaving the door open to the kitchen during cold wintery nights.

Trying to see out the small attic window, Lizzie discovered ice had formed on the panes overnight. *Poor Eliza, it's too hot in summer, an' too cold in winter.*

As she left the tiny attic, she gave her half-sister a gentle shake to waken her. Satisfied to hear Eliza groan in protest, Lizzie lowered the ladder to the back hallway, and made her way silently to the stairs. It was an eerie feeling walking through the upstairs, knowing everyone was still asleep.

In the kitchen, she fed the fire in the stove and began her morning routine. She peeked in her bedroom and saw Maggie's form on the bed. As she turned to go back to her duties, she saw Maggie's eyes fly open in confusion, then soften, as she saw Lizzie.

"Good morning, Sunshine," she said, stretching and grinning, using an endearment from Lizzie's childhood.

"Good morning, Maggie," whispered Lizzie. "Sleep as lang as ye like. I hope my putterin' around won't disturb ye. I'm settin' up fer breakfast. When yer ready, I'll have plenty fer ye."

Lizzie stepped quietly out the door without waiting for a reply. She hummed as she worked, setting out the breakfast trays, watching the oatmeal on the stove, and waiting for the smell of cinnamon biscuits to signal their exit time from the oven. Mister William had coddled eggs with home fried potatoes and rye toast every morning now, unless specifically noted, but the others had whatever Lizzie decided to make that morning. On occasion, bacon or ham was added to all plates. Coffee was served to everyone.

Maggie rolled her chair into the kitchen just as Lizzie was drizzling a maple syrup spiral on one of the servings of oatmeal. She made note to ask later what the syrup was.

"You kin sit at the table, Ma, an' I'll be wit' ye in jes' a moment."

She sat quietly prideful, observing her daughter attending the trays so efficiently. Each tray a study in elegance, the open cutwork napkins, silver utensils, Japanese-inspired bowls and small plates, were all arranged formally. Then, as if in a bid for a more relaxed style, a sprig of pine with a festive ribbon stood in a crystal bud vase, a reminder of Christmas. *Missus Twombly has taught her well. Lizzie has learned the tools of serving the gentry and could serve or dine with any of them.*

Satisfied with her handiwork, Lizzie took one tray and set it on the table in front of Maggie. "Enjoy. Missus Twombly says the Lord is present at ev'ry meal in this house. We should endeavor ta serve Him the best we have ta offer." She turned away, as she heard a knock on the door.

"Oh, excuse me, Ma. Our 'back-door' guests have arrived," said Lizzie answering the door. Lizzie carried three sacks of food and a jacket she took from one of the hooks inside the door. "Jimmy, you're no' warm enough. This jacket'll keep you warm t'day. Come back tonight, and I'll have some hot stew ta warm ye bones. Look in the bin fer mittens the right size and a scarf if ye need one. The ladies at the church haf' been busy knittin' all fall, jes' ta keep ye warm. Ye welcome, Big John. I hope ye find some big enough fer those fryin'-pan hands o' yers, too. Missus Twombly says ta heat up the church basement an' let anyone who wants ta, stay after evenin' service t'night. No one should be outside on these cold nights." A chorus of 'Thank yer, Miss Lizzie' followed her back into the kitchen.

On her way to the breakfast trays, Eliza asked, "Kin I git ye anythin', Maggie? Would ye like ta read the paper?" She set the paper on the corner of the table and continued with her chores. Placing the bud vases on one tray, she stacked two footed trays and carried them out of the kitchen. Lizzie took the other two and followed her.

When they returned to the kitchen, Eliza said, "The lil' bit o' pine looks nice, Lizzie. I wisht we still had some flowers ta use fer a change."

"I thought I could make some paper snowflakes or angels fer Christmas week, Eliza. I'm savin' some dried roses for Christmas Day. A ribbon bow perhaps? Any ideas? I can sift powdered sugar over the little molasses cakes, usin' paper cutouts of bells or angels.

Missus Twombly loves the lil' finishing touches, Ma. She says, it's lak' sayin' 'I love you' with ev'ry meal we make."

Maggie felt a little twinge of jealousy listening to the reverence with which Lizzie spoke of her mistress. "Perhaps, when I'm settled a' the boardin' house, I'll ha' time ta do some tattin' or crochetin' fer yer. 'Bout how big should each piece be? Ye will hafta be starchin' them, o' course."

Lizzie held out her two hands and with her fingers touching, measured an appropriate size of a decoration for the trays. She hugged her mother in appreciation. "Thank yer, Maggie. 'Twould be a nice surprise fer the family. The Twomblys are won'erful people, Ma."

Lizzie turned to the list on the table for her next order of chores. Sunday dinner would be roast duck, Franconia potatoes (roasted as the meat is basted), braised carrots, parsnips, onions, and apple-cranberry sauce, with warm cinnamon-apple cider or iced water to drink. Parker House rolls and hot johnnycake rounded out the main course. Lizzie thought through the timing of the meal components and began to assemble her pots and pans.

Maggie watched Lizzie with interest and read the list as she did. "Do they al'ays eat like this?" she asked incredulously.

"No, but 'cause they hafta entertain often, they have an allowance fer food from the church. Missus Twombly's verra frugal with the food allowance, but, she says, 'we mus' no' skimp on our guests, answered Lizzie. "When we dinna have guests, we eat soups an' stews, jes' like our 'back door' guests. Food is never wasted, so I add it to the stew on the back of the stove," she said proudly. "T'night, we'll have verra rich stew, an' whatever breads are remainin'."

"An' what is Eliza doin' nae?"

"She'll be dustin' the parlor and the office while she's waiting fer the trays ta come back inta the hallway. She'll bring them all down ta me ta wash, an' she'll see if the ladies need help gittin' dressed, an' pick up the laundry fer t'mara. They leave at nine o'clock sharp fer Sunday school. Eliza and I usually start walkin' ta church fer the worship service by ten-thirty.

"My goodness, I'd better get ready. I'd like ta meet them afore they leave. D' ye think they'd mind?" asked Maggie.

"Missus Twombly said she's lookin' forward ta it, Ma."

291

Maggie went back to Lizzie's room and her daughter continued her cooking preparations. When Maggie reemerged, she was perfectly groomed and radiant as ever. Just as she rolled her chair into the kitchen, Missus Twombly and Isabelle arrived to meet their guest. Lizzie stood up from her hot stove, her face flushed and her red hair escaping from her cap. She introduced the women, noticing Maggie's speech had changed to one she reserved for the gentry.

Isabelle was caught by surprise at this beautiful well-spoken woman, a mere ten years her senior.

Missus Twombly, ever the gracious hostess, did not blink an eye, but welcomed her warmly. "Missus Heenan, you are welcome to join us in the carriage and arrive for Sunday school, or you may choose to go with your daughters later. I've asked Mister Bachelor to borrow a carriage from Mister Baker to take you all at half past ten for the main service. He says it will be no trouble at all to bring you into the sanctuary himself, if you don't mind. You could then leave the chair here for when you come back."

"Thank you so much for your kindness, Missus Twombly. It would please me to attend with my daughters and Mister Bachelor. He is a most charitable young man and attentive to my needs."

"Excellent. You will join us for Sunday dinner, I hope. We have a small, but lively group including Mister Bachelor. You will find that your Lizzie is an extraordinary cook and is eager to show you her skills. Eliza is a wonderful server and sees to our every need. We have been most fortunate to have them with us this year and we thank you for allowing them to be here."

Lizzie felt like she was listening to a script on how to teach etiquette to young ladies. Smiling, she bent over her stove and let their words wash over her as she concentrated on her tasks at hand.

"Mother, William and father are waiting," nudged Isabelle. "It was very pleasant to meet you, Missus Heenan. I am delighted you'll join us for dinner." Even as she smiled, Isabelle had a strange look on her face as if she could not reconcile the sophisticated woman seated before her with the servants who had lived in her home for the past year.

No matter, Miss Isabelle. She will hold her ain wit' ye at dinner. Jes' wait an' see, thought Lizzie.

When she heard the carriage drive off, Maggie asked her daughter, "Miss Isabelle is not married, then?"

"No, Ma. She's had several suitors, but prefers no' ta share her life with any o' them. She takes wonderful care o' her mother an' father an' she is an artist, as well. Their son, William, is no' married either. He is the minister o' this church, but sometimes Doctor Twombly preaches in his stead."

"I'll enjoy gittin' ta knae them," Maggie said, her tenant lilt creeping into her voice again. "Dinna let me interrupt yer work, dear. I'll gae put away my bag fer this afternoon."

For all her tutoring in fine cooking, Lizzie was a little nervous as she orchestrated this meal.

Why am I sae frazzled? I knae wha' ta do. Where's thet list agin? Take a breath, Lizzie. She's yer Ma. She'll love what e'er ye do! Ye've made this meal afore. One step at a time like Missus Twombly says. Lizzie tried to chase the doubts away, to no avail. *Well, ye will have nothin' done if ye don' git started! Onct ye start, ye will be fine.*

Eliza popped in the kitchen to ask, "Lizzie, is there somethin' I kin help ye with? D' ye need anythin' from the cellar?"

"Oh my, what a wonderful offer. I have my hands in this stuffin', an' I need some good an' some bruised apples, about a dozen in all. Also, some cider for the ice box, about a dozen small round potatoes, a hand o' carrots, and parsnips... three onions, two handfuls of cranberries… oh, and two oranges, if there are any. Here take this sack with yer."

Eliza took the burlap potato sack and headed down the stairs. She returned just as Maggie entered the kitchen again. "All I could get was one orange an' not a verra good one, I'm afraid." she said to Lizzie who was washing the large duck and pulling a few errant pin feathers from it.

"That will do, Eliza. If you would like ta core an' quarter the bruised apples, maybe four. Then core an' skin the rest thet would be helpful."

"May I do somethin', Lizzie? I'd love ta help, too," Maggie asked.

Lizzie hesitated just a second, then acquiesced, "Ye must promise me ye won' tell Missus Twombly I had a guest help prepare her ain dinner. She would faint dead away. If ye take these parsnips an' carrots I've washed, peel them an' chop off the heads leaving as much of the meat as possible, I would be ever sae grateful. This duck was no' cleaned as nearly as I would like, so he's takin' more time than I thought he would."

"Lovely. I've ne'er used one o' these peeling things, but Eliza kin show me how. You go on an' teach thet duck a lesson in cleanliness, eh?" The three women laughed.

"It's good ta have ye here, Ma," said Lizzie sincerely, noticing how relaxed she felt now.

Eliza and Maggie chatted as they worked and Lizzie prepared the duck. She took the quartered apples and pushed them into the duck's body and craw, and added celery and a quartered onion.

Next, she wiped down the outside of the duck, rubbed it with the orange, and threw the rind into the body of the duck. Salted, peppered, and floured, the duck was trussed and ready for roasting. She bundled it up and slipped it into the ice box. Lizzie would put it in the oven after church, while the Twomblys were still saying their farewells to the congregation.

Lizzie set up a tray of small ceramic fruit bowls, another with two bread baskets lined with napkins, and yet another with relish dishes to receive orange marmalade, sweet pepper relish, and corn relish. She checked the rising dough next to the stove and began to roll it out, buttering the layers and cut out circles for the rolls. Each circle was folded, placed in buttered muffin tins, and washed with egg white. She let them sit, while she mixed the sweet corn bread. To the corn bread she added half a can of sweet cut corn. She placed the two pans of rolls and one of Johnny cake into the oven.

Maggie watched with wonder. Those chores done, Lizzie put the parsnips and carrots in a heavy cast iron pan with butter and some finely chopped onion. The potatoes were in the pot for boiling. All that remained was to boil the cranberries, add the sugar and cinnamon, then add the chopped apples. At just the right moment, she would turn the relish into two small bowls and place on the tray to cool.

"Lizzie, Charles is here! We have ta git ready fer church," said Eliza, anxiously heading for Lizzie's bedroom.

"I'll be right there. Maggie, kin ye let him in? He'll come ta the back door. I'll be ready in jes' a second. Thank yer."

"Of course, I'll get the door, Lizzie. Now, hurry and git dressed fer yer young man."

Lizzie shot her mother a look of gratitude as she raced out of the room. She could hear Charles climbing the back steps as she left.

Maggie maneuvered her chair to face the door and answered it just as Charles was about to knock. "Hello, Missus Heenan," he said pleasantly, with just a hint of caution. He looked around the kitchen for the girls, and said, "It smells like heaven in here."

"Hello, Charles. The girls should be ready shortly. I am so happy to see you again. Thank you for your kindness on our little trip," said Maggie, politely.

"It was my pleasure. I see you are being indoctrinated into the world of fine cookery. Lizzie has learned many things since cooking on an open fire in your fair Ireland, Missus Heenan."

Oh please, Charles. Lizzie won't mind if you call me Maggie."

"I would, Missus Heenan, but we are having dinner with the Twombly family, and they may not like my being that familiar with Lizzie's mother and a guest in their home. I promise in private, away from the family, I will call you Maggie, and you may call me Charles. I do not want to cause Lizzie any discomfort with them."

"Of course, how inept of me, I beg your pardon. I did not think of the consequences. Thank you," she said with a self-deprecating, but charming smile.

"Not at all, I do it for Lizzie," he said rather primly. ...*And for my own sense of decency. It is easier for me to hold you at arm's length, Maggie. I am hoping your spell does not reach me more than it already has. Lizzie is the one who is real. She has no need of false charms and hidden agendas,* he thought, suspiciously.

"Very well, how is your quest for algebraic knowledge going? I found that although I did not understand it at first, there was a sudden revelation and it all came together at once."

"I'm still in the dark at the moment, but I keep praying one day it will happen just as you say. I guess it is the expression of letters for numbers that confounds me. $x + y = z$."

"Perhaps if you say the number of *sheep* plus the number of *goats* equals the total number of *animals*, it will be clearer to you?" laughed Maggie.

The stunned look on his face told Maggie, she had opened another portal for him. "Perhaps, I will try that," he replied in wonder. "I'll stop thinking of them as strange letters with no meaning, but as entities I haven't yet discovered. Intellectually, I knew that, but I was making more of a mystery of them than was there. Thank you, I think that may help," Charles laughed at himself, and his look at Maggie softened as Lizzie came into the room.

"Hello Charles! I hope we haven't kept you too long. Eliza and I are ready."

"Lizzie, it's still early. Although it's almost ten-thirty, the ride is only a few minutes by carriage. Shall we?" Charles kissed her hand and opened the door for her and Eliza.

"Ready, Missus Heenan?" At her nod, he picked her up, and carried her out the door. He stopped on the top step for her to close the door, and then went on to the carriage. Outside, the girls were surprised to see Garrett in the driver's seat.

"I come with the carriage," he said cheerfully. He nodded to Maggie, winking surreptitiously at Eliza. "You kin ride inside, old man," he added to Charles. "It's very cold out here."

Charles placed Maggie on the seat inside and sat opposite her, next to her daughter. "If he's going to allege I am an old man, he can very well freeze out there by himself," he said wryly to Lizzie.

Then, he said, "Now, I know Lizzie is your daughter, Missus Heenan. How do Eliza and James fit into this family?"

Maggie smiled good-naturedly and replied, "My darling Eliza may be called by others, my stepchild, and James is my husband's brother's child or his nephew. However, they are both children of my heart, with no *steps* added. I proclaim them all my own children." Maggie leaned over and hugged Eliza warmly.

"Forgive my brash question, Missus Heenan, Eliza, and Lizzie. I was confused and I sought only to satisfy my own rude curiosity. I speak before my brain is aware at times. I must endeavor to find a cure for that or I will be a poor minister indeed," Charles flushed.

"Not at all, Charles," said Lizzie. "They asked me that when I started school and I didn't quite know how ta answer them. We're not the usual family, but it doesn't matter ta us, 'cause we love each other. People who don' knae us, say I am jes' an only child, raised by my grandmother. I have a cousin, two brothers, and two sisters whom I've loved without question, and a mother whose a heart is big enough fer all o' us," she said gently.

297

Charles thought, *it's as if Lizzie's rehearsed her story, having to tell it over and over. I can tell she believes it. She loves them all. She is the one who holds them together. Raised by her grandmother? Not her mother? No wonder she is so different from Maggie. This is definitely not the ordinary family. Let your curiosity rest, man. It's your Lizzie you must concentrate on, not who her mother is. Maggie should remain an unsolvable puzzle or you chance being swept up into her beautiful web. Lord, give me a battlement to throw up against the enticing mystery of Maggie Heenan's deep green eyes.*

He turned to Lizzie and watched her animated face as she spoke to her mother and sister. For the rest of the ride, until they arrived back at the house, he was silent but for the polite conversation required of him. When he carried Maggie back into the kitchen after services, her nearness nearly unnerved him, but he resolutely guarded his thoughts.

"Lizzie, I am going into the parlor to study. I hope you don't mind. You have a lot of catching up to do with your mother, so I will get out of your hair." Lizzie looked at him strangely, but nodded.

He seems so strange today. I hope he's feeling well. I'll check on him in a minute. Right now, I have ta get this dinner cooked an' ready afore the Twomblys come home in thirty-five minutes. First, the duck...

Lizzie tended her meal and Eliza set up the dining room, while Maggie sat at the kitchen table, amusing herself with the previous day's newspaper. When her dinner was roasting, boiling, and braising to her satisfaction, Lizzie stole a moment to look in on Charles.

"Lizzie!" Charles rose as she entered the room. "Is anything wrong?"

"No. Are you all right?" she asked. He strode toward her, pulled her into his arms and kissed her soundly.

298

"I am just fine, thank you," grinned Charles. "I missed you, is all."

"C-Charles," Lizzie sputtered. "They will be home any minute. What could you be thinking?"

"That I love you. That I still have about twelve and a half minutes before they come back. And, that I have the cook in the parlor all to myself," he said with a devilish grin. This time when he kissed her, he spied Eliza peeking in from the dining room and waved to her. It did not escape him that Lizzie returned his kiss with equal fervor.

"I must get back, Charles. Shame on you, you've got flour on your suit!" Lizzie blushed and ran to the kitchen door. Charles noticed she stopped, fixed her cook's cap and clothing before she entered the kitchen. She heard him laugh in the parlor and wanted to curse her fair skin for blushing yet again.

"And is your young gentleman in good health, Lizzie?" her mother teased.

"Aye, Mother. He's fine an' I need to tend to these vegetables," she said, stirring her braising pan. For several minutes she stood very business-like at the stove, checking one pot, then the next until she was satisfied with results. She placed the rolls and corn bread on the shelf over the steaming potatoes and took out her dessert pies to place on the swivel trays at the back of the stove. Shortly, she heard the Twomblys come bustling in the front door, chatting and saying 'hello' to Charles who took their coats.

When the initial noise died down, Lizzie said, "Maggie, you can go into the parlor now. You are expected to wait there until dinner is announced. Here, I'll get the door."

Lizzie watched through the open door to see if her mother could negotiate her chair through the obstacles in the hallway to the parlor. She saw her scrape her fingers against a side table, but her mother waved her off and managed to get around the umbrella stand to the room of people in the front of the house.

299

Good fer you, Maggie. Ye made a fine entrance on yer ain, without the kitchen help. Charles will take yer ta the dining room wit'out a problem.

Lizzie wondered if it would always be like this, her mother, the invited guest of nobility and her, forever the kitchen help. She wistfully wondered what it would be like to switch shoes with her.

Well, I canna think it would be pleasant ta be bound ta a chair fer a lifetime. It would be nice to be a guest fer a change, though. But, if I'm no' cookin', it surely won' be as good, would it?

She indulged herself with a prideful chuckle as she changed into her 'company' apron.

The skillful orchestration of the meal performed by Eliza and Lizzie was completed with no missteps. At the end of the main course, Lizzie was called to appear as usual for her accolades.

This day was particularly sweet because Maggie could see both of them were appreciated by the Twomblys. They raised their cider glasses in salute to Eliza and Lizzie for a grand meal. The servants beamed with pride as did Charles and Maggie. "We'll have dessert in the parlor, if you would. I think it's warmer in there. Coffee, tea, and perhaps even a cordial would be nice, Lizzie. And whatever you've prepared for an after-dinner treat, of course."

Lizzie had prepared the dessert cart, just in case. She added the cut-glass cordial decanter and glasses to the tray with the silver tea service. A second tray held a coffee urn and china. Below the beverages, were warm fruit pies, hermits, and variously decorated tea cakes. Added to these was a small bowl of candies. Eliza placed all the delicacies on the low table in the parlor. Then, she served the cordials and other beverages as requested.

Eliza stood at the edge of the doorway, smiling as she watched the two ministers competing to serve Maggie and seeing to her comfort. They were drawn like bees to her honey.

To Eliza, Charles seemed immune to her charms. *Perhaps the long trip made him weary.* Although distant, he too, seemed to be watching the beautiful Maggie commanding the room.

At the beginning of the dinner, they were polite and ingratiating. But, as they engaged her in more serious conversation, she held her own. Even Missus Twombly and Isabelle seemed taken with her. She offered a well-founded opinion of painting, botany, and poetry to each of them. Whatever the theme, she seemed to have something pertinent to say. When they forged ahead to theology, they were stunned by her knowledge of the subject.

I knew she read books upon books, but I had nae idea she knew sae much o' what ta say. These people are verra well-educated. She's in her glory, her with a grammar school education. She musta been wishin' someone could talk ta her about this stuff. Laird, I wouldn't knae what ta say. Lizzie's smart, but even she wouldn't knae what they were talkin' about.

In the kitchen, Lizzie was cleaning up, listening to the murmur and laughter of the guests in the parlor. Humming to herself, she didn't hear the door open. Up to her arms in dishwater, she jumped when Charles put his arms around her. "Oh my, 'tis a dangerous thin' yer doin' Mister Bachelor," she said as she spun around in his arms. "I had my hand on a kn—."

Her mock anger, interrupted by a kiss, she forgot what she was saying, and her arms held mindfully away from his suit, dripped soapy water on the floor beside them.

"Oh my," he mocked her with a grin. "It's such a terrible thing, to have a man besotted with you."

"Charles." She pretended to be stern. "I am *workin'*. I have no time fer play. 'Sides, someone will come in an' see us." She grabbed a dish towel, stooping to mop up the wet floor.

"Eliza, won't mind, Lizzie. She's guarding the door. She also took a whisk broom to my suit before your mother came into the parlor. She is a first-rate conspirator." He put a finger under the chin of her upturned face.

"Lizzie, dearest, you seem to be the only one who hesitates to make this a match. I am more convinced everyday that you want this, even though my schooling makes us wait." The slightest hint of a frown made his features look more tortured than in love.

"Charles, it's *because* we must wait fer your schooling, is why I hesitate ta declare myself. You're a wonderful, gifted man an' I am hypnotized by you. But, I hafta be willin' ta live my life apart, waitin' fer four years. I wan' ta be the kind o' person ye need at yer side, a minister's wife. I jes' don't knae if I kin be." To Lizzie's consternation, her eyes filled with tears threatening to overflow.

She was standing facing him now. He put his hands on the sides of her face and looked deep into her eyes. "I am not mistaking the feeling you show when you return my kiss. I'll cling to that for hope." His lips touched hers gently. "I will play this your way. I have no right to demand your love, but do not deny me the right to hope for it. I will wait for it. I do not want you to change for me. You are exactly what I want, who I need. There are no shadows in you. You do not hide in secrets, layer upon layer of pretense. It is you, Lizzie Heenan, that has captured my heart."

Lizzie was about to rejoin him with another argument when they heard three small raps on the door. Charles kissed her forehead and quickly sat in the rocker. Lizzie's hands were deep in the dishwater again.

Missus Twombly entered the kitchen looking from Charles to her cook. "It was a fine meal, Lizzie. You've outdone yourself. Your mother and I are both very proud of you."

Turning to Eliza, she said, "You may clear, Eliza, I think everyone is done. Charles, would you like another cup of coffee? Missus Heenan is engaged in a lively conversation about the theoretical future of the sciences with my three geniuses out there and it looks like it could go on for a while.

"Lizzie, if you are anxious to get her to her new home, perhaps we should set a time limit on the debate," Missus Twombly said cheerfully.

"Let us know when you are ready, and we will reluctantly release your mother to your care. She *is* a delight, my child. This is the liveliest conversation we've had since last summer with Doctor Jacobs, our visiting theologian from Nova Scotia."

"I'm sure she's delighted ta have people as knowledgeable as you with which ta converse, Missus Twombly," Lizzie said, bent over her sink.

"Knowledge is what we use, to compensate for lack of talents, Lizzie. You have many talents. You are a spectacular cook and laundress, two practical talents you will use throughout your life. I can show you how and give you recipes, but I have not one-tenth the instinct you use to pull it all together. You can't get that from a book, my dear."

"Thank ye fer sayin' so, Missus Twombly," said Lizzie, humbly. "I'll get this all done, then I will have ta git Ma to her room afore dark."

Within the hour, Lizzie and Eliza were gathering Maggie's belongings, preparing to leave.

Maggie said her goodbyes, donned her coat, and Charles whisked her out the door to the waiting carriage. The girls struggled with her luggage and chair. Garret ran up the back steps to get the bag from Eliza, who helped Lizzie position the chair to be strapped on the back. They cheerfully bantered back and forth while at their tasks. Finally, the girls piled in with their mother and the two men rode atop.

Around the corner at the boarding house, the whole process was performed again in reverse, while Lizzie rang the door bell. Missus Stanhope stood before them, with an arched eyebrow and hands on her hips. "Well, I hope you're not *all* tramping through m' house," she said unwelcoming.

303

"Only for a moment, Missus Stanhope, I assure you. As soon as we get my mother settled in her room, we will be gone." Lizzie turned on her brightest smile and hoped for the best.

"I am very pleased to meet you, Missus Stanhope," said Maggie. "Please forgive my needing so many people to assist me. These are my two daughters and their intendeds. Once I am settled, I will be happy to introduce myself properly. I am anxious to make the acquaintance of the proprietress of so gracious a home."

"Hmph, ah, thank you. Won't you come in?" The disgruntled boardinghouse owner's stern appearance transformed to a half smile of curiosity and pride.

Hidden from the view of Missus Stanhope, Charles looked over Maggie's head at Lizzie and winked.

Maggie's weaving her spell already. This fearsome woman won't know what hit her.

Once in the house, the group was very quiet. Lizzie suggested her mother try taking the chair through the doorways that would give her access to the rooms downstairs. The chair was maneuvered through her bedroom doorway, the water closet, and the dining room with relative ease. The parlor doors were narrow, but when both doors were opened, there would be no problem. They were told that only one door was opened as a rule, so only on very special occasions would she be allowed in there. Lizzie suspected it may take her mother until the next day before Missus Stanhope would invite her in there for a private tea.

The men went out to sit in the carriage, while the girls unpacked her bag, and put the items in the bureau within her reach. "Maggie," Lizzie asked, "Can you get from your chair to the bed?"

"Oh yes, it's not too high. I can stand for a brief moment, so I will manage just fine. Don't worry, my dears. I will manage. I hope you girls didn't mind my saying you were intended for Mister Bachelor and Mister Johansson. It somehow seemed more appropriate, if they were at least spoken for."

"Well, we may have questions ta answer from them, but I don' mind, a 'tall," said Lizzie. "Garrett may be no' so willin' ta be committed yet, but he's interested, fer sure."

Eliza's face turned crimson. She made a mock face of surprise and playfully swatted at her half sister. Lizzie ducked, laughing at her. Maggie, grinning, looked from one to the other enjoying this exchange.

Lizzie heard the hall clock strike half three and stood to leave. "I'm sorry, Maggie, we hafta go. We'll be back Tuesday at two, an' Thursday fer sure, an' other times, as we kin." She kissed her mother and slipped out the door. Eliza hastily kissed Maggie and followed Lizzie.

The shadows were long and the air was cold when they reached the carriage. The men were inside the cab, protected against the wind, engaged in serious conversation. Lizzie knocked on the cab and the door flew open. "See that, Garrett? We won't have to freeze our bones out here for another moment. They have come to save us!" Charles hopped out and helped the women into the carriage.

"It's all right old man, you can ride with the girls, I'll handle the drivin'," rejoined Garrett from the driver's seat.

"You kin call me an old man all you want, while I will ride with the girls and stay warm, my young friend. To the Twombly abode, sir," Charles laughed, jumping in beside Lizzie.

"Your mother is all settled in the witch's coven, Lizzie?" he asked.

"Fer the moment Charles, she'll have charmed them all an' be runnin' the place by t'marra," Lizzie laughed.

"No one is immune from the spells of Maggie Heenan," added Eliza.

God willing, I will stay out of range of her wiles, thought Charles. *God grant me the sunlight of Lizzie's truth, and keep me safe from her mother's shadows.*

305

Chapter Nineteen

Christmas Day was quiet at the Twombly house. Lizzie made the breakfast trays especially festive for the family, and when the family came down stairs, they gathered in the parlor, chatting.

Eliza poked her head in the kitchen, while her half-sister was washing dishes, "Lizzie! They want us in the parlor," she said, excitedly.

Lizzie sighed, *Kin I jes' git the dishes done all a' once, wit'out interruption,* she groused to herself. She dried her hands, straightened her cap and put on her clean apron.

"Here's our girls, now we can begin. Lizzie, Eliza, come in. William, please present them their gifts," Missus Twombly was beaming. "I hope you like them, my dears."

Lizzie took the proffered package cautiously. Am I supposed to open it? Or wait until I'm back at my room?

Eliza did not worry about order of propriety, but tore through the paper impulsively. Inside, was a bookmark with The Lord's Prayer on one side and a hand painted bird with flowers on the other. A thin yellow cord with a tassel on the end adorned the top.

"To help you remember your time with us, Eliza. Open your gift, Lizzie, dear. I hope you like it and know how much we appreciate your service."

Lizzie undid the ribbon and unfolded the paper carefully. She found a similar bookmark with the prayer and on the other side, a pineapple and her name in elaborate calligraphy.

At the confused look on Lizzie's face, Missus Twombly explained, "The pineapple is a symbol of hospitality, Lizzie. I thought it was fitting because my student has surpassed her teacher, in presentation and cookery." Lizzie was so humbled by the sentiment, she bowed her head, her eyes misting. "Thank you so much," she said, her voice cracking.

"Now Mother," said Doctor Twombly, "Perhaps we can find a home for this present?" He handed her a gift with her name on it. Eliza and Lizzie stood back as the family exchanged gifts and Lizzie slipped out the door to the kitchen. She put the bookmark in her room, looking it over carefully as she placed it in her *Book of Common Prayer*. She saw it was signed B. Twombly.

She thought of the last nine months, working with her family, and her struggle to master the art of indoor cooking. She put the wrappings and the ribbon away and returned to her dishes, humming to herself, mentally ticking off the items she needed to prepare for Christmas dinner. *There will be seven for dinner: the Twomblys, Big John, Maggie, and Charles. A great goose, apple, onion, and sage dressing, mashed potatoes with gravy, Hubbard squash, apple-cranberry sauce, creamed onions, Christmas pudding, and Christmas cake. What'll we serve for beverages? I'd better check the list. Charles and mother are coming. It'll be good to see Big John, too.*

Soon, the full operation of her holiday cooking regimen engrossed her thoughts. She heard her family setting out to church and Eliza rushing upstairs to get her work done. A knock at the back door caught her attention. Her hands covered in stuffing mixture, she peeked through the door and saw Charles. "Come in," she said, and went back to her work.

"I canna talk nae, Charles, I hafta concentrate on gittin' this bird in the oven."

"Ah, I'll have to be content to merely stand and admire, I suppose." He stood by the table, opening a package. Lizzie trying to figure the timing of roasting the large bird, paid him little mind. He walked up behind her and loosely tied a ribbon around her neck. "It's not complete, but this will have to do for now, I'm afraid. When I am financially solvent, I will buy you a gold chain to match it."

Lizzie rushed to wash her hands. Wiping them furiously on her apron towel, she picked up the bauble on the end of the red ribbon. It was a tiny golden angel. "Charles! It's beautiful. I-I..."

"Sh, Lizzie, I want you to have it. It is not your promise, but mine to give. Whether your answer is yes, or no, it is yours." Grinning at the surprise in her eyes, Charles raised her chin with his finger, kissed her gently on the lips, and said, "Merry Christmas, my darling."

"I-I have a gift for you, though it's small and not sae special as this, Charles," she said shyly. She picked up a package from several others on the table.

Charles held the plain butcher's paper tied with a ribbon in his hands for a moment. He turned it over, shook it and pretended to listen to it. "Is it a Winchester carriage? I've so longed for one of those, or perhaps a pure white Arabian steed? An Encyclopedia of Mathematics for The Dull-witted?"

"Jes' open it, Charles! It's taken longer fer ye ta open it, than it took ta make it," Lizzie exclaimed, exasperated, but laughing.

"Oh Lizzie, this is surely nectar for the gods," Charles exclaimed as he popped a piece of the gifted fudge into his mouth.

"Of course it is," she giggled. "Nae, let me git back ta my work. Are ye bringin' mother here or straight ta church? Do ye need help?"

"I would love to take you all to church, but can you manage? I'll have to leave no later than ten-thirty or half ten, as you would say. That leaves no extra room for waiting. Even so, it may be difficult to get a seat, being Christmas, so it should probably be at least by quarter past. What do you think?"

"Well, if it looks like I won' be ready, leave at quarter past. It'll still gif me time ta walk an' git there in time."

"Very well, I'll sit and keep you company, until then," said Charles. "Garrett will be bringing the carriage around..." He looked up as he heard a knock. "Look, here he is now."

"Well, let him in. I'm all a mess," said Lizzie irritably. "Please," she added, her voice softening. *I'm runnin' around, tryin' ta git my work done, an' they want ta converse!* She took a deep breath and turned to smile at Garrett. "Good ta see ye, Garrett."

"Sit here at the table and keep your voice down low, man. You'll take your life by your own hand, if you interrupt the cook at her work," said Charles, his eyes twinkling.

"Jes' keep each other comp'ny, while I git this ready. There's coffee, if ye want it. I canna stop, but Charles kin git it fer ye. Would ye do thet, please, Charles?"

Charles bit his lip, to prevent a retort he knew would set her irritated at him. He let the rejoiner go and poured a cup of coffee for his young friend. Together, they talked about the weather, horses, and the village news, watching Lizzie work, checking the time.

Eliza breezed into the kitchen, said "Hello" and breezed out to the bedroom to change her clothes for church.

Lizzie paused to check the counter and the stove for all the dinner components, and then left the room. In the bedroom with Eliza, she said, "You better hurry up and git out there. Garrett's anxious ta see ye. There's a packet o' fudge on the table wit' his name on it, ye kin give him, if ye like."

"Lizzie, could I? I never finished embroidering his initials on the handkerchief fer him. I kin give him that fer New Year, I

309

suppose. Oh, thank ye Lizzie, yer so good ta me. T'night when things quiet down, I've a little somethin' fer ye," She stopped suddenly and stared at the little gold angel. "What's *this*?"

"It's from Charles. He shouldn't have spent money on me, but it's sae pretty."

"It surely is. When ye put yer apron back on, ye will hafta put it inside yer dress though. It won' do ta drop it in the soup, would it? An' ye knae how Missus Twombly is about presentation."

"I knae, it will hafta hide until dinner's done, but I should be able ta wear it ta church, so Charles kin see it on me," Lizzie said. "Nae git out there, an' give Garrett his fudge afore he eats all o' Charles'." She gave her half-sister a hug and turned to the little mirror to fix her hair and admire her present.

She could hear the banter in the kitchen and smiled. She quickly popped her hat on and hurried out the door. "What's the time, Charles?"

"You did it, darling, with a minute to spare. Let's be off."

Lizzie's mother was ready when they arrived and they went on to the church to see crowds of people filing in the open doors. Garrett stopped the carriage in front, the girls disembarked and Charles took Maggie. The crowd parted when they saw his charming burden. He gratefully made his way up to the balcony, the girls following. "Eliza, save a seat for Garrett on your end of the pew," he said, winking. The pew was nearly filled with Charles, Lizzie, Maggie, and Eliza. Then Garrett arrived, his coat still chilled from his walk. Owing to the crowd allowing them through, they were able to have the second row seats in the balcony, overlooking the beautifully decorated sanctuary.

"It's always so grand when Christmas is on a Sunday!" said Charles to Lizzie. "You'll have to excuse me though. There is a lady in the back who doesn't have a seat. Garrett, I guess you and I are relegated to the back today." The men rose and invited two women to take their place.

The elderly woman, who sat beside Lizzie, took her hand and said, "He is such a lovely man. I thought he'd never marry. I'll wager he was only waiting for the best to find him." Her beaming smile was infectious. Lizzie chuckled and did not draw her hand away. She looked back to see Charles talking to another older woman. She rose, excused herself, and joined Charles while inviting another older woman to take her seat. As the woman passed her, she said, "Bless you child. I don't think my bones would have held me up for the whole service."

One by one, the men seated gave up their seats. Soon, Lizzie was surrounded by men of all ages. "Well, my dear," said a well-dressed man to her left, "you are a rosebud among the thorns, and we are all the better for it."

She blushed and nodded. Turning toward Charles, she drew the pendant from its hiding place under her coat so he could see. Smiling broadly, he rested his hand at her waist and pulled her close. As the music floated up to them, building as the choir sang, Charles and Lizzie looked straight ahead, grateful for the pressing crowd that drew them so close together.

The service seemed like it was orchestrated for them alone. When it was over, they awoke as if from a deep sleep, yet aware of every nuance of their nearness. They stood slightly apart as the congregation filed out around them.

When he saw the two older women leave their choice seats, Charles escorted them up to the hallway. Lizzie sat next to Maggie, resting her wobbly legs. "Charles will be back in a moment, hopefully he'll only have to carry one of us out," she said, wryly. Childishly she wriggled her toes in front of her to get the blood flowing again.

"It's lovely dear, from Charles?" Her mother picked up the little angel, admiring it.

Lizzie nodded, shyly. "Aye, isn't it beautiful? I was sae surprised." She took the bauble gently from her and tucked it inside her coat.

Eliza and Lizzie gently wove their way through the exuberant Christmas crowd, wishing they could stay and greet everyone. They hurried home to finish the last responsibilities for the holiday dinner so it would be in complete readiness when the Twomblys and their guests arrived.

The carriage was waiting out front of the church, but Charles was delayed in the balcony, hoping the crowd would thin out, so he could take Maggie safely down the stairs.

At home, Lizzie finished up her dinner tasks and Eliza set the table. The trays stood ready with tureens and serving bowls to be filled at the first sound of the Twomblys arriving home.

Each one checked her list and saw nothing undone. Eliza said, "How many did Missus Twombly say they would have at this dinner, Lizzie?"

"Just seven: the Twomblys, Maggie, Charles and Big John."

"That's what I thought, but today, she changed it to eight! It is so unlike her. She plans everything out sae thoroughly."

"I'm sure it will be fine, Eliza. She said ta make extra fer Big John ta bring ta the men in the church basement tonight, sae there is plenty o' food. It may be a little cramped in there wit' the tree, though."

"Oh, no' at all, Missus Twombly had Mister William an' Doctor Twombly move the tree into the parlor. I'm surprised ye didn't hear them. It was jes' before they left fer church. I had ta clean up the remnants, put a new leaf in the table an' rearrange the chairs fer eight. I can't imagine a last minute guest, an' she ne'er told yer?"

"I'm sure she jes' found out someone was goin' ta be alone fer Christmas an' ye knae how she feels 'bout thet. Thet's why Maggie, Charles an' Big John were invited.

"Well, I think I heard them pull up front, sae it's time ta start the gravy." Lizzie returned to the stove. When everything was set, Eliza announced dinner to the Twomblys and their guests.

Lizzie could hear the chatter as they filed into the dining room. Unexpectedly, the kitchen door opened and Eliza poked her head in to say, "Lizzie, you are urged ta come in fer grace."

Changing her apron once again, Lizzie sighed at the inconvenience. She could be working on the finishing touches of her special Christmas cake. She carefully tucked her angel inside her shirt, to keep her uniform appropriate.

Eliza and Lizzie stood in their corner as usual, but then a strange thing happened. Isabelle came to Lizzie and told her to take her place at the table. Then Mister William invited Eliza to take his place. The brother and sister stood behind their seats at the far end of the table. The two confused girls stared at each other then at Missus Twombly.

"It is a tradition we hold at Christmas, that our servants are seated at the table while we wait on them. It reminds us of your valuable service to us; and of the humility and grace with which you perform that service. Lizzie was seated between Maggie and Charles, while Eliza was seated between Big John and the still empty chair.

"Oh my, it seems we have one more chair. Is there someone we forgot?" Doctor Twombly smiled as he raised his voice.

"I suppose that would be me," said a voice from the hall. In the dining room, to the great surprise of the Heenans, was James, smiling and laughing. Maggie, Lizzie, and Eliza's faces held shock and surprise, as one by one, James kissed his family.

"Shall we begin?" Doctor Twombly interrupted gently, "Oh God, our Everlasting Father, we come together to praise and honor your name. On this blessed day, we celebrate the birth of your son, Jesus. Give us open hearts and minds as we gather at this feast prepared by gifted hands. Even as Jesus washed the feet of his

313

disciples, let us serve those who have served us so faithfully. Bless all our guests, dear Father, as they are reunited in family and fellowship around our humble table. Bless this food from your bounty to our use, may it nourish our bodies and make us ever-mindful of our God, who grants our every need. We ask all this, in the name of the Father, the Son and the Holy Ghost. Amen."

"Please, be seated. William, your father will carve the goose now. Isabella, you may serve the soup."

"Yes, Mother," Isabelle replied in her most humble voice. Lizzie and Eliza were nervous at the prospect of Miss Isabelle serving, but they needn't have been concerned. She was well practiced, and seemed to have no problem with the task.

"Thank you, Miss Isabelle," Lizzie said, using the name she preferred.

"You're very welcome, Miss Lizzie," she replied, her eyes dancing, playing her role fully.

The table chatter rose joyfully as the newness of the service faded. James regaled them with stories of the journey west he was planning for the spring. The men at the table plied him with interested questions and advised him on the dangers of the trail. Missus Twombly asked him a few questions about his ability at farming, and he replied, "My father taught me how ta make somethin' grow out o' mos' any ground. I jes' hafta find what the ground is best for. I am a carpenter first, however."

Big John was very interested in the young man's quest. "Maybe I should try my hand at land chasin' and farmin'. Hit can't be worse than findin' work 'round here. I'd like ta know more about this plan o' yours. Perhaps I kin be a help."

"I was hopin' James would love the work around here sae well, he'd be wantin' ta stay, but I guess that hope was doomed from the start," muttered Lizzie, sadly.

"Don' worry, Lizzie, when I make my fortune, I'll be sendin' fer ye, an' Maggie, an' Eliza, straightaway."

314

"An' what about yer Swedish lass, cousin, is she goin' ta bring the tribe wit' her? I don't think they'll be room fer us with all those children hangin' in the rafters."

"Lizzie, perhaps we should change the subject before the Twomblys think we have no manners at all," admonished Maggie. "Reverend Twombly, the service was lovely this morning. Do you and your father always share the services on Sunday morning?"

"Often, Missus Heenan, but not always. We spell each other on the sermons, but it is primarily my responsibility, so we try not to abuse the concession they grant us. The congregation enjoys my father's worthy contribution to the service and, as long as he enjoys it, we are the richer for it." William smiled and looked at his father kindly.

Lizzie sat picking at the sumptuous food on her plate. The lively conversation fading into the background, she was somehow distracted. Her thoughts wandered from the ribbon hidden under her shirt, to James' careless announcement to join the chase for land in the west, and the fact that she was seated at the very table she served all year. She was also becoming painfully aware that this wonderful existence of living with the Twomblys was drawing to a close.

As yet another tear coursed its way down her cheek, Charles broke from the conversation and leaning close to her, asked, "Lizzie, what's wrong, why do you cry?"

"Many things, Charles, ye an' I will talk later. I will stop being sae silly." She smiled wistfully, brushed her cheek dry and turned to Maggie, who held the group in awe of her tales of the days when she was young. It was Blaeberry Sunday and she was riding like the Mourne wind itself, and everyone at the table was riding with her.

Excep' for me, thought Lizzie. *I rode wit' her many times, but she always stopped the story before she answered my questions. What happened on the way hame? Why were her parents no' scandalized to see their daughter come hame with a handsome laird*

315

nearly twict her age? I do no' believe this 'friendship' o' theirs. Da was verra put out when e'er he saw the laird look her way.

Finally, she heard Charles say, "I believe she's still in shock to be waited on by others."

Suddenly aware of what was happening; Lizzie took the offered dinner rolls and passed them to Charles.

"Is there anything else we can get you, Lizzie?"

"Oh, no, Missus Twombly, can I get you anything?" Lizzie rose from her seat, intending to go back to the kitchen.

"Sit, child," said Missus Twombly. "You are our guest. Isabella will pour sweet wine for one last toast." Smiling, she leaned over and patted her husband's hand. He stood at his seat until his daughter had finished.

"To Lizzie and Eliza, who have served us so well. To their loved ones, whose company they share with us. To Charles and Big John, more dear or loyal friends, I have never found.

"To my children, who care for us and love us, even though they know all our faults. To my darling wife, who endures and adores me, and who is the best influence on my life, excepting God, Himself. She is my love, my intellectual superior and the kindest, most patient person I know. God bless you all." He hesitated for a moment and said, looking tenderly at his wife, "Missus Twombly says we can join her in the parlor. Bring your wine if you wish."

In the parlor, the tantalizing smell of coffee and tea, Christmas cake, and sugar biscuits assailed them. Everything was according to the standards set by Missus Twombly. Isabelle had invisibly slipped out from dinner, setting up the cart and tea service while they were all engaged in conversation.

Lizzie watched the scene as if from a place apart. Miss Isabelle was pouring tea and William taking it from her to serve Eliza, who sat near the decorated tree. Who could have dreamed such a vision — this Christmas gathering sae upside down! Kin they possibly no' knae what truly remarkable people they are!

As if reading her mind, James standing next to her said, "If being a servant is what you had ta be ta come ta America, how fortunate ye are, Lizzie Heenan, ta be servin' this lovely family."

Lizzie nodded, her emotion choking her speech. She looked so fragile in that moment, that James put his arm around her to keep her from falling. "I think ye had better perch yerself over here on this footstool, afore ye drop."

Missus Twombly, seeing the exchange, came to Lizzie and asked, "Are you quite alright dear?"

"Missus Twombly, I have ne'er had sech a Christmas as this. I dinna knae wha' ta say."

The radiantly smiling woman took Lizzie's face in her hands and replied earnestly, "We are meant to be servants to all God's children, Lizzie. Not merely because they may have need of our service, but because we desire to serve in His name. On Christmas Day, this little humility and service to you and Eliza, teaches us to be mindful of your quiet, loyal work throughout the year. It is a selfish token, my dear. We receive more from this gift, than the service we give, Merry Christmas, Lizzie."

Doctor Twombly stood behind his wife, with his hand on her shoulder, grinning. "You have the rest of the day off to spend as you wish, Lizzie. You may use the parlor as long as you like, or go out with your family, anything you wish. We will take care of the kitchen and packing the baskets for Big John's 'Basement Club' at the church. We can even manage to make a light supper tonight for all of us."

"We thank you sae much, Doctor an' Missus Twombly. I have a package on the work table fer the men comin' ta the church tonight. It's the big one with no name on it. There are lots o' cookies in the jar, too."

The good doctor, his wife, and children retired to the kitchen, leaving their guests in the parlor. A few minutes later, Isabelle came back with a tray. The rest of Lizzie's packages of fudge for Eliza,

317

James, and her mother were presented to her for distribution. Isabelle made a little curtsy and winked as she stood in front of Lizzie. "Oh my goodness," laughed Lizzie, taking her gifts, "I dinna think I kin get used ta this."

Eliza disappeared for a moment and popped back in the parlor with little packages for her sister, cousin, and mother. "Ye should see them in the kitchen! Missus Twombly is in the rocker, issuing orders, left an' right. Doctor Twombly is at the work table, carving what is left of the goose. Miss Isabelle is wrapped in an apron, washing dishes and M-Mister William…" Eliza melted into paroxysms of laughter without finishing. Every time she began again, she would be hit with another spasm of giggles. "M-Mister W-William has an apron on too! He's d-drying d-dishes and putting them away!" Eliza's voice though soft, rose in pitch with every word through her infectious giggles. Soon the whole group was laughing uncontrollably, trying to be quiet enough not to be heard in the kitchen.

"Children, please hush…," said Maggie, clapping her hand over her own mouth.

"Perhaps we should take our leave. Maybe if we get some fresh air, we could maintain some sense of decorum," Charles offered, his eyes full of glee. "Let me ask permission for the carriage."

Returning from the kitchen with a formidable pile of coats over his arm, Charles told them, the Twomblys agreed to let them use the carriage. Big John said he would stay with the 'kitchen help' and later, head back to the church with the baskets for the men. It was decided that Charles would drive, so James could have some time with his sisters and mother inside the coach. As they were leaving, Lizzie and Eliza picked up wrappers and crumbs in the parlor and brought the dessert cart back to the kitchen. Missus Twombly thanked them for the cart and shooed them out. "Bundle up warm, dears! Go enjoy yourselves."

318

The afternoon weather was milder than that morning. The sun played on the ice bound trees in an array of rainbows and sparkles as if to celebrate the holiday.

Lizzie had insisted on riding with Charles over his protest of propriety. "Charles there are few people out riding to see us an' I want ta spend some time alone wit' ye. If we take the carriage around ta the falls path, I don't imagine we'll see another living soul ta wag his tongue 'bout us. At any rate, you'll soon be off ta school again, an' I will be in Boston, seekin' work. I want ta see ye as much as possible."

"I should know better than to argue with you, Lizzie. I always seem to acquiesce what e'er the cost," returned Charles, smiling.

They rode for a while, and then as the shadows lengthened and the gray clouds gathered, Charles turned the carriage toward Maggie's boarding house.

"You must be frozen. We'll take James to catch his train, bring your mother home, and return the carriage. It's been a most pleasant Christmas Day, Lizzie Heenan."

"It has," she replied. "May I ask ye a question, Charles? Did ye knae the Twomblys were going to give us Christmas Dinner an' serve us, an' give us the day off?"

"They didn't say so, but they have done this every year since I have known them. They are who you see they are. I don't imagine the elder Twomblys will be able to do this much longer and I cannot guess whether the younger Twomblys have the ambition to do it without them. But for now, it is a testament to their faith, that they practice all they preach. I hope to emulate their fine example when I am a minister."

"I think it is a fine thing, ta emulate the Twomblys, but ye have many wonderful qualities o' yer ain, Charles."

"Ah, Lizzie, you are most endearing. I cannot imagine being as good a minister without you by my side." Tipping his hat to

319

shield their faces, he kissed her gently. "I live in hope, my darling, for the day you decide you cannot live without me." Replacing his hat, Charles pulled up to the platform of the train station. Smiling, he swung down from the driver's seat and guided her to the ground. Winking at her, he rapped on the carriage door, "C'mon, James, this is your stop, time to say goodbye."

After a moment's hesitation, James emerged from the coach. He hugged Lizzie fiercely and kissed her cold cheeks. "God be wit' y', Lizzie-girl, I'll see y' when I see y', an' no' a moment afore."

Lizzie smiled at the old saying her father used when saying farewell. "An' I ye, cousin, God keep ye safe an' outa the devil's eye 'til I see ye agin."

He shook Charles' hand, and with a wave, he bounded up the steps to the station without looking back. "Wha'…," Charles uttered in confusion.

"He doesn't want yer ta see the tears in his eyes, Charles."

Charles opened the carriage door and helped her in. "Here, git in away from the cold, Lizzie."

He brought Maggie into the boarding house, with the girls following with her packages. She was sad to have the day over, as they all were.

Back at the Twombly home, Charles unhitched the horse, leading him back to the barn across the street. "Come over to the house, when you're done with the horse, Garrett," he called over his shoulder as he left the Baker's home.

Soon, Lizzie, Charles, Eliza, and Garrett were in the kitchen, warming their hands around hot cups of chocolate. The kitchen was in its usual tidy condition with no evidence of an exchange of workers that day. Lizzie noted she had a full laundry basket to work on, and a few misplaced items to find, but for the most part, everything was as she had done it herself.

The house was quiet except for the quiet chatter between Garrett and Eliza. Lizzie took Charles' hand, leading him to the darkened parlor. Finding it empty, she stood by the tree, raised her arms around his neck and lifted her face toward his. He kissed her deeply and whispered, "What were you going to do if someone was in here, Miss Lizzie?"

"I would have thanked them profusely, as if that were my intended mission, of course," she whispered back saucily.

"Who's there? What are you doing here in the d—. Oh my, excuse me," Missus Twombly said as she saw them spring apart.

Without another word, the elderly woman turned and went into the kitchen. Out of the muffled conversation, Missus Twombly heard Lizzie say, "She's m' unwittin' conspirator. She wants ye ta be happy, my dear."

"Then she has succeeded, my darling," Charles murmured and kissed her again.

"I'm sorry ye canna stay, Charles." The startled question in his eyes, made her add, "I've much ta do ta prepare fer t'marra an' I'll no' abuse the privileges awarded me on this day."

He picked up the angel on the ribbon around her neck and kissed it, then her. "Until I see you again, Lizzie, think kindly on me."

She hugged him one last time then returned to the kitchen for his coat. The glow on her face revealed her reluctance to let him leave. Garrett, Eliza, and Missus Twombly looked up from their conversation. "I'm sorry if I disturbed you, dear," her mistress said.

"No' at all, ma'am," Lizzie said, kissing her cheek. "I have things to do an' he mus' leave."

Turning to the man putting on his coat, Lizzie said, "Will ye be joining us fer New Year's Eve services, Charles?"

"I would be delighted. Missus Twombly, would that be all right with you?"

"Of course, Doctor Twombly and I will probably not attend since it's in the evening, but William will be performing the service and I suspect Isabella will be there. You young people may have a

321

little gathering in the kitchen if you wish to stay up to greet the New Year. We will not be having guests on New Year's Day, so Lizzie and Eliza, if you would like to go out in the afternoon, I think we can spare you for a few hours to visit."

"That's very kind of you, Missus Twombly. Is there anything I can do for you this week?" asked Charles, bowing to take her hand.

"I'll think of something, Charles," The elderly woman smiled knowingly at him. A chore, or any excuse would bring him back to see Lizzie. "Why don't you plan to come around on Tuesday and I'll have an errand or two for you."

"It would be my pleasure, Missus Twombly." Charles stood, nodded to the group and left.

"Well I guess that's my cue to clear out, too, Eliza. Enjoy your evening, Missus Twombly. I will see you again, Miss Eliza, Miss Lizzie." Garrett bowed regally, and slipped into the coat Eliza held for him.

"I do hope you've enjoyed your Christmas, young ladies. I know I did. I hope you know how dear you are to this family." Missus Twombly rose, and stifling a yawn, left the kitchen.

Impulsively, Eliza hugged Lizzie tight. "This has ta be the most surprisin' an' wonderful Christmas I kin remember. They surely celebrate different in America, don't they?"

"Fer sure an' they do, Eliza, although I don't think all Americans celebrate the way of the Twomblys. Nae, what was I going ta do?" Her eyes misted and the kitchen was out of focus, but Lizzie made herself busy with the breakfast trays.

Uncharacteristic clumsiness seemed to take over her hands, as she hunted through the cabinets for misplaced dishes.

It's gonna be a sad day when we leave this lovin' place. In only 'bout three months, we'll be on our ain. We'd best start lookin' fer jobs in the paper. There won't be any money lef' in March fer Ma, an' I won' be beholdin' ta the Earl fer money ta keep her.

322

Chapter Twenty

The week between Christmas and New Year's Day was filled with the memories of special moments. The angel around Lizzie's neck, hidden under her daily uniform, dangled tantalizingly against her chest, reminding her of Charles' love-struck grin. She would unconsciously reach for it during the day, humming softly to herself. The impossibility of her being a minister's wife seemed not so great an obstacle to her these days. She dared to dream of being married to Charles.

Missus Twombly announced on the last morning of the year that they should be prepared to pack up the lesser used items of the house quickly, since their ministerial contract with the church may be rescinded at the end of January. "It is a year-to-year contract and we must not assume we will stay for the foreseeable future. The board always meets the first week of the year to assess its finances, its ministry, and the needs of the congregation. We will keep the decorations up until Little Christmas, and then they will be packed away promptly."

"As you know, April is the month of the Methodist-Episcopal Convention, so January is the time for all the committees and sub-committees of all the participating churches to consolidate their reports, proposals, and positions in the world today."

323

Doctor Twombly entering the kitchen as she was speaking, added, "It's also when they decide where their moral outrage should best placed, and how to protect their position of power against fair and equal privilege for women." He winked at Lizzie, and put his hands on his wife's shoulders and spoke gently to her, "It is my dearest desire that your voice be heard with equal interest throughout this convention, my dear. Perhaps one day, my fellow buffoons will learn that they have nothing to lose and much to gain in recognizing the creative and intelligent mind of the other half of God's human creation, probably the better half, at that."

"Yes, dear, right now, we must tend to more practical matters. I do not want to be premature in preparing to move, nor do I want to be having to do it in a haphazard fashion. Anything you haven't used in the last three months can be packed away in the trunks. We will not be entertaining this month, so be judicious in what we keep in the dining room drawers. Two sets of linens only to be in active use, one to use and one to wash. All others can be packed away. If we *are* going to stay, they will be unpacked as we need them, much as we did this past year." She went on describing the methods of paring down the household items in preparation of moving.

Doctor Twombly sat at the kitchen work table as Lizzie poured him coffee and put some biscuits on a small plate. "Can I get you some tea, ma'am?" she asked the older woman in her rocker.

"That would be lovely, dear. Now where was I?"

"You were telling this young lady, that we will lose our livelihood at the whim of the board, my dear."

"I was not, Doctor Twombly, I was only letting her know we should always be prepared. Do you think I am being overly cautious?"

"Not at all, dearest, please do continue." He smiled gently at her and pretended to read the paper.

324

Her eyes flashed at what she perceived as a dismissal, but she went on writing her daily list.

Later, having finished his coffee, he said, "Come Betsy, we can leave Lizzie to her chores and I will read my Sunday sermon to you while you rest. It will be our New Year's Day message and I want to set the right tone for the year. You have a wonderful ear for my sermons."

She did not protest, but went with him, leaving her list unfinished.

Lizzie smiled as she tried to picture Charles and herself twenty or thirty years hence, with a similar exchange. *'Twould not be sae bad, would it, to be a minister's wife, if he was as carin' ta me, as Doctor Twombly is ta her?*

Lizzie knew the Twomblys were worried about Mister William, who stayed in his room for several days after Christmas with severe congestion. The doctor said he would most likely develop pneumonia if he didn't rally soon. He had a bout with pneumonia several years prior and nearly died. Isabelle was to keep her parents and servants away from him, hoping they would remain healthy. Eliza was instructed to leave the trays for William and Isabelle outside his room for all meals. She piled nightshirts and bed linens outside the door daily while his fever rose. Lizzie added horehound drops and strong tea with honey to each of their meals. She wished she had more of Móraí's herbs to give him.

The whole household was hoping he would be well enough for the New Year's Eve Service, but he showed no signs of the full recovery he would need. Doctor Twombly would have to conduct the service. A snow squall had blown up that afternoon and the elderly man insisted that only he and Charles need go out that evening. "I promise I will return home right after the service and yes, I will deliver the soup for our Basement Men's Club. Did you know several small families have joined them this week? We really must do something to provide some private areas down there. Big

325

John hasn't said so, but I think we'll have to bring them more blankets and warm coats. Maybe I should suggest to Big John that he bring them upstairs to the anterooms for more warmth."

"Do you think we can send Charles to see if the Bakers have any more blankets to spare? I'm sure we don't have any more than what is on our own beds at the moment," said Missus Twombly. "Perhaps Ladies' Group can start a drive for more, when we meet again. It's a shame. We have organizations to take care of widows and orphans, but sober men who need work and whole families who have recently lost their homes have nowhere to go. I would think society would want to preserve the unity of even our poorest families and the virtue of men not dragged down by demon rum."

"You are right, my dear. Unfortunately, the poor we will always have with us and the poor house is overfull. It is up to us to bring attention to the situation. I think I'll add that little thought to my sermon tonight."

Doctor Twombly pulled out his pocket watch, and said, "I hope Charles gets here a little early so he can have supper with us before going to church."

Lizzie's heart skipped at the thought of seeing him again. Oh, I hope sae too, Doctor Twombly. Perhaps he'll have ta stay here after church if the snow keeps up. Her fingers reached for her angel again.

Later that afternoon, Charles and the cold wind blew into the kitchen. Careful to stay on the door mat, he stamped his feet and shook the snow off his shoulders, reminding Lizzie of a huge wet dog.

"Charles, give me yer hat an' coat. The weather seems ta be gittin' worse. How 'bout some coffee ta warm ye up?"

"That would be lovely, Lizzie. The walk from the station felt the longest it's been in quite some time. It was barely flurrying when I left Boston, but now it's coming down in earnest."

"Charles, I'm going ta put a pan of warm water in the water closet. I want ye ta gae in with these warm towels an' Mister William's stockin's. Put yer wet ones an' boots outside the door. If ye don't warm up those frozen feet, ye will catch yer death."

"Yes, ma'am, a gentleman would say, 'Oh no, don't trouble yourself,' but I can't think of anything more heavenly at the moment, than doing just what you tell me," Charles said grinning. "Thank you, my darling."

He watched her as she carried the pan of water and towels by him, and as she left the tiny room he kissed her cheek. Shortly after, he set his sopping boots and stockings outside the door as instructed. The boots were set behind the big cast iron stove and before the stockings went into the laundry basket, Lizzie sewed a stitch of bright red thread in the tops to identify them.

Lizzie hummed to herself as she stirred sautéed onions into the chicken stew. It would be a simple supper tonight. *'Twill keep him, er' them, warm when they go out fer church.* She smiled as she corrected herself. *Tonight, when they come hame, I will tell him 'Aye. I will be a minister's wife.' Please, God, help me, an' I will be the best one I can be.*

Missus Twombly and Eliza were in the kitchen when Charles emerged from the water closet with the empty pan in his hands, William's socks on his feet, and damp towels over his arm. They both turned in question toward Lizzie. "His feet were near frozen. I had ta do somethin'."

"Of course, dear, where are his boots?"

"They're behind the stove. They won't be dry in time, but they'll be better than they were."

"Well, we'll give him some of William's boots. He shan't be using them tonight, will he? Eliza?"

"Aye, ma'am, they're in the hall closet."

"Charles, it's so good of you to come early. We'll have a little supper before you and Doctor Twombly have to leave for church. Please sit and have some coffee to warm your bones."

Charles shot an amused look to Lizzie over Missus Twombly's head as she whisked out the door. Lizzie smiled back and turned to her stove. Eliza poked her head in, then handed Charles the requested boots.

"Charles, let me put 'em by the stove too, so they'll be toasty warm when you hafta gae out," Lizzie suggested.

"I knew I choose the right girl for me, Lizzie. You're already taking such good care of me."

"I'd do the same fer anyone in yer frozen condition, Charles," she said laughing.

Charles dramatically held his hands over his heart as if mortally wounded. "Well!"

Charles walked over to her and slipped his arms around her and gently whispered, "Ah, Lizzie, Do I have any chance of capturing your heart? Am I Don Quixote tilting at windmills, thinking I am winning the battle for your love?"

"Ye have my heart, Charles. Ye are the best, most decent man I knae," Lizzie whispered back. "Now, if ye will allow, I need ta finish here or we'll have no supper." She attempted to slip out of his grasp, but he spun her around deftly and kissed her soundly. Breathing together, he kissed her again, barely touching her lips.

"Now, I will sit down here and drink coffee, my dear." He watched her over the rim of his coffee cup, smiling as she straightened her cap and apron, trying to regain her composure.

She made herself busy chopping cooked potatoes and carrots, throwing them into the stew. Their eyes met in easy communication, requiring no speech. These were the moments she savored and remembered while they were apart. Her lips still tingled with recent kisses. Her eyes darted to him with secret glances, pregnant with meaning. Her heart was still racing, her body warm

328

and excited. Her hands moved unconsciously to the angel dangling from the ribbon circling her neck. She fought for reason.

Think, girl! Ye hafta git supper ready. What do ye do next? Make the biscuits. Set up the trays fer Eliza. Just three in the dinin' room, two upstairs. Ah, look at him! Sae handsome, sae self-assured, an' me all knotted up, wit'out the sense God gave a goose! My word, nae I'm talkin' like Garrett! Ye've completely addled my brain, Charles Bachelor. Laughing at herself, Lizzie shook her head and went back to making biscuits for their supper.

Charles put his feet on the register and being warm and content, began to doze. He was startled awake by Eliza, rushing in for the upstairs trays. "Lizzie, Miss Isabelle says Mister William's fever's broke an' he's hungry. She says hurry afore he changes his mind. Are ye thawed out, Charles?" Eliza spun back to Lizzie and asked, "Are we ready?"

"Aye, Eliza. Those trays just need silver. If they require a bit of dessert, ye can bring it up after. Blueberry cobbler or 'nilla drops."

Eliza stacked the trays and was gone. "Charles," Lizzie prompted gently, having seen him napping earlier, "Ye should probably gae into the dinin' room, nae. Eliza'll be callin' the Twomblys in fer supper soon."

Charles stifled a yawn, and asked if he could bring something in with him. They kept their voices low, so they would not be overheard.

"No, Charles. Missus Twombly would be terribly put out if I allowed ye ta do thet. Ye are our guest." She looked at his reflection in the dark kitchen window. "Oh dear, it looks like the snow is startin' up agin. I hope it's only a passin' flurry."

"I'm sure it'll be nothing. If it looks like it's building up, Doctor Twombly will cut his sermon short, and we'll come home early. Would you like to come to service tonight?"

329

"I daren't, Charles. Wit' Miss Isabelle upstairs with Mister William, I don't want ta leave Missus Twombly alone. If William got worse, I'd hafta gae after the doctor, an' Eliza would hafta stay wit' her."

"There should be a telephone in this house! I've begged them to put one in, just for occasions like this. The church just won't spend the money," Charles whispered with exasperation.

"I knae, there's money fer entertaining, but no' fer emergencies,' as ye've said before. I hope ye take thet lesson fer yer ministry," Lizzie said pointedly.

Charles nodded, and went into the dining room.

Supper was over quickly and the two men prepared to leave. Lizzie stood by the back door, knowing Charles would exit there to get the horse and rig to drive it around to the front for the elderly minister. Receiving a kiss on the cheek, Lizzie hugged his neck and repeated her caution about the weather. When he opened the door, the snow and wind blasted through. "I'll be back in little more than an hour, dear."

In a few minutes, he was at the front door, to help Doctor Twombly negotiate the front walk. Lizzie stood near the front door watching them. "Maybe that was just a small squall. It seems ta have calmed down nae," she said hopefully.

Having seen them drive off, she turned back to the kitchen. She filled the dish pan with hot water from the stove and began to wash the supper dishes. Her eyes wandered to the chair he had occupied earlier and saw the folded wool on the seat. *Oh dear, he fergot the extra blanket I gave him fer the ride. Well, he's gone nae. I hope he'll be warm enough.*

Just then, Lizzie heard a strange distant thud and the windows shook as if from the wind. She ran back to the front door with the blanket still in her hand. Eliza threw the front door open peering into the blowing snow toward the barely visible street lamp

330

down the road. Then they heard the terrifying scream of a horse in the throes of agony.

"Eliza, stay here wit' Missus Twombly!" Lizzie threw the blanket over her head and shoulders, and with caution abandoned, she dashed down the snowy steps and down the deeply-covered sidewalk toward the noise. As she ran, doors of the neighboring houses opened and men were shouting, as they ran toward the sound of the panicked horse.

Struggling with her skirts and the deep snow, Lizzie's heart beat hard in her ears. *Oh Laird, don't let it be...*

But it was. The carriage that had just left the Twombly home was split by a tree, severing the roadway with the injured horse on one side and the remains of the carriage on the other. The men closer to the carriage were gently lifting the elderly man out of the wreckage. He was not moving, but one man announced, "He's alive! Get him to his house."

To Lizzie's increased horror, another shouted through the storm, "Where's the driver? Somebody shoot that horse, for pity's sake! Careful of the river bank, you'll slide right into the water."

Charles! Where are you? Lizzie finally found her voice and began screaming, "Charles! Charles!"

"Here he is, over here, on the other side. Have mercy, man! Shoot that accursed horse, will you!"

Lizzie climbed over the fallen tree in time to see the horse felled by a single shot. Beyond the now-silent beast, Charles lay bloodied and barely alive, broken in the circle of men.

"Charles!" Lizzie uttered, forcing her way through the men. She threw the blanket from her shoulders over him and knelt in the blood-soaked snow.

"Lizzie," Charles struggled to speak. "I'm sorry. I love you. I—"

"Sh-h, Charles, you knae I love you. I want ta be yer wife. I was goin' ta tell ye t'night." She turned to the men around her, and

331

screamed. "Did ye send fer the doctor? Kin ye no' help him?" She felt a coat settle on her shoulders as the men murmured and shuffled in the trampled snow.

As she turned back to Charles, she felt his head get impossibly heavy on her arm and saw the light disappear from his eyes. She bent over his chest to hear the last beats of the tender heart she had learned to love. She began to moan sadly, rocking with his head still in her arms. She kissed his lips and closed his eyelids.

She no longer heard the voices around her, the ambulance siren, and the murmuring crowd of onlookers. Someone covered his face, but she drew the blanket back and kissed his forehead, running her fingers through his wet hair. She stared at him, unseeing, unfeeling and hummed the hymn they had sung together in church: *Blest Be the Tie That Binds*. The words fleeting through her mind were not recognized as significant at that moment, but later, reliving Charles' mortal departure, she wept.

> *When we asunder part*
> *It gives us inward pain;*
> *But we shall still be joined in heart,*
> *And hope to meet again.*

As they removed the inert body of Charles Titus Bachelor, it seemed to galvanize the action of her companions. A familiar voice in her ear brought her back to the reality of the moment. Mister Baker and Garrett helped her up from the grizzly scene. They tried to get her to board a wagon, but she balked violently, refusing their efforts. Mister Baker raised his hand to ward off Garrett's attempts to persuade her, instructing him to go ahead. Mister Baker gently put his arm around her waist and supported her. "We'll walk. It isn't far." Turning his head toward the men behind them, he added, "I'll return your coat tomorrow, Jim, thank you."

As they entered the yard, Lizzie pulled toward the path leading to the back door, but Mister Baker held fast. "Today, we'll go in the front door, Lizzie. No one will mind. We need to get you warm."

As they passed the parlor, Lizzie saw a group of people surrounding the couch where Doctor Twombly lay. It didn't seem to register that he, too, was dying.

"Eliza, bring her into the bedroom and get her out of these wet clothes, right away. Dress her warmly and wrap her in a blanket. I'll set the water to boil. She'll need a cup of tea and a pan of water to soak her feet in. We have to bring her temperature up. Quickly, now, bring her out here when she's ready."

"Aye, sir." Eliza took in Lizzie's ashen face, wet half-frozen curls, and the limp icy cold hands. "Come, Lizzie, come wit' me," Eliza said in a soft, slow mesmerizing voice. Lizzie showed no sign of hearing her, but she did as she was told.

Eliza dressed her in a nightgown, slipped a robe on her, and led her back to the chair near the stove. Mister Baker had prepared a washtub with warm water and a cup of tea for her.

He stood by the door and asked, "Eliza can you take care of the women in this house? Do you want me to send Missus Baker to you? I have to cut up the tree and haul the carriage away before everything is frozen in place. Will you tend to them?" Awkwardly, seeming embarrassed by his lack of action, he edged toward the door.

Eliza looked up from her kneeling position and replied, "I kin do it, but if Missus Baker could help, I would be grateful fer it." She returned to the chore of getting Lizzie's feet in the pan without getting her gown wet, all the while talking softly to her.

There was a noise at the front of the house as Garrett arrived with the doctor. They made no effort to silence the stamping of their feet, trying to get as much of the snow off before entering the parlor.

It seemed like everyone was speaking at once. Lizzie stood and tried to step out of the pan, headed for the door.

"No, Lizzie, sit down. You kin do no good in there," Eliza forced her sister into the chair.

"I need ta get tea an' biscuits fer them, Eliza. What are ye doing? I need ta get things ready fer our guests. Missus Twombly...," Lizzie said angrily. Her head was swimming and she was very cold. She couldn't make sense of where she was. Why was she in the kitchen with her feet in a wash bucket and in her nightgown? Where is m' apron, m' cap? We have company an' I am just sittin' here! I can't get up! The colors in the room were flowing together and she watched them fade into black. There was so much noise, but she couldn't understand what anyone was saying. Her head seemed to bang against a scratchy wool blanket. Her eyes slowly focused on a world upside down. She heard someone moan, far away.

Garrett ran into the room when he had heard Eliza's cry of distress. Seeing Lizzie falling hard on Eliza, he lifted her over his shoulder and carried her to the bedroom. Unmindful of her wet feet, Garrett gently laid her on the bed and pulled the blanket over her. Lizzie just stared unseeing at him, then closed her eyes. He stood for a minute watching as her breathing returned to normal and she turned away from him.

Garrett returned to the kitchen as Eliza still struggled to get up from the wet floor. Missus Baker entered, knocking Eliza down again. Garrett stood her upright and held her for a moment. Missus Baker just quietly nodded her head and began to pick up the chair, the bucket and mop. With her coat still on, the carpenter's wife methodically mopped up the water.

As Garrett held her, Eliza began to cry. "I'm s-s-sorry. I've never seen Lizzie like this. She's the strong one. She came in all bloody an' out o' her h-head. I didn't knae how ta help her."

334

"She'll be fine. She's had a terrible shock, but she'll be fine. *You'll have to be the strong one fer now, Eliza.*

She's sleepin', but when she wakes, she may still not be herself. But you'll be here t' help her." His voice crooned as if she were a baby. He kissed her hair, now uncapped, unrestrained and wild from her fall.

Still in his arms, Eliza seemed to pull herself together. Her hands flew to fix her hair and straighten her apron. "Thank ye, Garrett." She sniffed, backing away. "Thank ye, Missus Baker. Lemme take yer coat."

She hung the coat, and then turned to the task of making tea. *Lizzie's right, they need tea an' biscuits in the parlor. It's gonna be a lang night.* "Garrett, would ye count the number o' people in the parlor fer me? Missus Baker, if ye would, pull out thet tea cart an' set the second shelf with teacups an' saucers? I'll get the water boilin' an' put biscuits out." Eliza was almost calm and back to herself again.

Garrett returned with a count of fifteen. He suggested after they had some tea, she should encourage the lookers-on to go home. The family, the doctor, Missus Baker, and Eliza were all that needed to be there. He would leave shortly, he announced, to check on the children and see if Mister Baker needed help. "If you think that's best, Missus Baker?"

Missus Baker put her hand on his shoulder and said, "You're a goot young man, Garrett. We are blessed t' have you in our family."

Garrett looked at her, nodding. "I'm the one who's blessed, Missus Baker. I've ne'er had anyone care 'bout me before." He turned facing the door, trying to hide his emotion, and said, "I'll go check on the children now. I don't want them wake an' find we're all gone."

"Mary-Margaret next door is watchin' 'em. If you could help Mister Baker wit' the haulin' though, I'd be grateful."

"Of course, put a light out the back door when you're ready t' go home an' I'll come fetch you, Missus Baker. G'night, Eliza. Lizzie will come around in the mornin'. You'll see."

"G'night, Garrett. Thank ye," said Eliza shyly. Now that she was calmed, she was embarrassed by her lapse in taking charge. "I'll be fine nae. Please be careful."

Garrett kissed her cheek and slipped out the door. Eliza stood staring at the door until Missus Baker interrupted her reverie. "Shall I take der cart oot to der parlor, Eliza?"

"Oh heaven's, where was I? No, I'll tend the cart. Could ye peek in on Lizzie fer me?"

Without waiting for an answer, Eliza pushed the jingling cart down the hallway. The men in the parlor were murmuring among themselves concerning the grave condition of Doctor Twombly. The physician was speaking quietly to the family.

"Gentlemen, if ye would please take yer tea into the dinin' room? The family needs some privacy wit' Doctor Jameson. I will bring yer more biscuits there." The men shuffled almost as a unit to the other room, still retelling the gruesome details of the accident. Eliza quietly closed the dining room door against the voices that rose as each told the story from their vantage point. Her stomach lurched as she heard their description of the tragedy.

She surveyed the parlor as she poured tea for the grieving family. Isabelle sat weeping in the chair by the fireplace and Missus Twombly sat by her husband, clear-eyed, if shaky, listening to the doctor. Eliza stood by Isabelle and asked quietly, "Shall I help Mister William downstairs ta be wit' the family?"

Isabelle looked up at her and realized for the first time, William didn't know what happened. She tried to think what to do. "His fever broke this afternoon. Eliza, if he is sleeping, let him be. If he is awake, tell him what's happened, wait in the hall for him to get dressed, and then help him downstairs. I don't think I can tell him. I don't." Her tears freshened in red-rimmed eyes and she could no longer speak. She waved her hand toward the stairs and started weeping again.

Before going upstairs, Eliza ducked into the kitchen to tell Missus Baker to bring more biscuits to the dining room and instruct the gentlemen there to please leave by the back door. There was no sense in disturbing the family with their tramping out the front by the parlor. Mister William would not want the men to see him in his condition either.

Satisfied with that, she mounted the stairs quickly. She dreaded this chore and prayed Mister William was asleep. She knocked timidly and her heart sank when the minister answered. He was sitting up in bed, reading.

"What is all the noise about downstairs, Eliza? I thought we were not having company tonight."

"Mister William, Doctor Twombly's been in a terrible accident tonight. He's in grave condition an' the doctor's wit' him. Yer mother an' sister need you. Are you well enough ta gae down stairs?" Eliza added, "Kin I get anythin' fer you? I kin help ye on the stairs."

"Step into the hall, Eliza. I will be out in a minute." His panicked look frightened Eliza as his eyes darted about the room, planning his task of becoming presentable.

Eliza flew from the room. She heard several bumps and thuds in the room as the ailing minister bumbled around in his weakened state, trying to get dressed. She resisted the urge to forego his dignity and burst into the room. More frightening than the noise, was the sudden silence on the other side of the door. *Oh my, what if he fell an' is unconscious! What should I do? I—*

Her thoughts were interrupted by the opening of the door and Mister William standing there with not a hair out of place, resplendent, if pale, in his evening suit. He leaned on the door frame a moment, catching his breath. Then straightening, he smiled grimly and said, "Shall we?" He put out his arm as if they were going to promenade the Common on a Sunday afternoon.

Eliza took his arm and soon noticed the heavy weight he entrusted to her. "Slowly, my dear, I am not as steady as I had hoped. I'm sorry you will have to help me. This accursed body does not function well enough to hold its own weight, it appears."

"We all have our frailties, Mister William. Mine is a severe lack o' courage."

"You hide it well, my dear. Now, do you think we can negotiate the staircase?"

"I am right by yer side, Mister William. I'll no' let ye fall." Eliza had no choice but to venture forth on the strength of her own words. She prayed for renewed vigor at each step. When at last they reached the bottom, the younger minister stood up straight and with a masterful effort, strode into the parlor. Eliza marveled at the transformation. She hoped pretense of calm strength would not tax him to the point of falling into a faint, thereby disappointing his ambition. His mother and sister needed his inner calm to withstand their anticipated loss.

Eliza ran to get him a cup of hot tea to bolster his fading strength. William found the nearest chair to his mother and collapsed heavily in it. Isabelle woke from her sad despair just long enough to cross the parlor and sit on the floor at her brother's feet, her head on his knee. One hand stroked her shoulder while the other extended to hold his mother's hand.

Eliza reentered the room, watching the tableau before her. The family was linked by touch, one to the other, all listening to the doctor's low words of caution. Caution against hope, caution against miracles was his theme. He listed the injuries, the loss of blood, and the weakness of the heart that struggled to perform.

William gently retrieved his hands to accept the comforting tea. His deeply hollowed eyes looked into hers and murmured, "Thank you, Eliza."

338

"Kin I get you anythin' else?" she whispered. Receiving a barely perceptible shake of his head, she stood vigil at the doorway, waiting for any request to push her into action.

After a long half hour of standing, Eliza saw William look at her sadly and say gently, "Eliza, you've been very helpful. You may retire if you wish. I don't think we will need anything more."

"Thank yer, sir. I will be right in the kitchen, if ye need anythin'." Isabelle lifting her head, looked first at her brother and then at Eliza. Slowly, she returned to her position at William's knee.

Eliza checked the darkened dining room and entered the kitchen. Missus Baker sat in the rocker, reading the paper. The dishes were done and put away.

"Missus Baker, thank ye fer ever'thin'. I kin handle thin's from here on. I'll put the light on a' the back door an' Garrett'll come ta walk ye home."

"You did well t'night, Eliza. Lizzie is sleepin' soundly fer now. I suspect Doctor Jameson slipped her a potion when he first came in. She hasn't moved a'tall since I first saw her abed. I'll be back tomorrow t' see what is t' see. *De toekomst is een boek met zeven sloten.*"

"I'm sorry, Missus Baker, I don't knae wha' thet means"

"*The future is a book with seven locks.* As you might say, no one knows der future, child. I forget sometimes, not ever'one knows my mother's tongue. She vas Netherlander, from Almere. She never learned English. I was born here, but didn't speak English until I vent t' school. Mister Baker came here ven he vas nine years or so. They had long conversations together before I even knew him."

"Is everyone in America from somewhere else?"

"If you go back far enough, I guess. Even der savage Indians mus' haf' come fum somewheres," Missus Baker said with a twinkle in her eye. "Ah, there's Garrett. I'll be goin' now."

Eliza wished Missus Baker was not so willing to leave, so she could have the comfort of Garrett's arms again. In the absence of company, she felt overwhelmingly tired. She looked in on Lizzie, who still seemed to be sleeping deeply. She took a warm wrap and settled in the kitchen rocker. With her feet near the stove and the lamps down low, she dozed intermittently.

She woke with a start. *The church! Surely someone told the congregation that there would be no service. The soup! It never made it to the church! Nor do they know to go upstairs where it is warmer. She busied herself adding more vegetables to the little broth left from supper. More water, more broth, seasoning. Lizzie would bring life ta this sad, watery soup. What would she do? She looked in the ice box. Leftover mashed potatoes, carrots. She threw them all in the boiling concoction. Stirring the potatoes until they were blended, Eliza spied the burnt flour on the back of the stove. A little of this for color, some scraps of meat should make it palatable.*

She went to the parlor to check on the family. Mister William slouched back in the chair while his mother and sister leaned against him for comfort. *They will be fine.* Eliza silently signaled the doctor to the doorway, telling him she was going to fetch Garrett to bring food to the church. He agreed that the family would be fine under his watchful eye and she should go.

She peeked in on Lizzie once again and seeing her sister hadn't stirred since they put her there, Eliza donned her coat. It wasn't far from the manse's back door to Mister Baker's barn where they had hauled the larger pieces of wood. She persuaded the master carpenter to let Garrett deliver the soup to the church basement.

Watching him ride into the night with the soup, Eliza prayed she was not sending Garrett to his doom as well.

Chapter Twenty-one

Back in the warm kitchen, Eliza shifted her achy body in the padded rocker to find some measure of comfort while keeping her watch over the distraught and exhausted family. Drifting into a fitful sleep, thinking she had forgotten something important, she awoke several times, panicked, precipitating a hasty inspection of door and window latches, stoking the fires, peeking into the tension-filled parlor, her ears alert for the smallest sound of movement.

The family watched as the doctor hovered over the still body, listening for an arrhythmic heartbeat, or a telltale death rattle, watching for a fluttering of eyelids.

Isabelle slept, her face tracked by tears, her head on William's knee with his comforting arm around her, frozen in the same position since Eliza had last seen her. William, his face drawn, haggard from his illness and lack of sleep, looked more in danger of passing into the hereafter than his beloved father. Deep shadows under his eyes accenting his pallor, his body seemed to strain against the slightest motion, lest he wake his sister. Her body still leaning heavily against him, he feared precipitating another tortuous episode of her inconsolable weeping.

Betsey Dow Twombly held the immobile hand of the man who was her vibrant, intellectual equal, her husband for nearly forty-

341

nine years. She knew his journey to meet his heavenly Father had begun hours before. There was no turning back for him. Although his earthly shell was ravaged and spent, he seemed to smile, welcoming this new adventure and the culmination of his faith. She reasoned it was as it should be, quick, without a life incapacitated and frustrated. Yesterday, he was vigorous and about his work. Today, he was quietly leaving his work to the hands of others.

Eliza turned away from the family to the dining room where she had assumed they would have laid Charles. *Where could they have put him? This is the closest family he had.* She pictured with dread, Lizzie waking in the morning and asking where he was. She made a mental note to ask Garrett as soon as she saw him again. *Why didn't I ask? Why isn't he here?* A shiver went through her whole body. *This is no' a good thing. Lizzie will be sae upset.*

As she returned to the kitchen, she heard a plaintive cry from the parlor. Eliza ran to the front room. From the doorway, she saw Missus Twombly rise slowly, deliberately, kiss her two children who wept openly, and walk purposely toward her. "He is gone, Eliza. He is gone home. If you would help me up the stairs, I believe I will lay down now. Today will be a busy day. See if you can persuade my children to do the same."

"Aye, ma'am." When they reached Missus Twombly's bedroom, Eliza asked, "I don' wish ta disturb you, Missus Twombly, but do ye knae where they've taken Charles? Lizzie will want ta knae."

"I'm sorry, child, I should have told you. Mister Baker took him to his house for Missus Baker to clean him up and dress him for the viewing at the church. Missus Baker will help you with Doctor Twombly. Lizzie knows where his Sunday suit is. Good night, dear. Try to get some sleep."

Eliza shivered. "Whatever I kin do, ma'am." She held the old lady around her tiny waist to help her down the hall. "Thin's will ne'er be the same."

342

"From one day to the next, life changes, child. In the blink of an eye, we grow frail and old. Enjoy every moment, every day in the journey." Her every step seemed to mark the passing of time for her. By the time she reached her room, she was spent. Laying alone on her bed, Betsey Dow Twombly closed her eyes, willing her husband's gentle strength to enfold her in comfort.

Eliza hurried down the stairs, hoping to convince Isabelle and William to leave their father for an hour's rest. She found she did not have to cajole them at all. They were in the parlor doorway waiting for her. William dismissed her quietly. "Eliza, you can get Missus Baker to help you with my father. We are going to rest for awhile. We will call you if we require anything. I will check on Mother. Thank you, for your help."

Checking the clock in the hallway, winding it, Eliza wondered if she should stop its hands at the hour of death. *No, they probably don't do thet here. The curtains in the parlor are already closed. I have no mourning cloths ta cover the mirrors. When the shops open, I can buy black mourning bunting for the door an' perhaps a wreath, as I've seen done. Oh dear! Today is New Year's Day. The service! Mister William will have ta give the 11 o'clock sermon. There will be no shops open! Missus Baker will tell me what ta do.*

As she turned to the kitchen she heard a strange sound, the humming of an cheerful old Irish ballad. The clatter of pans told her who it was. *Lizzie!*

Rushing into the kitchen, she saw Lizzie preparing for breakfast as usual. She was dressed in her fresh apron and cap, her hair primly tucked in a bun. "Lizzie?"

Lizzie turned to her, smiled and said, "Eliza, ye surprised me. I awoke an' ye were already up. Strange, I didn't hear ye. Git the trays out, would yer? I canna imagine my havin' slept well beyond yer gittin' up."

"Lizzie. S-stop what yer doin', an' sit down." Lizzie looked at her, shocked at her tone, but did as she was told. "Lizzie." Eliza began anew, gently now, "Do ye remember las' night, a' tall?"

"What? It's funny I don't. I had this terrible dream. I didn't walk in my sleep, did I? I git sae wrapped up in my dreamin'. Ma said I used ta lash out an' e'en git outa bed. What's happened?"

"Lizzie..." Eliza walked over to her chair and put her arms tightly around her. "Charles and Doctor Twombly had an awful accident las' night." Pausing, she took a deep breath and let it out, saying, "They died, Lizzie. I'm sae sorry."

Lizzie jumped up. "Elizabeth Ann Heenan! How could ye sae sech a thing! Ye..."

Slowly the dream came back to her and the truth of her sister's words came alive in vivid pictures flooding her head. "Nay, Eliza, nay." She slumped back into the chair so quickly, Eliza almost fell. "Doctor Twombly, too?" she whispered.

"Yea, Lizzie, him too, less than an hour past, I'm sae sorry." Tears coursed down Eliza's face as she struggled to tell her half-sister the tragic events of the night. "The family is finally sleeping nae. They won' be disturbed fer hours, sae we are ta hold everythin' until they tell us what's ta be done." Calming herself, Eliza added, "Make some tea an' toast fer yerself. I have ta git Missus Baker, if 'n her lights are on."

Lizzie pushed Eliza out of her way and ran to the water closet. She emerged shortly, having emptied her stomach, remembering the bloody scene from the night before. She leaned against the door frame, her face blotchy and pale, watching her sister put on a coat and head for the door.

"Will ye be all right fer a while, Lizzie? I have ta git Missus Baker. She'll knae what ta do."

Lizzie nodded her head slowly, edging toward the nearest chair. She dropped heavily into it, allowing a shutter to tear through her body. Determined, she forcibly took charge of her body and her work.

Shakily, she filled the tea kettle, set out three cups and saucers, a plate of biscuits and jam. She was grateful for these routine movements not requiring thought. Her memory went from full recall of the last night's trial, to blank, foggy lapses. It was a merry-go-round where she could focus on a single scene in stark relief, only to have the memory blur until she returned to that same spot again. Over and over, she saw Charles' body in her arms bloodied and broken, and then she was at the house having no recollection of getting there. Back and forth the visions went, from Charles to the house. It occurred to her, although she remembered men shouting at her, she could not hear them.

The back door flew open, galvanizing Lizzie to action as she realized the tea kettle was fairly dancing on the stove. Vaguely, she remembered hearing the steam and the clattering of the kettle's cover, but the sound could not penetrate her fractured thinking. She rescued the kettle and refilled it as Eliza and their neighbor entered the kitchen. Missus Baker hugged her tight and entreated her to sit down.

"We'll haf' a cuppa tea, an' figure oot what t' do," the older housewife said, decisively. She chatted nervously, her almost forgotten Dutch punctuating her speech, betraying her apprehension as she looked from one stricken face, to the other one, with the tea kettle in her hand. "We haf' to be strong, noo? No giffin' in t' der sadness, not t'day, not vile dere's verk t' be done.

"We'll close der parlor doors, so's we can work in dere. Eliza, do we haf' Doctor Twombly's good suit and shirt for him? Mister Baker vill notify der undertaker, for der hearse an' livery. Mister Baker und Garrett haf' been working on der coffins all night. Better to haf' dem made wit' luffin' hands dan to buy 'em from der wretched Mister Gordon, wit' his fancy boxes und *fancier* prices,"

345

she finished with distain. "Lef' ter him, der expense off dyin' is gettin' t' be ootrageous."

"Lizzie, ye had his suit ready for t'day's service. Is it still down here or in his room?" Eliza asked.

"I-I don' remember." Lizzie eyes started to well up with frustrated tears.

"It's all right, Lizzie. I'll take a look. You jes' sit an' sip yer tea." She looked in the alcove where the freshly pressed laundry hung and found the suit. She picked up the suit, a shirt, tie, and his newly polished shoes, then brought them to the parlor. Eliza gasped as she saw the body lying in shadow on the couch, his face sharply illuminated in an eerie cameo of flickering lamplight. The cold reality of death seized her heart.

The two young women worked under Missus Baker's tutelage, readying the body for viewing. Experienced in the preparation of the dead, the older woman trimmed his beard and combed his hair. She sent the girls back to the kitchen as she removed his clothing, calling them back only when she had him sufficiently attired to preserve his dignity, avoiding an occasion of scandal to the two unmarried women.

She talked incessantly, keeping the work progressing at a steady pace. She attended the body while ordering the young women to remove the excess furniture from the room. "Ven der coffins arrive, ve'll haf' dem remove der sofa, to preffent our visitors und the family fum seein' remainders off der tragedy on der fabric. Mister Baker vill reupholster it wit' sumptin' appropriate.

"T'marra morning, der two coffins vill be brought t' der church for viewing. Der funeral vill pro'bly be held Tuesday. Den, der bodies vill be transported t' der funeral home und placed in a 'cold' room until der veather's varm enough t' bury dem. Der church vill pay for all dat. Mister Baker vill see t' it." Missus Baker talked on, telling them how to set up the dining room, by moving the

346

table and chairs to the walls in preparation for the food that would arrive with the guests who came to pay their respects.

"If the family isn' up by nine-thirty, we'll hafta wake them. Mister William has a sermon at eleven, don' forgit," said Lizzie. "It's nearly nine, so I'll start breakfast, then ye can wake them wit' the promise o' food."

Eliza could see Lizzie was coming back to her own efficient self. She resisted the urge to hug her, lest she fall back into the confusion she showed earlier. *She better off wit' somethin' ta do ta occupy her time. Oh dear, Maggie! She doesn't even knae an' she'll be waitin' fer Charles ta come git her fer church!* She quickly talked to Missus Baker while Lizzie was in the kitchen.

"Eliza, I vill go home, I'm just aboot done for now. I'll haf' Garrett go t' Missus Heenan, t' let her know. I'll be surprised if she hain't heard it fum som'one in the neighborhood. I'll arrange fer Mister Baker t' deliver der coffin fer der goot Reverend, an' the one vit' Mister Charles a'ready in it, vile you're all at church. Garrett vill deliffer you und your mutter t' church, den he'll hafta come back ta help Mister Baker und Big John set 'em up in the parlor."

Eliza stared at this woman who seemed to have everything in perfect order. "Thank you, Missus Baker. I canna imagine how ye always knae what ta do."

"Experience my dear. M' husband's a very methodical man und dereby *predictable* in his ways. I jes' do vat he tinks should be done, afore he expects it."

"Well, God bless yer both," Eliza said, thankfully. "I dinna knae wha' I'd have done wit'out ye."

"It's the least ve can do for folks who're sufferin'." Missus Baker patted her hand and slipping on her coat, she left.

The morning went as planned. The Reverend Mister Twombly took the pulpit with his father's sermon in hand and announced the sad news. Lizzie worried about his ability to deliver the sermon and found she was not alone. It seemed the entire congregation was breathing for him. When he coughed several times, his audience collectively held their breath. After the service, Garrett hurried them out, to get back to the house before the first guests arrived.

Peeking into the parlor, Eliza and Lizzie were amazed. Garrett and Mister Baker had been very busy in their absence. Set on saw horses were two white satin-lined pine coffins, skirted around with black satin. The bay window drapes were covered in black as a backdrop for the coffins placed head to head, tall candles at the apex, and shorter candles at the foot of each coffin. Three brocade-upholstered chairs were placed to one side for the family. A pine wreath with a black satin bow adorned the front door.

The dining room table was already laden with food from the nearest neighbors. Eliza set up the china, silver, and coffee urn on the buffet for their guests.

Eliza was exhausted, her head buzzing. Although nervous energy had kept her body going all night, she knew it was only a matter of time before she embarrassed herself and the household by falling asleep at her post or snapping at one of the guests.

"Lizzie, before the folks from church arrive, I'm going to lay down fer a bit. I haven't slept all night. Maggie will keep ye company. Wake me, if ye need me." She stumbled going over the threshold to the bedroom and fell on top of the bed. Lizzie waited five minutes and covered her with an afghan. She was already sound asleep.

Lizzie was pale and quiet, but seemed to have her wits about her and her emotions in check. Her hand wandered often to the angel Charles had given her, only a week before. The symbol, once representative of love and hope, now included sad remembrance, loss, and despair. She stood by the coffin staring at her handsome Charles, marveling at the peace in his face. She half expected to see his chest move with the breath that had abandoned him just hours before. '*Do not look for him here, for he is risen.*'

Also drifting into her thoughts were the words the good thief was told by Jesus on the cross, *'This day thou shalt be with me in paradise.'* She smiled wistfully, *Charles, ye served God well, wit'out yer education or yer church. Ye and Doctor Twombly must be there wit' Him nae, face-to-face. Goodbye, my darling. Ye made me hope I could be yer wife. God help me nae, ta live wit'out yer.* She took a deep breath to forestall the impending tears and turned away. As she did, her grandmother's voice came to her, *Dinna wish yer life away wit' wha' might haf' been, Lizzie. Take wha' God gaes yer on this side, an' appreciate its full worth. It may no' be here t'mara.*

Lizzie marched back into her kitchen determined to stave off her erratic emotions. She set up her stove for company. The tea kettle was boiling and coffee brewing, 'back-door' stew simmering, and biscuits baking. She heard the front door open and hastened to gather the coats and wraps of the family she served. She explained that Eliza was napping and Maggie was in the kitchen. She would send trays to their rooms if they wished to rest before the visitors came. They thanked her and went upstairs.

Maggie chatted with Lizzie about light local gossip, carefully avoiding the calamity of the previous night. She watched Lizzie's every move, wishing she could hold her and make the hurt go away like she could when she was a child. Garrett had said he would use the Baker's telephone to get a message to James, but she didn't know if he had done that.

Lizzie was relieved that her mother seemed content to prattle on and on about nothing. She kept her mind focused on her tasks, determined not to give in to the pervasive melancholy threatening to envelop her.

When the first guests arrived, barely three-quarters of an hour after the family came home; Lizzie went upstairs to announce them. As the family went down to greet their company, she used the back stairs to bring down the breakfast trays. As she suspected, the

349

trays were scarcely touched, except for the tea and toast. She would place the tea cart in the parlor to keep a steady flow of coffee, tea, and biscuits to sustain them. One at a time, she would coax them into the kitchen for a bowl of stew during the afternoon.

In the kitchen, she could hear Eliza rising. Wearing her best apron and cap, Eliza looked remarkably refreshed. She hugged her mother, kissed Lizzie, and headed for the parlor.

There were as many knocks on the back door as the front. Children delivered food and messages from their families almost nonstop all afternoon. Lizzie brought them in, offering small biscuits and milk, and then sent them on their way. Maggie kept them entertained, fussing over how good and smart and pretty they were. She was always able to entice a smile out of the shyest child.

Late in the day, the kitchen door swung open to a familiar face. James had paid his condolences in the parlor and came to see Maggie and his cousins. "Lizzie, I am sae sorry. I could hardly believe it." He wrapped her in his arms and held her for a long time.

"'Tis sae sad, James, an' I will miss him sorely," said Lizzie, hoping she could hold herself together. "Please sit an' have some tea."

Maggie, watching her daughter intently, immediately occupied James' attention with her questions about his work, his girl, and his travel to get there. When James mentioned that he promised to have a good long visit before he took off for the west in the land rush, Lizzie quickly interjected, "We won't be here, James. The Twomblys will be moving probably by the end of January, and I don't know where we'll be then. We'll write ta let ye knae where we are, pro'bly in Boston. Mother's lodging is paid up until February 1st, and then we'll likely have ta remove ourselves."

"Ye're no' serious, ye will have ta be gone sae soon?" James asked incredulously.

"'Tis true, perhaps it will be at the end o' February, but surely no longer. Wit' Doctor Twombly gone an' his son in ill health, it is unlikely we or they will be able ta stay beyond thet." James and Maggie were shocked at the news, no more so than at the coldly sensible voice with which it was delivered.

"*Is fada an bóthar nach mbíonn casadh ann.* 'Tis a lang road thet has no turning," said James.

Both women hung their heads and murmured in agreement.

Eliza peeked in the kitchen door just long enough to say, "Lizzie, we need more tea an' coffee in the dining room, an' more biscuits in the parlor."

"Aye, Eliza, right away." Lizzie returned to her work, and James turned his attention back to Maggie.

"Perhaps when you're in Boston, I can see you more often, before I leave. I want ye to meet Marianna, Maggie. She has consented ta gae wit' me ta the West as my wife. Her mother an' the children will follow when we have the land and are settled. Maggie, I will have a family o' six children, a mother-in-law, and a beautiful wife on a farm thet is my very ain!"

"Then it is as it should be, James. I will miss yer, but ye will always have my heart," Maggie said joining in his enthusiasm. "I hope yer lovely wife will be kind enough ta write an old lady ta tell her all the news."

"I'm sure o' it, Maggie. At least she will be better at it than I am. Isn't thet right, Lizzie?"

Lizzie didn't answer. She pretended to be too busy at the stove to hear him. She was afraid she could not make her voice steady and she would not keep from crying. She was losing everything she had found in the last year and she didn't want to talk about losing James, too.

When James was about to repeat his question, Maggie raised her hand to stop him. "Leave her be, James. She has enough on her plate as 'tis."

"You're right, Maggie. Lizzie, I'm sorry."

They talked quietly for awhile, and then James announced he

351

had to leave to make the train home before dark. As he donned his coat, Lizzie ran to him and hugged him fiercely. She hadn't said a word, but he knew how deeply she felt her loss and that he was adding to it with his leaving. He kissed her forehead and whispered, "I'm sorry ta hafta gae, but I'll be seein' ye again, cousin. Thet, I promise. 'Til then, ye will be in my heart, an' I in yers."

He quickly kissed Maggie and rushed out of the room. He paid his respects to the family again, then with a quick hug to Eliza, he was gone.

Eliza poked her head in the kitchen and looked from Lizzie to Maggie with a question in her eyes. Again, Maggie raised her hand to stop her from speaking. Lizzie turned back to the stove. "Would ye fix a plate fer Maggie, Eliza? Ye mus' be hungry, Ma."

"Some stew would be lovely, Lizzie, if ye have extra? Maybe ye would sit and have some with me, and ye, Eliza, if ye have a moment?"

"Very well, soon. I hafta get back in there. Someone's at th' door again."

Lizzie filled three bowls, and sat down with Maggie.

"Lizzie, it's all right to be happy or sad, or even angry, while ye're out of earshot of the family. For that, ye have every right. Just don't let it change who ye are. Ye'll find thet after the funeral, yer life will go on an' ye'll see many changes. Welcome them. Ye won't ever forget Charles or Doctor Twombly, but ye already have the best parts o' them in yer heart. Don't be afraid ta laugh an' be happy again. Don't let this make ye more cautious, or less willing ta give yer heart away. Someday, ye will give it again, an' Charles would want thet. He loved who ye are."

"M-Maggie, I don' *knae* who I am anymore. I'm sae confused. How could God take Charles from me, when I fin'lly wanted what he was offerin'?"

"Only He knaes what's next fer yer, Lizzie. It is beyond yer own dreams. Right now, the events o' the last year are still new an'

352

fresh. Years from nae, this will be a bitter-sweet memory fer yer. Ye'll always cherish the love Charles had fer yer. God will show us the road ye'll take tomorrow. Does the caterpillar knae he's ta become a butterfly? This may feel like the end, but it will become a new beginning. Mourn yer loss child, an' when yer heart is ready, move toward the new day."

Lizzie thought her mother's words incomprehensible, but a part of her knew to keep them in her heart for another day, when she could find the truth in them. She resolved to write them down that night, to put them away until they made sense to her.

The sun was going down, the lines of callers waning with it. The dining room still buzzed with visitors, but the constant rapping on the doors was subsiding.

Big John came to the back door to pick up the other pot of stew from the back of the stove. Lizzie strapped the lid on tight so he could bring it to the church to feed the families gathered there. He had a cart now, to transport several big pots to the church. The clusters of poor were growing weekly it seemed, as more families lost their livelihood. With the announcement from the pulpit, there were more parishioners who gave food and clothing to the needy in Big John's care.

When the final caller departed, the family retreated once more upstairs. Eliza brought trays laden with various food, hoping the family would find some morsel to pique their interest. William seemed to have regained his appetite, but Isabelle and his mother barely nibbled at toast and half-heartedly sipped tea.

The parlor was again silent. In the morning, the coffins would be loaded into the hearse and Mister Baker's new carriage would follow with the family.

A soft knock on the back door startled the three women in the too quiet house. It was Garrett, come to take Maggie back to her boarding house. Lizzie bundled up her mother for the trip home and added a small blanket for her lap.

Eliza slipped into the hallway and Garrett followed her. "Will ye come back afta droppin' her off?"

"I will, Eliza. I haven't seen yer by yerself, all day."

Eliza turned, heading upstairs and Garrett went back in the kitchen. "Are we ready, Missus Heenan?"

True to his word, he came back twenty minutes later to see Eliza. Lizzie, knowing they wanted to be alone, hurried to get her dishes done. As he came in, she went to her room. "G'night, Lizzie," he called softly as he sat heavily in the rocker.

"C'mere, Eliza, put that stuff down, come sit here wit' me."

Eliza smiled tiredly and sat in his lap. She lay her head on his coarse jacket shoulder and cried the salty tears she held back for fully a day now. He let her cry without comment, just holding her and letting the chair rock gently. When she seemed spent of tears, he sat up and kissed her softly. "My brave Eliza, ever'one's been dependin' on yer. Ye've done well. Missus Baker is quite impressed."

"It's good she was here. I wouldn't knae what ta do. She was sae amazin', Garrett. An' poor Lizzie, she didn't even knae what had happened when she got up this mornin'. She thought it was all a bad dream, her whole life, gone in a flash."

"No, not her whole life, she still has yer, James, an' yer mother, an' that's not jes' a small thing, Eliza. She'll need y' all t' get her through the next few months."

"I knae, she's always been the one in charge, though."

"Jes' keep your eye on 'er an' you'll do the right thing. She's uncommon strong mos' times, but she's a little fragile jes' now. She'll be fine, wit' yer help."

He kissed her and eased out of the chair, setting her on her feet. "I have t' go, but I'll see yer agin, t'marra."

Eliza stifled a yawn. "I need ta sleep, 'til t'marra, Garrett."

That night, Eliza slept without waking and when she rose, Lizzie was busy at work. It was Monday, but no laundry would be done that day. Missus Twombly had risen in the night, leaving her daily list on the kitchen work table as usual. The items were not usual, however.

Today: no laundry, save the pressing of Miss Isabelle's black crepe dress. My black cashmere wrap's been packed away and needs refreshing. Please bring my black gloves and bonnet to my room by 9 o'clock. My black silk matin dress, in my room from yesterday, will do. Wear your darkest clothing. If you have any problem with attire, please let me know. I have two other black bonnets if you need them.

Breakfast — 8 o'clock: Light fare, for an emotional day. Tea, Highland eggs on toast and sliced fruit. Lizzie, don't forget to eat. It will be a long day.

Pack a luncheon for church and place it in one of the ante rooms. This should be light fare as well, requiring no cooking. We will eat, one person at a time, as time allows. You will remain in the ante room, from the time the first of us eats, until the last. After you clean up, you may join us in the church again. Please pack a full dozen each: men's and women's handkerchiefs, the smelling salts, and a small vial of lavender. The lavender will offer a pleasant smell and will refresh the senses. Keep these items handy in a small bag with you at all times.

We will sit in the front pew and you will sit directly behind us for assistance. If one of us heads for the ante room, you will follow discretely with the purse. Leave a handkerchief and the lavender with Eliza. We will leave the church at 4 o'clock and return at six o'clock. We will stay until 8 o'clock, to give everyone a chance to pay their respects to Mister Twombly and Mister Bachelor.

Supper: hot stew, cold biscuits, tea. Refresh our clothing from today after we retire, pressing if needed.

Tomorrow: Same breakfast. 10 o'clock: funeral at the church, home by one o'clock. Bodies will be removed to the funeral home. Light lunch. Rest and a simple supper.

God bless you and Eliza for getting us through this day, in spite of your own loss. Please let me know if I can advise you or be of some small help.

Lizzie smiled at the sweetness of her offer. *I canna add ta yer burden, Missus Twombly. I wisht I'd yer courage an' gen'rous spirit. I will gif' yer the best I have.*

The viewing of the Reverend Doctor John Hanson Twombly, and the ecclesiastical student, Charles Titus Bachelor, was every bit as grueling an ordeal as Lizzie could have imagined. The smelling salts were not used for the family as she thought they would be, but for the parishioners who came to express their grief to them.

In their desire to convey their sorrow, several of the more dramatic women chose to display their delicate nature by collapsing in front of the grieving son of the deceased. Lizzie administered the smelling salts, and stifled her amusement at her patients' startled look when they "woke" in the arms of a female servant, instead of the planned embrace of the bachelor minister. She met the eyes of Mister William more than once, receiving his approval of this arrangement. Lizzie suspected that several unattached ladies in the long line were thwarted from trying the same tactic, seeing lack of desired response displayed before them. The Reverend Twombly sat between his mother and sister pretending not to notice the drama before him.

How ridiculous to subject their minister to this behavior! Lizzie thought, as the third woman fell into 'vapors' at his feet. *Have they no respect? I have heard these women read silly five-cent novels thet put these ideas in their heads. Do they think all men are stupid an' all is forgiven in the name o' romance? Poor Mister William!*

There were hundreds of mourners who conducted themselves in a manner suitable to the occasion. Several curiosity-seekers wanted to see a notable man under the pretense of having known him, but for the most part, the lines were orderly and well-meaning.

Dignitaries from educational institutions and colleagues from the Episcopal-Methodist church, paid their respects to the widow and her children.

The younger man in the next coffin seemed to be viewed as an oddity, there only by virtue of having died in close proximity to the well-known clergyman.

Lizzie did see a group of men her age stop at Charles' coffin to pay their respects, and then continue to speak to whom they assumed must be his mother and siblings. Lizzie was proud to hear how well they revered the man she thought she would marry. They said they looked to him for advice and admired his goal to become a minister at his advanced age. *Charles, are you seeing this? This is God's work, through you. See how you influenced these young men?*

Later that evening, after supper, Mister William spoke to Lizzie, "Thank you for your hard work today. I am embarrassed by the behavior of these otherwise proper young ladies. I'm afraid we have one more day of this before we're done. However, tomorrow will be shorter, and there will be less access to the family.

"Is there anything I can do for you, Lizzie? It has not escaped me that you have suffered greatly in this event. You have my deepest sympathy. Charles was a wonderful man. I can pray with you, if you like."

"Thank you, Mister William. I'll be fine. 'Twould be a kindness, if ye could say a few words 'bout Charles at the funeral tomorrow. 'It would mean sae much ta me. He's no fam'ly here, but you."

"Of course, Lizzie, It was in my thoughts to do so." He put his hand on her shoulder and bowed his head. "Heavenly Father, watch over your servant, Lizzie, in the days ahead. Lift up her heart from sorrow and grant her the peace that only You can give. Guide her footsteps as she continues in the path You have given her, that she will serve You in all her days. Grant her, oh Lord, the strength

357

and wisdom to live her life without Charles, until in joyful reunion, they meet again in Your presence, in Christ's Holy Name. Amen."

Lizzie trembled with emotion hearing his deep, melodious voice in prayer. She felt his hand tighten, but his voice was steady. When he was done, his eyes met hers, saying fervently, "Lizzie, Charles lived a richly fulfilled life. Too short, from our point of view perhaps, but fulfilled, nonetheless. He dedicated his life to serving God and knew a good woman's love. There are few enough men who have that, no matter how long they live. We are all blessed to have known him." Releasing her shoulder, he patted her folded hands and left.

Lizzie sat heavily in the rocker and closed her eyes for a moment, before tackling the supper dishes. *Mister William may be a man of strange moods*, she thought, *but his words comfort me.*

The funeral was a blur for Lizzie. Before she could steel herself to endure it, it was over. She heard the eulogy the minister had promised, then she was so deep in her thoughts, Eliza had to shake her arm to tell her they were leaving.

"It was a lovely service, Lizzie," her mother said, sounding worried about her daughter.

"Mm, aye, I can't believe it's over ... and he's *gone*," she replied woodenly.

Chapter Twenty-two

The following days were spent packing up the household in earnest. They were confident, now that the committee had held their emergency meeting; the services of the Twomblys would be regrettably terminated. The board was only waiting for a decent interval after the funeral to broach the subject to them. What the family did not know, was how soon they would have to vacate the manse.

Missus Twombly and Isabelle spent their mornings selecting the items they could do without, and those they needed to carry on the ladies missionary work in the regional and national church assemblies. The afternoons were spent working on their presentation to the *New England Conference of the Methodist-Episcopal Church* in April.

The Reverend Mister William L. D. Twombly had momentous decisions to make as well. With his father no longer part of the bilateral ministerial team, he had to decide how to maintain financial security for his family and still remain in his chosen profession. His health had never allowed him to be consistent in his capacity as leader of his flock. As a hobby, during the long hours of convalescence, he had begun to write a series of short sermons and Bible lessons. A local printing house who supplied pamphlets and Sunday school materials for a group of Methodist churches in New

England, purchased them as religious tracts. It had never been more than an interest, but perhaps since the meetings and deadlines were not demanding, he could take on more of this work. Once the decision was made, he felt an overwhelming sense of relief from having to appear as a sole minister to a church community. He was now sure he had finally found his calling.

He was nervous about broaching the subject to his mother and sister. It was financially risky and it seemed not a little disrespectful to the goals his father had labored so hard to achieve.

William was pleasantly surprised to find his family was whole-heartedly supportive. His mother said, "It seems the best solution to our situation, William! Perhaps you could gather them to publish an anthology of these works at a later date. There is a great need for teaching materials in our Sunday schools. With the backing of the Methodist-Episcopal Conference, you could even design a coordinated Sunday school curriculum for each age group. With the addition of Isabella's art lessons and paintings, and my small inheritance, I think we can live modestly." William had hoped he would not have to depend on Isabelle and his mother, but it helped to know there was more than one monetary life boat.

In the evenings, when her services were no longer required, Lizzie pored over newspaper classified advertisements, trying to find a situation for herself and Eliza. There seemed to be many opportunities for employment, but when she was in Boston, November past, she had seen the "Irish need not apply" and "No Irish" signs in the windows of the businesses there. In Quincy, she saw the tenements with similar signs, and where there were no such signs, the houses were in near-squalid conditions.

The prospects of finding a place to live with respect to the comfort of her invalid mother, was equally daunting. Maggie's bank account was dwindling. There was barely enough for one more month of room and board. Lizzie would have to hurry to establish employment and lodging before they ran out of money.

Her current anxiety made Lizzie realize how much she had changed in the past year. She was no longer the adventurous carefree child who ran off to America. She had a responsibility to her mother and half sister. She needed to find her own job, her own place to live. This time it would not be handed to her. She missed Charles' counsel, his matter-of-fact way of working as if everything depended on him, then leaving the rest in God's hands. The first part she had no trouble with, the second was a test of faith, in which she was sure she would be found wanting. *Nothing is as fearful as what we think may happen*, he'd say. *Do today's work today. Prepare for tomorrow, but don't let it make you stop you from enjoying the present.*

Painstakingly, she copied those classified advertisements that seemed to beckon her. Missus Twombly said she would allow them some time for finding new employment in the next two weeks. "We'll manage, dears. Just be careful to watch your purse and don't talk to strangers on the street." Then she smiled, "They're all strangers, of course. Perhaps Mister Baker would let Garrett go with you. Not just for the pleasure of his company, you understand," she said with a twinkle in her eye, "But to escort you young ladies around what can be a dangerous city."

"Aye ma'am," they replied. Eliza was now looking forward to the adventure of job-hunting. The prospect of spending the day with Garrett in no way dissuaded her, of course. Sadly, Lizzie recalled the lighthearted day when she and Charles had wandered the Boston Common.

Missus Twombly spoke to Mister Baker and it was arranged. The first excursion would be Tuesday. Garrett would work an extra hour per day for the next ten working days to make up the time lost to Mister Baker. Lizzie decided they would have to start very early in the morning to make every moment of the day worthwhile.

Armed with a dozen slips of paper, each with a job and an address, the escorted young women began their quest. "We'll start at Tremont Street and work our way out from there," said Lizzie.

"I'll take the first one, and we'll see how it goes. Eliza, I have a few sewing and maid situations for you to try, too. Mine are for a laundress and if that's not successful, I'll work as a cook. The first one is right up here, according to the numbers. There's a coffee shop on the first floor. The laundry is in the back. Don't spend all yer money, I'll be back directly."

Filled with trepidation but forging ahead, Lizzie walked through the dingy corridor to a door with frosted glass, inscribed, 'BAY STATE CLEAN TOWEL FURNISHING COMPANY'. Steeling her backbone, she turned the knob and strode purposely into the office.

She almost reeled back by the force of the heavy bleach-filled heat. It was as if she put her head into a steaming bucket of the stuff. Once she adjusted to the heat and smell, she pushed forward to the gleaming massive wood counter. Behind it, sat a little round man with a sour face. He slid off his chair and stepped up on a box behind the counter. It made him look much taller and more imposing than she supposed he would be.

"Glory be, it's another Irish child who thinks she knows how t' do laundry in the big city. What kin I do fer y', Miss?"

"I'm looking for work as a laundress, 'tis true. I have done fancy silk shirts for Londoners, banquet cloths with no crease and can remove stains from almost any cloth," Lizzie said in her mother's best "Queen's English."

"Well, from the fire in y' hair, y' look like Irish, but y' kin leastwise speak so's a man kin understand y', yer maybe too good fer us." He squinted his eyes suspiciously and took a long hard look at her. "We have linen towels and specialty cloths with pressin' and laundry done by machinery here. We supply men's toiletry boxes and towels to the biggest hotels, restaurants, and men's clubs in Boston.

"Working here means y' have ta stand the heat fer twelve hours a day, six days a week without havin' the 'vapors', child. Kin y' do that? I have thirteen to eighteen year olds thet can."

"I can, sir. I'm best at pressin', but I can do the rest, too, if it's a living wage."

"Are y' married, have children, a lazy husband, perhaps?"

"No, sir, I have a mother to support, and rent to pay, so I will need a decent wage."

"Child, did y' think I'd take y' word fer it that yer worth the money? Y' work on probation fer two weeks, durin' which time, y' learn the washin' and pressin' machines. If y' caint do that, then you'll fold. The good wages is in the machines, so y' best learn those well. If I see y' kin pass muster, then we'll talk money."

"If I'm ta work two weeks before we discuss a wage, I'll need some kind of pay for those weeks. If I can show you my worth by then, you'll have to raise that amount to keep me."

"Ah! Aren't we the hoity-toity ones now! You'll take what I give you or find somewhere else to work!" he glared at her. Under his breath, he muttered, "Who do these little snippets think they are, the Princess of Devonshire?"

"I beg your pardon, sir. Do you want a laundress who can do all I say I can do? If not, perhaps I *should* look elsewhere." Lizzie's face flushed at the manner of the little man in front of her.

"I am lookin' for someone who's as good as y' *think* y' are, who can also get these Irishers to do their job. One week at low scale, 60¢ a day, twelve hours a day, 8 to 8, Saturday, 8 to 12, Sundays off. Y' get a half hour fer lunch. An' if you can get these lazy Irisher girls to come up ta speed, we'll talk. I like your sass, little girl. Don't let me down. What's yer name?"

"Lizzie Heenan, sir. I will start in two weeks. One week probation at 60¢ a day, then I'll need a wage worthy of my hire. What is your name, sir?"

"G. L. Goulding. I am an owner here. Don't tell anyone you were hired off the street. Y' supposed to go to the main office."

"Well sir, your advertisement says to come here."

"What! I'll have that boy's hide. He can't do anything right. Humph!" The little man hopped down from his box and waddled to his massive desk and resumed writing in a ledger. "I'm not in this building on Monday, so's you'll start on a Tuesday. Let's make it January 24th, 8 A.M. *sharp.* If you're late, you're fired. Now, get outa here, I've work to do."

"Thank you, Mister Goulding," Lizzie said happily. Mister Goulding waved his hand as if swatting a fly, muttering to himself. She left the office, fairly skipping down the hall.

Garrett and Eliza could hardly believe her good fortune. "Well, I don't knae yet if it will work out. I haven't even seen these machines they're talkin' about. But at leas' I have a chanct ta have a job. Now let's see what we kin get fer you."

The first two places Eliza went to rejected her because she was Irish. Before they tried the third place, Lizzie said, "Perhaps if they ask where you're from, you should say Liverpool. It's not an entire lie. We had ta go there ta take the ship. If they ask where ye were born, ye'll have ta say Ireland..., or ye could jes' say Castlewellan. That sounds more English. Try to talk more like Maggie when she's talkin' ta the Twomblys. Mister Goulding thought I was no' Irish, because I pretended to be Maggie."

"I don't knae, Lizzie. What if I can't do it like you kin," Eliza replied.

"What's it goin' ta hurt? If they are rude ta y', it's no more than what the others have done."

"Yer right about thet, the last one wanted me to use a sewing machine. Lord help me, I've ne'er e'en seen one afore."

364

"In that case, tell 'em ye kin sew a hem thet don' show, make neat buttonholes, and ye kin take in clothes thet don't fit. Ye kin make lace edging, too. Show 'em yer handkerchief. If they still want yer ta sew on a machine, tell them ye learn fast an' yer sure ye kin do it," Lizzie said.

"I think we'll have good luck with either a millinery shop or a shop thet does dress alterations. What do ye think? We can probably get yer a job as a maid, if ye'd rather. Remember ye kin start on the 24th of January. If they want a demonstration, don' worry about us. They seems ta be a coffee shop on ev'ry corner 'round here. Remember ta smile, be pleasant an' confident."

"That's easy fer yer, Lizzie. I get all scared an' shy," said Eliza quietly.

"Ah, but ye're goin' ta be *Maggie*, remember? Just pretend. Stand up straight, smile an' be Maggie. She wouldn't get shy an' back down from anyone."

You can do it, Eliza, I know you can. Who wouldn't want t' hire a clever girl like you?" added Garrett.

Eliza stretched her petite frame as tall as possible, smiled and practiced her best "Maggie" voice all the way to the next shop. Lizzie and Garrett crossed their fingers and watched her enter.

Five minutes later, she came back to them with a sad face. "I didn't get the job."

Garrett and Lizzie both spoke at once, trying to reassure her that there would be other places.

"I didn't git the job," she repeated. "But the owner o' the shop used the telephone ta call her friend who needs a hand-sewer in her dress shop an' said I would be jes' perfect fer her. Here's the address. She said 'twasn't far."

"Wonderful! I knew yer could do it, Eliza." Lizzie hugged her half sister. "Let's gae afore she changes her mind."

"*Messenger Brothers & Jones* — Tailors and Importers, 388 Washington Street," Garrett read from the card. "Did the lady at the shop say who ye were to see?"

"It's on the other side of the card. Miss Penelope Jones, I think. She said take Bromfield Street ta Washington an' it's right on the corner. It's a big brick building."

The three hurried down the street, through a crowd of noontime shoppers. Mouth-watering smells tantalized their noses, and it was tempting to stop to eat but Lizzie urged them on. "We can't take the chanct the opportunity will still be there, sae hurry."

Arriving at the corner, Eliza gaped at the structure before her. The five story brick edifice bore a legend of giant brass letters across its entire width above the first floor, "*Messenger Brothers & Jones* — Tailors & Importers." In each of four huge windows in the front, were the words, "Women's Couture", "Men's Custom Suits", "Imported Furs", and "Exotic Furnishings".

"Oh, Lizzie, I don't knae." Eliza looked ready to turn and run.

Lizzie said sternly, "Would Maggie run from this? No. Jes' straighten up, smile an' be Maggie. Ye will be fine. Don' stop 'til ye meet Miss Penelope Jones. She's the only one who can say 'yea' or 'nay' to yer. Nae git in there, Eliza, show her what ye kin do."

Her pretty little nose elevated, Eliza stiffened up her back and strode up to the front doors. The massive portal magically opened, under the hand of a uniformed doorman. "Good afternoon, Miss." Eliza nodded to him as if she were royalty.

Lizzie and Garrett collectively held their breaths. "I feel like a mother sendin' her child off ta school fer the first time, proud, but scared someone will hurt her." Garrett nodded his head silently, still staring at the now-closed door. They crossed the street to a bench facing the building that just swallowed Eliza. "We'll be able ta see her come out from here."

It was nearly an hour before they spotted her. She was not at the front door as they expected, but walking down the sidewalk on the side of the building. Garrett and Lizzie ran to hear the news.

Eliza's face was flushed, excited by her adventure inside the imposing building. Wanting to savor the look of anticipation on their faces, she asked if they could go inside somewhere and warm up first.

"Make it someplace close, I am nearly frozen solid, but I can't wait to hear," said Lizzie. "Right nae, a cuppa tea an' a water closet would be like heaven on earth ta me."

"Lizzie, hush, Missus Twombly would faint dead away hearin' you."

"I'm with Lizzie on this one, Eliza. Desperation trumps elegant manners when yer freezin' and all ye have in yer gizzard is a gallon of tea," inserted Garrett. "We will return to yer as a polite lady an' gentleman when we've takin' care of the emergencies of the moment. Eliza, you hold the table while Lizzie an' I find the necessary." Garrett winked to take the edge off the coarseness of his words, took Lizzie's arm and hurried to the back of the tea room.

Eliza stood with her mouth open in shock until the man at the door asked amused, "Would you care to sit down, Miss? They will return shortly." She nodded, and followed him. *No wonder they think all Irishers are rude and have no manners,* she fumed.

The young man who seated her, whispered to her as if reading her thoughts, "They are the third couple in the last half hour who have rushed in sayin' very much the same, Miss. Don't let it fret you. It's no reflection on you, I assure you. It only speaks of the dreadful cold weather we're havin'. As hosts of Benningham's Tea Room, we are taught to ignore such comments an' not to judge. A girl will come to serve you shortly." He bowed slightly and backed away.

Lizzie and Garrett came back smiling and wound their way through the tables toward her. They sat and turned their attention to

367

Eliza. "I ordered tea fer ye both an' some meat biscuits." Then, leaning forward, she whispered, "I saw they cut the meat biscuits in two pieces, so I ordered two."

"You could have ordered three, Eliza. I intended to pay for our meal. Keep the money Missus Twombly gave you, an' allow me this grand gesture. My goodness, I am so delighted t' feel warm again!" Garrett looked so euphoric, that Lizzie and Eliza laughed. "Now, Eliza, tell us what happened at Messenger Brothers & Jones, Tailors an' *Importance*, or whate'er they are called."

"First, Miss Penelope Jones took me ta a room o' Singer machine sewers. It was verra noisy an' they were sewing yards an' yards of cloth in seconds. I was scared they were going ta tell me I had ta do thet. But no, she went through thet room ta a smaller room where there were two people sewing by hand. Miss Jones introduced me ta Miss Evelyn, the forewoman o' the hand sewing room. She handed me a dress an' told me ta hem it at the mark they made wit' thread. I asked her if she wanted a flat or rolled hem, since the cloth was silk. Did she want it corded, or self-rolled? Would there be a lace attached later or would this be the final hem? Then the forewoman said, 'Well, at least she knows what questions to ask, don't she?'"

"So you're hired? Don't keep me waitin' on yer story, Eliza!"

"Aye, I hemmed the dress. She inspected it, nodded, and then asked me ta make a buttonhole in the same silk cloth. That wasn't so easy. It was very fine silk an' I didn't have the button ta gae by. I didn't even have a backin' ta use, so I rolled the edges like I was goin' ta hem it, then put a button chain stitch over that. She seemed ta like it, sae I guess it was the right path ta take. I ne'er did one like thet before, but it worked. She said she ne'er saw one like it an' I pretended like I did them all the time jes' like it." Eliza put her hand over her mouth in amusement.

"She asked me about lace-makin'. Did I know how ta follow a pattern? I said I could learn new patterns, but I had only done a few patterns on my own. Jes' pineapple, clover, an' fan patterns in linen thread. Then, she asked 'bout other sewin' thet I'm not sure what she meant. She was satisfied that I had enough skills ta do what she wanted though, sae I got the job."

"How much money will you earn fer how many hours?"

"Oh my, I don't know! Oh Lizzie, I was sae busy trying ta please her, I didn't think ta ask."

"Well, I hope it's enough, Eliza. I'll have ta figure it's not as much as I'll be makin', jes' ta be safe, when I consider what we kin pay fer room an' board fer the three o' us."

"Eliza started to tear up, "I'm sae sorry, Lizzie. I'm sae stupid sometimes."

"We'll find out soon enough, Eliza. If it's no' enough we'll hafta try another path. Yer no' stupid, Eliza, I ne'er learned ta do *any* o' the things yer skillful needle will do. They should pay yer an honest wage fer thet."

"I hope so, Lizzie. Ye think Maggie could do some o' thet work a' home? ...when we have a home, that is? She always did some verra nice handwork."

"I'm hopin' she will, but she's no' seein' as well as she did once, ye ken." They continued chatting about sewing and wages while they ate.

"Ladies," Garrett interrupted finally, "We'll have t' move along, now. The host is lookin' ta see if we want ta take up lodgin' here in this booth. An' you'll be wantin' t' find a room this afternoon, if yer goin' t' be ready t' commence employment, come January 24th."

Lizzie took out her slips of papers for rooms to let. Some were boarding houses; some were furnished rooms allowing cooking; and some were rooms with no furnishings. None of them were listed as on the street floor. They took the electric street car to South Boston.

They gave the motorman the name of the street they wanted so they would get off at the right stop. It seemed like they were riding for a long time before he called the street name. The neighborhood was rundown and with the remnants of snow in the yard and bare trees, it looked even more bleak and sad.

"Number 125 Monks Street. I guess this is it," said Lizzie. The three story tenement house was unpainted and weathered gray, with two balconies on the side. Skinny, big-eyed children ran about the tiny yard shrieking and taunting each other in worn-out clothes. Two little girls with no hats or mittens, huddling together by the fence, stared curiously at the strangers knocking at the front door.

"We don' wan' any," the smallest of them said impudently.

Lizzie spied a turn bell in the center of the door and tried it. The door opened and a surly woman in a dirty apron and holey sweater asked, "So? Whadda ye want?"

"Do you have a room to let, ma'am?" she answered with her best 'Maggie' voice.

"Third floor rear, one room, no more than three occupants, fer six dollars a month. No music. No fights. No fires." Her mirthless jack-o-lantern grin startled them. "Ya wan' it or not?"

"I'm very sorry to have troubled you, ma'am. We need a room on the first floor."

"Well, good luck findin' thet one. It ain't worth rentin' if ye can't have the downstairs fer yerself."

"Yes, ma'am, do you know of another place with a first floor," Lizzie pressed.

"No' fer the likes o' yer, I doubt it would be good enou' fer yer."

"Perhaps it would, if we could get my invalid mother into it. We've no children, she's quiet and we would be working all day."

370

The woman's eyes softened a bit. "Nae, maybe there's one, at thet. There's a woman I knae who is very cautious 'bout who she rents ta. Don't knae what she'd charge, but it's o'er on Peters, number 10. Ask fer Missus Harrin'ton. She don' like the first floor. She's a widow an' scairt o' her own shadow. She usually puts the men on the first floor, so's no tramps break in lookin' fer food or valuables ta steal."

"Well, I thank you kindly, ma'am. I shall give it a try. I appreciate your helpfulness."

"Good Lord, I ain't had anybody talk thet good ta me since I were young an' pretty. An' that were a while back," She laughed heartily. "Ye sure ye don' wan' thet third floor room?"

"Thank you, no, ma'am. We'd best be going now," said Lizzie backing down the steps.

"Tell her, Sallie sent ye! A block over thet ways," she said, pointing east.

"Thank you, ma'am!"

The three fairly ran down the street in the direction 'Sallie' had pointed. As they crossed over to the next block, Lizzie noted the houses were even closer together, and if possible, more run down. In almost every tiny yard, ragged children ran, tumbling through scraggly bushes, tripping on rubbish abandoned before the snows came.

Finally, they found 10 Peters Street. The three story house was typical of the neighborhood, only in shape and construction. Although old, it stood out because it was well-maintained, painted light yellow and white, with flower boxes in the second story windows.

Now more hopeful, Lizzie turned the bell in the front door. They waited for a few minutes, then as she was about to ring again, the door opened just a crack. An older woman asked, "What can I do for you?"

371

"Are you Missus Harrington, ma'am? Sallie of Monks Street sent us to see you. We are looking to rent a first floor flat, one or two rooms for us sisters and our invalid mother. Do you have such an accommodation?"

"Well, I don't have first floor for you right now, but perhaps I can move someone to the third floor, if they're willing. It has to be the first floor?"

"Yes, ma'am, my sister and I could get my mother into the first floor, but it would not be possible to get her up and down a full flight of stairs."

"Do you have a telephone where I could reach you, or a card? If you're serious about rentin' on the first floor, I'd have t' move someone an' I'd have to charge you more for the inconvenience, you understand. I don't even know if they'd be willing."

"We do not have a telephone. I can write down the address where we now reside, if that would help. If you have a telephone, perhaps I could call you in a day or so, if that is convenient. We would need the rooms by January 29th. How much do you think you would charge for the rooms?"

"It would depend on which one I can empty for you. One room is five dollars and two rooms would be six-fifty each month, due on the first of ev'ry month. You should know, it's a shared water closet an' the rest of the tenants on the first floor are men. The second floor is the women's floor where I live. If you need furniture, that'll be another fifty cents a month. Any damages to the room or furniture will be added to your rent for the followin' month. I run a decent home here. If there is any cause for scandal, you will be set out on the street." The sweet-faced woman seemed to gain confidence and suspicion as she listed her terms. She handed Lizzie a card, with her address and telephone number on it, 165 R, South Boston.

372

"Thank you, Missus Harrington. I will call you on Thursday, if that is convenient for you, around three in the afternoon?"

"So be it. I should have an answer for you then. Good day, Miss." The door closed. Lizzie shrugged her shoulders and said, "Well, let's get the trolley before what little warmth in this day fades with the light."

The three went back to the trolley stop, waited about ten minutes and boarded for the return trip to Boston. By the time they reached home, it was already dark. Lizzie felt good about the day's accomplishments and was able to let go of some of the anxiety caused by the changes they were facing.

"Garrett," she said, "afore you gae, I'd like ta write a note ta Missus Baker, askin' her if I may use her telephone on Thursday ta call Missus Harrington 'bout the rooms." She noted with some amusement that Garrett and Eliza were so engrossed in each other, they paid little mind to her. As long as they had more time together, any postponement of separation would do.

Her note concluded, Lizzie went to the parlor to see if anyone required her services. Missus Twombly and Miss Isabelle had their heads together drafting a speech for the conference. Mister William was reading his Bible, making notes, presumably for a treatise on some moral issue. The women enquired about Lizzie's day and what kind of fortune she had in her employment quest. She told them the story of their two successful work enquiries and left the rest for another time.

The family had eaten the stew, simmering on the back of the stove. Lizzie promised she would replenish it and make more for the next day's poor.

That night, she checked the passbook for her mother's account, and the few coins she had left from her day off, hoping with Eliza's coins, it would be enough for the first month's rent and food. She would begin work on January 24th, just days before they would move into their own rooms. Hopefully, they could continue at the Twombleys until the end of the month. Their first week's wages would have to pay for food and transportation. Lizzie's twelve hour day, plus another hour for transportation, would not end until she set up meals for the Twombleys each night. The long hours were no more than she was used to as a cook, but she thought the new job would be much more physically demanding than her work as a house cook.

We'll have ta see Maggie an' tell her the news. She'll work her charm on Missus Harrin'ton, I'm sure. It'll be a new challenge fer her. I'm hopin' she'll be able ta make lace durin' th' day an' Eliza kin sell it ta Miss Jones.

She does lovely work, Lizzie thought. *My clumsy fingers are good fer cookin', pressin', an' liftin', no' delicate work like thet. Still, the Laird gives each one of us our ain talents.*

She'd see if she could steal an hour or two to see Maggie the next day. *We've a lot ta do in two weeks. We can't knae where the Twomblys are goin' ta, yet. I wonder if they will have a new maid or cook comin' from Ireland. She said she didn't think they could afford both without the church's support. I hate leavin' them nae, wit' Doctor Twombly gone. Life surely changes in the blink o' an eye, don' it?*

Lizzie slept that night dreaming of Charles, great vats of laundry, and scrawny urchins yelling curses at her. Upon rising, she wished she were already into her new routine, with each new day following one much like the day before.

Later that day, Maggie took the news of the move to her new surroundings well. Although they had no real assurance that they would be living with Missus Harrington, they knew they had to move by January 29th. Lizzie hoped they would be allowed to move by then.

"Wherever we live will be fine, I'm sure," said Maggie optimistically. "I'll be able to see you every morning and night. I'll be glad to have work for my hands to do, so making lace will be fine. If there are children, I might even have a child or two to tutor as well."

"Well, thet would be wonderful, though I doubt the parents o' the children we saw could or *would* pay for sech tutoring."

"We'll see. They will provide some entertainment for me if they play in the yard, at any rate. It would be nice to have some youngsters around." Nothing seemed to dampen Maggie's sense of adventure.

"Oh my," Lizzie exclaimed. "I ne'er asked if they had electricity in the house. Or gas. They must have lamps o' some kind. If they have electricity or gas, I don't know if it is included in the rent. The furniture stays, if we need it, but she will add to the rent fer it ev'ry month."

Lizzie was becoming more anxious with all the questions she didn't think to ask. *"How stupid kin I be? We don't know where ta buy food. We don't know how big the rooms are. There could be a thousand things we don't knae about this place. How can I knae how much more will it cost ta have the things we need?*

"Lizzie, do not chastise yourself. Let's write a list o' questions ye kin ask when ye telephone Missus Harrington. It couldn't be thet bad ta live there, if she has her ain telephone. We'll make do wit' what we have. In Ireland, we've had a whole lot less," Maggie reminded her.

I jes' don' want yer ta be uncomfortable, Ma. I also wan' ta be sure we've enough money ta eat. Lizzie was quiet while Eliza and Maggie chatted away in excited voices about the coming events.

I kin call Missus Harrin'ton t'marra, an' if ev'ry thin' gaes well, I'll gae ta the bank and close Ma's account. I'll look at the house an' if it's suitable a 'tall, I'll pay her first month, then an' there. Lord, help me, I'm puttin' all my eggs in one basket.

The next day, Lizzie went to the Baker house to make her phone call. "Dis here is the listenin' part, listen t' see if they's talkin' already," instructed Missus Baker. "Den if 'n dey's not talkin', turn the handle on the side, there. Wait 'till yer hear der operator speak, then gif' her der number."

Lizzie was fairly shaking in anticipation. She didn't hear anything. "Jes' a minute, let me git y' started, honey," Missus Baker said, taking the receiver. "Oh, there ye be, Mary. My friend Lizzie has a number for yer. She put the tall thin cup-like piece to Lizzie's ear again.

"What's the number, honey?"

"Um, 1-6-5 and R."

"The 'R' means it will ring four times for your party, Miss," answered the disembodied voice named Mary."When she says 'hello,' you can start talking."

Lizzie heard four rings. Then, she heard four more before she heard a tinny 'hello.'

"Missus Harrington, this Lizzie Heenan. I talked to you on Tuesday about some rooms on the first floor."

"Yes. I was able to talk two men into moving to the third floor. When do you want it?"

"Missus Harrington, I have a few questions, I hope you don't mind…"

"What is it, dear? Do you want the room or not?"

"I am very interested in taking the room by January 29th. Is it one room or two? How big are the rooms? Is there electricity or gas? Are there furnishings, and a stove? How much is it?"

"Slow down, child! It has two rooms, a big 'un and a small 'un. There is gas lighting and a wood stove, water closet down the hall. There is furniture if you want it, for fifty cents a month. The two rooms with furnishings cost six dollars. Wood for the stove is another fifty cents. I don't provide linens. Anything else?" Missus Harrington was beginning to sound irritated.

"I-it sounds lovely. All thet remains is to see the rooms." Lizzie noted to herself the price had gone down from the seven dollars she first quoted. *Fifty cents less, plus the wood!*

"It's one month in advance. You don't move in until it's paid. If you move out before the end of the month, you forfeit the rest of the rent. I do not tolerate any carousing', sinful acts or loud noises in my house. Such behavior will revoke any agreement to rent. Understood?"

Hearing the tension in the woman's voice, Lizzie grimaced with the prospect of asking yet another question. She forged ahead in her most charming voice, "Yes, ma'am, I am so happy to hear it. Do we have use of the back porch and the laundry lines?"

"Yes, of course, but you'll have to work out an agreement with the other roomers to share them, is that all?" Lizzie understood it was all the questions the woman would tolerate at the moment. She didn't know what the telephone call was costing the Bakers, so she made her goodbye brief and businesslike. She exhaled deeply, realizing she had been holding her breath during the entire conversation with her would-be landlady.

"How much is the fee for making a telephone call, Missus Baker? I don't want to presume on our friendship," asked Lizzie.

"Nonsense, Lizzie. The Good Lord put us here t' hep each odder. You mus' allow us der privilege."

"Then you mus' allow me ta repay yer kindness in another way, Missus Baker." *I'll have ta think on thet,* she mused.

"De Good Lord balances things oot, Lizzie. If 'n yer do a kindness fer som'one else, der debt be paid." Missus Baker smiled kindly and gave her a warm hug.

Chapter Twenty-three

Tuesday, January 24th, was upon her before Lizzie could quiet the butterflies in her belly. The prospect of leaving her safe haven of the last year, abandoning her job as an accomplished servant, careening blindly into new employment, wrestling with loud, frightening machines, and relocating to a strange new circumstance, was more exciting and scary, exhilarating, and daunting, than coming to America.

This was the last week they would be living with the Twomblys. Lizzie was up at five as usual, setting up the kitchen for breakfast. Foremost in her mind was catching the 7:05 train to arrive at work before eight o'clock. Missus Twombly came downstairs at six to wish her two fledglings well on their first day of work.

"Don't worry about what you don't know. You're both bright. Look how much you've learned this past year. You'll catch on in no time," she said. "Please do be careful going to and from work. Keep your wits about you and pay attention to those around you. Garrett will take you to Boston in the morning, and come for you at eight when you are finished, during the time you have left here. By the time you move on the weekend, you'll be able to get around on your own."

"Aye, Missus Twombly," the girls chorused.

Lizzie could see a shutter go through her half sister. She assured Eliza, that while they were living in South Boston, she would meet her at Messenger's before catching the trolley, so she would never be alone.

Soon, Garrett came for them and they were off to Boston. Lizzie arrived well before eight and marched into the office of Bay State Clean Towel Furnishing Company. *Will I e'er git usta the blast o' hot air openin' this door?* Lizzie wondered. *Whoops. I've got ta remember ta use my 'Maggie' voice here.*

"Mister Goulding, sir?"

"Ah, it's the Queen of Sheba whose great desire it is to do laundry. Alright, let's go. Hang yer coat an' put yer purse inside yer clothes. Y' don' want it caught on the machin'ry. Step lively, I've got other things ta do t'day." He opened the door to a roar of the mechanical beasts all vying for her attention. "These lazy Irishers don' get here 'til eight, if then, so I'll give y' the tour. I'll start y' on the mangle. Mind y' fingers on it. If y' do well, y' stay on the mangle, if not, y' go on to the other machines. If y' can't handle the machines, y' can fold, but it's low wages for that. We also have packers, who earn more than folders because y' still have to use y' brain. They're two inspectors. They keep us from lookin' the fool to our customers. Manglers, piece pressers, and inspectors carry the most responsibility an' git paid accordingly. Y' ready?"

"Yes sir, show me how it is done and I'll do it."

Mister Goulding grinned. "Sure thing Missy, roll up them pretty sleeves and let's get to work." He went to the back of the room, picked up a bucket and waddled back with it. You'll have a runner to keep you supplied with buckets. You'll get the rhythm after the first couple of buckets. Don't let there be more than two buckets ahead of yer. If you run out, holler 'bucket', and they'll bring another."

He went on to explain how to stretch the front edge of the towel, pull her fingers back and let it feed into the mangle, then stretch the sides of the linen so it is flat as it is pulled in. "Pick up another and start again. Got it?" He put his hand to his back and moaned. "God, I'm too old for this."

"Mister Goulding, is there any reason why you couldn't put a box where the bucket is to raise it about a foot? It would seem like it would ease the strain on your back, and get more towels through the wringer."

"Now, she's telling *me* how to do the job! The way for me to ease the strain in my back, little lady, is for me to have *you* do the job." He stomped off toward the office. Lizzie shrugged her shoulders and continued working, her tortured ears trying to adjust to the shrill scream of the monster she fed. She smiled as the steam seemed to admonish the fiend with an angry "Sh-h".

By now, the other workers were filing in, sizing her up and taking their places. A big red-faced woman stood at the next mangle and yelled above the steam and the chattering women, "What's yer name, Red?"

"Lizzie, an' yours?" she hollered back.

"I'm Molly, like a dozen or so others here. Hah, we're mostly Mollies and Maggies and Mary-Katherines around here. It's nice ta have somethin' different, Red. *Buck-et!*"

A little girl of about twelve with her skirts tied up through her legs came running with a heavy bucket. She dropped it at Mollie's mangle and ran back. "Bucket!" "Bucket!" "Bucket!" echoed the other workers down the line.

"Make sure y' make her put thet bucket right up ta the mangle, like she done mine. She gits tired an' leaves it behind yer if y' don' keep on her. Then yer all tuckered out from pickin' it up an' puttin' it where it should be. Next thin' yer knae, y' get yer fingers caught an' y' lose yer job."

380

"I'll remember that," said Lizzie. *Poor little thing, she's hardly bigger than a minute, an' she's luggin' buckets almost as big as she is.*

By mid-morning, Lizzie took Molly's advice in earnest. Lettie, the bucket girl was putting the buckets farther and farther behind, and Lizzie's back was beginning to twinge from twisting. With the next bucket, she told the girl to bring the bucket up snug to the mangle. Lettie let out a string of invectives that shocked her to the core. Some of them, she had no idea what they meant. Mollie threw her head back and laughed heartily.

"I wondert how long 'twould be, afore y' heard thet 'un's tongue. She's only a half-pint, but she swears like a sailor hame on leave. Yer more stubborn than mos'. Mos' o' the new 'uns give up afore an hour's past. We al'ays pull thet on the new girl. Don' report 'er though, we're all ta blame."

The little girl stopped halfway back to her station and gave Mollie a proud gap-toothed grin.

Lizzie laughed good-naturedly, saying, "I've always been my worst enemy. Stubborn as they come."

Soon, it was lunchtime, and Lizzie followed the women out. It seemed strange to leave the machines running, but Mollie said it would take too long to shut them down, then start them up again when the lunch break was over. The women stood about in the frosty air, eating their lunches. Some took turns sitting on barrels and broken crates in the alley, allowing only their allies to share in the blessed relief for their sore limbs. Others sat on their haunches against the building and talked in small clutches.

A fight broke out amongst three women in the back. At first shouting obscenities, then physical blows were exchanged. The squabble ended as soon as a fourth, much larger woman waded into the fray, elbowing each one in turn. *This is dreadful. No wonder they fight. Their feet are cold and wet from standing in water all morning, breathing the stench of bleach and lye soap, then taking their lunch out here with freezing weather with no place to sit!*

After lunch, she picked up the rhythm of feeding the machine again, allowing the rest of the day fly. Although she was tired and her newly-aggravated muscles were complaining, Lizzie was pleased she accomplished her set goal for the first day, not jamming her fingers in the machine and keeping up with Mollie. One of the last going out the door, she stopped when she heard the bellow, "She-*ba!*"

The stubby round man stood with his arms akimbo, glaring at her. Lizzie walked slowly to the front desk, her hands trembling. "Yes, Mister Goulding?"

"Office. Now," he growled.

Oh Lord, now what did I do? Don't tell me I'm bein' fired after only one day.

"I beg your pardon, Missy. If I don't yell atcha, the girls will think I'm favorin' you and then they start makin' up stories. I personally wouldn't care, but my wife believes them stories, so don't be frettin' y'self about my hollerin'. Y' did well today, a good count. Whatever ye've got I hope it's contagious and the Irishers yer workin' with ketch it."

"Sir, I want to do a good job. If I can speak, frankly . . ."

"I know I'm goin' to regret this, but go on."

"If you put that stand I mentioned by the mangle for the bucket to sit on, the bucket runner would likely put it in the same place every time, and the mangle worker could produce more. What's more, if you could make a slatted floor above the regular floor, the girls' feet would stay drier."

Lizzie could see she over-stepped the privilege of speaking her mind. Mister Goulding was turning red in the face and clenched his fists by his sides. *He's mad for sure, nae!*

"The bucket stand I'll think on, 'cause it may increase production. The floor is too expensive. I'm not in the business of coddlin' these women."

"How many of them are out sick? How does that affect your production, sir?" Lizzie could have bit her tongue off for allowing it to run away with her mouth. *What are y' tryin' ta do, Lizzie? Git yerself fired on yer first day?*

"The drains in the floor will have to do for now. I *knew* you were goin' t' cost me money. Hirin' a woman who thinks above her station, always costs money."

"I am sorry, Mister Goulding, but I think if you can make a few little changes, these women will produce more for you."

"So putting in a new floor is a little change? Never mind, git outa here. Next, you'll be wantin' som'one ta mop your dainty little brow while y' work!"

"Good night, Mister Goulding, I'll see you tomorrow." Lizzie said, subdued.

He didn't answer but went back to the workroom, muttering something about *him* working for the Queen of Sheba.

At least he said I had a good count. I wonder what it was. We'll see how it goes tamarra.

As she left the building, she saw Eliza and Garrett waiting for her. They cheerfully chatted on the way home about their respective jobs. Eliza said she had some variety in her work. In the morning, she made dozens of buttonholes for bridal gowns and in the afternoon she hemmed three gowns. She went into the salon to adjust a gown for a very heavy Beacon Hill woman, who had an invitation to the Governor's Ball. Eliza said she was told not to speak, but to take her orders from Miss Jones only.

"I was sae nervous; I stabbed myself three times in one finger. My biggest fear was that I'd bleed on the gown. Miss Jones worked wonders wit' both the gown an' the client. She convinced the woman thet the gown was made twa' small fer her, an' thet she was the perfec' size fer a woman o' her station. When we went back ta the sewin' room, Miss Jones said ta scrap the gown. She'd design a gown thet would be flexible in size. The old gown would be cut down ta a smaller size, 'when the appropriate client arrived.' The trimming's would be removed ta change the look o' the original gown, so Missus 'Beacon Hill' would no' hafta face a thinner, more petite version o' it at the ball."

"Sounds like ye had a verra int'restin' day, Eliza," said Lizzie tired, but smiling.

They hurried back to the house from the train station. Garrett hung back as the two girls told their stories. The brisk winter air felt good to Lizzie after working in the steam all day.

"If it snows tomorrow, an' it looks like it might, I'll ask fer the wagon," Garrett broke in. "See the haze around the moon? There's no star in the halo, so we've only hours before snowfall. Perhaps it won't amount t' much. But, we may hafta leave earlier in the mornin', t' git yer there on time." It occurred to Lizzie, these were the first words he had spoken since she had seen him after work. We've been sae busy with our ain stories, we hardly said hello ta him.

They were at the back door by then, and Lizzie struggled to convey some pleasantries to Garrett. "Thank you Garrett, for keepin' us safe today. I'm afraid we've been sae full of ourselves, we haven't been very polite."

He just waved his hand as if it was nothing, kissed Eliza's cheek chastely, and bounded off to the Baker house. Lizzie met Eliza's eyes in an unspoken question.

"He said after this week, we would probably not see each other very often. We'll be movin' away. He'll be workin' ever' day but Sunday, an' he hasta help the Bakers wit' the children. He seems sad about it, but doesn't seem willin' ta make a plan thet involves seein' us. He says he'll miss us, an' wishes us well. Oh Lizzie, I don't want ta ne'er see him again. I thought we were close."

"If he truly has deep feelings for yer, he'd find a way ta see yer," said Lizzie gently. "We can't tell what he's truly thinkin' if he doesn't say, can we?"

He knaes he only has until Friday, ta make up his mind whether to pursue a real courtship or no'. Garrett, don' jes' let it slip away, by no' sayin' anythin' 'bout it. It's harsh ta think ye don't care enough ta tell her, one way or the other.

Lizzie kept quiet about her thoughts. It was their business after all. For the duration of the week, she saw every day they had a new chance to talk about their prospects of a future, but they were silent. The silence burgeoned into a gloomy cloud of enveloping sadness.

Friday morning, Lizzie was pleasantly surprised to see box platforms up against the mangle to hold the buckets. Lizzie said nothing, except to instruct little Lettie to place the buckets atop the platforms. The ease of picking up the towels, without deep bending and twisting, made the work go quickly and it was lunchtime before she knew it.

Lizzie donned her coat and scurried out the side door and down the street. This was the day she had to go to the bank, close her mother's account and get back before lunch was done. The bank was not far, but Friday was a busy day. She was disheartened when she saw the long lines inside. She nervously stood on one foot, then the other willing the lines to open up just for her.

Finally, she stood before the teller. "Yes, miss?"

Lizzie stated her business and waited anxiously watching the teller count out the last of her mother's account. She signed her name, put the money into her purse, and carefully wrapped the strings around her wrist, and put hand and purse into her coat pocket.

As she left the bank, she looked both ways to cross the street. The sidewalk was crowded with jostling pedestrians, each intent on their own business. A man in front stepped back, pushing her violently, threatening her equilibrium. As she pulled her hand out of her pocket, to catch her balance, the purse still attached, her arm was pulled back hard behind her by a man in a rough wool jacket, his unshaven face scratching her cheek, his foul breath reeking of cigars and vinegar. Her purse strings cut, her arm suddenly freed, her body was thrown into the surging wave of people crossing the street. The disheveled hoodlum snorted a short guttural laugh, reversed his direction, ran down the street, and turning a corner, he disappeared.

Lizzie screamed, "My purse! He's stolen my purse!"

The crowd, turning as one, staring at her, continued on their way. An older gentleman, holding her elbow, seeing her eyes fill with tears, smiled gently, and asked if she were hurt.

"No," she shouted, stamping her foot angrily, desperately, "He stole my purse!"

"I am so sorry, my dear. Well, he's gone now," he said, as if it were of little consequence. "Can I drop you anywhere? My coach is just up the street." Something in the hard glint of his eyes warned Lizzie of his less than stellar intentions.

"No, no, I'm fine. But it was all I had in the world." Breaking away, Lizzie ran through the crowded sidewalk, red hair flying, skirts swirling about her, unmindful of the attention she drew.

She ran through the front door of the laundry building and down the dismally littered corridor. A ragged shadow lurched out of the darkened corner, grabbing her arm, said, "Hold on there, Honey." Without a second thought, Lizzie swung wildly at him, catching his jaw with her fist. A drunken oath escaped with his mouth bleeding, as he fell in a crumpled heap, scrambling to get out of her reach.

She stopped in front of the door to straighten her clothing, took a deep breath and entered. She took her place at her station and began to work.

386

"Hey Red, slow down, you'll catch yer fingers. What's happened ta yer?" Mollie asked, worry creeping into her voice.

At first, Lizzie didn't answer. She was still fuming from the events of the last twenty minutes. Her head was abuzz with a myriad of emotions, anger, panic, worry, fright, and self-castigation.

"I'm sorry, Mollie, I'll talk ta you at break time. My head's all turned around right now."

Mollie didn't reply, her unasked questions multiplying in her head. At break time, the story came tumbling out, along with the panic and distress of losing the money. Mollie's face revealed an inner battle of ideas, each fighting for a voice.

"Well, thet part is o'er an' done. I hope y' learnt there's a lesson in ev'ry bad thing thet happens. Ne'er go ta the bank 'thout another body, a man, if y' have one. They's cut-purses hangin' around jes' waitin' ta separate their quarry fum the pack at ev'ry corner. They's fast an' they're mean. Y' could no' hae stopped him, if 'n y' tried. T'mara, stick wit' me afta work, an' I kin git y' money back fer y'. Y' may no' like it, but if y' truly need the money, I kin git it fer y'."

At the look on Lizzie's face, Mollie laughed. "I'm no' askin' fer y' ta sell yer body, girl, only yer hair. Rich folks love red hair, curly hair, 'specially." She watched Lizzie's hand unconsciously go up to her hair. "It'll grow back, Red! D' y' need the money or no'?"

"I-I do need the money... but my *hair*?" The plaintive tremor in her voice betrayed the vanity she held for the red-gold crown she wore. Her demeanor changed from sad to determined. "Of course, I'll do it. I *have* to do it."

"It's settled then. I'll talk ta m' friend t'night an' see if he kin get yer the money t'mara. Bring a warm kerchief wit' yer. It'll be breezy around yer pretty noggin afta." She smiled, but her eyes were sad with sympathy. "I had ta do it onct mysel' afore I got this job."

"Thank you, Mollie. Is it far from here, where they take your hair?"

"No, girl, it'll only tak' a minute. Have yer sister an' her man wait a' the coffee shop an' ye'll be back afore they order 'nother cuppa. An' hide the money in yer bosom, Red."

"Come, it's back ta work fer us. Thank yer, Mollie. I din't knae wha' ta do."

"Careful, Red, yer losin' thet hoity-toity speech o' yer'n," Mollie said, her eyes dancing.

"Ach, he refused to hire another Irish girl, so I'm the baron's poor cousin whilst I'm here."

"I'll no' betray yer, Red. The old Jew is makin' money whether we have the sod of Ireland on our heels or no'."

"He's a good man, Mollie. I'll no' speak ill o' him."

"Nor will I, as long as he pays me fair wage."

The women returned to work in silence, each mulling over their conversations.

Soon, it was eight o'clock and time to go home. Lizzie told Eliza and Garrett what happened at the bank and Mollie's solution to the loss of their money. With the money they would earn this week and the money from selling her hair, Lizzie hoped they would have enough to pay for the first month's lodging, buy food, and still save for the next month's rent. *It will take a heap of prayin', savin', an' scrimpin' ta make this work,* Lizzie thought. *Oh, Lord, I have ta tell Maggie! I hate disappointin' her. I lost all her money, what little was left!* The memory of it caused her face to flush anew. *What a green Irisher I am! Stupid girl!*

Eliza put her arm around Lizzie and admonished her, as if reading her mind. "Lizzie, stop it, Ever'thin' will turn out all right. It could've happened ta any o' us, isn't thet right, Garrett?"

"She's right, Lizzie. Yer no' a careless person. Y' couldn't have prevented it. He oughta be horse-whipped wit'in an inch of his life."

"Should I sell my hair too, Lizzie?"

"No, Eliza. We'll need somethin' ta fall back on if we get in trouble later on, won't we?" As pretty as Eliza's hair was, it was not the red hair that would fetch the price they needed now. "Hang onta it an' keep it growin' fer now. I ne'er thought o' hair as a crop ta be sold at market afore," said Lizzie, smiling for the first time she told them. "Who knaes what t'marra will bring?"

"Garrett, will you be ready ta move us on Sunday? We don't have much, 'cept fer Maggie's chair, her trunk, our two bags, an' ourselves."

"I've already asked fer Mister Baker's wagon. Sorry, I can't take the new carriage, but they need it fer church. I'm sure 'tween Missus Baker an' Missus Twombly we kin git enough blankets or cushions fer Maggie to ride comfortably."

"Thank yer, Garrett, I'm sure 'twill be fine," replied Lizzie, her mind buzzing with preparations for the move. She counted the milestones of the next two days, the last meal in the Twombly house, the last night, and the last time she would brush out her long curly red hair. She didn't want to think about saying her goodbyes to the Twomblys. It was difficult to say goodbye to the house where she learned so many things, where she learned to love the family and...*Charles*. She felt a heavy weight of sadness where the angel still rested over her heart.

Lizzie pulled her body up straight in the train car. *Faith and strength overcomes trials and sadness. Look to the future, Lizzie! Unbidden tears slipped through her lashes. For heaven's sake, what kind o' strength is that? If you're going ta melt at the prospect o' movin' before ye even git hame fer the night, ye will be a sorry mess, come Sunday, won't ye?*

Later that evening, Missus Twombly came into the kitchen as Lizzie washed dishes. She took cups from the cupboard and set them on the table quietly. She took out the teapot and prepared tea. "Come, Lizzie. Sit with me for a while."

389

Lizzie dried her hands to pour the tea. "No, Lizzie. Let me do this for you. I enjoy pouring tea and I so seldom get to do it. Indulge me, child." Lizzie sat opposite her and watched as she poured.

"I have no great words of wisdom for you, except to trust in God. He knows who you are and who you will become, all according to His plan. You will have many choices in your life and if you trust in Him, you will not put one foot in the wrong direction. We do not see the whole of anything, but He does. We will not understand until we meet Him face to face."

"Beggin' your pardon, ma'am, I've been sae confused an' sae angry, and sad this whole month. My thoughts are no' worthy o' God's grace."

Missus Twombly reached her hand over to cover Lizzie's, and said, "God has understanding beyond our own, child. Rail at Him, if you wish. He is always and ever will be there, to forgive, to listen and guide you. Even when you turn your face from Him, He is there waiting for you. I say these things to you, because I have said them to myself. You and I have lost much. I still believe we have yet much to gain here on earth and in His kingdom. Put your trust in Him and you'll not fail."

They were silent then, sipping their tea, each comfortable in the presence of each other. Lizzie felt blessed and humble to know this great woman who favored the least of those around her.

The diminutive woman rose from her chair. "Good night, Lizzie. Sweet dreams." Lizzie rose as well. As she passed her, Missus Twombly kissed her cheek and left the room. The young cook gathered the cups into the sink and continued to wash dishes.

She slept soundly that night. As she woke in the morning, she went over the events of her day: get the family's breakfast, work until noon, have her hair cut off, tell her mother of her mishap, help her mother pack, then go home to prepare supper for her first American family, for the last time. With a groan, she forced her body and mind awake, to get dressed, to face her day with determination. *There's no help fer it, ye might just as well git it done an' o'er with.*

Lizzie was glad for the automatic movements of her hands that allowed her to reflect on how she would approach her mother about having lost the remainder of her money. That money was her mother's security and pride of independence. Maggie now had neither in her new country and it was Lizzie's fault. *I kin only make it as right as I can, an' hope she can forgive me.*

Lizzie moved through the morning as if she were back in Charles' funeral procession. She was mournful, quiet, and moved with forced determination to accomplish the tasks at hand. She acknowledged the people around her with a half smile, but had no idea what words they spoke.

Mollie called her name again, "Lizzie, it's no' the end o' the world. Let's git it o'er with." Lizzie nodded and raised her head.

"Of course, I'm ready." With a forced smile, she picked up her things and followed her friend.

It wasn't far, as Mollie had promised. The four walked from the laundry on Hamilton, down Tremont to Stuart to Washington. Eliza and Garrett stayed at the coffee shop while Mollie brought Lizzie to the *Gilbert & Company Wig Manufactory*. There was a small store front window with three mannequin heads, one with a man's wig, and two with female wigs. The front of the shop had a very formal waiting room with plush settees, and toward the back, several small dressing rooms with doors. Peeking in, Lizzie could see vanities with chairs, three-quarter length mirrors, hand mirrors, and vases of flowers on the vanities, combs, and hair accessories. A gentleman, dressed as a valet stood at attention. With one glance, he took in Mollie's coarse clothing and flushed face saying, "Please use the next entrance down the block if you wish to conduct your business."

"Oh, beggin' yer pardon, yer lordship. C'mon, Lizzie, we need ta go down the block. This is fer the buyin' lot, no' the sellin' sort, lak us." Turning toward her, she whispered, "I jes' wanted yer ta see the posh area where they'll sell yer hair. It'll be on the head of some uppity-puppity ta wear a' the Gov'nor's Ball, fer sure."

Lizzie's face flushed deep red. "Thank you, sir, please forgive us for disturbing you," she mumbled, as she fled out the door on Mollie's heels.

"Mollie, we were not supposed to be in there. I'm so embarrassed."

"Ach, don' be sae touchy. Ye got ta see it din't cha? Here's our door."

Lizzie giggled, shaking her head at her friend's audacity. *Leastwise, I'm no' quakin' anymore. No harm done.* The next entrance was less welcoming. It was a solid door with worn green paint and small painted words: *Solicitors and Gilbert & Co. Employees Only — Deliveries at the rear. Ring bell for service.*

Her friend rang the bell and a neatly-dressed young woman answered. Mollie explained that Lizzie had an appointment to sell her hair. The door swung open and Lizzie heard the noisy commotion of men, women, and machines. They followed the girl to a room to the left and as instructed, waited. The room was brightly lit by two floor to ceiling windows and was set up as a barber's shop.

In the next twenty minutes, the activity was both fascinating and difficult. A young man arrived, hung up her coat, draped her in a voluminous cloth, and then set a brimmed tray around her. "To catch ev'ry piece of 'air, Miss," he said in a low considerate voice. "You may look or not, but if you please, do not move. I'll cut as close as I can 'thout 'urting you, but you must stay very still. If you need ta speak, jest move your 'and so's I kin see."

While he went about his work, she paid close attention to what he was doing. He tightly bound sections of her hair with twine,

392

and then cut each one very close to her scalp. The bound end of each section was then dipped into a jar of hot wax to glue the hank together. He lay the tresses flat on the counter with the waxed end resting in a dish. As he clipped each section, he continued a calm, almost mesmerizing speech, rendering Lizzie quite content with the whole proceedings.

When he clipped the last of her hair he said, "I'm going to even out your hair now, so it will grow out just as beautiful as it was when you came in here." Mista 'arris say, we mus' always treat our sellers as gracious as we do our buyers, 'cause they are jes' as responsible fer the success of our livelihood."

Just as he was finishing, a black man entered the room. His bearing was straight and proud, his eyes darting around the rooms, and his mouth set in a thin line. "Very good, Mister Dunnington, carry on." He turned on his heel and left the room.

"Who was thet? Why is he sae black? What happened ta him?" Lizzie blurted out the words before she could hold them back.

"That is Mista 'arris, Miss. He owns this company. As to why he is black, he was born black, as are all chil'ren where 'is people come fum." The young man smiled.

"I curse m' mouth, fer m' outburst, I thought he had the plague. I ne'er saw a man thet was black afore. The only time I e'en heard o' a body bein' black was when they talked o' the Black Death in the olden days. My, he gave me sech a fright. Where do his people come from?"

"'E says fum Nigeria, on the cont'nent of Africa. 'E wus once a slave, 'e say."

"Where the elephants an' monkeys come from?"

"And black men, Miss. Mista 'arris be a genius wit' wigs. The best wig maker in Boston, black or white."

"Oh, I'm sure he is. Again, forgive my ignorance. I'd no idea."

393

"No matter, Mista 'arris would be pleased you are now enlightened. Please see Miss Markella when you leave, fer your payment. Thank you fer letting us serve you today." The young man's smile was threatening to degrade itself into a smirk, as Lizzie covered her shorn head and retreated. After the door closed, she could swear she heard him laughing out loud.

Lizzie and Mollie collected the money, rejoining Garrett and Eliza with barely a half hour elapsed. Lizzie held her kerchief tight. She was afraid the wind would blow it off and the world would see her red fuzzy head. 'Twill take a lang time ta git usta this breeze around my ears. Still, it's over a month's rent. Wryly, she thought, *my hair will gae places I could ne'er hope ta go.*

The girls bid Mollie farewell and thanked her for helping them. Lizzie looked toward her next task of the day, telling her tale of woe to Maggie. "Eliza, you an' Garrett, gae hame. I'll gae directly ta Maggie's house ta explain the money. I'll pack her trunk sae she'll be ready in the mornin'." When she saw Eliza about to protest, she added, "I've gotta tell Maggie on m' ain, Eliza. 'Sides, 'twill give you an' Garrett some time alone."

Lizzie's stomach was churning as she entered her mother's room. She chastised herself; *don't let the shame o' it cripple you. Ye made a mistake. Let it be done with, as Mollie said. Let her think it was the most natural thing in the world ta haf' all yer hair cut off. Try bein' as strong as she thinks ye are, an' we won't have ta be weepin' an' wailin' all night.*

Lizzie, with her head covered tightly, told Maggie her story. Her cold and unemotional telling had the effect she had hoped. Maggie took it seriously, but without admonishment or tears.

"The primary importance is yer no' harmed, except perhaps yer pride. Yer a good and practical girl, *mo cridhe.* But even ye cannot prevent the world from turning. Yer strength is in how ye handle the terrible moments thet happen. Good an' evil will always be. I'm sorry fer yer hair though, 'twas a proud mane. Now, let's see

394

yer bald pate." Her mother smiled kindly and slipped the kerchief from her head. Her fuzzy red curls revealed, her mother said, "Have ye looked in the mirror? It's not nearly as awful as ye imagine!" She wheeled herself to the bureau and picked up her hand mirror to hold it for her. "Think of how cool it will be fer the summer."

Lizzie peeked in the mirror and saw her strange red fuzzy head. She sighed, "It is what it is, I suppose. I'll hafta git usta it, won't I? At least we have our rent an' we kin eat. It'll grow out eventually." Lizzie laughed in spite of herself. All her worry disappeared with her mother's smile. "I guess I won't hafta fight off the men fer my honor, will I!"

"I dinna think ye kin depend on thet, Lizzie. The hair hid the true beauty of your face. Without it, your eyes and your smile are even more beautiful, brought into the light."

"I kin always depend on my Ma ta think I'm lovelier than spring. True or no', I'll take it ta m' heart an' I thank ye kindly fer thet." Impulsively, she kissed her mother soundly on the cheek.

She opened the trunk her mother brought from Ireland, packing her clothes from the bureau, chatting happily. Leaving out just a few things she would need for the night, they were finished quickly. Lizzie reached for the envelope she saw on the end of the bureau, but Maggie stopped her. "Lizzie, it's a note for Missus Stanhope. She's been so kind, I wanted to say 'thank you' and that I will miss her company."

Lizzie smiled to herself, remembering the crabby woman who was so worried about her house. Maggie had her dancing to her tune before the first week was out, as they had all predicted. "Ye always brin' out the best in people, Mother."

"The sternest people hide their best qualities inside to protect them. It's like a present ta unwrap. Everyone has a tender heart inside them. They jes' have to knae when it's safe ta reveal it, and ta whom."

Lizzie shook her head at her mother's words. *She makes it sound sae easy. Like everyone in the world should knae how ta do it. Maybe it's the chair that makes her sae patient wit' the people around her. Or, maybe it's the chair that makes 'em patient wit' her cajoling nature. All I knae is, she made me feel comfortable enough ta show her my naked head. I thought 'twould kill me ta show anyone, an' even more sae, her.*

Lizzie soon took her leave to prepare the last supper for the Twomblys. Another *last* ticked off in her mind. She would cook as if there were company coming, so the Twomblys would have plenty of food for the next few days. *I wonder if they will have a maid an' a cook where they are goin'? Probably just one servant, since they won' be entertainin'. I'll hafta double the stew pot, too, so Big John will haf' enough fer the church 'guests'.*

She served their favorite lamb with roast potatoes, mint jelly, and asparagus with hollandaise. *Missus Twombly said no dessert tonight. Thet seems very odd, an' disappointin'. Why...? No matter. Jes' git crackin' ye've no' much time.*

Soon dinner was concluded. Lizzie was called into the dining room as usual to receive the obligatory compliments to the cook. After some lovely words from the family, which she barely heard, she helped Eliza clear the table. They were both in the kitchen again when they heard a bustling at the front door. That's strange, thought Lizzie. *I didn't hear the door knocker or the bell.*

Mister William poked his head into the kitchen and said, "Lizzie, Eliza, step into the dining room please." The two servants looked at each other questioningly, and then did as they were told.

Chapter Twenty-four

Having been summoned by Missus Twombly, an unusually cautious Lizzie slipped silently into the darkened room. A single candle lit the center of the table, its glow encircled by floating faces, faces made into amorphous and grotesque moons by its wavering light.

Her eyes anxiously darted around the dining room. Her confused and apprehensive brain trying to make sense of the strange tableau. Her cold, shaking hand sought comfort in her half-sister's warm one. Her chilled spine steeled itself in anticipation of evil tidings. Her tense body visibly jumped when the smallest of the assembly shouted, "S'pwise!"

The group burst into choruses of "Best wishes.", "Good Luck.", and "God bless you." The grinning faces floated into focus as they spoke, Mister and Missus Baker and their children, the Twomblys, and Garrett. The candle sat atop a beautiful white cake, its frosting topped with raspberry preserves, and trimmed with candied orange slices. The entire confection was atop a footed glass dish, occupying the center of the lace table cloth like a celebrated trophy.

Eliza poked her, urging her to say something. Lizzie cleared her throat and blurted out the first thing that came to her jumbled mind. "Gracious, how'd ye all git in the door, 'thout us hearin' yer?" After a burst of laughter, she added, "What a wonderful surprise! I should have done this fer you. Ye've all been sae kind ta us, I hate ta leave. Please sit, while I git each o' ye some o' this lovely cake."

"You and Eliza sit. Missus Baker and I will tend to the cake," said Isabelle, somewhat imperiously. "Everyone else please be seated." Lizzie and Eliza sat, nervously. They dared not argue with her. Isabelle busied herself with the cake, but looked at her honored guests and said, "Do tell us about your new ventures in Boston, Eliza?"

Eliza told them about her new job as a seamstress. "I'm jes' feelin' my way, but I like doin' the handiwork. Miss Penelope says, she don' wan' me on the machines," she added conspiratorially, "an' I am sae grateful. Those things scare me!" The eldest Baker girl asked her questions about going into the showroom. Did she know who the ladies were that shopped there? What was the featured color going to be this year? What do the new fashions look like?

"I didn't really git ta see many o' the frocks, Eula. Jes' the ones I was hemmin' or makin' buttonholes fer. One bridal dress had twenty-nine buttonholes! The cloth was embroidered silk from China, I was told."

"When I grow up, I wanna own a dress shop an' sell only the finest fashions from Paris," Eula declared dreamily. "Someday, maybe you'll have your own dress shop too, Eliza."

Eliza lowered her head and said, "I'm jes' a maid who can sew, Eula. I couldn't haf' a shop o' my own."

"But Papa says, in America, you can do anything you want to do. A woman can become a doctor or a shop owner if she wants."

Mister Baker laughed softly. He took his daughter's hand and looked into his daughter's impassioned eyes. "...if the girl is willing to work long enough and hard enough, Sweetie. You have the right to do it, but no one is going to give it to you. You must earn it."

"Well, then I will work very hard, Papa." The little girl proudly returned his gaze and added determinedly, "Maybe Eliza will one day work for me and together we will create our own fashions."

"I would be most delighted, Eula."

The group then engaged Lizzie in conversation about her new employment. The boys were fascinated about the steam mangle, steam engines being their favorite topic of the *New Age*, as they called it. Steam was second only to the combustion engine they had heard would power automobiles in the future. "My teacher says, someday every man in America will own a motorized carriage."

Missus Baker said, "Oh my, I hope not! I saw one of dose tings in town an' it vas noisy, smelly, an' stopped ev'ry twenty feet. I don't tink dey should be allowed on the road wit' der horses. It frightened de poor tings half t' death."

Her comment curtailed the topic of combustion engines for the moment. After a while, Lizzie rose, picked up the dishes nearest her and asked if anyone would like some tea or coffee. The offer was politely declined and Mister Baker announced that they would have to go home. When the children groaned in unison, he gave each of them a mock look of scathing menace, voicing his oft-repeated maxim of child rearing, "Children are difficult enough to civilize on a Sunday morning, without having them up until all hours the night before." Even the shyest of them giggled at this pretense of sternness, but moved to get her coat.

"Well, Eliza and I thank each one of you for your kindness and I hope we will have occasion to see you again." Lizzie was aware of the stiffness of her words, but her emotions were beginning to overwhelm her.

Missus Baker hugged each of them. One by one, the children shook the hands of the parting servants, giving their rehearsed speeches.

"It's been very nice to know you."

"Good luck and I hope to see you again."

Clarence, only two, chose to forego the handshake and threw himself against Lizzie's apron and wailed, "I don' wan' chu da go!" Lizzie picked him up, kissed his cheek, and gave him back to his mother.

Don' make him any promises ye canna keep, Lizzie. He's only seen me a few times an' he's reluctant to let even me go, poor thing. Perhaps this small letting go will prepare him for the bigger ones in his future.

A sudden vision of Charles floated before her. "You have to let *me* go, Lizzie," he seemed to say. Knowing she was about to lose all sense of propriety, Lizzie made her escape through the kitchen into her bedroom. There she sank to the floor and wept like the child she just held in her arms. *Charles, this is sae hard. I don' want ta leave this place where I knew yer an' loved yer. I kin feel yer love around me here. I don' wanna lose yer.*

After a minute, she gathered her scattered thoughts. *Git up, Lizzie. Git hold o' yersel'. Ye've work ta do. Ye canna sit here whinin' o'er yer lot. Yer no' a child.*

She fixed her cap, straightened her apron and went back to the kitchen. Eliza had been gathering the dishes and piling them up by the sink. "We wondered where ye'd gone off ta, Lizzie," she said, concern creeping into her voice. "Wha' happened?"

Lizzie's answer was sharper than she intended, her mouth a grim straight line. "I jes' couldn't tolerate any more good wishes, Eliza. Give me some peace fer nae. Lemme jes' do my dishes, please."

"Very well," Eliza replied softly, a little hurt at her abruptness.

I'll have ta apologize later, but give me this moment wit'out questions an' concern, Eliza!

They worked silently, thoughtfully. When the dishes were done and the kitchen cleaned, Eliza went back into the dining room. Garrett was still there, waiting.

"Lizzie's gone t' bed. We can have the kitchen, I think. Come." The sadness in her voice was like a deep ache in his heart.

He sat in the rocker and pulled Eliza into his lap. Her warm proximity intoxicated his mind as he grappled for words.

"Eliza, dear, I can't be the man you want me t' be. I have ghosts that chase me an' vengeful people who are searchin' t' do me harm."

When she opened her mouth to protest, he said, "Please, lemme finish. I am besotted with y', but I hafta say g'bye. My heart isn't in it, but m' head says it's the only way t' keep y' safe. One day soon, I'll hafta tear m'self away fum this fine place. The Bakers will be safe enough. These men will think I'm runnin' a ruse on them. But if they find me wit' you, they'll know the way t' git t' me. These are dangerous men, Eliza, an' I've cost 'em dearly. I wus hidin' out when y' found me an' they were gittin' close, even then."

He continued, watching her face crumble, "I've neva' had so won'erful a sojourn, than this time wit' yer. I neva' had a family like the Bakers. This seems the best time fer me t' go. I wan' yer t' know thet m' heart will al'ays be with yer, but I'm not free t' marry yer." His eyes filled, watching the raw emotions move across her face.

"But...." she protested.

"No, *mon chere*, I'll not see yer harmed. I cannot. Can't y' see how hard this is fer me t' say? Do yer think I want t' give yer up? Can y' possibly think I don't love yer?" His voice broke. They were silent for a while, just holding each other, each trying to rationalize their wishes and finding no way to make them happen. After a long time, when her heart, though aching, returned to an almost normal beating, she spoke in hesitating whispers.

401

"Garrett, will ye write ta me? Will ye let me knae ye are all right?"

The agony of regret shone in his eyes as he fought for the words to soften his words. "I will, but y' cannot write back. These men are very good at findin' people an' I don't want 'em findin' yer. They'll search my belongings ta find yer letters."

"Garrett, what did y' do, that they'd hunt y' down sae?" She trembled in his arms, shocked at his concern of her safety.

"I don't want yer t' know, my love. 'Twas deep in the past an' I din't choose t' do it, an' I'm not proud of it. I want y' ta know only what y' already know of me. Y' kin know thet fum now on, I'll be the sort of man y' would want me t' be. Y' an' the Bakers have done thet fer me. I'll someday pay fer my past sins, but I'll not repeat them."

Eliza kissed his lips and drawing away, whispered, "Let's no' speak o' this anymore. If I can't knae, then don' let m' imagine the worst. Jes' hold me fer a moment more."

They lapsed into a quiet sadness again, wrapped in each other's arms in the rocker. Then Eliza moved, facing him, asking with a smile playing on her lips, "What does this *'mon chere'* mean?"

"It means, 'my dear.' My Ma called me thet when I was a small child, I'm told. I don't 'member her, but som'one tol' me it when I was very young. It's the only thing I have of hers an' I gladly give it t' you."

"It's lovely, Garrett. I'll al'ays think *mon chere* when I think o' yer."

He kissed her deeply once more then stood, still holding her. His voice husky with emotion, he said good night and left her. She touched the lips that still tingled from his kiss. She sat back down in the rocker and felt his warmth lingering in the wood. When his warmth left her, she sighed, pulled herself up and went to bed.

As she climbed into bed next to Lizzie, she heard her sister's sleepy voice say, "I'm sorry Eliza, fer snapping at yer."

"It's all right, Lizzie. Gae back ta sleep." Eliza had greater hurts to nurse.

That night, Eliza in fitful slumber, dreamed of chasing Garrett with an overwhelming sense of longing. But, every time she came close enough to see him, it wasn't him at all. It was a faceless man wearing Garrett's clothing.

When she finally woke, she wondered, *how could I have loved someone, I didn' e'en knae? Was I in love wit' the notion o' bein' in love, or jes' wantin' ta be married? Am I thet fluffy-headed thet it dinna matter who it was? No,* she corrected herself; *I loved the man he showed me. An' he showed me only what I wanted ta see. I don't knae if I'm sad ta lose him or angered a' bein' sae deceived! He said he's no' free ta marry? Does thet mean he's already married?*

To belay the war in her head, Eliza tried to focus on the tasks she would have to accomplish before they left that day. Hearing Lizzie in the kitchen clattering dishes as she set the breakfast trays for the family, Eliza hurried to don her apron and cap to help her. She heard six resonating bongs of the grandfather clock in the hall.

In the kitchen, she gave a last buffing to Mister William's shoes. She hung his Sunday shirt, freshly starched, and pressed on its hook, and placed his newly-shined shoes on the shelf outside his bedroom door. Isabelle's Sunday dress hung on her hook and Missus Twombly's dove-colored boots sat on her shelf.

Eliza's soft knock on their doors signaled them to don their robes and make themselves presentable. As soon as she delivered the breakfast trays to each room and poured their coffees, she would be allowed to bring in the clothing items for the day. *I'll miss this little exercise,* she thought. *It's funny, how much pride an' pleasure I take in these simple steps ta help the family be prepared fer the day.*

Her sad demeanor seemed to leave her, taken over by a lighter, almost joyful spirit, as she went downstairs to inspect the carpet under the dining table for any spills she may have missed the night before. She swept the carpet carefully, returning the chairs to their original position, checking the fine china, the silver, and the linen drawers until all was in order. She moved to the parlor, stoking the fire once again, sweeping the hearth, and restocking the wood bin.

By the time she returned to the kitchen, Eliza could hear the family, descending the stairs, talking low. Mister William opened the kitchen door, asking the girls to step into the parlor.

Lizzie and Eliza changed to their fresh aprons, hurrying down the hall to the front of the house.

"We want you to know we will miss you girls and this house will not be the same without you." Missus Twombly gave them each an envelope and said, "I hope you will enjoy these. It is but a small token of appreciation for your service." One by one, the family shook their hands and wished them well. "William, dear...?"

William stood to his full height, raised his hands, placing them gently on the heads of Lizzie and Eliza and prayed, "Dear Heavenly Father, bless these, your children, as they go forth into the world, protect them from all harm and grant them the strength to do Your will in all things. Amen. May the Lord watch between me and thee, while we are absent one from the other."

As she saw his hands retreat to his sides, Isabelle added brightly, "Godspeed, girls. If you ever need us we will be in the area. Seek us out and whatever we have to offer is yours. Thank you to taking such good care of us. We will miss you sorely."

"Thank you all," said Lizzie. "We could no' have come ta America ta a more gracious family."

"We are truly blessed," Eliza added, shyly.

"Well, ladies," said Mister William, "I hate to cut this short, but we do need to leave now, if we are to be at the church on time.

Mister Baker has been waiting the carriage for us outside for fully five minutes now."

Once the family left, Lizzie could not believe how crushingly quiet the house had become. "Come, Eliza. We have ta finish up. You git the trays an' I'll start on the dishes. The family is going ta the Bakers fer Sunday dinner, sae all I need ta do is make sure the stew is on the back of the stove, one fer the family's supper, an' an extra large pot fer Big John. While I'm doing the rest o' the dishes, you kin set the dining room table. It'll be jes' the three settings fer luncheon.

"After thet, we kin change an' git our stuff packed. I'll quick wash our dresses, caps an' aprons. Since we can't hang them on a Sunday, I'll soak them in the tub under the sink, sae Miss Isabelle kin hang them in the morning. I'll leave them a note, tellin' them where they are. If it were warmer, I'd leave the tub outside, but it'll pro'bly freeze tonight."

The girls rushed around and made short work of their final tasks. When they were almost done, Eliza leaned out the back door and rang the bell for Garrett to come with the wagon. Lizzie put the bags on the back porch and was surprised to see Big John there.

"Hello! Come in, come in. I'm sae glad ta see ye afore we gae. Oh John, we'll miss yer sorely."

"An' me as well, Miss Lizzie. Y've been very kind t' us."

Lizzie stepped into his big bear hug. "Kin I git ye some stew while ye here? I made a double batch fer you, plus some fer the Twombly's supper. They's plenty in here."

"Oh no, thank y' kindly. Missus Jacobson down the street gave us breakfast at the church this morning. I sent a couple men over t' clear out the snow from in front of her barn last month an' she's been most accommodatin' since. I make sure the men work fer their supper, no matter the weather. Makes the givers know these men aren't lazy or moochers. They're jes' out of a job."

405

"Thet's good. I hope the boys git some payin' work soon. It'll be easier when the weather warms up. I heard Titus got a job up at the mill last month."

"Yes, Miss, he's workin' steady. He's been comin' back t' the church, bringin' mittens an' mufflers every week fer the little ones."

"Oh, here comes Garrett. He's takin' me, Eliza an' mother ta our new place today. Kin ye join us? It would give him comp'ny on the way back."

"Sorry, can't. I kin ride wit' you t' yer Ma's an' git her settled in the wagon, but I bes' be goin' t' church. I can't have them thinkin' my presence is not required." He raised an eyebrow wryly and added, "We might appear t' be ungrateful heathens." Lizzie joined in his laugh. "Lemme git yer bags out to the wagon, Miss Lizzie."

"Thank yer, Big John. I'll go in ta see if Eliza's ready." She swung into the kitchen and didn't see Eliza. She didn't see her in the bedroom, but saw the bed was made. "Eliza!"

"Up here!" Eliza called from upstairs. "One more bed an' I'm done."

Lizzie ran up the stairs and saw the only open door. "I'll help you. Missus Twombly hardly makes a dent in her bed, does she?"

"Nope," her sister replied. "She's droppin' a lot o' stuff on the floor though. Why don't ye pick up her floor around the chifferobe? I don' think she kin see as well as she usta."

"Hm-m, maybe I'll address m' note ta Miss Isabelle instead. "Ye may wanna take one las' a look around afore ye come down."

In the kitchen, Lizzie wrote, *Dear Miss Isabelle, Please convey our gratitude to your gracious family for the generous employment that allowed us to come to America. We have received from your family more than we could ever give. As we commence our lives independent of our dear benefactors in this country, we*

406

will endeavor always to conduct ourselves as if we were in your presence.

With regard to your supper, I have one pot of stew on the back of the stove for your family, and a larger pot for the "church visitors." Our day clothes are in the wash bucket under the sink, ready to hang in the morning. There was a small tear in the right sleeve of one of my dresses, which has been repaired.

We pray for good fortune in your new home and ventures. May God grant you the happiness you so richly deserve. It was our honor to serve you and your lovely family.

Your Humble and Obedient Servants,
Eliza and Lizzie Heenan

"Eliza, read this an' tell me if it's satisfactory. I tried ta write it as Maggie would."

"Oh, Lizzie, it's as if she wrote it! The penmanship is lovely. I always write as if I was using a stick in hard ground."

"Your penmanship is fine, Eliza. If you took as much care ta write, as ye do ye needlework, it would be far superior ta mine. Nae, let's git goin'. Garrett's waitin' fer us."

As if he heard them, the young man came in to see what the holdup was. "It looks like we'll need the extra blankets to wrap around us, instead of having Maggie sit on them. Brrr-r."

The girls hopped into the back of the wagon with the aid of a box Garrett set out for them. There they saw, as promised, the heavy blankets. Lizzie and Eliza huddled together in the raw cold on the way to pick up Maggie. "Looks like snow," Garrett shouted back to them over the noise of the horse and wagon.

The girls watched as Garrett and Big John went in the boarding house to get Maggie and her chair. They left Maggie in her chair, holding her bag, and lifted her, chair and all into the back of the wagon. Big John said, "We're gonna tie the chair t' the wagon seat an' let Maggie stay in it. Y' kin take my belt to strap 'er in. 'Zat

all right, Missus Heenan? Thet way if we hit a bump y' won't be
flying out of the wagon!"

Maggie laughed good-naturedly, and then whispered to Big
John. He laughed even louder in return, winking at the girls. When
everything was secure, they wrapped one of the blankets around
Maggie, and said goodbye to John. As he walked away, he hitched
up his pants and Maggie chortled with laughter.

"Maggie, what did you say to Big John?" her daughters
asked, curiously.

"I asked him how he would keep his britches up without his
belt," said Maggie, wickedly.

"Ma, ye didn't." Lizzie clapped her hand over her mouth,
giggling.

"Eliza, come sit up here wit' me, girl," called Garrett. "Y'
can't be havin' all the fun back there, wit' me not one part of it."

Eliza hesitated then took her place beside Garrett. Lizzie
gave her one of the blankets and took the last one herself. Lizzie sat
beside her mother's chair and Maggie's hand rested on her shoulder.
The only noise came from the steady clopping of hooves and the
occasional snort of the horses.

Lizzie watched the changing scenery from small town to
pasture, then bustling city. Even on Sunday, the traffic was
congested. Ahead, a horse was spooked by a child darting across in
front of him. The driver cursed the boy with a flaming list of
invectives. Then as if he just remembered it was Sunday, he took off
his hat and bowed his head. The pace resumed.

The buildings they saw now were older, smaller, and wood-
clad instead of brick, and not as close together. "We're almost there,
Mother. I hope you'll like it. Oh dear! It's snowing."

"It's a welcome sign to our new home," said Maggie,
cheerfully waving to some children lagging behind their mother.
Lizzie was grateful that the snow covered the barren rocky ground.
Now, she could see the house standing alone — pale yellow, like

winter sunshine, apart from the run down weathered tenements around it. *Will yer be happy here, Maggie, lookin' out on these sad dwellin's an' scruffy children?*

As if she read her mind yet again, her mother said, "Lizzie, 'tis a lovely house. ...and a porch! You chose well, *mo cridhe*."

"I'm hopin' ye will like livin' here, Maggie."

As they stopped in front of the house, two strapping young men came out in their shirtsleeves, grinning from ear to ear. "Are you the Heenan family? Kin we help you?"

"Help would be most welcome, boys," said Garrett, just trying to figure how to get Maggie safely up the steps an' into the house wit' her chair. "I'll take her in if you would kindly take the bags an' the chair. Lizzie, Eliza, please lead the way."

Eliza and Lizzie scampered up the steps to the front door where Mrs. Harrington was waiting. "First month's rent in advance, ladies. Seven dollars, then you'll have the key," she said haughtily.

"Aye, ma'am." Lizzie pulled an envelope out of her purse and handed it to her. "That's fer two rooms, and furniture, and wood?" she asked, warily.

"Yes, miss. It's what was agreed upon."

"Thank ye, Missus Harrington, I jes' wanted ta knae I understood correctly," Lizzie replied, not wanting to offend her. The key was pressed in her hand.

"Your door must be locked at all times, except when you have company, in which case the door will stand open. There is a list of rules on the back of your entry door. Please understand, any breach of the house rules will be deemed just cause to evict you from the premises."

"Aye, ma'am," the girls chorused.

"If you need me for any reason, knock on my door on the second floor, apartment four, between nine in the morning and seven in the evening. If I am not at home, leave a note in my mail box. Your rooms are the first in the hall to your right, number one."

Then, once her business had concluded, Missus Harrington smiled, and the brilliance of it, was as if the sun suddenly broke through the clouds. She turned on her heel and climbed the stairs.

"She's really a bit of all right, y' know," said one of the young men in a low voice. "She's careful about her tenants, is all." Lizzie noticed he carried her mother's heavy chair and her bag with the irons in it, without complaint, as if it were a bag of feathers. *We'll knae who ta call on if we need ta move furniture,* she thought, amused.

The snow was falling heavier now, as they bustled into the rooms. Maggie was seated in her chair, talking to one of the young men, and surveying her domain. Lizzie saw the furniture was serviceable, if dark and more than a little threadbare. There was a full size bed and a cot in the second room, with a light curtain hanging across its wide opening for privacy.

Lizzie inspected the little stove and saw that it was out. It was much smaller than the cook stove she used at the Twombly's house, but enough for the three of them. The oven would hardly hold a tray o' biscuits or maybe two small meat pies. There were two burners and two warming lids, with one small attached shelf for her browned flour and sugar. It would be a week before they could do any serious food shopping, and they would have to make do with the bread, potatoes, some canned tomatoes, and peas, and the few spices Missus Twombly gave them, along with the small pot of stew for that night's fare. Sharing it with Garrett for his help was one thing, but sharing it with these two hardy young men would stretch it beyond its limits. *We wouldn't have anythin' fer the rest o' the week! Perhaps I kin go out durin' my lunch an' git somethin' each day? Oh dear.*

While she was pondering the problem of food, the elder boy, said to her, "I understand you're Lizzie. I'm Charlie McNeill. I'm goin' out back t' pick up yer wood t' git the fire started fer you. If y' like, we already have a stew cookin'. Maybe we kin bring it over 'n have dinner together? It'll gie us a chance t' know each other. It's gonna be a while before yer stove is up 'n runnin' anyways. I'd invite yer t' our place, but it's only the one room, y' un'erstand. What do yer think?"

"Sounds very nice, Charlie. Let me see if Mother is up to it. In the meantime, 'twould be wonderful ta get some heat in here."

"Sure thing. Will, gie us a hand, will you?"

"Lizzie, do y' think it's all right fer me t' leave yer now?" asked Garrett. "They seem like good sorts. I'd stay if you needed me fer a while longer, but I should be goin'. I put yer bags in yer room. Y' seem t' have ever'thin' y' need. I gave yer Ma one o' the blankets 'til the fire gits goin'."

"Well, we were hopin' ye could stay fer Sunday dinner, since we made ye miss church. It won' be much, but we'd love ta have ye."

"I really should go, Lizzie. I don't know how much worse this snow will git, an' it's a long ways home." The worried look on his face emphasized his troubling words.

"Oh, Garrett, I'm sorry fer bein' sae selfish, I fergot about the snow. I won' hold ye any longer. Please be safe, God gae wit' ye. I wish ye could stay 'til it's o'er. It looks worse than e'er nae."

The shadow of remembered danger crossed her face and prompted him to say, "I will be fine, Lizzie. I'm sure this will blow over soon, but the longer I stay, the longer I'll be travelin' in it."

"Eliza, Mother, say goodbye ta Garrett. He has ta gae nae." Lizzie's announcement was met with a chorus of dismay. Quickly, he kissed each of the women on the cheek and shook hands with Will.

As Charlie returned with the wood, Garrett clapped him on the back and said goodbye. His arms full of wood, he turned towards the retreating figure in confusion. "Yer leavin' a'ready?"

"Sorry, Charlie, please t' meet yer, but I gotta git the beasts back home."

411

"An' fine beasts they are, Garrett. Sorry, you couldn' stay awhile longer, young man."

Lizzie smiled at that. Garrett was probably his senior by a few years. Ordinarily, she would be concerned being left in the company of two strangers, however friendly they seemed. These men however, were more than helpful and if they passed Missus Harrington's cautious standards, surely they could pass hers.

Charlie went to work lighting the stove, adjusting the damper and poking the logs, until at last, the heat could be felt in the whole room. Will set a generous pot of stew on the stove and their smaller one, next to it. She looked in her bag for the makings of biscuits. Soon they were seated around the table like old friends, laughing and talking.

"Will, say grace, if y' would, but make it a short one, I've worked up an appetite," Charlie asked.

"Oh Lord, bless this meal from yer bounty, bless yer children who eat it, an' may we e'er be mindful of those who have not ta eat or none to eat with. Amen." The echoes of 'amen' and the warmth of their company made Lizzie long for Ireland, just a little.

"Sae Charlie, what is it that ye do ta earn ye keep?" asked Lizzie.

Will interrupted and replied teasingly, "He earns his keep by tellin' *me* what t' do all day! An' I do what he tells me while he threatens ta send me home." Charlie playfully cuffed the back of his brother's head.

"If I may reply, I am a blacksmith, as is Will here, when he gits off his duff. We're hopin' ta git a shop of our ain one day soon. The man we work fer has a place here in the south of Boston, an' another in Malden. We're thinkin' ta take o'er the Malden shop. There's enough work there fer four, maybe five smithies."

"It's a fine opportunity fer us, if he'll take on a couple of strappin' boys from Nova Scotia. So, what are you young ladies all about?"

412

"Lizzie runs a steam mangle an' I am a seamstress. We've only jes' started. We earned passage from Ireland by bein' in service ta a minister in Newton Lower Falls, an' nae we're here."

The lively conversation ran on until the stew and biscuits were gone. Charlie made sure each person at the table had a turn to speak. Lizzie watched as Eliza leaned in to hear his every word.

Lizzie gathered the dishes, denying any offers of help from their guests or Eliza. This is the part she liked, company lingering around the table idly tellin' stories while she did the dishes. She took out her apron from home. A simple cotton skirt and bib, made from an old outgrown shift. Not starched or pristine white as her uniform at the Twombly's had been, but full of homespun memories of a two-room thatched house in the Legananny.

"Will, it's time to retreat an' let these ladies unpack their goods. Like us, they have work ta do in the mornin'. Ladies, if yer workin' in town, you'll be catchin' the trolley at the end of the street. It comes ev'ry twenty minutes. We'll be off two blocks away ta the shop, around seven, but we kin git you on the right one, if y' like." Charlie met her eyes, and she could see he was sincere in his offer.

"That's very kind o' ye. It might be a good idea, at least fer the first day or two. Thank yer, Charlie, an' thank ye kindly fer a taste o' yer lamb an' barley stew. 'Twas delicious. We're blessed ta have good neighbors sech as ye."

"Our mother would have us be nothin' less. If you care t' go at seven, we'll be here an' ready."

"Seven o'clock will be fine. Good afternoon, Charlie, Will."

Lizzie closed the door. As she did, she saw the list of rules Missus Harrington demanded. She smiled as she read the long list of possible infractions that could result in dismissal from the property. Most of the list was common sense, but the proprietress did not leave anything to chance.

"If we kin afford it, in the next couple weeks, I think we should purchase some cloth ta cover thet settee. If one o' those blacksmith boys has occasion ta sit down on it, I think the fabric will fall apart. At least wit' a cover, it will still look presentable when it does."

Eliza took her bag into the bedroom. "We can put our bags under the bed. An' there's room fer each o' us ta have a drawer in the bureau. There are hooks in here ta hang our shifts an' coats. The bottom drawer has some towels, thank goodness. Maggie, where will ye sleep? Do ye want the cot or share the bed?"

"I think I should take the cot, don't you? I don't wan' ta disturb you girls with my restless movements. Put the pot under the cot an' a wash basin on the little table there. That will be sufficient fer me. That little cabinet in the front room kin hold my handwork, if that's all right."

"That should be fine. By the looks of it, that window will have good light from mid-morning until mid-afternoon. You'll be able ta read or do yer tattin' an' crochetin' there. We'll leave thet area open fer yer chair an' drop the leaves down on the table while we're gone," said Lizzie. "In the warmer weather, we'll figure a way ta get ye out ta the porch."

They spent the waning hours of daylight arranging their few belongings and chatting about their new neighbors. "Charlie seems the elder one. I can't tell how old Will is. They are both formidable, but very friendly an' open," said Eliza. "Rather han'some, too," she added.

"I found them both engagin' an' helpful," volunteered Maggie. "Ambitious, too. Ye girls could find a good match in them."

"I wondered how many o' those wild stories they told were true," Lizzie said a little harshly. "The McNeills are good storytellers, I'll grant you thet."

"Ye'd have ta expect them ta put their best foot forward, wouldn't yer? If there was a little exaggeration in their tales, it would no' be sae likely ta impress ye, now would it?" Lizzie could see her mother's teasing eyes on her.

"Maggie, I think it cruel ta think o' matchin' us up. I've just lost Charles an' Eliza's dreams o' Garrett are dashed," Lizzie said, her voice restrained with emotion.

"Of course, dear, I do not mean ta minimize yer sorrow, but we canna tell the future. Please forgive me, yer mother is a hopeless romantic, who speaks wit' her heart instead o' her head."

"I've decided thet perhaps I kin very well live wit'out Garrett, since he seems ta be able ta live wit'out me," Eliza said, trying to lighten the mood. "I don't think I was sae enamored o' him, as much as I wanted ta be. So, dear Maggie, perhaps one day, I kin entertain feelin's fer one o' the boys, but no' jes' yet. We'll see what they're really like after a while o' gittin' ta knae 'em. Time will number the warts on the prettiest frog."

With her mother and sister settled down for the night, Lizzie reached into her bag for the envelope Missus Twombly gave her before they left. She had almost forgotten it with the flurry of activity unpacking and arranging her new living area. She would have to remind Eliza to read hers in the morning.

She opened the envelope carefully. There inside was another bookmark, beautifully hand-painted with a Bible verse, "*Be not forgetful to entertain strangers, for thereby some have entertained angels unawares. — Hebrews 13:2*" A short note accompanied the small gift:

My Dear Lizzie,

Accept this gift to remind you how when you came to us, we entertained you, and received many blessings every day you were with us. It has been so rewarding for us, I fear we have received the better part of the bargain for your passage to this country. America is blessed by your addition to this fair land.

415

As often as you can, entertain strangers. The time and effort you expend comes back to you tenfold in blessings.

You and I have both loved men of God. I like to think some of their devotion to Him stays with us and helps us to serve Him better.

God watches over you in all your trials and joys. I know this, because I ask Him daily to put His arm of protection around you.

In all you do, do your best, love God, and you'll not go far wrong.

God bless and keep you always,
Betsy Dow Twombly

Lizzie lay awake for a long time that night, her mind going over her last year as an Irish immigrant cook. She marveled at the many life-changing events packed into so short a time. Leaving her small village in Ireland, she embarked on a voyage to the edge of her imagination. America was more than she could have imagined. It seemed to test her abilities, her faith, and her maturity every day.

She smiled as she remembered her first sight of Lady Liberty. It was as if she had dreamed it. Perhaps Ireland and the slow predictable peace of her childhood, was the dream?

Who will watch the selfsame moon and stars for me now? Da and *Móraí* are gone, and Maggie is here. The comfort of Ireland and its simple way of life seemed so far away. Charles is gone and I feel so alone. *What is Yer plan fer me nae, Laird?*

The Truth and the Fantasy

Because this is a collection of stories based on real people, real events, and real circumstances, it is incumbent upon me to tell what is true, and what is merely literary license employed to connect those people and events. In all cases, the timeline of published events of all the characters of the book have been carefully preserved to the best of my ability. Descriptions of private events were extracted from family lore set in the culture and times they occurred.

The place names and companies are accurate for the time period, but I cannot verify that any of the people in the book went there. Boston was undergoing huge changes during 1892 and the ones to follow. Electrified trolleys, the subway, the Boston Public Library were all under construction or being planned at that time. The entire Boston business district was less than twenty years old, due to the Great Boston fire of 1872.

Elizabeth (Lizzie) Jane Heenan (1872-1964)

Lizzie was described by herself *(as quoted by her son, Raymond)* as "an only child of an only child, raised by a grandmother, tough as smithy's nails." Her mother was Margaret (*nee* Coburn, Cockburn) Heenan and as an invalid, turned her child over to the care of her mother, Elizabeth Jane Fraser Coburn.

We are still untangling the Heenan family lines at this stage. One theory is, Margaret Steele was Joseph's 1st wife and Margaret Coburn had Lizzie out of wedlock. On Lizzie's birth certificate, Joseph's name does not appear as her father, nor have I found baptism records to support his paternity. The name of Elizabeth Jane Heenan's mother appears as Margaret *Heenan* and the eyewitness to the birth was Elizabeth Heenan *(Joseph's mother's name)*. The certificate was signed with her mark. With four Elizabeths (the child, her half-sister and both grandmothers), the record could have been distorted in many ways. More research is needed to prove a marriage between Margaret Coburn and Joseph Heenan, and the resulting issue, Lizzie Heenan. Baptism records show Joseph Heenan was the father of Lizzie's half-sister, Elizabeth Ann Heenan, and other half-siblings, John, Joseph, Ann and James, so it would follow, Joseph is Lizzie's father.

Her trip to America with Eliza and James was described by Lizzie to her son, as stormy and disagreeable. Her alien cards noted that she came to America in 1892 through the Port of New York. Subsequent searches revealed her name, Eliza's, and James' in steerage on the *City of New York*, landing April 14th of that year at Ellis Island about three and a half months after it opened. Their names were transcribed incorrectly on the website by a volunteer, as *Keenan*. On inspection of the original manifest however, it is indeed, *Heenan*.

The mention of Lizzie's education is factual and was one of the stories my father told us. The Latin phrase was a direct quote and the indignation of the minister's daughter was also in Lizzie's account. It was this story that led me to find the ministers, the location of the house in Lower Falls, and the church, with thanks to the Newton Library Research team.

The immigrant group may have traveled by ship to Boston, instead of by rail. Lizzie told my father that she came "into Boston". I have found no information to support either theory. I thought it would be cruel after their rough crossing, to make them take another ship to Boston, so I arbitrarily had them travel from New York by rail instead.

Lizzie did have her hair cut off for the money to take care of her mother, according to several stories our father told us. Her first turkey dinner is also represented about the way it was told to him.

Elizabeth (Eliza) Ann Heenan (1868 - ca. 1956)

According to Church of Ireland records, Lizzie's half-sister, Eliza, was the daughter of Joseph Heenan and Margaret Steele. She is called Eliza in the story to separate her from Lizzie, but our father said his mother and his aunt were both named Elizabeth and both called *Lizzie*.

She is listed on the Liverpool manifest (*City of New York*) and the Ellis Island passenger manifest, as *Eliza*. She is listed as being 21, but she was almost four years older than Lizzie who was 20 at the time. Her siblings were Joseph (junior), John, Ann, and James. James died at the age of six. Eliza was the fourth child of five, and then Lizzie was Joseph's sixth child.

Her mother, we believe, died in childbirth having James in June 1871, eight months before our Lizzie was born.

Her paternal grandmother (or great-grandmother?), Elizabeth Heenan, died in 1889 at the age of 84.

James Heenan (1868 – unknown)

This James is likely a cousin of Lizzie and Eliza, since their sibling, James, died at the age of six. Joseph's (Lizzie's father's) siblings have not been researched, and we have no details of James' life.

When some of my cousins were researching the Heenans, they found a James Heenan who died in New York Harbor. They assumed this was Lizzie's father, but her half sister, Eliza's father was Joseph. It very well could be that *this* James (the cousin of Eliza and Lizzie) died in the harbor, but I elected to go with the research I had at the time, so Lizzie's father drowned in the story (The Winds

419

of County Down). In this volume, James goes off to the west chasing a land claim in Oklahoma, which is completely fabricated.

Margaret Jane Coburn (Cockburn) Heenan
(1845 -after 1893)

Margaret Coburn was said to have been an invalid. Family lore says she stopped walking at an early age. *(That story may have emanated from my having been born with dislocated hips, which were not discovered until I developed a limp at age five. The defect is hereditary, so it is plausible.)* Margaret was reputed to be very bright, but unable to care for her child after the first few months. Her mother, Elizabeth Coburn, raised Margaret's child, Lizzie.

Margaret did come to visit Lizzie in America, and was not detained at Ellis Island. She was an invalid and as such was never classified as an immigrant. She traveled on the *non-immigrant* ship, *The City of Chicago* and was probably issued a temporary visa. She probably left the United States within six months. The trip was probably precipitated by the death of her mother, Elizabeth Coburn.

There is no factual proof of a relationship with Lord Annesley except as the daughter of one of his tenants. The timeline for both of them is as accurate as our research allows.

The Twomblys
(Ministers of the Lower Falls Episcopal-Methodist Church)

John Hanson Twombly was an accomplished clergyman and educator. He was self-taught until he attended college at Wesleyan University in Connecticut. He was superintendant of schools of Charlestown and Sommerville Schools near Boston, was chaplain of the Massachusetts House of representatives, became president of Wisconsin University, received a Doctorate of Divinity from Wesleyan University, was a trustee of Boston University from its incorporation, and served as minister to several northeastern churches before his death, on January 1, 1893 at 79 years old.

Betsy Twombly was well educated, an artist, and poet. She was one of the first female teachers in a university, and was the first to teach a class in Mental Philosophy, (later called psychology) at the college level in 1837. She held many posts in the Missions Society for the Episcopal-Methodist Church. She had a significant lung deficiency as did her son.

She was known for her many dinner parties, inviting notable cultural groups wherever her husband was stationed. She had two children. She and her husband were instrumental in starting the Oak Bluffs, Methodist Campground. The Tabernacle built in 1879, still exists there today on Martha's Vineyard.

William L. D. Twombly, born 1850, graduated Harvard Divinity School, and became a clergyman. He was sickly most of his life and his father often spelled him in the pulpit throughout his career. He never married. After his father died, he remained a consultant and elder of the Lower Falls Methodist Episcopalian Church, and made his living writing religious tracts and Sunday school materials until his death in 1921. He owned a separate home at the campground.

Isabella Twombly, born about 1848, was an artist and devoted most of her time caring for her elderly parents and her brother. She was about 44 at the time Lizzie was the cook in their household. She inherited her parents' house at Martha's Vineyard.

The church at Newton Lower Falls no longer exists, but the house still stands, as does the house at Martha's Vineyard.

Other Characters in the Book

The name Charles Titus Bachelor is fictious, but such a man would have had to be the sponsors' representative to meet Lizzie, Eliza, and James at Ellis Island, and transport them into the care of the Twomblys and the shipyard.

Also, while we do not know the details of John Hanson Twombly's death, he would have needed a driver on that night. As such, we cannot know if Lizzie became romantically involved with this man or any other during her indentureship.

The Bakers were real. Mister Baker, a carpenter, did build the house where the Twomblys lived and resided around the corner. Mister Baker was a Dutch immigrant and a pillar of the church until 1921. Missus Baker was second generation American, but did not learn English until she went to school. They had six children as named in the story.

Garrett Johansson was invented to add color to the story, as was Marianna Petersen, James' girl.

Lizzie talked about the 'back door' guests of the Twomblys, represented by Big John in the story. The story of the 'baby ghost' was told by the old timers of Newton Lower Falls for many years.

Will and Charlie MacNeill, brothers and blacksmiths were from Nova Scotia and met Eliza and Lizzie as described.

We may never know the whole truth, but the known facts were lovingly arranged in their best light, so the generations that follow would think well of their ancestors and perhaps seek out the missing parts of the story as it really happened.

ACKNOWLEDGEMENTS

There are many people who helped me organize, research, and clarify the stories in this book.

My family may remember some of the stories told by my father, and although they may remember them differently, they have always been encouraging. Thank you, Janice, David, and Joyce, for your patience and kindness while I go on and on talking about this series.

I especially give thanks to Patricia J. Thompson who gave me her unpublished paper, *The Significance of the Life of Betsy Dow Twombly.* It gave me a remarkable insight to this beautiful lady.

Thanks to Cathy Norvish Voci who patiently consents to edit these books, for very little reward, but has my undying gratitude and friendship. My cheerleaders, Joe and Ellen Dutcher, encouraged me every step of the way to write and publish. I am blessed to have my lifelong friends, Mary Ann O'Connell, Beverly Bifano, and Gerry Testa who listen to me prattle on about my characters and their stories. They inspire me.

I extend my gratitude to the unsung reference staff of the Newton Free Library who spent their time, to find the right church, the right ministers, and the right house in which my grandmother lived for less than a year. Remarkably, we found the Twomblys who were at that church as ministers and in that house *for only one year.*

Roni Herlihy took me to Newton Lower Falls to see the house that my grandmother spent her indenture. Laura White took us to Martha's Vineyard to see the campground and the house that the Twomblys owned there. It still gives me shivers to look at the pictures of these houses. Thank you, ladies. My sister Janice went with me to Northern Ireland on a research trip sponsored by The Irish Ancestral Research Association (TIARA), a genealogical group in Boston. Together we were able to find the farm and the village where Lizzie was raised.

I am grateful to my readers, who have taken a chance that a new writer will have something of value to tell them.

My dear family, Tom, Anthony, Melissa and Daniel, you have my heart. Thank you for taking good care of it. I am so proud of each of you.

ABOUT THE AUTHOR

Dorothy MacNeill Dupont is a new writer, an amateur genealogist, a graphic designer, a water color artist, an avid traveler and an active volunteer at a local charity and her church.

Retired from the advertising world, she makes her home in a small town in Massachusetts. She misses her husband George, the love of her life, every single day.

The Selfsame Moon and Stars is the fictionalized story of Elizabeth Jane Heenan, the author's grandmother. It is the second of the *Legananny Legacy* series.

The first book of the *Legananny Legacy* series, *The Winds of County Down,* is the story of Margaret Jane Coburn Heenan, Lizzie's mother, and life in Northern Ireland.

The Legananny Legacy series, *The Scent of Smoldering Bridges,* concludes with the continuing story of Lizzie and her daughter, Clara Jane MacNeill. This book is scheduled for publication in the fall of 2015.

The Legananny Legacy series includes five generations of women from 1828 to 1970.